KAUSTIKWORLD
A DEBAUCHERY OF ONSLAUGHT

Written by

CHRISTOPHER J FENNELL

ISBN: 0615829910

ISBN-13: 9780615829913

DEDICATIONS

This book is dedicated to my family and friends for keeping me from coming unglued.

THE LORD IS MY LIGHT.

FICTION EMPOWERS THE READER TO JOURNEY INTO THE FANTASY REALMS OF ANOTHER'S MIND; SOME FANTASIES COME TRUE!

C.J.F

These 2 pages are dedicated to our son Scotty who we lost in an unfortunate accident back in 2006. And to all the others on this planet that have lost someone that they love.

SON

He was young, wild and free
But
Not an exact copy of me
Because he came before my time
But
That never stopped my undying love
for him
He was my son in so many ways
That no one could possibly see
His frame was not that of mine
Nor his features
But
His soul resembled a close match
with me
He will never be forgotten
For I will make damn sure of that
And

My love for him will endure forever

And

Forever is a very long time to account for

But

I am willing to travel that long journey

To ensure his memory

We are parted for a short time

And

Answers seem hard to find

But

The good times will never part my mind

You can't hear my words today here in person

So I yell them into Heaven

In hopes that the doves

Will carry my message to you

That message is.....

Love you Son!

C-ya soon

Love Dad

CONTENTS

PART 1: INTERCOURSE WITH EVIL

1 Walking death begins (**2008**) 11

2 The Plutarch conspiracy (**2008**). . . . 113

3 The birth of it (**1985**) 209

4 All wrapped up (**2008**) 263

5 The Crypt (**1996**) 297

6 The return (**2008**) 313

7 Echo valley (**1985**) 379

8 I.P.C.O viper program (**2007**). 391

9 Ascension complete (**1985**) 431

10 I see your bones (**2008**). 485

11 Cyclotron (**1987**). 501

12 Illumination confirmed (**1987**) 557

13 Dragons are lose (**2008**) 589

An acidic drop falls from Cyprus 621

INNARDS PART 1:

THE FORGOTTEN FILES ARE A GLIMPSE INTO A PSYCHOPATHS MIND.

Evil (e'vel) ; 1 morally wrong or bad; wicked

2 harmful; injurious 3 unlucky; disastrous-
n.

1 wickedness; sin 2 anything that causes
harm,

Pain, suffering, etc....

A Dictionary

INTERLUDE

In 2008 a filthy secret that has been locked away for thousands of years in the minds of a few on planet earths' surface has finally reared its ugly head. With the catacombs weakened the dirt below everyone's feet vomited out the vilest form of evil that this new generation has ever encountered. This hunger driven abomination so eager to devour our souls was to be locked away by the ancients never to be spoken of again. But one day on an excursion off the coasts in the country of Oman an unfortunate discovery was made by the Knight family that would unbalance the universe forever. No one had inkling that such a small black pearl, as some would call it; would make the dead rise or even worse make them eat their own hearts forcing them to mutate into the Dragons. The mythical beasts were designed in an Atlantis lab by the man with no face or as some know him as, Gentry Faust, to cleanse the surface of planet earth for rebirth.

The future is being manipulated by a fanatical group known as the Plutocracy. Unknowing by most it has embedded its roots deep within most continents with a grand scheme to thin out the herd of mankind. The world has become a very unsafe place for everyone on the earth's surface since Plutarch's main diet is humans, preferably younger more tender ones,' according to their emperor Cutlass Rush. The emperor who serves the Livid Mother awaits her awakening so that they may return to their home world as earth was supposed to be just a pit stop on the way. Plutarch, a Greek philosopher introduced the Plutocracy concept during Roman times and now it has erupted into a full scale religion but mainly by those who reside just beneath our feet. It is a belief in the powerful elite controlling the world through pain and suffering as the poor are used as cattle. The Plutocracy has many arteries that fuel the new uprising happening before the worlds eyes. The most widely known derivative organization connected with the Plutocracy is the secret society known as the (S.O.G) or Sons of God.

Cannon Knight being the most illuminated of them all is a unique type of spiritually graphed human hybrid known as a Reaper. These Reapers reap the heads of humans in search of more black pearls. The dark fluid according to the Plutarch's assembles itself right above the spinal column in the diencephalon just like a pearl in a clam. This hidden substance used for spiritual communication was placed into mankind's DNA almost a thousand years ago and has gone undetected until now. In the ancient Plutarch scrolls it is written that trace amounts of the dark fluid was scattered throughout the race of mankind to keep it hidden from those trying to reach the synagogue. The synagogue is a mythical place where if someone that was powerful enough to harvest all of the dark fluid on earth they could travel between worlds or so it is written.

According to the I.P.C.O database the Reapers are a soulless bunch of twisted sickies with multiple personalities bred to inflict torment against mankind. But unfortunately for the agents serving the law of man they are oblivious to the fact that what they are chasing is not really human anymore but merely walking death. And now more than ever it seems that thousands have emerged through the cracks of the earths' surface despite the barriers put forth to keep them below in Cyprus.

The academy at Quantico has long been forgotten. The cobwebs along the window seals could tell stories of less suicidal times. The majority of the baby boomers now run the newly funded organization known as the International Psychotic Containment Organization. V.I.C.A.P has now been discontinued and blended into I.P.C.O. This new government agency combines all of the countries elite branches throughout the world. N.C.A.V.C, The National Center for The Analyses of Violent Crime, B.A.U, The Behavioral Analysis Unit, C.A.S.M.I.R.C, The Child Abduction Serial Murder Investigation Resources Center and V.I.C.A.P have all combined through world government's complete cooperation.

Serial killing has now become an international art with millions going missing throughout all the continents. The horrific crimes once erupting from the fingers of a corrupt few have become a worldwide epidemic, a plague or sickness as it is described through the media. A plague soon to be depicted as the Black Death by all. And now with I.P.C.O being fully funded by the Optimal Intelligence Agency, it all has gone global.

The International Psychological Containment Organization with its new instituted Viper program to counteract the plague has produced specialized agents in the tens of thousands. They are an elite few trained in very unique styles of attack, restraint, interrogation and death. These newly created agents are designed to stop the Plutocracy uprising. They carry gear similar to S.E.A.L units but with a lot more jazz and techno savvy. With unlimited funds for backing, the sky has become the limit for research and development of weaponry in the I.P.C.O. organization. Being an executioner in the I.P.C.O's Viper unit has become the norm amongst the organization and now many young civilians being brainwashed by the NWS propaganda aspire to join them.

The coming about of this agency was fueled by the New World Sector. Now that all nations are committing to one world government and one world currency, containment and labeling of possible liabilities has become easier.

All Sickies as they are labeled have been implanted with a Deuterium based Intradermal Nano-Bacillus parasite that rearranges the extra "y" chromosome for rehabilitation purposes. The new eugenics technology developed and created by scientists studying the Darwin theory back in the 1900's were knows as "interventions", a term used for classifications of families and individuals who were deemed degenerates or unfit. The classifications were racial groups, homosexuals, promiscuous women, the blind, mentally ill, deaf, and developmentally disabled or anyone unfit according to the world governments. And now with the uprising of the Plutocracy the Plutarch people have been put on the very top of the list. When the results from the testing came in to O.I.A from the eugenics radiation experiments being performed on people going into the hospitals throughout the U.S for common illnesses back in the 1940's they finally obtained the secret knowledge to fuel operation Zeitgeist. The patients were unknowing and never gave any consent to the testing that eventually put them in the grave rather quickly.

After the initial concept was implemented by the International Eugenics Conferences in 1912 the program known as Action (Tiegartenstrasse 4) or just T-4 as it is known in the U.S now was put into effect from 1939 – 1945 by the hands of the Nazis in Germany where 250,000 mentally impaired men, women, children and even babies were stripped, placed in paper suits and then slaughtered with hydrocyanic acid gas and then placed on conveyor belts that fed into large crematorium furnaces where bodies were piled six feet high and decimated.

This was Hitler's first attempt to match Gentry Faust's accomplishments. He used his euthanasia propaganda to create a stronger race for breeding in Germany or so everyone believed. And although inhumane and terrible something reared its ugly head up from the slaughtering, something so powerful but yet enlightening to those who could wield its terrifying power.

Although tracked and controlled at the time no one knew of the long term side effects if there were to be any. All of this became possible through the research performed by Dennis Dangle- Senior Etymologist and his mostly silent partner Poyang Beria a weapons Professor as he has been labeled. The world seemed to run like a finely tuned machined to all those who were watching or so they believed!

CHAPTER 1 WDB (2008)

1

"WHAT THE FUCK IS THAT?" Dennis Dangle Jr. hollers as he abruptly looks over his right shoulder. Dennis who speaks with a Boston accent is a forty-four magnum of an age according to himself. He is the top etymologist of his time according to his peers. He sits in his luxurious office resting atop the penthouse section of the newly created Dangle and Beria building in downtown city of Pittsburgh Pennsylvania when something outside his window catches his eye but it was speeding by so fast that he could not immediately identify it.

He drops his father's pre-world war two phone down on his humungous Grand Mahogany desk that resides upon elephant skin legs, takes a deep breath, puts his feet into his alligator loafers, sucks in his fat peter belly and slowly rises to his feet to see what is swinging past the buildings windows outside. Supposedly the Mahogany wood used in the desk was harvested from the trees in Jerusalem hundreds of years in the past. The myth is that the desk was crafted by the hands of six ordained Rabbis working as carpenters to fund their Religion. There are two blood covered spikes inlaid in the shape of a cross dead center of the desk that are supposed to be the same spikes that were used to fasten Jesus Christ upon the cross by Pilot back in the biblical times but no such evidence exists. Dennis Dangle senior always used the spikes as a conversational piece with new clients. Littered all across the desk are religious artifacts from many continents around the world. A big owl is placed in the right corner near a small Buda figure; the left corner contains a granite Mayan rock tablet created from around 880 AD. It is propped up against a two foot bronze statue of the mythical Greek God Plutonius, the ruler of Hades and the grand center piece is a glass encased Monarch butterfly perched atop a twelve by twelve, twenty four karat gold pyramid which is engraved with Dennis Dangle seniors name directly in the center bottom and Danaus Plexippus, illuminate the world is inscribed right below it. Dust resides all around the edges of the pyramid as no one is ever allowed to lay their fingers upon it. This was a rule governed by death and forced into all of the minds of every employee before Dennis senior's sudden departure to the afterlife.

The stank laden air from Dennis's ass sweat can be heard hissing out from under the cushions of his twenty-thousand dollar elephant leather chair that has large ivory tusks for arm rests. The chair was originally created by Dennis Dangle Senior back in the 1920's when hunting elephants in Africa was legal. A Zulu tribesman named Akan which translates,' born on Tuesday,' fabricated the entire chair in a few hours. A .454 caliber Marlin bullet hole stares out from the top of the chairs head rest. The backing of the chair and head rest is crafted entirely from the head of the elephant's skin. The large animal's eye sockets have been replaced by large red rubies that stare out from each side just above the arm rests. The elephant's trunk had been split to make the seat area in a diagonal pattern.

Dennis Senior was an amazing shot. He still holds many records of long distance shots with a lever action rifle in the Guinness book of world records. His reputation still proceeds even in death.

With such a massive desk a special crane had to be constructed and perched atop the neighboring Russian

Czar building according to the big headed Dennis. The Pittsburgh city lifting certs was not an issue because as Dennis and his late father rose as business elites they gained ties all through the state and government. This allowed free access or passes to do pretty much what they wanted with very little consequences. In all reality though, two smaller buildings were having their tops removed for a fancier rebuild anyway but Dennis likes to believe that the entire world only moves when he speaks.

The May air on that Monday in 2008 is cool enough to erect your nipples but not so bad that you need a heavy jacket. It is now 3:17 PM, a day that Dennis and Monica Dangle will remember for the rest of their lives, if their lives continue to exist a minute past 3:17 PM. The sun has shifted to the East and the glare of the fading sun across the large windows makes it difficult to see without squinting just right. The phone receiver blurts out with a man's muffled deep voice as Dennis races to the north side of his office. He knows the importance of the meeting at hand but his curiosity is overpowering him. He thinks back to the bomb threat that he received last week from someone called Tickle. The thought makes his blood boil,' if anyone destroys my kingdom I'll kill them,' he thinks while tapping his expensive loafer on the marble floor just below the window. Dennis is right behind his desk trying to catch a better glimpse of what's going on outside. As he puts his ear closer to the window he hears sounds like that of a Sikorsky MH-60S Knight hawk helicopter echoing through the walls. It is close to the same sound of his father's Knight Hawk he thinks or maybe more powerful like his personal chopper the Sikorsky CH-53E Super Stallion. The sound is all too familiar he thinks while rotating his head to fully capture the noise coming from outside the window. The chopper sounds used to wake him from his slumber in the middle of the nights when his father would return from running all over the world on his long expeditions, the same expeditions where he would tell everyone that he was seeking the chalice or the so called fountain of youth.

"I'm getting close little Dennis, "he would say," and soon you will be in charge of the entire operation my son."

Dennis clicks the blue tooth ear piece on his right ear and yells." William, run your ass right in here now!" But the earpiece malfunctions. "What the fuck", he screams as he dials again.

Immediately William's number is dialed, passed through security and connected by Genie Dangle's personal watcher. Genie is the artificial intelligence that runs the Dangle buildings entire internal electronic networking. Dennis's earpiece is voice activated to every employee's desk in the entire building and linked to every computer monitor.

All computers are equipped with cameras so that everything can be monitored on a daily basis as Dennis hates slackers! He will hire and fire on a whim. An attribute he did not obtain from his father!

"William what the hell is flying out around the windows of my newly constructed building? I want to know right now. God damn it!" Dennis yells with spit propelling from his big mouth.

When Dennis doesn't get an immediate answer he clicks a button on the bottom of the head set. Unknowingly William's desk phone lights up red as Dennis's face appears on William's computer screen. A startled William leaps back from his chair as he sees the big rosy cheeks of an unhappy Dennis staring back at him. William clears his throat as he tries to speak without the usual tremble in his voice because Mr. Dangle doesn't like it. As he shuffles to his feet he spills a Master energy drink all down the crotch area of his pants, he jumps to his feet, brushes off the liquid and runs to the window in the lobby. His cheap plastic chair goes flying into one of the nearly cardboard made walls of his four by five foot cubicle right outside Dennis's office. The imprint of ass is evident in the chairs thin cushion as William has lived in it for hours upon days.

"Mr. Dangle sir I have no recollection of any other type of work that was supposed to be scheduled to your building but I'll get right on it now sir." He hollers back at the screen while looking out the window. But what William is really thinking is; Hey asshole why don't you dangle from my nut sack with your porn star name and comb over.

"Oh Ok," Dennis says in his usual sarcastic whiny asshole voice, "better recheck that fucking recollection then because I'm not imagining a big fucking orange ball flying around out there. It looks like another fucking sun orbiting around. And real nice dumbass," He says as he wipes the dandruff away from his shoulders," looks like u pissed your-self now, what a way to represent. Maybe you need a nipple on that can!"

Dennis chuckles, spins around and points to the window again.

"Look, there it is again, look damn it, "He hollers as he runs back over to the same spot in his office. Dennis swears that he caught a glimpse of a person swinging round outside on the last pass but quickly dismisses the thought,' how insane would that be he thinks, people can't fly.'

William rubs his hands over his forehead. When he sees all of the oil on his fingers staring back at him he realizes that he needs to change his poor diet.

"I can't see what you-, through the blue-." William quickly dismisses trying to explain how blue tooth technology works to limp dick Dennis, ' a nickname that everyone calls him behind his back since Bridgette his secretary told them all about Mr. Dingle's Viagra prescription,' that he cannot see what he sees through his earpiece. He can't believe that such an intelligent man is borderline retarded when it comes to common sense. But he persists on as it is his job.

"I will check right now sir." William replies.

Dennis walks over to the main camera in a wall mounted white tigers' mouth hanging on the west wall in his office. It is activated when the ear piece button is depressed. The motion sensors placed all throughout the building activate the hundred monitors on the wall occasionally.

"Oh and before it slips my mind go fire that little bitch Bridgette because her idea of a café mocha is shit, literally tastes like shit because now from just three sips

I am shitting my guts out! Hell I have to put on a fucking depends just to stay at work now!"

"Ok sir I'm on that as well. I'm moving as we speak."

Abruptly Dennis lets out a huge fart; he damn near shits his pants, squeezes his legs together and waddles like a duck to the thermostat to get some air moving.

William watches on the screen. He almost laughs but turns away before being seen by Dennis. He wants to avoid from being fired again. He was escorted out of the building five times in the last month but was always brought back in. William just dismisses it as one of Dennis's power trips trying to show dominance in the work place.

"Ooh. O-o-o-oh. Damn it." Dennis moans as he hunches over holding his stomach. He grabs a small bottle of anti-diarrhea pills but quickly finds that the bottle is empty. He takes a bottle of water, downs half and turns to see William wondering around outside his office.

"Excuse me sir. What is wrong?" William mumbles.

"Bring me some Imodium as well. I'm dying in here. And hurry now. Damn it

2

Dennis's spectacle of a northwest corner office is that of pure magnificence. It has two hundred and eighty degree viewing through the triple pane bullet proof gold tinted windows with exquisite tapestries from Egypt. The floors are the finest pieces of black marble shipped in from Ecuador with outlines in actual twenty-four karat gold trim. All the walls are finished in an antique swirl texture that resembles Roman art décor from past history structures. The tops are littered with many different types of animal heads from all over the world killed by the hands of Dennis Senior.

Just then Dennis's phone blurts out again.

"HELLO! DENNIS ARE YOU THERE?" It's the voice of O.I.A director Hatchet Grounder. He exudes strength in his words. He alone wants nothing more than absolute power! General Hatchet Augustus Grounder served his country for forty two years in the research and development division in the United States Army. His talent in reverse engineering just about anything was unsurpassed among his subordinates. To this day his reputation still precedes him. Many rumors arose right after Hatchet's retirement from the military that he personally had a hand in reverse engineering the bell spacecraft that fell in Kecksburg Pennsylvania on December 9th 1965. Rumor has it that the great Generals heart is actually enhanced with alien DNA that Dennis Dangle Senior modified for human use but to this day no evidence has surfaced to reveal the truth. Even the military doesn't have classifications to access the general's medical records any more.

"THE DAMN ZEIT-GEIST MEETING IS AT 3 PM! TEN MINUTES FROM NOW", the General yells into the receiver on the other end.

"HELLO! HELLO!" Where the hell are you son?"

"Dennis if you screw this up I will have your head spinning on a spit," the receiver blares out.

Hatchet slams his fist against the intercom module in the middle of the large granite table that resides in one of the meeting rooms in the spacious Augustus tower. It is located in downtown Detroit on the water front near the Ambassador Bridge. He stands up, puts his hands under both armpits and walks to the white board at the front of the room. He tries to think of a cover for Dennis. Most times the boy is reliable, he thinks but he's not sure what's up today. And he swore to Dennis Senior that he would always watch over his boy. While searching for the right answer he gazes down the long table to witness twenty sets of eyes staring back at him. They all watch his every move. The tension in the room can be cut with a knife.

"Listen up men," Hatchet says completely disregarding the woman at the table while showing his true chauvinistic tendencies," there must be something wrong down there in Pittsburgh because if I know Dennis and I do very well," he pauses for a second to rub his bushy mustache," well let's just say-"

The general is cut off by the sounds echoing from the movements of Elijah rummaging around. He lifts a phylactery up onto the table, starts throwing papers down to everyone in the room and then sits back down. When his eyes meet Hatchet's he swiftly understands what all the others warned him about.

"General we all have to look at these biblical documents that I received from the Papacy three weeks ago. They refer to an uprising of unclean beasts, a malignant plague or soul eaters that some call them." Elijah says with vibrancy.

The flustered General looks at him with cremating eyes. Hatchet hates to be interrupted. Especially by Jews as he calls them. One time he even beat a private near to death in his early years for the same reason but now a civilian he realizes that the army can't protect him anymore so he just stands there all red faced clenching his fists making his knuckles pop like popcorn. That private named Methuselah was the son of a Jewish pawn broker from Detroit. Methuselah Gold despised his father Seth for being a cheap ass as he ran off to the army back in the 1970's. What Methuselah didn't understand was the fact that many of the army men in that era still hated Jewish people. No one knew why it just happened and unfortunately for him General Hatchet was the leader of those hater mongers. He hated anyone not white. Some say it was his German upbringing or maybe his father's love for Hitler before they were forced to leave their homeland or he was just a human devil if something like that can exist. No one knew then but they will soon. The General had a select few of six that operated out of his platoon. His Viper unit consisted of Charles, Darwin, Hail, Pierce, Derek and his favorite young German mutt Christophe Schnur who had the same German roots as Hatchet. Christophe's great grandparents had a home just several miles outside of Berlin. The exact location was right across the street where Hatchet used to play as a little boy. Hatchet would always drink his scotch while off duty and beat Christophe's ear with, "I wish Germany would have won. And this country would be so much better if the eugenics program would have run a hundred percent", the general would yell to all of his men as he stumbled around piss poor drunk off his ass. During one of his usual rants and raves at one of the local bars during the war in Vietnam he screamed," I hate all those immigrant motherfuckers boys, now let's get back to killing them gooks and if a nigger, spic or Jew gets in front of your weapon, well just kill them too."

And the six did just as he commanded. Friendly fire wasn't even a term in those days. All six competed to see who could kill the most. And they did without hesitation or remorse. They're actions were like that of a programmed robot and poor Methuselah witnessed it firsthand. The six killed everything in their path, men, women, children, goats and anything with a soul. They're platoon burned through more ammunition than any other unit throughout the entire war and with that fact charges were slowly brought up on the six as testimonies poured forth by the thousands. Christophe won the Viper competition with the last victim being Methuselah. When the Military Police verified the fingerprints from the hundreds of fingers and toes that Christophe collected as souvenirs they quickly found out that Methuselah was murdered. Christophe did not get off Scott free like the other five that time because despite the hatred for his father,

Methuselah sent out several letters detailing how he believed that he was going to be killed for being Jewish. And when his father Seth received the letters he pursued Hatchet. Especially since Methuselah named him the king pin of the whole death squad operation. All six boy's names were listed right below the generals on the letters by Methuselah. He called the general Abaddon many times in his letters. And now looking back some think that Methuselah could have been a prophet. His father Seth gave him the name hoping that he would prosper and live to be 969 like the biblical Methuselah who was the oldest man in the bible ever mentioned. Darwin who's name does not reflect any genius was murdered in a back alley way while boning a hooker in Chicago. When he tried to run off without paying her pimp Kendal put a cap in his ass. Literally in his ass where the .25 caliber shattered his femur leaving him to bleed to death on the inside. Christophe is still in the brig serving a life sentence but he won't serve it all as Hatchet has enlisted him in the Zeitgeist trials without his knowledge. The general makes sure that Christophe's accommodations are the most comfy conditions possible. He visits him on a weekly basis to continue feeding him his bullshit propaganda. Charles, Hail, Pierce and Derek are four of the men sitting around the large table in the Augustus tower. The lines across their old faces look like an old road map. The elderly men continue to follow their general in hopes of capturing a small taste of the fountain of youth that he preaches about. Hatchet totally disregards Elijah. He can't stand to look in his direction because he wants nothing more than to knock the yarmulke from his skull.

"Well men let's get down to business," Hatchet says," let's face it, the city of Cyprus will never become a state, continent or whatever the hell they think is going to happen."

Autumn Duke stands; she slides a series of papers towards Hatchet. They are all signed by the presidents of the world. The General sees her rise. He is immediately disgusted by the fact that a woman is even allowed to be in the same meeting as him.

"Now General Grounder, we the New World Sect and speaking for the Zalaph division, we have signed a treaty that will most likely allow the Plutarch's their freedom to come above ground as they wish but only in their shifted human form as not to create a panic.

The general tries to speak over Autumn but she continues on louder. "And you were present when the document was signed as well, without any objection then." Autumn says. She is a beautiful young woman who believes that equality should be given to everyone, even the lesser educated races. It's her Jainism religious belief structures that keep her straight. Hatchet looks around the table for a minute. He wipes the sweat from his brow, cracks his neck to the right as he always does when he gets irritated and starts into one of his tyrannical escapades.

"Listen Autumn you have no fucking idea what you are talking about here. A little immature cunt like you shouldn't even be in here with the big boy-"

Autumn instantly leaps from her seat but does it with graceful motions. She closes her eyes for a second, controls her anger and lets Hatchet have it.

"Listen you fat bald fuck," Autumn cuts off Hatchet," you are not a general anymore so why don't you sit your old crippled ass down and let the real rulers at this table dictate the fate of a race."

Hatchet slams both fists down on the table. The entire table vibrates. Delilah's lidless water bottle tips spilling cold water all over her new pumps. She makes a little squeal as the cold water fills her shoe. The testosterone supplementation that Hatchet injects each week keeps him strong and it shows. For an old man at the ripe age of 88 he still sports 19" biceps and a large boner that repeatedly pops up when he gets excited. And he is sporting wood right now without even realizing it. He grabs a manila folder, spins sideways and almost knocks over his coffee mug with his boner. Dr. Delilah Lemon a nuclear physicist representing Rain Deer robotics attempts to restrict her smile. Autumn abruptly releases her laughter rather loudly. She sips her shitty government bought coffee, makes a puckered face and puts her Big-bird mug back on its coaster. Hatchet's face turns a different shade of red this time. He can hear his heart pounding through his ears.

"Do you people think I'm funny? Well Autumn, am I standing up here like a fucking clown or something?"

Zhang Song stands up, pushes his folder into the center of the table and heads for the exit. Zhang who represents the Japanese Samurai division despises ignorance and he almost refused the meeting until he heard that Delilah would be present. He turns and looks in Hatchet's direction.

"I will not tolerate your cursing any longer general," Zhang says in a heavy Japanese accent," we are all here to ensure the safety of mankind. You are not the only one concerned here."

Zhang walks out the door, dials his cell phone and begins chatting in Japanese, "Benedict we need to get a hold of Garvin Templeton and implement operation Pusillanimity because this Hatchet fellow is a joke."

"Hold one second Zhang while I put you through to Garvin," Benedict replies," Garvin is on a satellite phone somewhere in the Denver area."

The static on the other end of Garvin's cell signal is terrible but he is able to hold one bar. Garvin turns his head towards the water pipe exiting up from the ground under the Denver airport.

"I'm sorry sir, "Garvin replies," the entire unit is in the underground bunker beneath the Denver airport preparing the weapons support systems for the possibility of the first strike."

Zhang looks over his shoulder to see Hatchet eaves dropping so he walks further down the hall. Autumn turns her right ear in the direction of Zhang in hopes of picking up on his conversation. She is fluent in almost all languages and even a few of the ancient ones that have never been spoken on earth. Zhang catches a hint of Italian dressing floating through the air as one of the secretaries walks back to her cubicle with a sub covered in a dripping paper towel. She smiles, licks her fingers and heads into the office of Thorn Stuckey, the head of the department of biological investigations.

"Listen Garvin wrap it up out there because I just received intelligence that points to Grace Adams. She may be are only key to unraveling this mess at this point."

Garvin looks down to see that some of the gear lube from the massive turret gun spindles had leaked onto his new Foxfire boots. He kicks some floor clean on them as he repositions the phone to his ear.

"Ok sir, we are on it. Do you have a starting point?"

Zhang puts the phone back to his ear after pulling away from the large scratching sounds coming from the other end.

"Try Latrobe Pennsylvania first, our sources have her working as an agent in New York but after her accident she apparently went back to her home town. That's all I have. Don't disappoint the ministry!" Zhang can hear Garvin giving orders to his squad. Garvin puts the phone down beside his thigh as he walks over to the 60 millimeter Turret guns behind the ten foot thick cobalt covered titanium blast doors.

"Ok ladies wrap it up in here. The ministry has new urgent matters that need addressed. Drusilla, Ruthenia, and Viola load those new whistler rounds into the Humvee and Eunice, Uriah and Abigail grab the Midget Plunder canisters. Oh and definitely load those new SPEAR suits; we are trying those out on this mission for sure." The girls all follow they're orders to the t. They are one of the best covert black ops units in the world. And they are all built like brick shit houses. The Siren's as they call themselves are killers in heels. That is what their tats display. Garvin calls them bitches with big guns.

"Yes sir, they all yell back almost in unison, "hoorah."

Garvin turns away from the noise of the Hummers running diesel engine. The whining from the turbo makes it difficult to hear. He takes in a nostril full of diesel exhaust, coughs a few times and puts the phone back to his ear.

"Alright Sir we are all loaded, Garvin says," we will be in Pennsylvania momentarily. The girls are driving our truck into the Cessna as we speak.

Zhang smiles a little. He misses the days when he was able to lead his own squad of beautiful ladies. He stands there for a minute watching the sun set over Windsor Canada across the river. Zhang reaches into his pocket, pulls a slot machine ticket out and looks over it. "Shit $305.00 is too much money to let go," he thinks," I may never get to come back here if the disaster happens like everyone is predicting.

"Sir, sir are you there?" Garvin asks as he walks towards the plane.

"Sorry Garvin, yes I am. Did I hear you say SPEAR suits?

Garvin thinks for a moment because he knew that Zhang did not want them attempting to use experimental prototypes again since the last upset in Kuwait when the drone named Morningstar accidentally crashed into Sadam's pipeline and ultimately caused a war.

"Yes Zhang and I know what you-, "Zhang cuts him off in midsentence.

"Make sure that you pack one for me and get moving. I'll see you all tomorrow. And before I forget bring the Bucks Tears rounds because I think that we may need them too."

Garvin puts the phone down again, he smiles as he knows that Zhang finally trusts him. He hopes that the micromanaging training that Johnston gave him will finally stop. Garvin waves for the girls to come over. He orders them to grab cases of every experimental round that he has in stock. They obey and load the hummer.

"Bucks Tears sir, do you realize that without the proper suits or ventilation the acid will destroy any carbon life form it touches."

A smile comes across Zhang's face as he reminisces for a second about Iraq.

"I've melted a few enemies down with them. This isn't my first rodeo Garvin. And hopefully for you those new SPEAR suits are everything that Delilah says they will be, Z out."

Zhang slides the bar on his I phone to off, shoves the ticket and phone into his pocket, takes the elevator down to the lobby floor, catches a cab and heads across the Ambassador Bridge to Caesars Palace casino.

Hatchet returns from the doorway. He does not understand the Japanese language. The tent is still pitched in his pants. "Guess the Japanese will do things on their own then," Hatchet says.

Autumn coughs in her right hand. She is beautiful, witty and extremely intelligent. Her father Ahmed Sigler groomed her to be the best of what she does. But when she was first placed on his doorstep he almost sent her to a Muslim orphanage to be cared for by his sister Afia. With Autumn's Christian, Muslim upbringing she was allowed to gaze into the different worlds of two cultures but her two years of studies in India led her to the belief in Jainism. She studied counterintelligence with the beast in the world at an undisclosed location in Israel. When she turned sixteen she did her time for four years in the Israeli special forces program with a top honors in explosives. After Israel she enrolled in Yale where she graduated top of her class in foreign espionage, a class not listed in the enrollment manual. Her father a top C.I.A operative pulled a few favors to get her into the secret society of the Order of the Garter an all-women's spy network renowned for its secrecy all over the world. Autumn is a tough bitch. Her balls are bigger than most men's and many have no idea how she is so strong. Now at the age of twenty-nine she sits at the table with the big boys making decisions for the rest of the world. She is one of only twenty of the elite chosen few allowed to mold the world.

"Well Hatchet why don't you just send that missile in your pants underground?" Autumn says holding back a big smile.

Hatchet looks down at his groin. He then looks at Autumn, puts his arms up in the air and locks his fingers together behind his head. He then leans back a little. His boner seems to protrude out even farther in this position. He smiles at her with big pearly white teeth. Autumn tries to look away but cant. The thought of old wrinkled up Johnston makes a gag creep up her throat but the sheer magnificence protruding through Hatchet's green Ducky's pants keeps her gaze.

She possessed no thought in her head that later that night she would be perched atop Mt. St. Hatchet and no inkling of an idea that an older man in his eighties could rock her world like that. But if he even knew how old she really was he would shit, she thought. She can smell the Plutarch blood coursing through his veins and as his temperature rises the sweet Plutarch aroma tickles her nose causing insatiable cravings that are almost unbearable to withstand.

After the show Hatchet relaxes his arms, sits down at the head of the table and begins back where he left off.

"Cutlass Rush has presented his threat today," Hatchet says," as he grabs a paper from his briefcase. He reads on, "This is to all who oppose the Plutocracy. If we are not granted our freewill to operate as an independent state a war will surely ensue, a war that you surface dwellers will not rebound from. Fear the Black Death as it is upon you." Hatchet looks up over the paper, "It is signed by the City of Cyprus security council," He says," That means that the entire council has voted so there is no negotiation here. This is big as it took 1,000 signatures before that piece of parchment was even aloud to rise up from underground."

Hatchet throws the strange looking document on the table. Autumn picks it up, feels it in her fingers while smelling it and tries to speak again but is inadvertently cut off by Hatchet.

"Listen you little liberal bitch, watch the video and then tell me I'm wrong again. I know that your bleeding heart daddy boned a few pale faces after your mother's death and now you both love them all." Hatchet fires out.

Autumn stares at Hatchet with hateful eyes. She whispers under her breath," Fuck you!" She moves her lips enough for him to make out exactly what she is putting down. He feels the heat.

Hatchet smiles at her politely then waves to Farouche Zastabar who is standing in the back of the room. None of the others sitting around the table will speak unless spoken to as they fear the wrath of the Hatchet as he has the power to make people disappear, at least that is the rumor. Autumn is the only one that has spoken to the general that way in many years.

Farouche shuts off the lights, presses start on the laptop and returns to his seat near Darwin who is fondling a Rubik's cube under the table. When he sees the two folds of skin close in above Farouche's eyebrows he stops fondling. Farouche is equivalent to the right hand of God if general Hatchet Augustus Grounder was a god. He is the second in command and can take control of the Viper system if Hatchet should succumb to death. Farouche served with Hatchet but never fought under his command. He was almost a general himself before being dishonorably discharged for the Vrykolakas conspiracy.

The poorly filmed video projecting from 1987 reveals a type of large spherical machine that appears melted and burned to the platform in which it resided. The area all around it is scorched black and covered in body parts. Debris is littered all over the ground for miles. In the parking lot the National Guard set up perimeters to keep out watching eyes. They all witness two soldiers carrying a corpse over to a large pile of more corpses. They heave ho the body on top of the rest. Hatchet stops the video with a remote that Farouche slid down the table.

"There are eighty-three victims lying in that pile," he says," the National Guard responded within minutes of the accident. Now watch what starts to happen next."

Hatchet clicks the play button. When the two soldiers start walking away the corpse that they just threw on top of the pile rolls back down to their feet. The two soldiers look at one another with a puzzled face. When they lean over to once again grab hold of the corpse it somehow reanimates and shoves its hand through Private Elwood's stomach. Private Colchester tries to stomp it away by kicking it in the head repeatedly but it knocks him ten feet away with one swoop. Private Colchester lies there for a few seconds dazed from the fall. The reanimated corpse rips through Private Elwood's abdominal area throwing viscera everywhere until it has its entire head up inside his chest cavity like a possum that eats the ass out of a dead deer to get to the good stuff. Blood gurgling screams erupt so loud that the speakers on the surround system momentarily become a form of static. Delilah looks away from the screen towards the back wall until the screams subside. Hatchet watching Delilah enjoys her suffering.

Private Elwood flat lines when the corpse has hold of his still beating heart in its mouth, it retracts its head from his chest cavity and sits there eating the heart. Private Colchester hollers for help but it is already too late. Private Elwood is dead. When the rest of the small unit catches a glimpse what is happening they run to assist. When Private Colchester realizes that the rest of the corpses are moving around in the pile he immediately runs to a Jeep near the tent, pulls out a flamethrower and puts down fire all over their bodies. Hatchet hits pause again on the remote.

"Do you all see what we are dealing with now? This shit is serious. It's just like those stupid zombie movies that all the kids are watching these days but this shit is real."

The entire group at the table nods in agreement. Autumn is especially sick to her stomach for cracking jokes at Hatchet. She thought that the meeting was a joke as usual; a joke just like the last seventeen meetings were he tried to get funding for stupid shit but now she realizes that it is a real threat. At that very moment she realizes that the Black Death plague is no longer a myth.

Hatchet pushes play again on the remote again. They all watch on in horror as one by one the corpses get up and run down through the neighboring field covered in flames. General Mustard jumps on a deuce with a .50 caliber machine gun mounted on the flatbed behind it and starts mowing down the corpses. When the camera zooms back around to the first animated corpse that ate Private Elwood's heart they see it start to change. Its pale skin turns black; it appears to have scales like an alligator. Its face starts to protrude like a dragon from mythical legend with hundreds of teeth sprouting out from its large jaws in all directions. The eyes enlarge to the size of soda can bottoms. They are orange in color like fire. The arms and legs rotate in their sockets; a three foot tail like a reptile grows out from behind its ass. The limbs finally come to rest when the entire creature stands there like a lion ready to pounce on pray. Only this creature is now four times the size of a lion. And from what they witness it has four times the appetite. When General Mustard sees the creature transforming before his eyes he sends a shower of hot lead into its direction. The rounds do nothing more than spark as they bounce from its hard flesh. Private Colchester takes aim with the flame thrower. He blasts the beast repeatedly but when he pulls back the creature lunges, knocking him to the ground. It then leaps onto the deuce killing General mustard instantly. The creature rips off the generals' head and eats it whole in a bite. It then rips through his chest cavity with its immense claws to get to the heart. When the beast looks up Sargent Thorn Stuckey launches a Midget Plunder canister into the bed of the deuce. The canister begins blinking with a red light to let you know that it is starting to operate. It tilts upward as four legs bolt themselves into the deuces wooden bed to stabilize it. The beast screeches like a wild banshee out of a horror flick as it consumes the general Mustard's heart. Within seconds a bright red light can be seen coming out from the top of the canister, smoke emits as sounds like a turbine engine wind up and then a roaring sound bellows out. The entire unit drop to their knees trying to cover their ears. The creature tries to pull away but its body is being sucked into the canister. Delilah turns her head away from the screen for a second. She looks around the table and realizes that she and Autumn are the only two women at the table. She looks at Thorn Stuckey who is in the video that they are all watching. He winks at her and points to the screen.

"The climax is happening right now." Thorn says in an inbred southern voice. He sits up with his chest out all proud.

Delilah nods with a shit eaten grin upon her face. 'This asshole believes that he is a movie star or something, Delilah thinks. She looks back up at the screen. The creature is being shredded limb by limb as it fights to get away. What's left of general mustards body is pulled into the can instantaneously. Wood shards are ripped from the deuce's bed; anything not attached goes in the can as it stretches to accept the contents. The scaly flesh on the beast is first to be ripped from its body. The creature is still trying to fight as it stands there naked. And within a minute or less

Farouche pushes stop on the laptop, slams it shut and starts handing out envelopes.

"That Midget Plunder weapon works like a whore sucking a bowling bowl through a garden hose," Thorn says. His opinion just showed everyone in the room his IO.

Autumn looks at him in disgust. She immediately knows now how he got his lead biological position.

"Thorn you talk like Goofy the cartoon character," Autumn says," and hell you act like him too. I didn't know that old Walt made people too." She hates ignorance and has no problem addressing it when the time is needed.

The entire table chuckles except Hatchet. Thorn flips Autumn the finger.

"Can we please get back to the issue at hand?" Hatchet barks, "And you too Goofy."

Hatchet smiles at Autumn. Despite her being a little bitch to him he knows that he has a shot at nailing her. Age doesn't matter if you have a big cock and balls according to Hatchet. He struts over to the south wall and turns on the lights. Mosby Hogg who has been sitting quietly in the back corner of the room takes a sip of his ice water. He passes on the shitty coffee offered because it tears up his ass in the evenings and he just learned that morning that he was fresh out of Preparation H. Mosby Hogg born and bred in the great state of Texas right here in the good old U. S.A. sports a huge white Stetson hat with a gold horn pegged dead center. He is 6' 6" of pure bad ass. He is an ex-marine who earned a purple heart for rescuing six guys. If you ask a Texan they'll tell you." everything is bigger in Texas."

According to the military records he carried two men at a time out of a biological munitions building in Iraq during the first Kuwait war in 1990. They all made it out just minutes before the building exploded. And now he sits on the council of the elite as one of the richest men in the U.S. He breeds stallions on his 2,000 acre horse ranch in Texas just for fun.

"So what you are showing us Hatchet, its zombies?" Mosby asks. His Texan accent gives him away that he is a true cowboy.

Orta Fife chimes in with his deep South African accent," Give me a fucking break people;

Zombies don't exist! Are you all serious here? What a joke!" Orta starts laughing out loud. He is one of those people that have those white saliva balls in each corner of his mouth that move around when he speaks. They are very apparent on his dark skin. And it makes you just want to hand him a napkin. Hatchet's face starts to turn a little red. Orta who is nicknamed Dr. Sheol by the parents of those he murdered represents the Zulu Order. He was first recruited by the C.I.A back in the 1970's for his involvement in the aids genocide research project used for population control in Africa. He is also the one responsible for the rumor of a man having sex with an orangutan that supposedly caused the aids outbreak. He put that propaganda in place to cover up the experimentation that he personally performed on in his people. His experience in mass infection of diseases has warranted him a seat amongst the rest at the table.

Hatchet walks over to the small refrigerator beside the sink; he reaches inside, pulls out a black satin bag and walks over beside Orta. He pulls out a glass box that immediately steams up from the heat in the room. He places the box right in front of Orta and returns to his seat.

"What am I to do with this?" Orta asks.

"Look inside." Hatchet responds.

Orta takes the napkin from under his water glass that he should use to wipe his mouth but doesn't, wipes the glass box and then abruptly jumps to his feet knocking his chair over. As he runs down to the other end of the table near Hatchet the others back away from the table.

"Is this some type of fucking joke Hatchet?" Orta yells. He is shaking profusely. The rattling of the door knob against his Rolex can be heard as Orta leans against it ready to flee at any second.

Autumn who is sitting right next to Orta leans over to see what's inside. And when the box starts sliding by itself over to her position she too jumps up and runs over to the door screaming.

3

Dennis puts his hand slightly above his eyes to muffle the suns gaze. On the top hundred fifty first floors the sun gazes directly in all the windows on this cool May evening. The penthouse section of Dennis's office stands fifty feet taller than the rest of the six towers attached to the lower platforms. He especially enjoys looking out the South side to see his helicopter.

"William! Get in here now! Hey William, William do you see this?" Dennis yells.

In milliseconds William comes running in as fast as humanly possible. He is drenched in sweat head to toe. As he adjusts his shirt he can feel the full out attack of a bad case of swamp ass.

"HOLY SHIT, Is that what I think it is? You better get nine one-one on the phone Dennis and quick" William hollers as the nails from his fingers make strange noises from his shaking hands tapping against the window pane.

William Whestle, a tall skinny man in a cheap green three piece suit jolts to Dennis's side at the other window does all that he asks in order to one day get back the Plutarch skin flute that Dennis took from his desk two months ago. The skin flute is the only remembrance that he has from his two dads. Dennis found out about it when everyone bragged how well William played his dads skin flute. And that is when Dennis decided to steal it. William Whestle was always called Mr. Whistle like the noise you make with your lips because that's how it's pronounced and he also addresses himself as so. He would always say call me Mr. Whistle like the sound only better just because he loved the attention from anyone. Being an only child in a gay marriage was very difficult for William. He was the only kid in school who had two dads and it was easy to explain until high school because then everybody knew. For years William endured the poop chute loving innuendos, the hey Willy Whistle can you play the meat whistle like your dads or his most unfavorable, let's all go to Willy's two dads house and have spunk tarts and faggots tea.

William is Dennis's office bitch, nothing more and he would sample Dennis's waste if asked just to be number one in Dennis's book. Not because of his gay parent upbringing or that he was queer or anything but just to climb the corporate ladder because that is how it's done in the corporate world. In just about any corporation it is who you know or who you blow to get ahead and those facts are proven with the whole Peter Principle littered throughout businesses all over the world and the governments abroad.

"Dennis is that your wife Monica strapped to that big orange wrecking ball?" William screams. He is now chewing on his nails rather than tapping them.

William takes off running to the secretary's office to try and grab another glimpse. He rubs his eyes while starring through the triple pane glass. And sure enough within a few seconds he witnesses the most horrific site possible. It is a fluorescent orange twenty ton wrecking ball with a big yellow smiley face painted on it and directly in the center is Dennis's wife Monica Dangle. Her mouth is wide open. The whites of her eyes are glaring bright. They could be seen from space in anyone was looking in her direction.

Dennis's big tank ass takes off running down through the office hallway to the west wing where he again witnesses Monica twirling around in the air.

"Monica. Monica," Dennis screams. He pulls his phone from his pocket dropping it on the floor and as he runs he is kicking it in front of him trying to get it back all the while still trying to look out the windows to see Monica's position.

"William. William what the fuck is this? Oh my God help. Help! Someone help her."

Dennis spins, and then darts back down the hall to his office in the East wing. His poke a dot socks make an appearance as his loafers almost collapse from the immediate force of ass pushing down on them. It is the quickest movement Dennis had made in some time. Accept for the taking of the chicken on the stick from a little girl at the Subic De Chinese buffet at lunch time. As he lunges forward the acid from the sweet sour soup burns his throat a little. He turns his head and sees

Monica through the windows spinning around the corner of the building again. Sweat is erupting from every pore in Dennis's body. Right before his office door he slams into Bridgette Clark. She goes flying into her office face first, spills her European gourmet roast café mocha all over her white blouse revealing big nipples and tumbles to the floor over Dennis. She screams shit all the way to the floor. But it's more like a never ending shiiiiiiiiiiiit. He grabs some composure and pulls himself up to try and see where Monica's position is.

"HELP, help her please. Someone help her."

Dennis puts his head into his hands and begins crying. He can't help to think about all the money he had just spent on those new fake tits. And then as the sick thought came in it went away with the whirling sound coming from outside. His hands are shaking profusely.

People all around the nearby offices are popping up like gophers from their shitty cubicles. It looks like a game of whack a mole with people.

"Please dear God don't let this happen. Please hear me." Dennis prays hysterically.

Dennis has never prayed for anything his entire life as it was always served on a silver spoon to him. For forty-four years Dennis Dangle Jr. never ached or desired anything as his families old money made sure of that. His father Dennis Dangle senior was a Master Chemist with a PHD in biology that invented a sub-atomic Deuterium based Intradermal Nano-Bacillus parasite that would feed on malignant cancer cells before metastasis could begin. With a magnitude of funding from a private sector only known at the time as three initials O.I.A, Dennis Senior researched every avenue in all DNA sequencing without any hesitation. He even experimented on human DNA to produce hybrid structures that revolutionized the world of today. No one knew where he had obtained the strands to cure some diseases. The mystery that perplexed millions would shine through this day in 2008.

His true purpose in life became apparent when his loving wife Mildred became diagnosed with Acute Leukemia. Her life began to diminish rapidly so he spent every waking moment in the lab and at Mildred's bed side. With all of the blood transfusions and bone marrow transplants Mildred was able to live on beyond her life expectancy despite the diagnosis from other doctors. Way beyond the typical 72 years of a spider. But the side effects were so severe that she never leaves her residence. In an unfortunate accident Dennis Senior succumbed to his own death in 1985 while Dennis Junior at the young age of twenty-three first introduced his medical breakthrough in frontal lobe psycho-therapy enhancement drugs to remove the extra Y chromosome from psychopaths. The newest achievement at Dangle research center gave the world hope that they would not have to abort their children or make them succumb to the new Cyprus rehabilitation program indoctrinated by O.I.A.

Since implementation worldwide; all newborns are now being inoculated before birth if any of their characteristics are found destructive in their DNA sequences. The mothers are drugged and the procedure is performed without consent. Dennis Senior's parasite based serum I-6 became a breakthrough in research worldwide and is still being used today. His isotope based serum was perfected from the original base that was first created during the T-4 euphemism trials in Germany during the 1920's. There were many miracles and monsters that came from that disturbing human testing experimentation period.

Just then Dennis's I phone residing in his silk shirt pocket begins to vibrate. His eyes capture the beauty of Monica's face on the screen as he quickly answers.

"Hello, Hello." Dennis cries.

"Dennis, oh Dennis I'm so-so sorry for what I have done to you. I love you." Monica screams. It is hard for her to hear Dennis with the wind whirling past her head at such a speed. When she looks down to see that one of her Cardigan high heels has fallen to the ground she erupts in a hateful passion of rage and rather than worry about her life she curses about how expensive those heels cost. Unbeknownst to her tiny brain she is getting closer to the building.

Dennis runs over to the window in Bridgette's office to see Monica fly by again. He can see her cell phone taped to her right hand.

"Monica, tell me who did this to you and I swear I'll gut the son of a bitch. I swear!"

Monica tries to rub her dry eyes with her left hand but the g force from the heavy ball is pushing back against her tiny frame. When she tries to speak the dizzying effect causes her to puke up the Dom Perignon that she had consumed by the bottle load earlier before meeting David at the waterfront resort in Pittsburgh.

"David, David Christopher," Monica replies, "look in the safe at home."

Dennis rotates his phone around in his ear trying to capture her voice but it is difficult so he turns on the record button to listen back in case she doesn't make it.

"What, what I can barely hear you with all the wind blowing." Dennis puts his hand on the glass window.

He knows that no matter what, the outcome is going to be devastating and right then at that moment he realizes that he has no power to control the situation whatsoever.

Monica comes swinging by again but this time she seems to be getting closer to the windows. It becomes apparent to Dennis when he sees her platinum incisor staring back at him. By now everyone on that floor is glaring out the window to see what is happening. They all witness the horrific act unfolding before they're very eyes. Cell phones are ringing and dialing all over the floors. Little Dickey Dong the mail room boy has been recording the whole thing on the other side of the building so that he can possibly make a claim to fame on Google or YouTube. Almost instantly pictures are being loaded all over the Facebook site. Pictures like Dennis's ass crack exposed as he falls against Bridgette. There are photos of Bridgette's nipples on the website secretaries gone wild. Joe Bob the smelly security guard on the 20th floor is masturbating to picture of Bridgette's nipples as he is a member to Secretaries gone wild. Bridgette who has no clue of the matter is sitting at her desk with an ice pack pressed against the lump on her head. And once the entire building learns of what is transpiring you can see people running from corner to corner trying to capture a video or a photo for their own personal gain. If the building was a ship it would have capsized fifteen times already. Some say that they could actually see the towers swinging back and forth from the amount of weight being shifted and those some being the witnesses calling the police from the various other buildings around Dangle & Berea. That morning the police dispatcher received three thousand phone calls all pertaining to some girl flying around outside an office building. At first the dispatcher took it as a joke but after the tenth call she dispatched a unit to the B & F building.

Both Dennis and William are standing with their faces glued to the big plate windows on the hundred fifty first floor of the Dangle & Beria building in the beautiful city of Pittsburgh Pennsylvania. Their heads go round and round as they watch in horror as Monica gets closer and closer to the windows.

4

The Dangle & Beria building is the brontosaurus of buildings to be erected in the city of Pittsburgh. The monstrosity houses six pent houses, eight indoor pools, nine-teen labs, two helicopter pads, thousands of offices and it is whispered secretly that there are negative number chambers that go beneath the city that can only be accessed with special clearances and riding the black elevator. Although it has been mumbled under the breath of a few past employees that human DNA experimenting was being performed, no evidence has ever surfaced.

Its mere magnificence is mesmerizing especially when standing below and staring up at the radius of the arc. The middle crest of the building resembles a serrated knife that smiles back at you. At least that's what Dennis thinks.

The structure was designed by the Wang Thorp engineering firm out of Derry Pennsylvania. Basically it is the only achievement that put the little town of Derry on the map. This great achievement was all possible with Dennis's genetic research and of course his small silent partner Poyang Beria's constant financial contribution. But Dennis was so blinded with his research that he never asked questions. He always left that part up to his lawyers. And his lawyers had their own interests in mind. Unfortunately with his big degrees came an even bigger head that swelled constantly but never contained any common sense or emotion and this all was especially apparent at the news conferences when Dennis would brag about his new developments in genetic DNA breeding sequences that led to the cure of many diseases and some cancers. But this was all just a little piece of Dennis's massive puzzle. The other dark pieces were hidden, hidden deep within. That was until today.

5

Hatchet walks over to the table. He picks up the glass container, looks at it closely with his good left eye and then shakes it at all the participants of the meeting. They all look at him with disbelief and fear.

"I cannot believe that you are all afraid of this measly little eyeball," Hatchet says.

He wipes away the frost from all of the surfaces and holds it up into the air for everyone to see. The hazed bloodshot eyeball spins around inside the little glass case trying to see everyone. It jumps back and forth in the case trying to get free. It looks like a little angry scorpion trying to sting. Archibald CaslteBerry gracefully walks over to Hatchet. He takes the little glass case from his hand. Slowly he rotates the case examining its contents from every angle. Archibald who has been nicknamed Spirit Licker by the Navajo Indians because of his dabbling with crossing human genetics with animals is at the meeting for his superior knowledge of necrosis. He has written twelve novels on anything from death to children's books. His New York's best seller book is a children's book called Whipple the whining walrus.

"Whose eyeball does this belong to?" Archibald questions in his low drawn out voice. His dry senseless humor is monotone. When he preaches among colleagues at college conferences they all have to drink Master energy drinks to keep from falling asleep. He turns to look at Hatchet. His facial expression shows that of intrigue but mostly fear. They are all afraid. Even Hatchet too but he hides it well.

Hatchet takes the glass case back from Archibald. He puts it back in the refrigerator from which it came but this time he enters a code on the security button screen where a large deadbolt slides down over the door. When the loud clicking sound invades his ears he knows that the semtex charge has been set. He stands back up from the bent over position and feels a small twinge in his back. He reaches back to feel the not bulging from his lower left disc above his derriere. He turns to face the others while massaging the knot. "The eyeball is General Mustards. It popped out of its socket when the creature bit down on his head. An anonymous private found it slithering away like a slug." Hatchet replies.

"Do we know how it infects us yet," Archibald asks," do we even know how it all got started because I didn't see anything on the video that showed what killed eighty-three people and ate their hearts?" Archibald who is ready now with his small note pad is ready for Hatchets reply.

Hatchet pulls back his feet in his boots to crack his aching toes. His nose captures a hint of baby powder that he sprinkled into his socks earlier that day to keep his feet dry. It is a ritual that he follows every day. Just like ironing every article of clothing before putting it on. The army trained him well. Trained him how to kill, be precise, neat and neat with everything, especially with disposing of bodies.

"We only know that if whatever it is or was eats your heart you reanimate into a walking corpse or Zombie as Orta stated .And then you try to eat other living people's hearts. And if you reanimate and eat living people's hearts you turn into a killing machine like we seen on the video. That is all I have right now but to everyone this whole thing is a mystery." Hatchet never gives a hint that he has a zombie chained up underneath the Viper factory where they experiment with it daily. And if anyone, including the mass of recruits signing up to join the I.P.C.O Viper program ever knew that he was synthesizing small doses of the creatures DNA to create a super race with the help of Dangle & Berea he would be eviscerated on national TV.

Elijah stands up, he points to the refrigerator yelling," Hatchet, I know that you don't want to hear what I have to say but tot bad. And oh don't think that I'm oblivious to your anti-Semitic beliefs!"

Hatchet shrugs his shoulder. He doesn't disagree with Elijah because he straight up doesn't give a flying fuck about anyone but himself. He especially doesn't give two shits about the same kind of Jew that almost made him lose his military career years ago, he thinks. Hatchet wishes that he could shove the eyeball down his throat to see what will happen but he realizes that it's not kosher and then laughs aloud. He envisions putting the eyeball on an aluminum arrow shaft with one of those expanding razor blade style tips and shooting it down Elijah's throat at three hundred feet per second. A half lit smile creeps along Hatchet's face while he watches the sick daydreams in his mind but then the whiny sound of Elijah breathing through his hair filled nostrils brings him back to reality. Elijah who is a fanatic on biblical history has some of the story right but his tiny brain could never comprehend what is about to unfold. Sure it's all words and decisions until the shit finally hits the fan so to say and the shit is just hours away from flying.

Elijah takes two very ancient scrolls from his phylactery. He gently unrolls them across the table. Everyone can hear the crackling sounds coming from the old shellac from the pines back in the day used to preserve papyrus sheets or so they think. But the only reason that the scrolls have survived is that they are actually made from human flesh that has been soaked in olive oil repeatedly. Those same scrolls have been written by the Plutarch's thousands of years ago. Elijah begins to read the ancient Hebrew text aloud. And he does it more so to shake Hatchet the evil German. Lester Pippin one of Elijah's colleagues steps up and deciphers what Elijah is reading, "Thee of little faith, fornicators of darkness, I your one and only God have poured forth this black plague to rid you vipers of the earth. Thee whoremongers bred from the loins of Satan, you an evil race will beg for death but It will flee from you ,"Lester reads." you will knash upon your tongues in pain and I the one true God will not answer your prayers."

Hatchet starts laughing hysterically. He especially likes the quote about the Vipers.

"Elijah put your bullshit away. This is not God's doing but human and that catalyst is the Plutocracy. The pale faces have been seeking their one up on us and by god they found it. And these are not just dumb corpses wandering around the world like in all those stupid zombie movies. These creatures are hunters. If they come into existence humans will become number two on the food chain in a hurry." Hatchet knows that they already are number two on the food chain because he knows that Plutarch's are number one but he continues to spin his web of lies and deceit. It will ultimately be his undoing.

Andre Wick slowly pushes back his chair against the wall. The rest of the people in the room look in his direction as the chair arm clangs against the air conditioning unit. He pulls out a little case from a digitally locked silver briefcase that is handcuffed to his right wrist. Andre depresses his thumb print onto a small screen. Two locks pop open and an alarm sounds. As it counts down from ten he enters a code that immediately halts the countdown. He sits it on the table pulling back the dark lid to reveal a little blue pellet the size of a Tic-Tac. "Listen up people, "Andre says," I don't know about all of you but I recommend isolating the Plutocracy from the surface all together. This little blue pellet is two hundred times more powerful than plutonium 240. So just imagine two-hundred times more powerful than any other nuclear explosion ever detonated here on earth but there is a catch. This little beast we call ICE implodes leaving behind a perfectly preserved frozen environment."

Hatchet holds both of his hands up in the air.

"Does everyone here agree that this could be the answer?" Hatchet asks.

Autumn walks back over to her chair. She sits down, gathers all of her documents while sipping her cold coffee. When the bitter taste bites back on her tongue she cringes.

"I have a question," Autumn asks," How do you know that the eye in that container is not infectious through airborne transmission?"

Hatchet laughs. Kneels down to tie his camouflage boot, walks over to Autumn and sits beside her. As he woofs down in the seat she catches a hint of scotch lingering on his breath.

"Well because I have had that in my possession since 1986," Hatchet says," and I am still normal."

Delilah almost spits her water back into her Fiji bottle. "Speak for yourself there Hatchet but you are far from being any normal that I am used too." She smiles and then looks away. Hatchet just smiles from ear to ear. He loves the attention from the ladies, even if it is negative attention. It's not that he is a woman hater but rather a woman should know her place in the world and that place being in the kitchen or the bed.

Autumn finishes packing up her documents. She rises to her feet. She knew about everything that was discussed before it even arose. The part that was missing was the name Grace Adams who she believes is a direct link to the possible side effects of a Plutarch experiment gone badly. But all of this she will not share because she knows that the tiny human brains sitting before her would melt down if they really knew what was lingering just below their feet.

"Listen Hatchet," she says," I am totally against wiping out any race but if they are biologically creating a race of creatures or a disease to wipe us off the planet then you have my vote."

She pretends to accidentally bump into Hatchet's chair; she drops a little rolled up note into his lap while walking off towards the door. Hatchet pockets the little note, rises to his feet as well and heads over to his laptop where Autumn secretly drops a Nano-worm onto the keyboard.

Delilah leans under the table. She pulls out a little blue sphere that looks like a bouncy ball. She plugs a wire into it, presses a button and a hologram appears above the table.

"Gentlemen and ladies", Delilah says in her sweet Georgian accent," before we get too hasty might I suggest an alternative solution to all of our problems?"

Everyone walks back over to the table. They all look on in awe as the hologram shows a multitude of weaponry.

Delilah starts again; "This is the R.A.Z.O.R or Remote Artillery Zombie Outbreak Rover. I wasn't going to share this until I finally viewed what was going on here. What you all don't realize is that the President of the United States has had our program into effect ever since that crazy lunatic ate that bums face of a few years back. I will also show you the S.P.E.A.R.S and B.L.A.D.E.S that you will want to acquire for this mission."

Delilah pulls the R.A.Z.O.R around with her interactive ring controls on her fingers. She shows the underside of the small drone carrying all the munitions and then shows the S.P.E.A.R or Special Plutonium Energy Armored Razor Suit used to control it and the more extreme of the two known as B.L.A.D.E.S or Bionic Lawrencium Armored Destruction Ending Suits and what is used to control them. When she shifts the hologram around everyone at the table can see the type of scientific technology that went into the designs.

Thorn Stuckey cracks his knuckles, sips his water and slams down the glass.

"Listen sister," Thorn says in his inbred hillbilly Kentuckian voice," I don't care what payload you have on that drone. It doesn't matter because once the corpse mutates into the Sluagh Dragon as we call them, you can't kill them. They have to be contained."

"Sluagh Dragon," Hatchet says," that's the name you came up with? Why not crawlers, splitters, soul eaters or flesh weavers? Much cooler names don't you all think?"

Thorn whips his big mullet filled head around to Hatchets direction. "Yeah, did you see how that thing crawled up inside Elwood? It only wanted his heart, nothing more. And according to myth the heart is the vessel that contains the soul." Thorn says.

Elijah buts in," According to Irish folklore the Sluagh Dragons are dead sinners that return as malicious spirits to steal souls. And according to Revelation 20:2 it reads, "And he laid hold on the dragon, that old serpent which is the devil and Satan and bound him a thousand years."

Hatchet throws his coffee mug at Elijah nearly hitting him in the face.

"I told you enough of that fucking biblical bullshit Elijah," Hatchet yells," I'm so sick of hearing about how God is going to punish the sinners."

Elijah slams his book shut and wraps up the three scrolls. He is trying not to show his anger. It is apparent to him that the general is an atheist or something. He looks up under his spectacles while pointing at the general, "listen up Hatchet," He says with a hard T," how would you military types like to know where Gods armor is hidden?"

Now all attention is on Elijah. He found a nerve that they all contained.

"Just what kind of bullshit are you speaking of Elijah?" Hatchet says.

Just then Lester stands up. He throws a large withered map across the table. There are red X's all over the map. Elijah points to a single location showing Philadelphia Pennsylvania.

"Right there is the spot supposed to house the armor of God. It is believed that the armor will stand up against the dragon according to biblical text so whether you believe or not I would at least exhume whatever lies down there in the dirt just in case it might be needed. But there is a catch as the prophesy states that the angel

Philadelphia who holds the sixth seal in place protects it from being taken."

Elijah stands back crossing his arms. Hatchet smiles while rubbing his chin. Autumn walks over and takes a photo of the map with her I-phone. "I'm going to send these coordinates to the Viper squadron immediately so that we can get a jump on this disaster just waiting to happen, Autumn says," and in the meantime why doesn't everyone else take all that we know and pass it along to only our dedicated teams so that we can come up with a plan of attack."

Hatchet looks down at the table. He knows that I.P.C.O thinks that they are chasing regular serial killers at large and he also knows that when whatever team gets to the coordinates that Elijah gave them that they will encounter a heavily armored Plutarch legion because he has a copy of the same map. And despite all that he knows he will just let things fall where they may because he wants to see the world implode. Farouche packs up his laptop. He has heard enough bullshit for one night. All the talk of zombies and soul eaters is enough to make a stupid movie, he thinks. Hell he hoped that someone recorded it because when all the bullshit rolls over they might be able to make a million bucks if the Secret Service will release the files twenty years from now. All the rest follow suit. The meeting lasted six hours. It was the longest meeting in the history of the new organization. Just then the fax machine in the far left corner of the room spits out a few papers. Gerard Weed the record clerk recording the meeting walks the papers over to Hatchet. Once again he waves for everyone's attention.

"According to the orders from the President of the United States we as a team are supposed to first isolate, contain and destroy any and all involved with the creation of such abominations on earth. We are not to destroy the entire Plutocracy race nor hurt the city of Cyprus unless it becomes infected like those creatures in which we saw on the video. Good luck and God speed," Hatchet reads from the papers.

The entire group now stands around the table awaiting the final word. Hatchet stuffs the papers and Elijah's map into his leather briefcase.

"Ok so first of all I have to let you all know that we have an operative that has penetrated the Plutocracy S.O.G program," Hatchet announces," she is equipped with ten of those little pellets that Andre has shown us. And if she catches the slightest whiff of what we have seen on that video today the entire city of Cyprus will fall. And on one last note, if her identity is blown everyone in this room including myself will be destroyed."

Mosby thinks that he didn't just hear the general threaten his existence. He stomps over in his big cowboy boots to confirm. "What in the hell are you rattling on about? I hope for your sake that I didn't hear you correctly." Mosby asks.

Hatchet sees the look in Mosby's eyes so he motions Farouche with his pinky finger to get prepared.

"Well everyone in here signed the secrecy act with their thumbprint when they walked through the door," Hatchet says," and in doing so you volunteered to let us install little Nano parasites into your bodies."

Orta slams his fists on the table, "What the fuck are you speaking of Hatchet? I didn't sign on for any death sentence." Orta never curses but this time it is acceptable. It's almost comical to see the vertically challenged man yell like that. His scream is like a kindergartener hollering for a cookie before nap time.

Everyone snickers a little as they watch the Zulu man holler. Autumn already knowing that the water was spiked asks the question anyway. "How did you put something into us without our knowledge Hatchet?" Autumn asks.

Hatchet walks over to the water cooler. He taps it on the top and smiles. "I didn't have to. We all stayed in here long enough that every one of you drank from the fountain."

Mosby grabs the drum of water and throws it out through the window. It smashes the glass in the building window and plummets right down on top of Hatchet's new custom canary yellow 2008 Mustang Cobra. Hatchet runs to the window. He looks down at the mess below him. His car is almost totaled. Everyone can see tears forming in the old mans' eyes. "Mosby, that damage is definitely coming out of your ass." Hatchet screams. At the end of the scream his voice goes hoarse to the point that ass just sounded like a. When he finally runs out of breath the big mad Mosby grabs Hatchet by the neck. He lifts him six inches off the floor holding him there with his feet dangling in the air. Hatchet is gasping for air as he tries to pull Mosby's big mitts away from his neck but it is no use as Mosby is too strong. Hatchet's face is turning blue as he starts to slide out of consciousness. Mosby is the only man that has ever laid a hand upon Hatchet. Delilah screams for Mosby to not kill him because they all might die if Hatchet isn't there to help them get the parasites out of their bodies after operation Z is over.

"You fucking asshole you have no right to play God with our lives," Mosby yells.

Farouche slyly slips up behind Mosby with a Taser in hand. He jolts 50,000 volts into Mosby's neck but the man does not budge. He smacks Farouche to the ground with his other arm. He knocks into Delilah who falls onto the water cooler base. Farouche doesn't want to use the Torrent since everyone is watching but chooses to do so anyway. Immediately the big man crashes to the floor with Hatchet falling right on top of him. Mosby is convulsing uncontrollably as saliva pours form his mouth and he bleeds from his rectum through his pants. It was the first time that the Torrent had ever been tested and all Farouche did was aim the small device hitting the button for a second. He looked around to see if anyone saw him and supposed that no one did but Autumn knew exactly what he used as she had the only other one on the planet.

6

Odd noises can be heard echoing throughout the walls of the 88th floor of the Dangle & Beria building. Faustino Styx has no idea that a huge iron ball with a woman chained to it is spinning right outside his window. He doesn't know this because his blinds are down and his security monitor is off so that he can teach a punk a lesson or two.

"Butch this is the last time that I will ever write you up for some bullshit childish stunt like this," Faustino says with his strong Italian accent," you are a great analyst so why are you jeopardizing your career like this?"

Butch puts his hands over his face. With his breath heavy rubs his hands back and forth over his cheeks. He is trying not to laugh but it bursts out.

"I'm sorry I just can't help it", Butch says," when I saw Tim's bald melon staring back at me I just-. Well I, I just wanted to draw on it damn it. I'm not sure why I did it."

Faustino shakes his head in a no fashion. Cracks his knuckles, pulls out a Cuban and lights it up.

"Well ok then finally an honest answer from you. Grab one of those stogies and get over here by the window with me so I can congratulate you in your new position." Faustino loves the way a real Cuban's smoke draws in so smoothly against his tongue.

Butch looks on with a strange face. He chokes as he sucks in a smoke cloud coming from Faustino's direction. He thinks that Faustino is pulling some bullshit trick like if he fires up a smoke in the building he will have grounds for an immediate dismissal.

"No I better not sir." Butch says with a serious face. He doesn't trust anyone working at D&B because he knows how the management team works. They do as they please even if it means losing millions of dollars but still somehow seem to get promoted with large bonuses. And he can see that Faustino is no exception with his expensive jewelry, Dingo boots and his gold teeth. Butch fears that Faustino may have caught wind of some of his anarchist charades that he pulled at a few other companies.

Faustino spins around to look at Butch. He takes in a long smooth drag and blows it back at Butch. Large round smoke burst come out from his mouth, six to be exact float through the air like little clouds.

"I know how your mind thinks kid. You think that I will have grounds to remove you for smoking in the building and I would but I am serious about the promotion. I still can't believe that you drew on Tim's gourd with a sharpie marker. I mean what did he do? What the hell is wrong with you, are you on drugs or something?"

Butch starts to full out laugh. He doesn't care if he gets fired because he knows that his rich daddy Farouche will bail him out again like he did all of the other times when he screwed up.

"I'll tell you what Faustino," Butch says in his new found arrogance," I'm going to smoke one of these fucking Cubans and if you want to fire me then quit fucking around already. I'm not kissing your ass or blowing your cock like everyone else in this joint does."

Faustino busts out laughing. He even starts to choke on his cigar so he runs over to his scotch collection and pours a glass. He quickly downs it, runs over to Butch and cracks him up alongside of the head with his left fist. Butch flies off the side of the chair but never loses the stogie out of his mouth.

"You little prick do you think that because your daddy got you this position you can do or say whatever you want? Well son, daddy isn't here today and you are a little bitch that will suck my Johnston if I wish for it."

Abruptly a loud knock comes from the office door. In comes Tim dressed in his black leather attire but this time he is also wearing a leather mask with zippers for the eyes and mouth area. Instantly Butch jumps to his feet, he runs to the corner closest to the window in Faustino's large office. "Wait a minute what's going on here? I'll call my father and he will-." Butch is immediately cut off By Tim. He knocks Butch's phone out of his hand but it is in the process of dialing his father as it hits the ground. Tim grabs Butch's head from behind and stretches open his mouth with his fingers. Butch is screaming as loud as he can with fingers in his mouth. Tim who sports 287 pounds on his large frame is quite a beast to reckon with but his slow drawn out soft voice would never let you suspect that he is a masochist who loves to be hung in the air with large stainless steel hooks shoved through the flesh in his back.

"Well, well little bitch," Tim says," you thought that old bossy poo was going to protect you from little old me huh?"

Faustino walks over to the Ivory blinds covering the windows and starts reeling them back. He turns to Tim and Butch. "Be quiet for a minute there is something cracking outside the window."

Just as he pulls back the blinds far enough to see the wrecking ball with Monica facing forward it plows through the side of the building at an ungodly speed.

7

Farouche is pushing buttons on his phone frantically. Hatchet climbs up off the floor pulling himself up by Farouche. "What is wrong, "Hatchet says," you look like someone died." Hatchet's voice is coarse, almost faded.

Farouche looks into Hatchet's eyes," Butch sent me the warning signal from his phone so I'm not sure if it's one of his bullshit tricks or if it's real."

"Where is the signal coming from?"

Farouche shows Hatchet his E-phone. "It's the 88th floor at the Dangle & Beria building. What do you think?"

Hatchet looks at the phone display. He is more impressed with the new E-phone military technology than what is happening with Butch because Butch has exercised Farouche and his team at least a dozen times over the years for nothing. One time Butch got a little too frisky with a dancer by the name of Holley Hussey down at the Squeaky Peach gentlemen's club where a few bouncers roughed him up a little. In the middle of the much needed ass whooping Butch pushed the call button. Within seconds a Viper team arrived and leveled the place. The only survivor was Holley.

"Farouche I would say that Butch is crying wolf again," Hatchet says," let's get old Mosby here downstairs and then will run over there. That building is impenetrable Farouche, I know because I helped install the turret guns in the bronze head statues out front."

Autumn gives Hatchet a cup of coffee to tame that throat smashing. "Farouche do you need me to run by there," Delilah says," I'm going in that direction anyway.

Farouche agrees with a nod," If you see anything out of the ordinary will you please call me?" He hands Delilah his business card. She takes it while entering the elevator. Autumn joins her but then holds the door as she slips her head outside," Hey Hatchet your lucky it was Mosby and not me." Hatchet flashes her one of those go fuck yourself and die smiles. Farouche grabs Mosby by the arm and drags him to the elevator. Hatchet puts a special key into the top of the control panel, turns it left and they descend rapidly. In three seconds they are in the basement of the Augustus building. Three guards and Thorn Stuckey come over to help with Mosby. They load him into a wheel chair zip tying his arms, legs and neck so that he is restrained. As Mosby starts to come back to reality he realizes that he is restrained and being wheeled down a long dark hallway. He can hear Hatchet, Farouche and Thorn discussing some kind of test.

"Listen you assholes you do not know who you're dealing with here," Mosby yells," my wife will not rest until I am found. And my brother Cage will destroy all of you"

Farouche looks at Thorn," Did you know about Cage you idiot?"

Thorn waves his hand in the air," What I'm supposed to do everything around here? You're the trained assassin Farouche why didn't you know about the brother?"

Hatchet smacks Thorn up the side of his head," Would you shut up please and go hit the lights in the cells. Hatchet pats Mosby on the top of the head. "Look to your left tough guy. Isn't that your wife Priscilla in that cage right there?"

Mosby goes nuts. And that's an understatement. He breaks all of the zip ties as he flies up from the wheel chair with arms swinging. He blasts Thorn right in the mouth and he goes flying to the ground. Thorn spits out four of his teeth as he drift in and out of consciousness. Farouche tries to use the torrent on him again but Mosby is already choking the life from his body. His saliva is dripping onto the green marble floor as his eyes roll almost all the way back into his skull. He gets huge nostrils full of Mosby's Dakar Noir cologne that is helping choke him.

Hatchet starts hollering to get Mosby's attention. "Hold on, hold on big boy we are just playing with you here, look I'm opening the door for you to get Priscilla out, just calm down would you. This was all just a big joke that was taken for a misunderstanding."

Just then Hatchet flips a switch on the wall and a door opens to Priscilla's cell. Mosby gets up off Farouche. Mosby lunges toward Hatchet and he runs back a little down the hall. Mosby swiftly runs into the cell, pulls the gag ball from her mouth. He starts to free Priscilla from her restraints when he swears that he catches a hint of death. The smell of a rotting human corpse is undeniable to anyone that has been in a war. He disregards his gut instincts. It will ultimately be his undoing. Mosby puts his full attention back to his hurt wife.

"Are you alright sweetheart?" Mosby asks as he caresses Pricilla's face. He can feel her warm tears pouring down over his large fingers. The fear across her face angers him immensely.

Priscilla starts crying loudly when she sees Mosby. The Brompton compound makes it hard for her to speak, so hard that she thinks that she is in a dream or rather a nightmare.

"I, I think I'm ok Mosby," Priscilla says in a soft voice," but they put a shot in my neck and there is something in the cell next to us making god awful noises."

Hatchet flips a switch on the wall closing the door on the cell housing Priscilla. He then knocks on the glass case around the cell with a bottle of Coke to get Mosby's attention. He cracks of the cap sending out a swooshing sound, takes a big gulp and then burps for what seems to be forever. Mosby jumps around to see Hatchet staring back at him wearing a huge grin. He pulls a Springfield .45 MDX from his boot. He fires four rounds at Hatchets head. Hatchet does not even flinch. He taps on the glass again with his bottle. "Listen dummy I installed the bullet proof glass myself," Hatchet says as he turns to look down at Farouche and Thorn pulling themselves up off the floor," Thorn use that intercom over there and ask Captain Sykes to bring those chairs on wheels please. Thorn looks up bleeding from his mouth. He swishes his tongue around to realize that a few teeth were persuaded to leave by Mosby's huge fist.

"And oh make sure that he puts butter on the popcorn this time because last time it was dry," Hatchet says.

Mosby quickly realizes that the glass is impenetrable so he pulls a Taurus Judge from his other boot. He hands it to Priscilla, "Listen honey we only have one way out of here and that is going down shooting," he says while staring into Priscilla's beautiful eyes," remember all those times we practiced out by the corn-field shooting at watermelons?" She nods her head yes.

Priscilla takes the gun from Mosby, pulls back the hammer and kneels down near the far corner of the cell. Ungodly shrieking sounds can be heard coming from the cell next to them and screams of other people echo up from the hall below. Hatchet, Farouche, Thorn and now Captain Sykes all sit outside the cells drinking soda and eating popcorn waiting for the action to unfold.

8

The steel strand cables from the crane wrap around the building thirteen times before the ball plunges through Faustino's office. The ball impacts like a me-teor crashing to earth. It impales the wall with such a great force that Monica's body explodes like a grape under someone's shoe. Her head, limbs and viscera give Faustino's office a new paint job. The ball peels through Faustino's office taking him and Tim with it. Tim falls, he slides under the ball being undressed from his skin and as it continues to travel his brain launches from his skull. Butch is showered with shards of skull frag-ments and Tim's tiny brain. The stink of meat gags the vegetarian bred man. Faustino is being shredded by shards of glass as the heavy ball projects him straight through the entire 88th floor right out the other side of the building where he plummets to his death. His loud screams can be heard all the way down to the 63rd floor where Bessie Bungalow catches a glimpse of his plummet. She drops her creampuff on her desk to call the police.

The entire 88th floor on the west tower has been ripped open like a sardine can to reveal all of its bones. Immediately alarms start sounding all throughout the floor. Hundreds of people are running for their lives trying to get down hallways or to an elevator which is forbidden in a crisis scenario. Butch was gently pushed out of the way into the far corner of Faustino's office. He slowly pulls himself to his feet while wiping brain matter from his eyes to witness the huge whole in the side of the building. He sees what is left of Tim who now looks like a deflated blow up doll lying out in the hall from what is left of Faustino's office. For a minute he thinks,' well that's one way to lose a few ugly pounds Tim,' but when the reality gears start turning he knows that he must exit the building quickly. As thoughts of the 911 tragedy bounce through his head he turns around to see that the ball has pushed straight through the entire floor. He sees something in the top of it glowing purple as it hangs out the other side of the building. Creeks and plucking noises like those coming from a guitar string can be heard all the way up from the 88th floor to Dennis's penthouse. Smoke from burnt electrical wires pour out the large windows. The thirteen wraps around the entire upper floor squeezed all of the windows until they shattered. Glass all over the ground below looks like snow. The entire building is in a panic. A tall blonde covered in blood picks up an office phone and dials the authorities. Instantaneously sirens can be heard echoing throughout the City of Pittsburgh. People are running around everywhere like ants on a mound hill. Butch sees that his phone has miraculously survived so he runs to it. He dials his father again.

Dennis makes his way down the stairs from the penthouse. He pushes the fire door open to see one of the biggest disasters in history. He cannot believe that his beautiful building just completed a few months ago now sports an orifice right in the center of it. As he walks over to the hole where the wrecking ball now resides he sees fragments of Monica's clothes left behind from its path of destruction. He notices the gold butterfly locket that he had given here for Valentine s Day lying near one of the shattered desks. It was the same one that his father had given to his mother when they first met. As he picks up the bloody locket he also sees her arm with the phone taped to it and one of her breast implants. Dennis pulls a small penknife from his pocket, cuts the phone from her hand, puts it in his pocket, grabs the breast implant in his left hand and then retreats to the elevator. When he sees Billy standing over in the corner of Faustino's now blown open office he calls for him to join him in the black elevator, "Billy did you see my wife before she died," Dennis asks while tears are poring forth from both his eyes," I mean did she look scared? Do you think she suffered much?" Dennis is shaking uncontrollably. Billy can see that he has the bloody breast implant in his trembling hand.

He puts his hand on Dennis's shoulder. When he sees all the white flakes he almost pulls his hand back. It is his OCD that makes him do strange things like that, even in times of agony. He knows that if it wasn't for Dennis allowing him to work in his building, he would never have been able afford the Porsche 911 that he loved to drive so much. He wasn't much for pity or remorse but he felt that he owed the man something.

"I'm really sorry about your wife sir," Butch says in a low voice," if it's any constellation I'm pretty sure that she was knocked unconscious." Butch lies straight to his face and he hopes that the cameras got destroyed before Dennis can witness his wife screaming as she was ripped to pieces coming through the side of the building. Butch has to close his eyes for a second as he can still see her eyeballs popping out from the heavy ball smashing her.

Dennis slides down against the back of the elevator wall. The doors close and a loud robotic voice from Genie asks for a code. Dennis stops his sobbing for a second, sucks up his snot and blurts out Monica's birthday. The elevator descends rapidly to the basement of the Dangle and Beria building.

"Where are we going?" Butch with a little concern asks softly. He can see that the sadness in Dennis's face is rapidly becoming something more.

Dennis looks up at Butch," Well son let's just say that you really are getting promoted and you will be able to do more than just write on someone's bald head when we are through here today." Dennis realizes that the boy standing in front of him may shit his pants once the doors open. No one employed in the building has ever been to the basement of the building before.

Butch can't believe his ears. He had heard rumors that the whole building was bugged but hardly believed it. He was always told by the older workers to beware of the wrath of the Genie,' whatever that meant,' he thought. And now here he stands with the boss who knows exactly what he had done to Tim's melon just hours before the accident.

The elevator hits the floor with a louder than usual thud. The doors open and the white lights in the elevator go red. The stink of burnt wires seemed to follow them into the elevator. The smoke irritates Butch's nose. He rubs it erratically to make the itch stop.

A blinking green strobe light flashes as a voice in the elevator warns them to get out immediately because the power is fluctuating.

Butch exits the elevator stopping dead in his track. He backs up a little bumping into Dennis.

"Oh my God what the hell is that?" Butch yells.

9

Farouche takes a swig of his cold Dr. Pepper. He almost chokes on it when he sees the upper half of Private Elwood's torso crawling towards Mosby and Priscilla dragging its spine like a tail. When Priscilla sees it coming she goes irate.

"Hand me the tub of popcorn Thorn," Hatchet says," your being a damn hog." He points at Priscilla going nuts. They all chuckle while watching her wiggle the big Judge in her small hands.

Mosby blasts one of his 410 Federal disk rounds into Elwood's skull. Hatchet offers Farouche some popcorn but he refuses. He is sick to his stomach from watching what is unfolding before him. Mosby blasts two more rounds at Elwood's head and the skull peels open as brains fly all over the glass making a splat sound directly in front of Farouche and the others. Captain Sykes jumps back a little in his seat. The entire thing is like a 3-D movie. Burnt hair and gunpowder linger throughout the air. The loud burst from the Long colt 45 caliber shells is drowned out by the thick glass on the outside. But on the inside Mosby's ears are ringing. Mosby looks out through the glass as he squashes Elwood's brains under his boots, "Is that all you got general?" Mosby screams as he loads a few more 410 shotgun shells into the cylinder of his Judge. Just as he flips the cylinder as an incredible beast knocks him over. He looks up to see it ripping open Priscilla's chest cavity. She doesn't even get a round off before the beast rips out her heart. Mosby screams. He starts blasting at the beast as it is feasting on Pricilla's meat. The 410 rounds bounce right off its tough flesh.

Thorn nudges Farouche." Watch this part," Thorn says," it's like once their heart is gone the bodies reanimate and they just wonder around all zombie like an shit."

Mosby shoots off all five rounds. When he attempts a second reload his heart is ripped from his chest by Priscilla. Blood is all over the cell walls. It looks like a red paint bomb went off.

"Holy shit that's sick," Thorn screams," Imagine the one you love the most eats your heart." They all watch in horror as Priscilla's body that was once zombie like transforms into the same kind of creature that killed her.

Hatchet stands up, eats a handful of buttery popcorn and walks over to the glass to see the dragons inside. They repeatedly ram into the glass trying to get to him. "You see boys I have figured this creature out and the zombies that it leaves behind," Hatchet says, "they all can zero in on our heart beats and for some reason that's the only part that they want to eat."

Thorn gets up out of his chair. He downs his Coke and stands beside the general. He acknowledges him as general because Thorn has joined his new faction against the world. He knows that with the dragon technology the general will most likely take over the planet.

"General," Thorn says," what is the plan now sir? I'm ready for my first set of orders"

The four of them watch on as both Dragon's pace back and forth in the cell trying to figure out a way to get to them. The dragon's squeal a high pitched sound as it knashes its jaws. Mosby a zombie and Priscilla now a Dragon are also pacing aimlessly back and forth through the cell bouncing into one another.

"I'll tell you Thorn," Hatchet says," If you all remember my main man Christophe Schnur or if you don't you are going too because he is going to demonstrate a technology that may one day save your lives while on the battlefield. Hit the switch Captain Sykes please."

Flood lights come on in the cell to the left of the one that the men are facing. And there they see Christophe walking towards the original dragon, Mosby and Priscilla. He is covered in a heavy combat armor that looks almost robotic like. He walks right through the cell and into the next one. None of the beasts take notice to his presence as he paints an M on Mosby's head and a P on the new Dragon that Priscilla turned into.

"You are insane Hatchet," Farouche says," I would lay down my life for you but I would not have done that for anyone."

Hatchet pats Farouche on the back, "I know my old friend and that's why I didn't ask you too. Christophe was more than eager to win back his freedom."

"But I thought that Christophe was a free man after yesterday's trial, "Thorn buts in.

Hatchet wipes the butter from his fingers on his pants. He pulls a Cuban from his inside jacket pocket. He lights it up, takes a few puffs and then pulls it away from his mouth. "Well Thorn let's just keep that between us guys or you will be walking through that cell without the armor, comprende amigo?"

Thorn spins so quick that his military issued boots squeak against the tile floor. "Yes sir I would never jeopardize our mission at any cost," Thorn says," and besides I want to see the president try to stop your Dragons.

Farouche looks on in horror as he knows that Hatchet is out to destroy the world in which he loves, "Hatchet, what exactly are you planning with these beasts? I mean if they get loose the entire population could be wiped out."

Hatchet takes another long drag from his stogie. The scent of peach erupts through the air. He can sees the concern in his face, "Farouche my brother you have been at my side for as long as I can remember and you know that I always value your opinions but opinions are like assholes, everyone has one. But that being said I will take your comments into advisement."

Farouche brushes off the shitty comment as he has taken the abuse from Hatchet before. The part that Hatchet doesn't know is that Farouche vividly remembers how Hatchet cut the throat of Mishmi a beautiful Vietnamese woman that he fell in love with during the Vietnam War. And when Hatchet starts talking about how he can make the men turn into gods from the blood of the dragon Farouche quickly jumps at the chance. He knows that it may be the only failsafe that h can put in place to stop the general. Hatchet goes on to tell the men how the entire I.P.C.O Viper unit has been graphed with the DNA from a less powerful dragon. But the part that he doesn't share is that the so called dragon blood used on the Viper's is really Plutarch blood. In all reality the dragon's blood has never been obtained until today.

10

Cannon Knight one of the S.O.G's elite is traveling North on route 60 towards Pittsburgh airport. He looks down at the god particle in his left hand. Sadness comes across his heart as he thinks about chaining Monica to the wrecking ball. The look in her eyes when he removed it from the gold locket around her neck will forever be embedded in his mind forever. The Hemi roars as he mashes the pedal to the floor. The Jeep instantly races up to 110 MPH. It seems as though after killing Cassandra he is still hungry. His thirst for pain just can't seem to be quenched by any old whore of the world anymore. He wants something more, something special to fill the hole in his soul. A special someone that would let him touch their heart both emotionally and physically you could say. The scent of death is aching to line the inner corridors of his nostrils despite the fact that Cutlass will kill Celeste if he fails again. Death is an aphrodisiac to him. Just then Cannon is pulled from his dreamlike rage as rain begins to trickle against his windshield. The sound of the little pellets is hypnotizing. It almost slows his lusts for flesh and before he realizes his actions, he has his hand massaging his member as he drifts off into another unknown bent reality. As the rain pounds harder his mind drifts deeper and deeper into the past where he is fifteen again and alone with his first love. He remembers how she was always cold. He tried everything to warm her body but it was no use. She would always listen to him and never talk back, not even once. Her silence was so soothing.

She never judged him for the things that he had done. He often times thinks of her all alone in that tomb and plans one day to revisit her if he gets the chance.

Just then the sounds of racing engines pour into his car. When his eyes peel open he sees several police patrol vehicles trailing up on him at a high rate of speed. He can't believe his eyes. 'There is no way, how on earth they could know, he thinks. I worked the scene like a magician. Oh shit! Maybe the Jeep is out of inspection. Keep cool. Keep cool. We just won't let them look in the back hatch. That's it. No back hatch.' He returns his gaze upon the rearview mirror. Both units are on his ass so he slows down just under the speed limit. Sixty-four, that's a mile under. No harm no foul,' he thinks. When he looks upon the rearview mirror again he sees something different. He begins slowly touching his face. *"You stupid son of a bitch how could you be so idiotic? HUH! Answer me dickhead."* Cannon can't believe his eyes. It can't be happening again. It's been so long since that evil beast reared its ugly head,' he thinks.

Abruptly he begins banging his head off the steering wheel, "NO! NO! Go away. GO away damn it", he screams," my god Osiris is back, Osiris the worst of his multiple personalities if that is what you could call them but they are more like souls competing for the joystick in the same body with Cannon's soul. Abruptly he reaches past his Judge in the center console to pull out his rosaries. He begins praying profusely," Dear Lord, my Father in Heaven please forgive me-." He is cut off by a big rig carrying farm animals. The stink of pig shit envelopes in the car. He kisses his rosary beads several times in hopes of a reclusion. The first patrol car flies past but the second car lags behind a bit. He can see the officers face plain as day. The brown haired thirties man has a face of content. Cannon looks in the back seat but no one is there. He thinks that the rosary beads scared the others in his mind away for the moment.

The officer pulls up on Cannon's side. He peers through his drivers' side window to Cannon looking over out of the corner of his eye. Cannon's years of espionage help keep him from being suspicious but the reappearance of the old beast that has haunted him for so many years makes him more nervous than ever. And just then out of the blue the officer announces on the loud speaker, "Sir pool over your car please. " Cannon finds a large enough berm to pool into. He slows the Jeep to a halt. Within seconds the officer is at the window, "Sir please let me see your driver's license and registration." Cannon reaches to his glove box but there is no registration. He forgot to put in in the glove box. When Freckle interrupted him in the bay area of Cyprus he lost track of the priorities. He looks up at the officer, "here is my license sir but I'm not sure where my registration is. This is a new car. I must have left it at home. "Cannon replies politely.

The officer takes his license back with him to his patrol car. Cannon's mind is spinning out of control. So many voices are talking to him at once. He tries to maintain a stand up presence.

"Shut up you sons of bitches. Just shut up for a minute while I think." Cannon yells.

Without Cannon realizing it, the officer returns to his drivers' side of the Jeep. He put his right hand on his side arm while he witnesses Cannon becoming irate, "Excuse me sir," the officer says." but who are you talking too?"

Cannon a little disorientated looks up in shame, "Sorry officer, It's a song I like to sing or uh…"

The officer walks around the car to inspect the outside. Cannon looks in the rearview mirror again. His face expression portrays utmost fear. He says under his breath, "Gentry Faust." OH NO! Then without hesitation he slams his head off the steering wheel again. This time it doesn't work. The officer immediately runs back to the driver's side window, "Sir, are you taking medication or have you been drinking today?"

Cannon who is now transforming into Gentry shakes his head no. The officer writes something in his little tablet. Cannon closes his eyes trying to keep them all back, way back in the deepest corridors of his mind where they can't hurt anyone.

"Sir, would you please step out of the vehicle for a minute?" The policeman leans in closer towards Cannon. He turns his head trying to inspect what is in the car.

Cannon tries to explain that he did nothing wrong but the officer insists that he exit his vehicle for a sobriety test. He flips the snap on his holster and gestures for Cannon to exit the vehicle or else. For a second officer Callahan swears that he sees the man's face staring back at him change into something else. Cannon acts as if his seat belt is wedged and will not release. He waves for help. Officer Callahan's gut instincts tell him to call for backup but instead he cautiously goes at lone ranger style approaching the window. As the officer peers down into the back floor area of the Jeep he sees Cassandras bloody head. The immediate rush widens his eyes. He immediately draws his Glock .40 Caliber pistol putting it to Cannon's head but it's already too late as Cannon had already seen the reflection of fear in his eyes. Cannon depresses a button on his Stinger Taser. Two darts plummet into the officers' chin delivering 75,000 volts of electricity. Officer Callahan's body trembles out of control as he falls back to the ground twitching. Cannon can hear the officers teeth chattering as the voltage flows freely through his body. When Cannon feels that the officers ass has puckered enough he releases the button. The jingle of officer Callahan's cuffs against the pavement is music to Cannons ears. He even moves his finger through the air like a symphony instructor. The officers Glock blasts off a round when it falls to the ground. The loud burst pulls Cannon from his musical masterpiece. And then without the blink of an eye Cannon leaps upon the man like a lion. The cop bucks and kicks from the juice that just raced through his flesh. After a few seconds Cannon realizes that Gentry is fueling his lust. The entity inside him tells him that he is Lord, Lord to all. It tells him to embrace the feeling of power. This man had no reason to pull him over,' he thinks. Hell he was the goddamn king of the earth. The chosen one, the master, he is one of the "*Sons of God.*" Without hesitation he hits the trunk button on his key ring, kneels down and stares into Officer Callahan's stunned face. He can see that the juice dried up the officer's eyes a little.

"Motherfucker, do you know who you just messed with?" Cannon or Gentry or even maybe Osiris yells.

The one controlling his body probably isn't even sure who it is at the moment. This is the first time in a long while that the other's residing in his mind have erupted so freely. Usually the medication that Dr. Freckle provides Cannon with holds the voices at bay. The entities residing in Cannon's mind may be realizing that their days of interference are coming to an end as they seemed to rise up to the front of his brain when he looked at the god particle.

Cannon picks officer Callahan up off the pavement with one hand. His 200 pound body is nothing for Cannon to hold. The officer tries to talk while dangling in the air and when Cannon whips him into the back of the Jeep officer Callahan's urine flies all over his hand. The grin on Cannon's face becomes apparent when he sees his reflection in the window of the back hatch. He especially enjoys hurting the corrupt ones pretending to be law abiding. And Callahan would be just another statistic soon enough.

"Oh yeah, waste not wants not that's what I always say."

As reality pokes back a little he realizes that all patrol vehicles have cameras. And becoming aware of this fact he rummages through the back of the Jeep until he finds the green box that Freckle gave him before he left that morning. He punches Callahan in the balls six times.

"This will do nicely Callahan you fucking invalid." He mumbles while turning the dial on a metal flash light looking object. At least that is how it is described by other officers when they observe the video. Unfortunately for the Pittsburgh police department they never even find a trace of it after its detonation.

He walks back to the patrol car, opens the door and grabs the twelve gauge shotgun from the console. Then carefully and neatly he places the cylindrical device on the center console. Abruptly the patrol radio sounds off about terroristic activities sited in the City of Pittsburgh. The loud intrusion makes Cannon smack his head on the door rail. "Shit goddamn it!" He yells.

But then almost immediately the inner windings of his complex brain begin to wield thoughts of wicked torment as he reaches for the radio. He depresses the switch on the microphone," HELP, HELP officer down," he sounds off in a feminine voice," Were on route 60 North near the airport exit just past the 189 mile marker." He drops the receiver exiting the vehicle.

The Dispatcher sounds back, "Mam, mam, please state your name."

Cannon walks to the back of the patrol car, pulls several flares from the trunk. He then lights three and then throws them onto all four lanes of the highway just in front of his car. After gazing at the blood splatter marks laying across the pavement he sighs a bit, jumps in the Jeep and drives slowly up the highway. As motorists slow to a stop near the officer Callahan's patrol car he pulls a trigger mechanism from his pocket. He looks back to ensure the perfect timing has arrived and when the large smelly rig hauling pigs that he passed a few miles back pulls directly beside the patrol unit he flips the switch. Aggressively the blast ricochets into all the vehicles near the patrol unit. The back end of Cannon's Jeep lifts two feet into the air forcing his Jeep to squeal tires into the guardrail as fire, smoke, metal; human flesh, pig viscera and other debris rain down on top of his vehicle. Cannon hits the button on the windshield wiper to only leave behind a smeared mess of lard across the windshield.

He abruptly exits his car to absorb all the chaos that his hands have inflicted. He dances through the piles of flesh around his jeep. The squishing sounds of bloody meat against concrete fuels his desires to move. He is hollering like a wild man as blood and chunks of meat fly through the air. He closes his eyes, puts his face up in the air and opens his mouth as if a child does to catch a snowflake when a blizzard hits. As he stands there with the fireballs reflecting in his eyes larger pieces of pig carcasses' rain down in front of his feet. One, two and then three pieces come crashing down slowly skidding several feet in front of him. He picks up the charred pigs head, rolls it around like a puppet while starring into its burned out eye sockets. Cannon peers at it for a long while as if he can see into its soul. Then with a new wicked face he starts screaming, "This little piggy went to market, this little piggy stayed home but this little piggy got blown, whoop, whoop." He then goes to the Jeep's hatch where he pulls officer Callahan out to show him the carnage. He lifts up his head towards the burning rig while pulling back both of his eyelids. "Look asshole. Look what you did. You killed all those people just because you were too damn nosey." He starts punching the officers' face repeatedly. And then when he sees fire trucks speeding up the highway underpass he throws Callahan's body against the guard rails. He slams the Jeeps hatch and as he walks back to jump in the drivers' side he slips on the pig viscera painted all over the highway. The molten lard is like ice. Route 60 has become drunken with the blood of many creatures. As he pulls himself up from the ground he takes hits from the smoke rolling in his direction. "Ooh Bacon," he whispers with his sadistic voice. Cannon grabs the flaming head of a burnt hog that slid into his direction. He pulls a cherry swisher sweet blunt from his pocket and lights up using the burning hogs head as his lighter. Slowly he slides into his vehicle and speeds away towards the airport.

11

After Hatchet gets wind of what has happened at the Dangle & Beria building he and Farouche rise to the top of the Augustus building where they hitch a ride in a Blackhawk special ops chopper to the Pittsburgh airport. They are coming in North bound when they see black smoke bellowing up into the air from a massive 63 car pileup below them. Farouche points to the devastation below. The stench of burnt tires reaches out to their nostrils.

"I wonder if that is part of the terrorist attack that happened to the B & F building," Farouche yells through the chopper headset.

Hatchet shrugs his shoulders. "Maybe we better drop below the airport and take the transport directly underground to Dennis's building. We can also make sure that Juniper is finishing up the final transdermal implementation on the imprinted army." He pulls a little glowing vial of fluid and hands it to Farouche. "You said that you want to be immortal my brother so I have just handed you the chalice." The imprinted army being produced is not cloned or grown but literally printed out like a 3-D model on a household printer. Hatchet's printer utilizes the same technology with the exception of where the ink and resin would go human liquefied DNA canisters reside. A complete human being can be printed out in six hour flat. The testing revealed that any longer or slower produced an imperfect being. Hatchet's final ingredient was obtained when Priscilla mutated into the Dragon. Ports were embedded into her flesh before her transformation that allowed Hatchet to pretty much tap her like a beer keg. She is pressed between two large hydraulic cylinders to keep her contained and is fed people to be kept alive for experimentation processes. The original Dragon and the now Mosby zombie are traveling with Hatchet below the chopper in a sealed canister.

Farouche spins the little chameleon colored vial in his hand. "What do you mean Hatchet? How can this little container of juice make me into anything but a senseless monster?"

Hatchet puts his hand on Farouche's shoulder, "Oh my brother it's not without pain and suffering I assure you. After the injection into your brain you are going to have to take a ride on the Graviton."

Farouche shakes his head no. "Not gonna happin cappin," he yells above the chopper noise," I saw what happens to people that take a ride on that thing. You shit out the wrong end of your body, no way sir not me."

A pissed off Hatchet slams back into his seat on the chopper, "It's your prerogative Farouche but don't be crying you want some when it's gone. I guess that I will be taking the first ride then."

Hatchet leans forward. He tells the pilot to land on the reserved pad rather than out in public. When the chopper bucks right they see a Jeep parked in the Admirals parking spot.

"Did the Admiral get one of those new SR8's," Hatchet asks the pilot. He shrugs his shoulders and replies," The Admiral is supposed to be in Florida sir."

The chopper lands on the secret pad out on the tarmac but this time the entire chopper doesn't descend underground as they fear eyes are watching so Hatchet and Farouche exit the chopper. They walk out to the middle of the tarmac and dial a number on a phone sitting on the ground. Just as the ground below their feet begins to shift a 747 jumbo jet touches down. It comes barreling right over their heads. Within a minute they are underneath the Pittsburgh airports runway in one of the U.S government's secret nuclear bunkers. There is a nuclear bunker under every airport according to Hatchet.

They are walking down the hall when the ground below them shifts so abruptly that they fall to their knees. When Hatchet realizes what is going on he takes off sprinting towards the Graviton bay. Farouche is surprised when he cannot keep up with the old man. Electron particles sparkle through the air as a metallic taste enters Hatchet's mouth. He rolls around his tongue and immediately spits it out onto the floor. The nuclear base is not as cozy as the structure under Hatchet's building.

"Cannon falls out of the Graviton's seat. He is gasping for air as he tears through a large cocoon that has engulfed the whole of his body. As he rips through a little hole the cocoon vomits him out onto a metal platform. Cannon is reborn! He can't believe that after he placed the little red pellet into the Graviton's particle accelerator console it just took off before he could even get the seatbelt on. Just as he pulls himself to all fours he hears a beautiful melody ringing in his ears. The blinding light show from the particle collision into his body has temporarily blinded him. His body has been weakened from the quasar forces passing through his flesh. He staggers towards the direction of the mesmerizing sounds. As he gets closer the sounds seem more elegant. It's like nothing that he has ever heard. When he slips and falls into a wall the jarring effect jostles his eyesight back. From a distance he can see a glowing white light so he crawls towards it thinking that it is an exit to the outside.

When Cannon finally reaches the light he feels a small warm hand caress his face. Immediately his vision returns to normal and there he sees a little girl not more than eight years of age he thinks standing over him behind a cage. Her hair is like snow, her eyes are as a flame dancing atop a candlestick and her voice that echoes in his mind is like the sound of many waters rolling down a rock bed.

He rolls his tongue around his mouth to taste stickiness like u get when you dose off for a few minutes and then wake. "What are you," He says," as he stares at the most beautiful thing that he has ever laid eyes upon.

The little girl puts her finger to his temple," I am Life and you are death."

When visions of millions of people being shredded by unimaginable creatures enter his mind he jolts away from the little girls touch. He rubs his hands over his face trying to remove the visions," Why are you doing this to me?"

The little girl reaches towards Cannon, closes her eyes and pulls him up against her cell with her mind. She levitates up to his face level and whispers in his ear," You did this Examinan's."

Cannon's body falls back to the floor. He pulls himself up onto his wobbly legs. "What has happened to me?"

The little girl floats down on the floor. She takes her pointer and burns signs into the metal lining the floor. She points to one of the four symbols on the outside of what looks to be a planet, "This is me. I am Uriel, one of the four holding the winds in our palms," She points to the six sign in a line of seven," You are here, the sixth seal."

Cannon drops back down to his knees. The weight of his body is just too much for his legs. He feels like he has just walked for the first time, "I don't understand what you are talking about! Quit talking in riddles damn it!"

Uriel's face changes to that of a lioness. Her body bursts into flames. The metal cell around her becomes molten metal. Cannon looks down to see his skin burning away from the bone so he quickly slides away from her position as fear starts to takes over his mind. But when he realizes that there is no pain he puts his arm down away from his face. The burst of energy subsides and Uriel steps down out of the molten cell. She walks over to Cannon to help him get to his feet." You have created an abomination that will exterminate human kind." She takes his hand in hers.

Cannon looks down to see his burnt flesh repairing itself," Are you God?" He whispers.

Uriel looks up at him with a big smile, "We can be gods if we choose so! Your stumbling block is gone but when you seek death Abaddon, it will flee from thee!"

The warmth emitting from Uriel is unlike any feeling that Cannon has ever been exposed to. The only thing that he can relate it with is when he prayed in church and that warm feeling of energy came over his body like a warm bath or warm chills down the spine if there is such a thing.

"What am I supposed to do Uriel? Please tell me what to do?"

She pulls Cannon down the hall into a plane hangar," I cannot tell you how to proceed. We have already interfered enough." She lets go of his hand while levitating away from him.

Hatchet and Farouche follow the slimy trail left behind Cannon to Uriel's cell. Farouche wraps a sash around his mouth to keep the smoke from the cooling metal at bay. He steps into the cell to see what is glowing on the floor. He breaks a piece of wood out of a small table and presses it onto the floor. The glowing symbols burn into the wood. He exits back out of the cell and hands the wood to Hatchet.

"It has begun Farouche," Hatchet says," don't sound the alarm but rather turn on the infrared cameras to find their position and execute them both. We don't need her anymore!"

Farouche hands him a radio," It's already done sir. They are in the experimental plane hangar on the surface. Should I send the code to Juniper Sir?"

Hatchet with a face full of concern looks at Farouche. He nods his yes and then speaks into the radio.

"Wait, wait a second please I need to know what to do," Cannon yells.

Uriel who is now twenty yards in front of him looks back as she opens two big doors with her mind," Mankind's future rests in the palm of your hand Cannon." She propels into his conscious.

When he looks down to feel a burning sensation in his right hand Uriel disappears in a bright flash of light. He looks everywhere but she is gone. He runs to the exact area where she was standing but there is no trace of her existence. Cannon looks back down at the baseball sized metallic sphere in his right hand. As he inspects the device a sharp edge pierces his finger. Instantly the sphere seems to come to life. It magically floats above his palm like it has its own soul. He feels heat emitting from it as Uriel's voice enters into his mind," My Guardian will guide you Gentry."

Cannon swiftly turns around to see where the sound is coming from. He has so many more questions to ask. But as he spins around and around he realizes that no one is there.

When he peeks out the doors the sunshine warms his face. As he takes in a breath of fresh air he picks up on the sounds of boots stomping in his direction and when he spins around six soldiers dressed in what appears to be a type of black armor surrounds Cannon. Out from there ear pieces Cannon picks up Hatchet's voice. It says," Kill any intruders at will." Without hesitation they all open fire at Cannon, the loud bursts of their P-32's echo throughout the hanger. Cannon closes his eyes waiting for death to take him. All he can think about is here I stand naked as a Jay bird about to become Swiss cheese and I'll probably get my junk blown off so no one will even know if I was a man or a woman. He continues on in his mind as he puts his arms over his face to protect himself but then he quickly realizes that the bullets are not even penetrating his body. When he peers through his arms he witnesses a glowing field around his body. The soldiers all look at one another in awe. After they check to make sure that their shells are not practice blanks they start chambering more magazines but before they can even lock them in place the Guardian rips through each one of their heads. Their bodies slump to the ground as warm blood ripples across the hangar floor to kiss Cannon's toes. The Guardian hovers around his body several times and then places itself on his right forearm. When he reaches down to touch it again the Guardian changes into a type of fancy looking watch.

Without another thought Cannon darts to his Jeep where he climbs into a spare set of clothes. He repeatedly looks down at his right forearm in disbelief. The last few moments are still replaying in his mind. When he sees more military personnel approaching he jumps into his Jeep, once again hammers down on the Hemi and heads out onto 376 West.

CH 2 THE PLUTARCH CONSPIRACY (2008)

1

The time is exactly 4:15 AM. The sun is slowly rising up over the City of Pittsburgh on this beautiful cool May morning of 2008. Dennis Dangle reaches for his alarm as it bangs out the early AM bells. He has played the zeitgeist meeting over and over in his mind even while performing his latest sexual tricks on his wife. Last night's fanatical escapade is what keeps his youth going according to Dennis. Without young pussy, well he would just wither and die,' he always says to his entire cigar smoking click.

Slowly Dennis drags his tired pale ass to the edge of the bed to begin his usual morning ritual. He peels the satin sheets from his sticky balls. It makes a cracking sound like a cracker crumbling. He whimpers as a few pubes disengage with the sheet. The shitty taste of old caviar mixed with vintage wine lines both of his lips.

As he stumbles to the bathroom in the dark he nearly trips over the multitude of sex toys lying on the floor and drags a set of shitty anal beads with his left foot towards the bathroom with him. It's too early for him to remember whose bunghole they fell from last. The smell of raunchy sex and cherry Lick-A-Lot lube lingers in the air. It is very invigorating to Dennis as he inhales a breath or two while reminiscing about last night.

Just as he reaches the bathroom his ass nearly rockets out the prairie dogging log before his cheeks hit the toilet seat. He leans forward around the wall where glances back in awe to capture a glimpse of his hot young wife Monica Dangle lying half naked across his bed. Monica Walker the daughter of Johnny Walker,' not the whisky but a dead beat father from Detroit who was a rubber butler at a local brothel posing as a gentlemen's club. The Fuzzy Carrot Club near eight mile is unfortunately where Monica got her start into the entertainment industry. At just sixteen years old her old man got her a gig at the club singing back up for Infibulation, a local punk band out of Kalamazoo Michigan. It was there that her career took full swing when an industry leader known as The

Sofa King Sexy signed her to be the lead singer with his creation Coprophilous.Monica now twenty-three with a tight body of a goddess lay's in Dennis's Dangle's bed by choice but sometimes her choices aren't always in her best interest despite what she believes. Her hair is crimson like a magnesium fire, just like her personality. Her fake D breasts were perfectly installed by Patrick Gardner associates out of Chicago IL and paid in full by Dennis. She has skin as white as milk and just as smooth as cool butter sliding a crossed a hot tongue. But Dennis hates her tatted up sleeved arms. The only tats that he enjoys the most is the silver mechanical heart impregnated with internal gears right above her shaved beaver or the fluorescent green four leaf clover tramp stamp with curly blue swirls right above her left ass cheek. To Dennis it is a spunk target that he rarely misses.

He still wanders if it's true love or her love of his money that keeps her with his old ass. At the ripe age of Forty-four Dennis is no magnum. Monica pleaded with Dennis time and time again to stop his childishness and just let things fall where they may. But he just can't. Dennis's insecurities have always got the best of him. It especially is apparent in this instance. Dennis has never trusted anyone, not even his own mother. His rough childhood, the abandonment he felt as a kid and mostly the gay innuendos that the media used to drag down his reputation. So marrying a voluptuous up and coming punk singer seemed like the right thing to do at the moment. And he cherished her more than anything in the world. Even his own life!

Slowly Monica lifts her naked body off the bed and stumbles towards the bathroom. Dennis opens his arms. "Good morning love!"

Monica blows right past him dropping to her knees in front of the toilet. She reeks of stale beer and dirty sex. Dennis whine's like a little bitch. "What the fuck. "You are too good to give me a hug?" He doesn't have the heart to tell her that he just dropped Paul's family off at the pool minutes earlier.

She waves her arm at him while chunking into the toilet. Her face is completely buried in the porcelain god. She pulls back her hair, looks up at him with her lips curling. "Go fuck yourself Dennis!"

The stink of bleach and shit from Dennis's fat ass coming up of from the toilet water burns her nostrils a little but she thinks that it is more pleasant than the sour stench of beer erupting from her stomach.

Now with that dumb pouty look that Dennis gives to anyone that doesn't give into his way, he storms off to his twenty foot wide closet where begins aggressively laying out his office attire. He rips the clothes from the hangers with such an attitude. The metal clangs against the plastic violently. He tries to concentrate as he selects a soft blue silk shirt, a bright red Armenian tie, black khakis, green and red poke a dot cotton socks and his infamous alligator loafers that were bought by his father years ago in England at Dixons. It is the only place to buy real handmade shoes he thinks as he stares at the shoes looking for defects. Dennis never did have a sense of style. It really shined through when he sported the Vanilla Ice hair back in the day. His head was just way too large to make that look a cool one. The poor stylist ended up making him appear like Bert the Muppet. In his younger years people would blurt out,' Hey Bert where's Ernie.' But the dumb founded Dennis never caught on. He would even laugh with them pretending to know.

Monica screams from the bathroom, "You better not have knocked me up asshole. I told you not to blow it in me, you ass hole"!

Dennis runs back into the bathroom. He kneels down beside her. He hopes that he can comfort her while containing her fiery attitude. He loves it but sometimes it's just so damn unbearable to tolerate but he knows what it's like to try and tame and immature young girl like Monica as he is on his third attempt with someone her age. Unfortunately the other two girls went to the Cyprus rehabilitation clinic after he slipped a little LSD in their lip gloss.

"I'm sorry honey", Dennis whispers, "I love you so much that sometimes it seems like you don't feel the same. It just makes me crazy. Damn it!"

Monica pulls herself off the floor. She pushes through Dennis to get to the sink. Dennis stands there with a blank stare on his face with his hands crossed. All Monica can think is,' what a little bitch. How can this older man act like such a child?' She brushes her teeth, washes her face then runs over and kisses him to put out the flame of wander. She knows that her career is dead without his money and her band Coprophilous would most likely go to shit.

"Oh my little baby do you want to suckle from mommy's teats? Would that make it all better?" She bellows out like a whiney violin.

Almost immediately Dennis's frown turns to a smile. He begins to rub his naked body against hers. She gently pushes him away knowing the outcome, "Whoa! Whoa, down boy. Save a little for later." Monica spits out.

Now Dennis is pissed off again. It takes very little to set him off when it comes to sex. The redness can be seen in his cheeks, "Are you for real? Every Friday you pull this shit on me. Thursday night you screw my fucking brains out but Friday nothing."

Dennis slams the Crest tooth paste on the counter and the cream shoots all over the mirror. Instantly the mint scent starts lingering in the air. He grabs a bottle of Imodium from the medicine cabinet and heads back to his closet.

<h2 style="text-align:center">2</h2>

Two-thousand feet below the earths' surface the air is warm and pleasant as long as the gigantic turbine fans are circulating but the smell is always a bit dank with a hint of saltiness. That is as long as the East corridor waste fans are also blowing at full capacity, blowing the stink of rotten corpses out the stack to the top outside. It is indeed stink to humans but mouthwatering to Plutarch's. The time below ground is the same as on the surface, you just can't see or feel the sunshine but to some the constant 65 degrees year round is wonderful and the sunshine is your enemy.

Cannon Knight who also addresses himself with alias names such as David Christopher, Arcane Tact or none other than the craziest of them all Gentry who also frequents under the name Centaur, a well-known artist on the surface gyrates in ecstasy. His multiple personalities go right along with each name and they rear their ugly heads from time to time. Over the years he has been able to control them with pain infliction, hypnosis and a lot of mind altering drugs, especially knell weed.

He as in Cannon this very minute of time and Celeste a Praetorian Plutarch guard are making love like a couple of animals. The sounds of flesh smacking echo throughout Celeste's quarters. Celeste's bloodline runs deep into the ancient families who first came forth from slavery to start the Plutocracy back in biblical times. It is said that the blood coursing through her veins comes from the Livid Mother herself now reigning over the City of Cyprus but she is never seen.

Cannon's body smashes against Celeste's as the two look like they are at war against one another. Their motions don't seem normal according to Cannon. Plutarch woman move so much better than human woman. And her genitals seem to spin. It's the only way he can describe the feelings going on down there.

"Celeste we are floating in the air again," Cannon says," you are the only Plutarch woman that this ever happens with."

Celeste bites his upper lip. She stuffs her split tongue into his mouth. She massages his tongue with the two pieces. He looks down to see her forked tongue caressing his tongue like two small legs walking slowly. He kisses her back hard. Her mouth tastes like candy. She flips him over and rides him through the air until he puts his hands against the wall to keep form hitting his head.

Plutarch's are rumored to possess telekinetic powers that range from all levels. Celeste can read minds, shape shift and levitate, especially during love making but it really goes wild when she and Cannon mingle. As Cannon hollers in ecstasy while erupting into Celeste the two fall to the bed below. Her hot sticky milk flows all down over his package onto his thighs. She is quivering profusely. The moist squishing sounds make him continue to thrust upward into her.

"You need to be quiet Cannon; If Cutlass finds out that we are interbreeding you will be destroyed. Oh and what do you mean the only Plutarch woman?" It's hard for her to speak while the fifteenth convulsive orgasm consumes her body. She tries to control her body as her eyes roll way back in her head. Cannon is the only one who hits her G spot.

Cannon rolls over, caresses her face and runs his hands down over her lean body. Her pale grayish blue purple skin is beautiful to him. She wears it with pride. He thinks that is why she attracts him so much. Her scent also makes him spring forth uncontrollable wood. Her pheromones are like that of lavender mixed with honey. Almost all Plutarch women are irresistible to humans. That's how they lure us in to consume our flesh.

"Well uh-", Cannon tries to speak but is at a loss of words. He doesn't want to piss off Celeste like he did two years before when she ripped his arm out of socket.

"It's ok silly. I know that you slept with Lily because she told me." She stares into his face with a devilish grin. The black lining of her mouth really makes her teeth glow bright. Her eyes are hypnotizing. They don't have retinas like humans so their entire eyes are brightly colored.

"What she told you?" Cannon abruptly sits up in the soft bed.

"Yeah she didn't want her arm ripped off too." Celeste laughs lightly.

The Plutarch women are like surface woman in most ways except that all of their joints are doubled and they are most notably unreal in bed because their pleasure organs can be adjusted to each partner. Many of the other Plutarch women all bleach and tan their skin in hopes of someday rising to the surface. Almost every Plutarch under the earth yearns to one day feel the sun shine upon their faces. Everyone but Celeste, she is content with her simple life of guarding the Livid Mother's quarters. Cannon opens his mouth but before he can get out another word Lily barges into the room. The mercury liquid like barrier for a door seems to float in the air. Cannon quickly rolls to the floor pulling the jasper covers overtop his body.

"Come quick Celeste something is wrong," Lily says," oh and I know your under there Cannon cause I can smell you. "Lily looks down at her sidearm, pulls it, chambers a shell and turns around, "Ok bye," Lily mumbles as she runs back out the door.

Cannon pulls the covers off his face," what was that all about? She smells me?"

Celeste smacks Cannon's right ass cheek protruding out from the covers," of course she smells you dummy, we all can. You have to remember that you are only half Plutarch and half-."

She stops her speech dead because she for one knows that Cannon contains the demon deciduae inside him. It sometimes reveals itself through the night.

She has been awoken by it talking to the other entities residing in Cannon's body. She recorded several of the conversations but hasn't given the copy to Cannon yet as she feels that his undeveloped brain couldn't handle it. She realizes that when these beings come out the true Cannon that she loves takes a back seat to their actions sometimes. It is something that the two have been working on and it has helped for six months. Cannon waves in the air to break her trance like gaze.

"What were you going to say Celeste? That I'm half monster?" Cannon smiles and reaches for her hand. She quickly pulls away while pulling her legs up to her chest. She sits there flexing her peck muscles. Her fun bags dance up and down like small puppets. She is playing the wan ton with Cannon as she always does and he knows it so he makes his member jump up and down under the covers like a puppet too. He raises his eyebrows up and down in sync with his member. She tries to smack it like on one of those whack a mole games at the arcade but he is too quick. She winks, sticks out her tongue and pushes him back, "It is not funny Deekadue. I can hear them talking inside your head when we make love." She peers at him with all seriousness.

"Why do you call me that?" Cannon slides up around her body. She can feel the heat from his breath on her chest.

Celeste runs her soft hand down along Cannon's face. She leans in kissing him softly. Cannon pulls back a little afraid. It's like Celeste is kissing him for the last time. She steals a quick peck anyway and smiles, "My father told me a story about angels from above called the Deekadue that came to earth to save the people many years ago from the Deciduae. Oh what am I saying? Cannon you know that there are other races because here we are. You can't believe that we are the only two types of races do you?"

Cannon's eyes open a little wider. She can tell by the strange look on his face that his cage has been rattled. It wasn't what she was going for in anyway because this was one hybrid that she actually cared for. Celeste knows that it is forbidden to fully illuminate a lower breed of race but her love for Cannon goes deeper than she has ever encountered.

"Cannon you have the same black markings as the Deekadue on your tongue that they had all over their bodies. At least I hope that I have it right or we are all doomed."

Cannon stares into her beautiful red eyes. They are mesmerizing like staring into a raging bonfire. Celeste pulls her face from his gaze. She gracefully flips over backwards onto her feet. It was always something that she did to show off and just as always she looks back with a shit eating grin like; bet you can't do that human. It is an attitude that every Plutarch houses. An attitude of greatness, like look at us we are better than you. Hell Cannon remembers vividly of encountering some humans that are the same way and when he did he just cut off their heads. Cannon watches her every move. Celeste slides across the room like she is making love to the air. It is the sexiness that she exudes that drives Cannon and all the other Plutarch men crazy. Cannon knows that if Knox ever catches wind of the two he will kill him. He knows for a fact because Knox told him to his face that if he touches any of the Plutarch women he will be destroyed. The rules were laid down to Cannon when he first entered the Reaper program at age sixteen. And on that day Cannon encountered the biggest culture shock of his life. It wasn't like just trying to shit in a hole in the Middle East without so much as a sheet of TP or succumbing to the hose for cleansing your rectum but a shock of holy shit we are not alone in the world. It was a shock that made him a little mad in the head for a few weeks. So mad that he and the others ran and hid from them or at least tried.

Interbreeding is punishable by death in the Plutarch arena. The arena is where all Plutarch's solve their issues. If a problem arises that cannot be worked out through discussion then an arena match is booked between the rivals. This also acts as free entertainment. A few Plutarch's like the overgrown Knox actually get paid to compete in the arena where he slaughters beasts from other planets but mostly the weaker bred humans. There are no court systems to judge them for crimes like on the surface. And if a Plutarch or human is just too crazed they are dropped into Hades. It is a true lake of fire beneath the City of Cyprus that is fueled by all the toxic waste poured into from the factories on the surface.

All the Plutarch colonies watched as Cannon grew into a man. From seventeen on he performed all of their bidding without question and even consumed a few of his own kind during Cutlass's wild dinner parties.

Celeste looks out her door to see what all the commotion is about. She sees several of the guards running down the corridor. Echoes of someone screaming can be heard throughout the corridors.

"Boom", a large explosion rocks the ground below. Salt dust drifts through the air.

"Cannon quickly wash my scent off your body and get your clothes on."

Celeste walks in and back out of her steam shower. She looks down at Cannon while running a brush through her long silver strands of hair.

"I have to show you something Cannon," she says," I can't let happen to you what has happened to all the rest. So let's hurry because we don't have much time."

Cannon is steaming off when he turns to Celeste. He stands up from his routine prayer to the one God as he does every morning. "What are you talking about all the rest?"

She walks over. Hands him a towel made from a kotare hide and heads towards the kitchen area. She reaches into her cooling unit, removes a few human protein bars and places them in her bag. Plutarch's have a metabolism that burn's calories three times as fast as humans do.

"What is this Celeste? This is the softest material that I have ever felt in my life," Cannon says," Is this new?"

Celeste puts on the finishing touches to her body armor, the P-636 Hawkeye aerial grappler that Lily configured for Plutarch use.

"That's what I'm talking about Cannon. I have to show you the truth. It's an ancient animal that once roamed the surface long before any of our times on earth."

"What do you mean truth Celeste?" A deep look of concern comes across Cannon's face. It seems that every time that someone has a secret to tell him the outcome ends in great peril.

"Well my dear I just found out that the council believes that you are a spy for the red bloods and that you are trying to undermine the elite reaper program." She hits the button on her boots and they conform to her feet. She spins a dial on her arm band that temporarily makes her invisible.

"What the hell are you talking about Celeste? Where did you go? I have dedicated most of my life to all of you. My God I'm fucking 38 years old now and I'm over the hill according to the people on the surface. We all can't age like you living into the hundreds of years!"

Celeste walks over to him, kneels down and puts her hot tongue into his ear. He jumps a little from the wetness. Her breath is scolding to his sensitive flesh.

She would like nothing more than to tell him that she is thousands of years old but knows that his mind will detonate. She reappears whispering in her usual sexy voice, "Yes you can Cannon, oh yes you can and I'll show you how." She smiles and reaches for Cannon's hand, "Now I want you to know one thing. If we get caught you and I are going to be mutilated in the arena by one of the genetic beasts that Freckle has created, most likely a Fang, a Zipper head or a Thrasher."

Cannon slips on his boots, rises up and grabs her hand. He is not allowed to wear armor or carry any type of weapon while in the City of Cyprus. No human is allowed too.

"What on earth is a fang or zipper? You're making this shit up Celeste just to test me."

Celeste squeezes his hand tight. She leads him to the back of her place where he sees the outline of a small square protruding through one of the human hair rugs on the floor. She flips over the rug, presses a code into the security panel and the door slides open. A stale scent rushes up from the gaping hole in the floor. When Cannon looks down he cannot' see the bottom.

"Celeste, where are you taking me? I'm not going to fit down that hole."

She rubs her hands down over his chest. "Well Cannon now is the best time to test those new found skills that you keep bragging about. You have to shift your body because I can't do it for you. And I know that you have only been allowed to change your face but no one is here to see."

Cannon stands there as Celeste is already climbing down inside. He closes his eyes as his body starts to contort. He envisions that his body is like taffy. Slowly his body contorts thinner.

"Hurry up, "Celeste says," We need to move quickly." She is literally flying down the ladder.

Cannon can hear her echoes drifting up from roughly a hundred feet below him. He quickly shifts enough to get down the ladder where he reaches Celeste. She once again grabs his hand and pulls him several hundred yards through the dark. He tries to see where they are going but his eyes have not developed to see in the dark yet.

"Celeste where are you taking me and what is all this about?"

"Just keep up. We are almost there."

After three rights, two lefts, a straight dash above the arena and at the top of a rock chute Cannon comes to a halt. He leans over the edge of the arena wall to see unimaginable creatures devouring humans a hundred feet below. Almost the entire City of Cypress is there cheering for their favorite warriors. Just then he sees Knox come barreling out on top of some kind of Triceratops dinosaur looking beast, "What am I seeing Celeste? Is this the secret that everyone has kept from me all of these years? Your sick love to kill and eat humans?"

Celeste grabs his hand again," Come on damn it before we get caught. Quit getting all sentimental all of a sudden. You brought most of those assholes down here. "She rips him down into the tube with her. The two of them spin round and round for several minutes until they finally reach the bottom. Once there the room is lit with a tremendous amount of light. All of the walls appear to be quartz or diamonds. The light is so bright that Celeste puts on a pair of shades. Her eyes are sensitive to light as she has been underground her whole life while living on planet earth.

"This is what I'm talking about Cannon. You are in the chambers of the ancients. Now hurry, get over here because we don't have much time. When the arena battle is over the guards will return to their posts and well I don't really want to climb up that tube all the way back to my room."

Cannon quickly joins Celeste in front of a large control panel. She pushes a few buttons and the entire room lights up with solar systems. She points to the center of the universe to show him earth. She then moves her hands back and forth to pull the universe in tighter.

"Ok Celeste your light show is beautiful but what is this all about?"

Celeste takes his hand and moves it around the air until Pluto rests in the top of his palm. She points to the distance right above it which states 3.57 billion miles.

"Ok so it would take 8,500 days to get there. What is the point to this?" He asks.

She points to a door to the left of their position, "In there is a transportation machine called the sword of God that can beam you from Earth to Pluto or any other planet within seconds; however the council needs enough dark fluid to create a power source." The same lie that Celeste utters is identical to the one that Cutlass has told everyone in the City of Cyprus but in all reality Cutlass wants to use the dark liquid hidden in the brains of a few on earth to travel to the Synagogue of Satan where he plans to steal the sword called; The word of God, a biblical sword that can kill anything on any planet, even gods. It is the one thing that can destroy a soul and a Dragon if needed.

"Why would you want to go there it's an uninhabitable planet?" Cannon shakes his head in disbelief.

Celeste pulls the planet down into her palm. She expands the atmosphere to show the surface.

"Cannon you cannot believe what you have been told by the Red Bloods above because we implanted almost all of the lies into every aspect of your education programs for hundreds of years. We helped to write your religious beliefs and most importantly we have placed the stumbling blocks into your minds right after your birth to ensure that your race doesn't ascend to fast. Where do you think that internet and cell phones came from? It's a program to track you all in real time. We know everyone's position that owns one at all times. The Keepers of the light monitor everyone." Celeste rubs her hand through his hair. She knows that his tiny mind cannot even comprehend a small particle of what she is preaching, "Now look at this scan of the planet's surface it is in real time just like the ones on Google earth coming in from the satellites revolving around earth."

As Cannon looks on he can see Trillions of Plutarch's all over Pluto's surface. There are huge cities scattered abroad for miles. He can see small disc shaped objects flying back and forth between the cities. Celeste points to a certain point on the planet.

"This is where I am supposed to be from but it's been so long that my memories are not much more than fragments anymore. Cutlass told me that my mother still remains there. It is called Areopagus and next to it is Ptolemais the capital of the planet"

Cannon slides his hand against her arm. His mind is about to pop. It is so much to take in and after 38years of believing that earth was all there was. And his religion belief not being correct is a little too much to handle. He pulls away from her. A little bit of anger lingers across his face. She sees it glowing back at her but it's not her prerogative at all. Cannon takes a deep breath and blows it out slowly, "Well then why don't you just transport back there?"

Celeste can feel his pain as she had the same done to her by her mother Aquila when she was only five. She only believed in Plutonius the one and only God until she read the universal scrolls of order.

"That's why I brought you down here to show you. If any of us Plutarch's transport back to our home world the entire armada will come here and wipe your civilization off the planet."

Cannon looks on in disbelief. He grabs Celeste's hand and pulls it close. The mind detonating torment is almost unbearable. His eyes are starting to tear up.

"Why would they do that? Don't we pretty much live in harmony as one now?"

Celeste stares into Cannon's face. "We eat your kind Cannon. You are our food source but we have evolved over the years to incorporate other things into our diets to preserve your race. When I was younger I could eat and entire person per day and we including everyone on Pluto triple your numbers here on earth. Figure that one out genius."

Cannon pulls his hand away from hers. His eyes have been ripped open, "So why don't you all just come down here and wipe us all out then?" Cannon is more than pissed now.

"Well that's what I'm about to tell you if you let me. Your biblical story of Noah is true to a certain extent. The flood was not of water but of hybrid dragons a genetically designed beast to clean off the surfaces of planets. And the beasts were created by an Atlantis scientist by the name of Gentry Faust or as humans know him as the Serpent. We Plutarch's call him the faceless man. He was cast down from the planet Heaven for trying to take over the enlightened elder council.

Cannon puts his hand up to her face," Hold on, hold on. The planet Heaven you say? Please enough bullshit already."

Now Celeste is pissed a little that a puny human man put his hand in her face. As she pushes her anger down deep and takes a deep breath she starts again," Please don't interrupt again, ok? He vowed to one day return, to decimate everyone on the planet. A great war ensued in Heaven while he was there killing millions and only the Plutarch ancients have details about the war. Gentry and a few others of his likeminded kind were transported onto earth after their defeat. At once he quickly started playing a god by rearranging the entire DNA sequencing protocols of all the samples that he collected to produce a superior race of everyone combined or so he thought. His motive was the same as Cutlass's to make humans create more of the dark fluid in their brains. And on one day a machine similar to the Cyclotron malfunctioned just like it did with you in it and an unimaginable creature came from it. The beast ate the hearts of millions and it converted millions more until only a few of us were left on earth. That is Plutarch's and humans."

Cannon kneels down to crack his knees, "So what are you saying that everything about the history of the planet and our Christian belief system is untrue?"

Celeste shakes her head yes, "Cannon I was there when this all happened believe me I would not lie to you. Didn't you ever wonder why your bible is incomplete or why there are strange names like Thessalonica, Apollonia or people called Epicureans? Cannon these are the names of planets in similar solar systems and names of other beings in the universe. Didn't you ever wonder why there are so many different religions? It's because many races of beings from other planets visited here. Your Jesus took human form so that you all would not freak out. Look here." She pushes another button on the console. Trillions of numbers appear in the air.

"These are all the DNA samples of every living creature from many different worlds. Cannon the ARC is down here with us. We were using the great pyramids to beam hydrogen to the ship and when the power source dropped off we jettisoned Noah and his family to the earth's surface as we plummeted hard into the ground. And that is why we are thousands of feet below the Earth's surface. The others on Pluto think that we are all dead and that the Earth is still uninhabitable. They all know and fear the Dragon as it killed millions of our people. It is nicknamed the black death plague and no one will come here in fear of spreading the infectious disease to the home world but if Cutlass doesn't get his way with the Red Bloods he is going to transport one of us back to Pluto to tell everyone that Earth is ripe for the harvesting."

Cannon turns around to face the North wall. He walks over and puts his right hand on the cold surface. Sweat drips down into his eyes leaving a stinging sensation behind. He then rests his head against the wall trying to gain some composure. The thoughts of all the lies and the visions of the 83 that he killed haunt his memories. Every day he struggles with the fact that at any moment he could lose control and never return to his true form. A form that he wasn't even sure what was at this point. And now he stands there being told that everything is a lie.

"So let me get this straight. Everything that I ever knew in my entire life is a lie? Is that what you are trying to tell me here? It can't be there is no way. Someone would have known about it and told others after all this time." He drops to his knees; he pukes up all of his dinner from the night before. Fluid drips from his nose as the acid burns his throat. The rancid taste tears up his eyes. He swears that he can taste a hint of flan way back in his throat.

Celeste can see the shock in Cannon's face. She walks over to him to provide a little comfort. She almost hates to hurt him like this but she knows that he must know the truth or Cutlass will use his power for his own bidding. She hugs him tightly. He hugs her back but with a little disgust. He has known Celeste for 12 years now and wonders why now all of a sudden.

"Cannon according to your human bible, Ephesian 6: 10-18 and Hebrews 4:12 there is ancient armor that you must obtain to protect your planet against the cosmic powers. The apostles spoke of a shield of faith, a helmet of salvation, a belt of truth, a breast plate of righteousness and a sword called the word of God. The only weapon in the entire universe that can kill anything, even destroy the soul so that not even a hint of its existence remains. Even destroy the Serpent Gentry when he returns."

"Why are you telling me this? You could of just ate me years ago and saved yourself a shit ton of trouble."

She wipes away the food particles from his mouth and nose. Her compassion for this human hybrid is evident. And despite the consequence of death she feels that the risk is worth the weight.

"Cannon I care about you. You are not like the others who came before you and we have the same blood coursing through our veins. I know because I put it there personally. And I'm sorry that I didn't tell you earlier but you weren't ready, I know it. I just feel it in my soul that you are destined for greater things! We have to move because the battle in the arena is almost over. I can feel the excitement of everyone floating through the air."

"Well why know? What has changed all of a sudden?"

Celeste pulls his face into her hands. He can feel the warmth resonating from her body. He closes his eyes as he to can feel that it may be the last time that the two ever get to share a moment together.

"Cannon it's because Cutlass has decided to destroy you after you get the God particle. And I know that your mind is probably mush now but I have to show you something that will quite honestly probably make you a little sicker."

Celeste grabs him by his wrist and leads him to the Graviton room.

3

"It's like you have to save that pussy for someone else on Fridays," Dennis shouts aloud in a fit of rage," It can't be too stretched out. Don't want him to know that someone was already there, right!"

Monica disregards the ear beating. She jumps in the shower to wash away the previous night's filth from her body. The crust of Dennis's fluids cracks between the folds of her thighs and ass as she cranks one of the ten knobs in the large rock encrusted shower stall. She accidentally turns one of the knobs towards the cold direction. The ice water pours forth but it doesn't even faze her because her body is aching so badly from all the hard booze that she consumed. Once the warm water is regulated she leans out from behind the shower door, pulls a pregnancy stick out of her purse from on the floor, pulls the stick from the plastic cover and pees on the end. She then puts the test up on the upper soap dish mounted on the back of the shower stall wall. She then slowly squeezes out a quarter sized dab of coconut vanilla body wash onto her wash poof, lathers up real good and cleans all areas of her body. The scent of vanilla always seems to relax her. She is thinking her way out of the conversation but knows that Dennis is relentless. It's been the same old fight for the last year or so and she knows that if David even catches a hint of another man's odor on her there will be hell to pay. It is becoming extremely taxing on her mentally and physically trying to juggle two men at the same time. She is always texting or leaving to talk to one another of the men in the restroom wherever she is at the time.

And all of the lies are starting to catch up with her. Monica wanted to end the relationship a long time ago but fears the consequences. All she wanted to do was dabble a bit with the bad boy but the sex was out of this world. She just couldn't stop the cravings. David was like a drug.

It was all fun until the night of **October 17th, 2007 at 3:22 AM exactly.** The time and date are forever etched in her brain like a cancer that eats her away every day. It was supposed to be a night of pure ecstasy. A pleasure experiment with another woman or two but it did not go as planned. The scent of the vanilla wash gel takes her back to that night in Vegas. And as the fragments of that encounter slowly begin to enter her frontal lobe she catapults into a dreamlike state from the past were she relives the David encounter all over again. Her legs begin to weaken, she crouches down to her knees before falling. Her body is trembling out of control. Dennis hears her feet squeak on the fine onyx shower floor as the shampoo bottle bounces off the shower floor.

"Hey are you alright in there, baby?" Dennis hollers from the bedroom.

Dennis's voice fades out as she drifts off into a bent reality in her mind. She sees David's face appear to her as if in a dream. She reaches out her right hand to touch him but he disappears into the steam.

"David Christopher", she says under her breath with her lips now quivering.

Slowly Monica begins to remember that night vividly.

4

When Celeste pushes the security code into the air tight cylindrical door, the hard metal turns to a liquid mercury type state. They both pass through the door like walking through water but only dry. And there they see standing before them a slightly green glowing figure locked in a cage twenty feet or so from the Gravitons underbelly. Odd noises can be heard coming from below the beings waist.

Cannon looks on in awe. He can't believe his eyes. The Graviton is enormous as he can see it going for miles down through the corridors. It is more amazing than the rumors give it credit for. Energy particles can still be seen emitting light energy like lightning bugs floating through the air on the earth's surface. The energy still exists from the previous start up a week ago.

The static electricity in the atmosphere makes their hair stand straight up. Celeste pulls Cannon from his awe inspiring gaze. Her fingertips get lightly shocked," ouch," utters from her mouth as she gently pushes him in front of the cage where he captures a hint of stench. He can see fecal matter all over the floor, on the bars of the cage and a yellow substance dripping from the cells roof.

"Cannon I want you to meet your twin brother Lox Knight." Celeste says.

Cannon puts both hands on the cage to peer through the bars. He can quickly see that something is not right with the person standing in there. The fecal matter squishes through his knuckles.

"Celeste, is this another joke or what? I only had one brother and that was Mitch."

"Cannon, try to think back to the lies that I told you about," Celeste says," It was all lies my dear, you weren't even really born like you remember but more like blended like a shake in a test tube to be superior for Cutlass's needs."

Cannon looks down at the floor shaking his head.

"So what the fuck Celeste, you brought me here to see a guy with an ass for a face for what to get some kind of secret knowledge of rectums or what?"

Just then the Lox runs over to them. Fecal matter splashes up from the floor all over Cannon. Lox bends over and pulls down his pants to reveal his face where his ass should be. Shit covers almost all of his face and Cannon can see the brown waste hanging from his teeth. The site is so overbearing that Cannon almost runs away.

"She brought you here dumbass," Lox says in a garbled voice," so that you don't turn out like me. Oh, oh, oh shit hold on a second." Lox turns his face sideways away from Cannon and vomits out a huge turd. The gurgling sounds echo throughout the walls as the stench rises up to bite Cannon's nostrils. Lox spits all over the ground and then farts from his mouth a few times, wipes his face with some toilet paper and then returns to Cannon's position.

"Ok idiot do you want to end up like me shitting out of your mouth? You know that I have to be fed from a tube shoved down my asshole right? You see it up there hanging out"

When the stink from Lox's breath hits Cannon and Celeste the two take a step back to try and capture some clean air. Cannon cannot believe what is standing before him. He doesn't know whether to be sad for the creature or laugh. It just so unreal, he thinks.

"What did they do to you," Cannon says," I thought this Graviton machine was perfected."

Lox turns sideways and farts from his mouth again. The loud noise echoes out through the corridors like one of those big chili cheese dog trucker farts. It even smells just as ripe too.

"I swear they put lactose in that feeding tube just to be funny. Can you imagine farting from your mouth man? Do you have any idea what shit taste like?"

Cannon cringes. He puts his hand up over his nose to repel some of the stink, "I can't say that I do Lox, guess I just never had the pleasure."

Lox hobbles around in the cage like an elderly man. It appears to Cannon that all of his limbs have contorted in the opposite directions. He has one big leg and one big arm like a person with elephantiasis. His flesh looks like it drips from the overly large bones lying underneath.

"Well I'll tell you. It tastes like shit!" He screams.

Cannon grabs Celeste by her hand. He pulls her away from the cage over to the Graviton controls. He can hear Lox ranting and raving about corn and peanuts getting stuck in his teeth and how terrible the hard toilet paper blisters his lips. Where's the Charmin?" He yells.

Cannon pulls Celeste closer to him, "What happened here Celeste?"

Celeste gently squeezes his hand, "Cannon your mother gave birth to twins. It is how it is always done in our world, one is usually born for service and the other is for spare parts. The Plutarch's are born the same way in order to keep the race thriving. You were concocted in a test tube by someone and then placed in your mother's womb for birth on the surface. You will have to find out who decided on your creation Cannon."

Again he cannot believe what is being said. He wants to scream to the top of his lungs,' what the fuck,' but holds back all that energy in fear of changing, "Well ok I think that I can accept that but can you tell me why my so called brother shits out of his face?"

Celeste tries not to laugh. She doesn't really care about Lox's feelings as he has always been Cutlass's bitch. She always thought that he had a terrible attitude toward everyone and as Cutlass's pet he could pretty much do what he wanted below ground. Even beat up on a few of the Plutarch women a time or two. That was before he became ass backwards of course.

"Ok Cannon but you will not like it. When you brought the God particle back with you it turned out to be something else. Something inorganic and that is why Lox's gene makeup shifted so uncontrollably."

"So you brought me her to show me that I could be the one shitting from my mouth is that it?"

Celeste drops to one knee to chamber a shell in to her AR-19. She quickly picks up on the sounds coming from above. She looks up at Cannon with a look of concern, "Precisely you were to be the test subject but Lox refused to go second so Cutlass agreed to let him go first. And this is the result that could have been you. Now you might want to take a knee as this could get messy."

"What get messy?" Cannon asks as he kneels down beside her. He can feel the heat from her body radiating into his flesh through his jacket. Plutarch's body temperatures are way hotter than humans and that is how you can distinguish them from real humans when they shape shift. Then from the South bay area a large thud is heard from the upper elevator dropping in to the Graviton corridor. Out marches Cutlass with a bloody Knox at his side and a few other armed guards with Lily being in the center of them. She smiles, and then winks at Cannon. Celeste catches it and returns an evil eye in a pissed off gesture. Knox feels Celeste's anger as he grinds his teeth at Cannon. He can hear the loud grinding noise approaching form Knox's mouth. Knox is dragging a battered human man that has wheels for legs. He hollers at it," Come on now Jacques. Roll faster damn it or I'll eat you." The poor mutated creature rolls along faster to keep up.

"Cannon my boy I guess you got to witness your handy work," Cutlass says in his usual angry deep voice," Knox, go let Cannon feel some of my pain will you my boy?"

Knox instantaneously drifts into Celeste and Cannon both sending them twirling into Lox's cage. Celeste's rifle goes flying down behind the large non unity rare earth magnet power generator. Lox kneels down beside Cannon to whisper into his ear, "Go find the elder Nicolaite, Crispus," but before he finishes Knox pulls his side arm, points it at Lox and fires off a round.

"Holy fuck you big blue oaf you shot me in my ass," Lox screams," what the hell is wrong with you, you stupid overgrown Smurf?"

Knox starts laughing wildly and points to Lox. "You have the same blood as this idiot before me," Knox says in his deep growling voice," and I forgot because I was aiming for your head."

Cutlass pulls Knox back by his big arm, "You idiot don't kill him. We need one more test from his body so he must be breathing."

Cutlass waves to Lily to go get the repair division to help fix Lox's wound before he bleeds out.

"Oh and Mr. Knight we heard the whole conversation between you and Celeste. If you try to deviate from my plan I will push this little red button on this here tracking device to alert the entire Plutarch armada. They will arrive here in three earth days and most likely eviscerate everyone on the planet in half that time."

Cutlass shakes a small watch like device in the air. It has a small yellow blinking light on it. Cannon wipes the blood from his mouth and sits up to face Cutlass, "What do you want from me Cutlass? Haven't I been a good little errand boy for you all of these years? I mean my God I killed thousands of my own kind to please your tastes. Is that not enough?"

Cutlass spits on Cannon, "You don't have a kind son. I'm sure you are confused and oh you look so hungry. How long has it been since you have fed?"

Cannon tries to speak but he is punched in the mouth by Knox repeatedly. Cutlass kneels beside him, "I will tell you when you are allowed to address me do you understand?" Knox moves Cannon's head back and forth in a yes motion for him.

"You are a mutt, nothing more than a hybrid of parts strewn together to make a servant. Nothing more than a modern Frankenstein you are. You and the many others before you are to be used and then put down after your services. Do you really think that we pardon half breeds to pollute the worlds? I think not!"

Celeste looks on in horror. She is a bit delusional from cracking her head against the wall.

Cannon leaps to his feet. He drifts through Knox almost reaching Cutlass before a paralyzing pain in his head drops him to his knees.

"Again piss ant, you the stupid human in you thought that we would grant great power without restraint and then let you run amuck between both worlds. Everything has order in the universe Cannon and every civilization bows before its creator. And Cannon I am your God not your friend!"

Cannon pushes through the pain. He digs deep into the souls inside his body and forcefully drifts into Cutlass knocking him up against the electrical control panel for the Graviton. Sparks fly from the panel as the lights blink.

A drift is a term used for reapers that can jump though a kind of wormhole to move to a place in milliseconds. Not all of them can do it as it usually takes years to master.

Cutlass falls to the ground dropping the remote for Cannon's brain implant. When the power surge in Cannon's head stops he begins to change. His mouth begins to elongate revealing thousands of sharp teeth protruding in every direction. Knox blasts him with a thunder dwarf round. The shell splits into 10 separate explosives. The miniature canisters embed themselves deep into Cannon's flesh. When they detonate the micro explosions blow large holes in Cannon's body. Blood is pouring fourth from every new orifice in his body but he still perseveres getting a good bite on Cutlass's left arm. Cutlass shrieks like a little girl.

5

David Christopher is like no other to Monica. She has no idea that his real name is Cannon Knight who is partially a Plutarch alien and can shape shift parts of his body at will. And there are many other secrets that she will unfortunately come to find out but it will be too late. To her he is a true vision of Godly Greek inspired perfection. She thought that he looked exactly like one of those marble statues carved at the Caesars palace in Las Vegas or at least from what was remembered on one of her drunken binges.

The two met at the Luxor Casino right after one of her shitty shows. With a small turn out and little to show for all her efforts she decided to binge at the Rusty Pickle 2 bar in the middle of the casino. Her wandering eye captures his pure magnificence immediately. With her mind two sheets to the wind already, it became apparent that it was on.

His 6'0" frame accented all of the 217 pounds nicely as he stands at the five hundred dollar minimum black jack table. He sports faded blue jeans, a nice maroon collared long sleeve shirt and what appears to be rather pricey leather dress shoes. His jet black hair is groomed perfectly to the right side.

First she sees beef and then all those thousand dollar chips piled up high. The gold chains layered around his thick neck with an odd center piece that looks like an old dried bean accent his appearance well she thinks. And best of all, no wedding ring, even though that hasn't stopped her before. She points him out to her guitarist Trudy and immediately begins stumbling into his direction.

"I'm eating that tonight." Monica says to Trudy as the two share a Newport cigarette while supporting one another coming through the casino floor.

Trudy grabs Monica; she pulls her close as she almost falls into the roulette table several feet from David, "Monica, pull your shit together, damn it girl you spilled Grey Goose all over your tits. No rich guy wants a drunken whore."

Trudy then grabs Monica's bra by both hands. She pulls it up over her spilling out breasts. Monica looked beautiful that evening. Even with almost two full sleeves of tats lining her arms she wore her black Hermes dress with class. Monica's true passion was art and her body proves it. She slyly stumbles into David trying not to be too obvious. He noticed her earlier but had to keep his eyes on the true prize of the night. Within an instance she is in his arms. David's glass goes flying, his Crown on the rocks spills all over his shirt and all down onto the blackjack table. He aggressively pulls her closer into his body. At first Monica shows fear but smiles as she feels his immense package throbbing against her thigh. He slides his strong hands down over her backside as his lips gently place upon hers. Slowly he licks her lower lip up to the top gently nibbling and then sucks her upper lip before releasing her back onto her own two feet. Her pineapple lipstick tickles his nostrils. The scent just turns him on that much more. It is the same kind that Grace Adams wore when they first kissed at the big oak tree,' David thinks. Pineapple blunts are also David's favorite. The scent always puts him at ease in tense situations. Immediately Monica begins to dampen her panties. Her eyes roll way back in her head if almost not to return any time soon. Once back into reality Monica stands up straight and adjusts her bra.

"I'm sorry mist-," She tries to say but before she can finish her sentence David vertically puts his right finger over her lips, like telling her to keep a secret. She can smell the hint of Crown on his breath, some kind of seasoned meat possibly and Gain detergent on his sleeve. His nails are perfectly manicured with not a trace of funk underneath. Not one.

"Sh-. No need for apologies my sweet. It appears that your extensive alcohol indulgence has rendered your limbs weak." When David he sees Monica's pencil eraser sized nipples protruding through her beautiful dress he becomes well aware of what is about to go down. He looks over Monica across the casino floor to see if the little Thai spinner that he has been tailing all night is still at the baccarat tables. When he doesn't see her anymore he activates the tracking device on his phones.

Monica starts to melt. She thinks, "my God rich, smoking hot and articulate, usually I either attract rich old farts, cave men with hot bodies or psychos. But damn I hit the jackpot tonight."

Trudy recognizes that the deal is going down so she retreats back to the room with Marco.

David gazes deep into her cerulean eyes, "Maybe we can go somewhere a little quieter. You agree?"

Monica nods her head all wobbly in agreement. All her extremities are still numb from the mouth licking. She doesn't even know his name and at that point she didn't care. It wasn't the first time that she met a strange man and had a one night fling. It was exciting to her, a game of sorts!

Just then a sexy waitress dressed in no more than thin black lingerie steps in. Shelly Stephenson wears her clothes well and David knows what she is hiding beneath. The two went a few rounds dancing to the horizontal mamba a few weeks back and by the look in her eyes she remembered that weekend vividly. She wasn't the first incomplete woman that he had bed. You couldn't even tell that she had a prosthetic leg. Not even by the way she walks. She tried to tell David about a psycho that cut it off and left her to bleed to death in the street but when she started balling uncontrollably he left. The cries start bringing back memories of Mitch.

"Here are your two fingers of Crown on the rocks Doctor." Shelly says.

David grabs the drink, shoots it like a shot and throws a thousand dollar chip on her tray, "Thank you beautiful!"

She gives him a peck with a hint of tongue on the cheek. As she walks off he admires how her leg comes up and makes an ass out of itself. David's cell phone goes off. This is the fifth time that night. He pulls it from his front pocket, looks and shakes his head.

Monica can't believe it. Her mind is about to detonate. She can't keep her hands off him and wants to let the waitress know that he is her dinner tonight, "My God a doctor, she mumbles.

David places his glass on the table and turns to the dealer.

Monica pulls David closer against her hot body.

"Don't you want to know my name love?" Monica asks.

David points to the pile of chips on the table, "Cash me out kind sir," and then looks down deep into Monica's eyes," now tell me everything baby."

Paul the dealer pulls David's chips in to the center of the table and begins to count, "Cashing out," Paul yells. He stacks the chips in rows of ten, "Ten, twenty, thirty and onto eighty eight thousand he counts out. Sir what would you like to do with your winnings?"

"Oh no Please don't ever call me sir if you want my respect. Just C-c-, David is fine." He replies.

David looks down at his Rado watch realizing that he doesn't have much time before he has to administer the serum into his parietal lobe. It's getting hard to concentrate and his words are even coming out jumbled. He grabs a stack of five thousand dollar chips. He hands them to Paul, "First this is for you. Please put the rest into my casino account if you would kind s-s-sir."

Paul nods. He is sporting a white sweaty pit dripping shirt with a red bowtie and mixed colored visor. His glasses are old and worn. Paul's discolored front teeth peering through his cracked lips appear to David like that of an addict.

Instantly Paul prints off an eighty eight thousand dollar voucher and hands it to David, "Thank you doctor and good luck."

David grabs Monica's hand. "Are you ready to go?"

Hand in hand the two head to the exit swooping right past the roulette table and out past all the penny slots. Jingles and jangles echo all throughout the area. Stink of stale beer and cigarette smoke lingers throughout the section of slots near the Kaboom machines next to the V-bar. The two stop to watch as a fat elderly man wearing a Depends adult diaper sinks a twenty into the diamonds slot machine, he pulls the lever and a bonus round starts up. Instantly a siren goes off as the echo of coins dropping starts to come out. As the old man squirms it can be seen that his adult diaper is overflowing onto the floor. Rumors have always went around about people who wear diapers while playing slots so that they don't have to leave their machines and the two just witnessed it firsthand. When the stench rolled out the two cringed.

David looks at Monica, tugs on her hand in a come on gesture and they walk out the door exiting to the valet area in front of the casino.

Mike Valencia the lead valet approaches their position quickly. He is a chubby Mexican fella with at least a six inch chartreuse goatee draping down onto his vest. The glow is almost mesmerizing. His stance is unbalanced but he's clean. "You all set Mr. Christopher." Mike says.

David tosses a thousand dollar chip to Mike. He puts his arm around Monica's waist pulling her in tight against his hart on. Mike walks over closer to David. He shakes his right hand leaving behind a small vial of honey oil. Monica witnesses all of this going down but acts nonchalant. She has not a care in the world as she loves the hemp probably as much as anyone.

Honey oil is the THC that is pressed from hundreds of pounds of marijuana. It is so powerful that one time when Monica and her band ended their gig in L.A they got the bright idea to empty a half ounce vial onto some raisins and then smoke them out of a six hose mermaid hookah. They all sucked, gagged and ended up mostly naked scattered through the Los Angeles zoo the next morning. When everyone started to come to it they found that Marco a true Italian drummer was somehow in the gorilla cage stripped naked of all his clothing. Marco who goes by the Italian nickname Scorcia for finding a piece of a tomato peel on the head of his penis after having anal sex with a hot milf one night in a Fiat in Italy laid there sporting huge morning wood as the male gorilla's flung fecal matter at his face. When the zoo park personnel tried to rescue him a big female gorilla named Swanky drug him back to her cave by his immense penis. When she began to mate with him people visiting the park took photos and videos that would later be uploaded to YouTube. Mother's covered their children's eyes as they sped away from the gorilla area at break neck speeds. Marco woke at the beginning of the dragging, "Help me, help me," He screamed on agony as the strong Swanky pulled harder on his big wanker.

But despite the craziness he was rescued without the zoo pressing charges. Poor Swanky had to be tranquilized in order to get him out. She just wouldn't let go of that big Johnston. And still to this day Marco is afraid to go to a zoo but he did acquire a new nickname that is Una Buccia Di banana which translates to banana peel. Marco did return to that same zoo to take his two year old daughter Fettuccine one time and on that trip Swanky climbed out of her cage and began chasing them down through the park. The whole spectacle was caught on camera and Marco is always reminded, even by his daughter. She would say, "Daddy that gorilla Swanky really loves you huh?" It can only be believed that Marco's hairy body is what Swanky was so attracted too but no one may ever know.

David rolls the vial up against his carbide Rado watch in order to conceal it from the many cameras watching, "Oh yeah Mike, get my prize out here."

Mike runs down into the lot and within seconds a brand new two-thousand seven Lamborghini Diablo with a color that resembles the blue green tip of a flame in a titanium fire pulls up. Its V-12 engine resonates like an F-16 turbine cranking up the afterburner into the night sky. The million dollar piece of hand crafted artwork demands respect and all who peer upon its glistening surface smile and nod. Mike exits the driver's side door, walks to the passenger side where he lifts the gullwing door for Monica.

Monica damn near shits herself! She kisses David's lips softly and then runs over to the passenger side door. "Oh hell yes, she screams.

David assists her into the racing seat. He shuts the door behind and then runs to the other side, stops, smiles at Mike and jumps into the driver's side, shuts the door, pushes in the clutch, drops the leather accented chrome skull shifter into first gear and races out onto the Vegas strip.

He looks at Monica while licking his lips, "Well gorgeous now what do you want to do? You hungry, want to eat or?"

Monica grabs David's right hand, she slowly puts his index finger in her mouth and sucks it like a lollipop deep down her throat. She can taste the sweet Crown that spilled all over him from earlier that night. The taste erects her nipples so she sucks harder. Crown and soda is her second favorite concoction to get lit up on, "I don't have any gag reflexes. So what do you think?"

David's groin area begins to pulsate. He reaches down to correct the position of his Johnston as all men do when beginning to sport wood, "Let's head to my place."

6

Cutlass pushes Cannon's limp body up away from him as crawls back to his feet. He wraps a piece of his torn shirt around the large hole in his right arm. He hopes that Cannon didn't shift enough into the Dragon to infect him. He realizes that he is playing a dangerous game housing such dangerous creature within the confines of his home but is blinded by his ignorance. Cutlass puts on his face of no concern as he retreats away to inoculate himself.

"We are going to pretend that this incident didn't happen Cannon," Cutlass says," mostly because we need you to go to the surface to retrieve the real God particle back from Monica Dangle. But if you fail us this time," Cutlass pauses for a second as he pulls a canister out form lily's back pack, and then pulls out a human arm. He begins licking it between the fingers with his massive tongue," Hmm this is so good Cannon. So good because it is Grace Adams left arm." Cutlass pulls a photo from his left pocket. He throws it onto the ground beside Cannon. He then takes a big bite from Graces severed hand eating all but the thumb. The crunching sounds of bones reach Cannon's ears. As he chews he shows the meat between his teeth to Cannon. Drool is pouring down all over his chin. Most times Plutarch's don't eat meat from the bone or whole in front of any human help as it would destroy their moral character according to the high council of Cyprus so just about every Plutarch eats the human meat after it is run through the processing facility. Basically a person is processed into a patty of some sort that looks like a breaded chicken nugget. The breading on the human meat is salt which helps to preserve it like beef jerky but all Plutarch's including Celeste binge on live subjects every once in a while to keep from going ravenous. The liberal Plutarch's who only eat the human nuggets and never live subjects are nicknamed hedgetarians.

Cannon regains his composure as he slowly crawls to the picture. He picks it up to view the contents. Quickly he sees that it is a photo of Grace lying in a hospital bed getting her left stub wrapped up. Freckle is the doctor performing the repair work. Immediately he gets hot again. They all can feel heat resonating from his body like it did that first day in the hospital. Even Freckle doesn't understand where the heat comes from as Cannon is the only Reaper to give off such a phenomenal untapped power. Cutlass rubs his eyes to alleviate the dryness.

"What the fuck do you want from me Cutlass," Cannon hollers," I've always done everything that you have ever commanded me to do. Always, I have completed all 6,924 missions that you have put before me. That's ten times any other Reaper that ever came before my time."

Cutlass in all of his glory just continues chomping down the arm savoring every last bite. Cannon watches in horror as he rips the meat from the bone like eating a greasy chicken leg from KFC. The Plutarch's have four times the teeth of a human that help them tear through the stringy human flesh with ease. He rips off the last of the meat while putting his large green tongue through the radius and ulna. He chews on the elbow for a few seconds and then throws the bones to Cannon. Cannon knows that Cutlass is telling the truth as he can smell Graces blood on the bones. Cutlass burps, farts and then pulls down his zipper. He proceeds to urinate all over Cannon, "If you do not make this happen I will eat Grace right in front of your face especially since I have a taste for her now hmm." Cutlass burps and then licks his fingers.

Once a Plutarch tastes the flesh from a victim a kind of ravenous rage sets in and they can't rest until they have eaten the entire body. Despite what Cutlass says Cannon knows that he will not keep his word. No Plutarch has ever been able to stop the hunger after they have sampled a particular human's flesh. A week before Cannon came to this position on the floor before Cutlass he watched in horror as Blart tried to resist consuming a whole person after receiving a sequence of serum injections from Freckle. The result was absolutely horrendous. At first Blart was fed just a pinky toe to start. The young surface woman agreed to the experiment in hopes of gaining glorious riches. The experiment was published state wide,' it stated that a series of subjects would have their bodies tested on with no harm to their flesh and that the reward was a payment of ten thousand dollars. Two thousand people died that day. At first the injections seemed to work for Blart but after ten minutes he ripped through the young woman like a wet paper towel. Cannon watched in horror as the girl screamed and screamed for mercy but no one would help. Freckle grabbed his bag and left the room. The experiment backfired terribly. Blart was thrown down into the pit of Hades with the rest of the degenerates. Blart was the only male Plutarch that took to Cannon and he hoped that one day he could save him if he was still alive below. Hades as the Plutarch's call it houses some of the vilest creatures that mankind could ever dream up. Occasionally Cutlass generates a type of beast from the DNA sequencer and sends it to Hades to thin the herd just in case an uprising is assembling.

Cannon would like to rip Cutlass's hearts out from his chest but instead keeps his cool so that he can buy time to figure out a good game plan, "Ok Cutlass I will do whatever you want." He wipes the piss from his face while pulling himself to his knees.

Cutlass kneels down near Cannon's face," damn straight you will! Oh and one other thing, He looks up at the guards," Knox Celeste is now your toy. Do with her what you will. Also get this red blood out of here. He stinks like piss."

Celeste starts jumping around wildly. She drifts into Lily knocking her to the ground and busts Knox in the mouth sending one of his incisors flying to the ground.

"You are not my god Cutlass," Celeste yells," I am of higher ancient blood than all of you combined. And if you pull this shit I will eat the hearts from all of your chests."

Knox stuns Celeste with a lightning rod, binds her hands, puts a sack over her face and throws her over his shoulder. He then kneels down beside Cannon, "I'm going to ruin this little bitch. She will never want a puny Red blood like you ever again."

Cannon smells Nell weed on his breath. It is an albino plant that grows underground that the Plutarch's chew. It's almost like a form of tobacco but the opiates that it produces gives the feeling of euphoria unlike conventional tobacco. Cutlass, Knox and several of the other guards get in the elevator, the heavy doors slam shut and they ascend to the next level. Lily kneels down and picks up Cannon. She carries him over to the Graviton's control room where she starts cleaning him off. She pulls a freshly plucked human heart from her pack and hands it to Cannon. At first he tries to resist but inhales it in seconds. Lily steps back as she sees the ugly beast come out of Cannon to feast. The dragon pushes out through his skin to take shape. She knows that there is no one that can save her if he completely turns. Usually it's the other way around as the Plutarch's eat humans so fear is not something that she has encountered much. Almost instantly his wounds seal shut. When the Dragon pulls back up inside him she comes closer.

"My, my Cannon you sure do heal fast. You know that Cutlass fears you right? "Lily says in her normal soft voice," Come on Cannon I know what we need to do. Oh and don't worry, Knox is a big boy but when it comes to pleasing a woman his gear isn't so impressive."

It is hard for him to get past what Cutlass who once treated him like a father is doing to him now but he quickly dismisses the pain. He gets up beside Lily looking at her in the face. He can feel the warmth that she has for him. The two start laughing about Knox as they walk to the elevator.

"What do you mean Cutlass fears me Lily?

She pats him on his ass. "If you become a full blown Dragon, you will annihilate everything on this planet and I mean everything because I saw it before. You will eat anything that gets in your way."

Cannon pats her on her ass to let her know that he still cares. He loves all women and most times they all love him back, "So Lily how do I remove the stumbling block from my mind to control it? And don't pretend like you don't know what I'm talking about because all of this equipment down here has your signature all over it."

She smiles to reveal a full set of teeth. Lily is only one of a few Plutarch women that still have all of her teeth. Most are missing a lot. No one knows what is causing it but some speculation has arose that it's from the radiation that is given off from the human degenerates implants put into their brains before they are flushed underground by the O.I.A. The implants are designed so that they cannot return to the surface.

7

Just then David's cell phone rings again. After he views the screen he accepts the call. It's Idle on the other end, "I'm busy at this very moment. What is so God damn important at this hour in the morning? I told you that the situation is under control. No the package is not lost," David shakes his head, rolls his eyes and taps his foot against the car door, "Ok. Ok it is done but no more calls. I'm with someone. C- Out. Come on already are we done or what?"

Monica sits up while grabbing a handful of David's balls. She tried to hear who was on the other end of the line to see if it is a woman. She prays in her tiny mind that it's not David's wife but even if it is she would just live for the moment. It would only be her sixth home that she wrecked. In her mind that wasn't very many and anyway she got a whole bunch of nice things from the idiot's before. A deep Russian accented voice echoes throughout the car. It is almost robotic she thinks.

David pulls the phone from his ear exiting the call. He looks on the screen to see a blinking red dot. He rubs Monica's thigh as she peers out at the Paris casino's Eifel Tower structure. As he digs a little deeper he is surprised to find out that she is not wearing any panties and as he pulls back his warm sticky fingers to shift again Monica looks into his eyes and smiles, "I would love to go to Paris one day."

He smiles, throws the shifter into fourth and then licks his fingers, "Hey are you up for a little adventure tonight or what, because I'm thinking a ménage."

Monica laughs. She pulls down his zipper and slowly begins to prod, "Ok guy. But you are in for a real treat fella because I love woman even more than men."

Within minutes the car rockets the two in front of Treasure Island casino. David swiftly pulls the race car to the curb next to a beautiful Thai girl. She approaches the passenger side door while taking long drags from her Marlboro Light and then flicks it onto the road. The twenty-two year old Tang Come or professionally known as A.K.A Delicious is a total spinner. Five foot nothing and one hundred pounds soaking wet. Her eye shadow and lipstick match her flashy pink leather dress that barely covers her ass cheeks. David puts down the window. He waited for her to blow away the smoke as he doesn't want the smoke to invest in the leather interior. "Hey there, are you Delicious?" David asks.

The girl climbs half way into the passenger side window on top of Monica. The scent of cigarette smoke, spicy Thai food and vanilla bean body spray particles gently tug at the attention of David's nostrils. He hates cigarette smoke on the breath of a woman. Almost despises it. Unless they are so hot like this one. She kisses Monica and then sticks her tongue out at David, "In her heavy Thai accent Delicious replies. "Maybe you will have to taste me and find out Mr. Big time." Delicious slides her hand down into the same wet spot between Monica's legs that David had just visited moments earlier.

Monica's eyes roll back in her head," I like her David." Monica whispers. She grabs Delicious around her waist and rips her into the car through the window showing David her aggressive side. It is immediate that the sexual attraction is there. Instantly the two are licking one another's tongues, poking and prodding every crevice imaginable. Monica reaches for David's Johnston as David shifts to first, hits the gas and damn near crashes into a pimped out Escalade right in front of him. Both vehicles swerve coming to a complete halt. The driver of the Escalade throws a full can of Rolling Rock beer onto the car's windshield. He screams loud in German, "Fuck you asshole!" Fuck you Fucking American!"

Before anyone even knew what was happening David has the driver on the ground smashing his head into the pavement. His head splits open like a melon as blood spews everywhere. Three more Germans exit the vehicle and dash towards David. And as they all approach, one, two, three, they all fall hard. David explodes like lightning in a storm at such an expedited speed that none of them knew what hit them until they were staring up from their backs on the ground. David pulls an incisor out of his right fist as he looks down at the driver passed out in a pool of his own blood. He puts it in his pocket as a souvenir. He feels that the big tooth will complement the thousands of others that line his kitchen floor. The other three guys lay groaning, broken and battered as their bodies contort on the street. David notices the tattoo on the drivers arm. The two lightning bolts look like that of the Nazi wolf squads from back in the 1940's.

The wolf squads were created by Hitler to infiltrate behind enemy lines like spies or assassin's in order to spin the war in Germanys favor. For years rumors have surfaced that the wolf squads were set up to operate long after the fall of Germany. They were engineered to get revenge long after the war ended. Laying in dormancy and waiting to strike like a viper.

David jumps back in the race car and quickly pulls out. Monica saw everything out of the corner of her eyes but pretended not too. It really just kind of turned her on more seeing the fight. As they pull away the back drivers side tinted window on the Escalade lowers. A silenced barrel points directly in David's direction. At first he captures a glimpse of the license plate that reads BIG and then sees the gun barrel in his rear view. Immediately he starts grabbing gears as quickly as possible and the zero to sixty miles per hour in three seconds race car darts down the Vegas strip like a pinball in an arcade game. But it wasn't fast enough. The entire rear driver's side rear quarter panel got riddled with bullets.

8

Back in the bay area near the grand hall Lily helps Cannon pack some supplies into a new 2008 Jeep SR8. He loads a small weapons cache, two ammo buckets and a full Reaper armor suit with the newly liquid chameleon design created by Lily just in case he encounters resistance. Cutlass pulls up behind Cannon in his V-crest. It is the only one in existence under planet Earth and it is unique in its ability to hover over any terrain at lightning fast speeds. The chassis is all future technology with a 1935 Duesenberg SSJ body on it. The technology is far beyond anything that Cannon has ever seen before. His pet sloth barks at Cannon as Cutlass laughs, "Load the EMP canister into the Jeep as well Lily. It is just insurance if dick bag here fails that's all," Cannon rolls his monstrous head around as Creed blares from the speakers on his nifty ride," There's a beast inside us all, a beast inside us all," Cutlass sings aloud.

Lily takes the canister off the rack and loads it into the back of the Jeep, "Did you put fresh saltwater into the RFG reactor in your V-crest?"

Cutlass pets his sloth Giorgio as he looks up at Lily. "Yes Lily the Radio Frequency Generator produces hydrogen just like you said it would. Have you finished putting the last tweaks on the generators for the Knuckleheads?"

Lily smiles and shakes her head, "Yes sir they are ready for deployment and I have perfected the Thrashers for the next magnum tournament."

Cannon jumps in between the two. He just can't stand to hear another word come from Cutlass's big mouth, "What is the canister for, Cutlass? " Cannon yells.

The noise from the tram delivering fresh degenerates barrels past canceling out Cutlass's mumbling. Cutlass points at Cannon with his crooked finger. He sports a smile that looks like a muddy river with sticks protruding up from it. He hands Cannon a rolled up paper scroll and drives off. Salt dust sprays up from the floor in Cannon's face. It burns his eyes and coats his lips. Cutlass hollers from a little ways down the corridor," Cannon total power is not controlling the world currency but rather being on top of the food chain."

He busts out laughing," Hmm love to eat me some more of that Grace, hmm."

Cannon reaches for the phosphorous rifle in the back of the Jeep. What Cutlass and everyone else on the planet including Cannon doesn't know is that he as in being Cannon is already at the tippy top of the food chain. If the Dragon bursts through nothing in its path will survive. Lily quickly counters and puts her hands over his, "If you do what I think you are going to do than not only is Grace lost but Celeste is dead too," Lily says," you better get your compass set to due North and get hopping stud."

Cannon swiftly pulls Lily into his arms. He lays a huge kiss with tongue right up on her. She doesn't resist a bit. He knows that if he is going to get any information he has to succumb to her.

"Now if you want a ton more of that goodness than you better start confessing to me. What does the canister do and what the hell is a Knucklehead and Thrasher?"

Lily has already melted in Cannon's arms. The pheromones coming from his body force her into a state of euphoria. Lily was the first Plutarch woman to sleep with him. She has been in love ever since despite her romance with Nuke. Her eyes are immediately glazed over with lust. When Celeste heard Lily bragging about how wonderful a human was in bed while at one of Cutlass's lavish dinner parties on one evening she stepped in to sample the goods. And now that Cannon has been claimed by Celeste no Plutarch woman looks twice at him except Lily because a Plutarch's sex drive is just like their ravenous behavior for food. Once you sample the goods it's like crack cocaine you will do anything for it. But if a Plutarch woman commits adultery with another Plutarch woman's man the outcome is a battle to the death in the arena. Lily knows that she cannot win against Celeste as she is an Alpha breed and Lily's battle skills are not as great as Celeste's because she was not blessed with the ancient blood. She can't heal as fast, drift as quick or use her telekinetic powers to predict movements like the ancient bred babies but her lustful tendencies for Cannon are too overpowering so she indulges hoping Celeste doesn't find out, "Ok but you must make love to me before you go. That is the price!"

Cannon laughs with a crooked smile. It is something that he always does when a woman comes onto him. He always smiled like that since Sir forced Drano down his throat when he was a young boy, "If that is your price Lily I will agree but first you tell me what Cutlass is up too."

Lily falls away from Cannon's arms. She walks over to the canister putting her thumbprint on the security panel, "I helped build this device Cannon and I'm sorry that I ever did. Cutlass traded the schematics with the world leaders in the pact for food. We were starving down here after we all came out of sleep stasis so I had no choice but to agree. The Manta machines had long dried up and quit producing. I can't believe that I'm telling you this but we even resulted to eating some of our own kind. They were weak and wouldn't have made it but still I know it is wrong. The Red bloods altered the atoms in the chamber of my device and used the energy to produce a massive explosion. It wasn't what it was designed for. It ultimately gave them the power over the entire world and us as well. They detonated my altered version on Nagasaki Japan. We all watched in horror down here. Now I'll have you know that Tesla was one of us, do you know of him? Anyway he used it to try and give the Red Bloods free energy through radio electric frequencies in the atmosphere, pretty much like static electricity but the government killed him and- "

Cannon slides over to Lily's side. He places his hand over her motor mouth because she will just go on talking forever. It's like once you wind her up she doesn't shut up. She would take off like one of those vibrating dolls with the wind up screw in their back if you let her. Cannon can see a purple glow erupting out from inside the canister, "So what will this do? Kill everyone on the planets' surface? You want me to wipe out my own kind, Lily? Are you crazy?"

Lily shakes her head. She pushes another button to reveal the inside purple reflecting energy and then slides it back up inside the body, "Calm down, no Cannon this device will send an electromagnetic pulse through every creature on earth but it is specifically designed for humans. We want to stun everyone so that we can rise to the surface. It just short circuits their wiring for a little while. Why would we kill everyone then we would starve to death ourselves? That would be stupid!"

Cannon takes a step back. The conversation is almost ridiculous to think about. First he knew about the eating of human flesh as that was a given. He too sampled it many times but medium of course. And now here he was in the position to subdue the entire human population for God only knows for how long. And what a dilemma he either does it and the surface people will become slaves and eventually eaten or the Plutarch armada will be called in and the entire planet will be destroyed. It is a no win situation and only the Plutarch's gain,' Cannon thinks.

"Lily, would you please do something for me," Cannon asks," could you at least tighten the radius to Pittsburgh? You know that Cutlass is going to destroy the entire world anyway I do this."

She slides her hand up and down his arm tickling his flesh with her light strokes. Her gestures are all sexual. He wasn't sure why no Plutarch man has ever snatched her up. Maybe it was her neediness he thought. After all she was a prodigy genius according to all the others. Everything that she lacked in motor abilities sure shined through in her inventions.

"Cannon if I do this I will be putting my own race at risk. Just let the stun happen and it will wear off within a few hours. Cutlass just wants to get into the I.P.C.O tower to take back the arc of the covenant. That's all; it is the power source for our ship. He wants it in case we need to leave that's all. A long time ago a General Grounder snuck down here with one of his death squads and took it from us when we all were signing the feed treaty."

Cannon opens the scroll that Cutlass gave him. The first sentence reads; keep your word or Grace will be eaten alive. The rest reads on with orders on how to place the canister into a wrecking ball. The location and time frame has been laid out. Lily leads Cannon to her chamber just a few yards away. He makes love to her repeatedly. When he finishes his body looks like Slimer the ghost from Ghostbusters just ran over him. Cannon starts to wonder if that is why the Plutarch men stay clear of her because she is a squirter. He steams off, dresses and heads to the Jeep in the bay area where he encounters Dr. Freckle, "Listen asshole I don't have anything to say to you, you are nothing more than a conniving liar! I didn't sign up to be a slave to kill all of mankind! And I saw the photo of you cutting off Grace's arm."

The doctor puts his face down. He hands Cannon a small green box, a thumb drive and then starts walking away," Hogshead cut off her arm Cannon. I tried to reattach it."

"What is this Freckle another one of your con jobs? Where's my fucking brother Mitch Freckle, huh? Good job dick head."

Dr. Freckle turns back to Cannon," I did all that I could for you son. It could be worse you could have been food for these monsters down here."

Cannon drifts really fast, faster than ever before and Freckle sees it. The whites of his eyes show fear. Before Freckle knows what is happening Cannon has him lifted up in the air by his neck. He is choking profusely. Cannon's eyes begin to glow green," Listen you piece of shit," He says in a new dark voice," you started all of this. I read the documents that Sir had in his safe before Mitch died so quit fucking pretending." He then throws Freckle into the corridor wall. His old frail body slumps down on the floor. "Cannon I'm trying to fix it. Just listen to the recording on the I-pod and it will tell you everything that you need to do to put this mess back in order. I'm really sorry my son!"

Cannon jumps in the driver's side of the Jeep and races out of the City of Cyprus to the surface.

9

Within an instance they pulled up to what seemed to be an old casino under construction. The dilapidated dimly lit letters that spelled out Nugget near the roof were almost hanging vertically rather than horizontally in their once proper place. A large B & F monogram are perched right above the old hanging letters awaiting their locations.

David pushes a remote to enter the parking garage. He exits the driver's side, pauses for a minute, kneels down to inspect all the bullet holes, "seven point six two three", he whispers under his breath. A.K-47 probably he thought. When moans from the two hotties come from the Lamborghini he rushes to the passenger side where he pulls the girls out. In his mind he can envision all of the pleasures and displeasures that are about to begin but the big thought of wasting such a beautiful young woman tended to tear at his soul. Monica pushes Delicious out, leaps to her feet and then jumps onto David like a wild animal. She's licking and kissing all over his neck and ears as he awkwardly struts into the elevator. Delicious is right on his ass as well groping and prodding. The three look like an octopus out of water. David slouches down all the while still holding Monica in his lap as he slides his key card into the security slot. He pushes the top floor P button. It lights up and the elevator rockets upward.

"The penthouse suites, wow you are Mr. Big time aren't you?' Delicious whispers with her broken Thai English.

David turns smiling at Delicious. He doesn't have the heart to tell her how big of a trouble she's really in. Once at the top floor the doors open to an unimaginable sight. Grey marble floors smuggled in from Africa line the floors, golden silk drapes with red fringes hang twenty feet down in front of the large tinted windows and everything seems to be outlined in real gold. The girls look in awe as their jaws drop and hearts pound. David grabs Delicious by the hand while continuing to carry Monica to the bedroom where he softly plops her ass down. The two begin shredding David's clothes. Monica bites the buttons off his shirt one by one and spits them on the floor like a machine gun. They both look in awe as their four sets of hands caress his chiseled body. Each of the girls pulls up close to David chest and began to lick and tug on his platinum hoop nipple rings. Their hot breath makes his package throb as his head drops back in ecstasy. He pushes a button on a remote that makes a 70" TV monitor drop down from the ceiling. They all can see themselves behaving badly on the screen. Monica waves at the monitor to see herself waving back. Her puny brain is mesmerized.

"This is the biggest bed that I have ever laid upon," Delicious says in a low sexy voice.

David pushes Delicious onto Monica's face and steps to the dresser as he watches tongues dance against flesh. "Delicious you haven't been laid upon it yet but I'm fixing to take care of that real soon my dear," David replies. He places a small amount of herbal substance into the screen on a triple hose skull hookah, he then dribbles a pen head sized dot of honey oil on top and brings it over to the bed. All three of them take long drags, inhale deep and then exhale into one another's mouths repeatedly. Abruptly pupils dilate as the two girl's crash onto the bed. They all roll all over one another probing every orifice. Articles of clothing get ripped and thrown to the floor as David climbs in to join the fun. Monica un-wraps David's body like a gift on Christmas Eve and when she pulls out his twelve inch Johnston her body begins to convulse. When Delicious sees the sheer magnificence she quickly slides down beside Monica where the two fight to put it in their mouths. Back and forth the two take turns gorging their throats as deep as possible. At some point between deep moans of pleasure David looks down to see if the two are playing a game of who can go deeper. Quickly he realizes that because of the profession Delicious is in she is the winner. Clean to the balls she takes it as she looks up into his eyes as if asking for more. Abruptly he pulls away before he erupts and samples a taste from Monica's sweet spot and then samples Delicious the same way. The nectar glistens form his chin. His face looks like a glazed doughnut. David places the girls atop one another in face down and ass up fashion. The two girls continue to pleasure one another as David dominates their bodies. He takes turns pounding one for several minutes and then pulls from one and enters the other and continues to pound like a freight train for hours upon hours. He doesn't discriminate as he drills them both accordingly. The trio swims within one another's fluids. They slide all over each other's hot sweaty bodies as they all move and moan with pure ecstasy. David takes long nostril fills of ass mixed with poontang as he plunges deep inside Monica. The squishing sounds of David's root gorging deep inside Monica's tight fold make it hard for him to keep track of the time. In between bouts he tries to capture a glimpse of the large grandfather clock in the corner but the girls make it difficult. Both girls take turns squirting as David erupts multiple times over and over again. They mix it up repeatedly, in and out and in and hot tongues and lips, ass to Johnston and in and out all over one another for six hours or more and then as Monica erupts one last time all over Delicious's face the two girls fall to the bed just soaked to the bone in each other's sticky sweat.

Their bodies cannot take any more punishment from the big David. He parts the two girls like the Red sea while gently exiting from the bed, walks over to Delicious, pulls her head up to the base of his balls and makes her clean all of his Johnston with her lips. She gladly takes it all. He can see her eyes rolling back in her head while gagging. The swirling of her tongue tickles immensely and David's body convulses. Monica a jealous cat jumps over to assist. The sucking sounds beating Cannon's ears tickle as the heat from their mouths makes his ass pucker. His legs buckle a bit but eventually he regains the will power to pull away from their mouths. He heads over to the bar and rummages around behind the sink to find the bottle of Crown gold. He pulls three pineapple shaped whiskey glasses down from the cupboard above the wine rack, removes the whiskey bottle from the gold sack, cracks the lid and fills them all two inches high. Slowly he looks over his shoulder to see the two girls making out and when they aren't looking he pulls a small white bottle from the lower drawer, drops one of the yellow capsules into his left palm and empties the contents equally into two of the glasses. He grabs all the whiskey glasses with the two spiked glasses in his right hand, the other in his left and returns to the bed. He hands Monica and Delicious the two glasses from the right hand that have been spiked. Quickly Delicious downs her shot and falls to the bed. Monica sips and gags a little on hers before placing it on the night stand beside her. She drank about half but couldn't get the rest down. "David would you please grab me a bottle of water, I am so damn thirsty. I think that you drained me of all my fluids." Monica says with a hoarse voice.

David quickly obliges, runs to the stainless side by side refrigerator and quickly returns with three bottles of Crystal Springs water bottles. He uncaps one bottle, hands it to Monica and downs one of the bottles into himself.

"Wow Delicious must really be worn out. She's not even budging, Monica says as she places her bottle of water on the night stand beside her whiskey glass. She slides back into the bed, curls up against Delicious and starts to drift off.

David figured that half a swig of the whiskey was more than enough as half a capsule usually subdues over two hundred pound grown men. He climbs in between the two beautiful women and they curl up onto his body. Monica reaches down and jostles David's Johnston for a while before she passes out. Delicious is out cold instantly and starts snoring.

An hour or so passes before David realizes what time it is. He gently climbs out from the bed trying not to disturb Monica. Slowly he pulls Delicious from the left side of the bed. He walks off with her limp body over top his right shoulder down the hall to the clean room. David had no idea that Monica was awake and on his heels to see what he was doing. Her curiosity always seemed to get her in trouble, especially when she was in college. As David approaches a silver door resembling the elevator doors it opens and the lights come on. The entire room is bright white accented in stainless steel. The entire floor is stainless steel with a large drain right underneath an operating bed directly in the center of the room. There are ten monitors and several trays of operating tools. Around the edge of the thirty by thirty rooms are plush red chairs covered in clear plastic. Seventeen TV monitors line all the walls while a multitude of cameras lines the ceiling. The lights are so bright that sunglasses are almost needed. The smell of the room reeks of the cleaner Gone. David quickly places Delicious down onto the table, straps her in and pulls a tinted shield over her entire body. He pushes the start button which brings a laser scanner up to run down the entire length of her body. When the laser approaches her left breast a beeping noise begins to alarm. David then presses the yellow button and a torch like nozzle comes out from underneath the left side of the bed. It begins to cut into the left breast on Delicious. The plasma cutter is precise, it cauterizes the flesh before any blood can be lost and in three seconds her left breast looks like it has a smiley face on it right below the nipple. David puts his hand over his nose to hold back the stink of burnt flesh.

It is a stink that he remembers all too well. This was especially when he took in a large amount of the smoke back in 1987 while pulling himself from the ashes of the Blithe residence. The plasma cutter finishes the cut work and returns to its location under the bed. David flips over the shield; he reaches into the left breast of Delicious and pulls out a C-cup implant. As he holds it up to the light he can see a small capsule floating around inside of it. He places the implant onto a silver tray next to the bed and leans over into her face. He thinks that she is very beautiful. He hates very much what he has to do next if he finds the mark on her body. According to the texts on his I phone the S.O.G believe that she is a mule for the Wolf squad operating out of Phoenix Arizona. They feel that she should be terminated but David has been given permission to judge whether she lives or dies. Quickly he begins to look all over her body for the same mark that the driver had out on the Vegas strip. He hopes that it does not exist for her sake. As he narrows the search he finds the same signature burnt into the roof of her mouth. David rubs it with his fingers to be sure and realizes that some animal had forced her to be branded like cattle. Now with no choice he has to follow orders. He once again stares into her face while kissing her lips one last time before she is changed forever. He has no inkling that Monica is right outside the door watching his every move.

After a short pause David grabs a scalpel from the tray. He begins to cut a perfect circle around the neck of Delicious and then cuts two perfect lines from her neck to each of her shoulders. He then walks to the foot of the bed. He pushes a foot pedal on the floor where a small door in the floor opens. It produces a winch type device with several hundred fiber cables accented with hooks on the ends. When it rises to the top of the foot of the bed it rotates engaging the drive gear. After David hears the proper sound chime out, he slowly hooks her up. One by one David takes a hook and pierces it through her flesh, first all around her neck and then all down each of her shoulders. He steps back a minute to admire his handy work. He realizes that she looks like a fly trapped in a spiders' web. David walks to right side of the bed where he depresses the square blue button on the control panel and the winch slowly begins to tug on Delicious's flesh. Once the flesh is tight he wraps a large strap around her neck that is attached to a sky hook in the ceiling. He then pushes another lever on the floor that drops the bed out from under Delicious. She is now completely suspended in the air by the hooked fiber cables and the strap around her neck. David goes to the counter behind the bed area and pulls out a syringe full of a Brompton Mixture. He injects Delicious right in her neck and hopes that the 90 CC's is enough to keep her out until the procedure is over because he can remember the time that he placed Andrew Green the Jewish stalker through the stripper machine without any type of anesthesia.

Andrew who was born and raised in the Jewish community followed all the rules up until he was seventeen. When he killed the daughter of a high powered Rabbi named Cecil Gold he became a wanted man. Cecil was unique amongst the Jewish community in that he united all the Jewish communities throughout the U.S by only permitting them to purchase products with the kosher seal on the bags, boxes and boxes in which his company provided to all vendors. Throughout his years he quickly rose to be one of the billionaire elite who actually had a say in the molding of the new world sect.

It was believed that Andrew despite his upbringing possessed the extra Y chromosome that all psychopaths carry. Of course there was never any testing performed as Andrew was placed on the S.O.G Reaper list by the Keepers of the Seal. And then when the directive came in as a number one priority from the Livid Mother herself Andrew was detained, tortured and eventually executed by the S.O.G within twenty-four hours.

David looks over Delicious and can remember how Andrew screamed so loud that he had to put ear plugs in. But the difference was that with Andrew it took six people to hold him in place until the winch could get enough tension to suspend him into place.

That late evening in October 2004 Andrew was found gambling in the Circus-Circus casino smoking, drinking, gambling and fondling a whore despite his religion upbringing. David slid in real slick, flashed a wad of cash at Andrew and he followed like a lamb to the slaughter. When the trio turned into the alley behind the casino Idle and Lacey pushed Andrew into a fifty-five gallon drum, loaded him into a small box truck and took him to the exact room that Delicious now resides in. Although on the same table as Andrew, he was rapidly peeled like an orange rather than stripped which means that each limb was peeled of its skin in a series of fast instances. This in turn caused a substantial amount of pain throughout the course of the procedure. Eventually when Andrew was stripped of his face Cecil came in to see him one last time to castrate him personally. Cecil wanted to be the last face that Andrew saw before he succumbed to inevitable. Rumor has it that Cecil now in his late eighties still carries the change pouch made from Andrew's scrotum sack.

With a shit eating grin David once again depresses the blue button on the control panel and slowly and precisely the flesh is peeled from Delicious's body in a rather unique fashion. He sets the timer and heads to the bathroom right outside the operating room. He catches a glimpse of Monica climbing into the bed so he rushes to the door containing Delicious and locks it. David now worried that he may have to destroy Monica as well rushes to her side in the bed. He starts to kiss her neck and when she doesn't even move an inch he decides to let her live. He sets the alarm on his I phone for exactly one hour and texts Idle to be ready for pickup. He tries to take a nap up against Monica's warm body. But the scent of her vanilla arouses David so he slides down a little lower behind her backside and once again enters into her. He makes love to her while she sleeps and ejaculates for the tenth time before the alarm goes off. Abruptly he jumps up, throws on his boxers and runs down the hall. He peeks in on Delicious to see how far the machine has moved. When he enters the room the last of her flesh is pulling off from in between her toes. As the winch gets close to finishing the table slowly rose to accommodate her body. Once the skin is removed from her toes it makes a popping sound like when u put your finger in your cheek and pull it out real quick. David grabs the flesh suit, detaches the hooks, turns it right side out, sprays it down with saline and places it into a vacuum sealed clear plastic bag. He then returns to Delicious, sprays her entire body except for her face down with a burn cream and wraps her in bandages. Gently he dresses her body in a business suite and places her into a wheelchair. He gives her one more kiss on her soft supple lips. Only her face has skin now.

As David stands there looking at Delicious he starts to get sick in his stomach. He can't believe that possibly he might be becoming soft so he swiftly goes to the right corner of the room where the Optimizer contains the elixir to keep him straight. He looks down at the face of his watch and realizes that the inoculation was to be administered 7 hours ago now. David sits down in front of the machine, places his head into the holder and hits the button. Within seconds a large needle protrudes from the center of the machine, a fluorescent red liquid uploads into a small chamber behind the needle with a swooshing sound. A small clamp comes out from the side and opens David's right eye wide as the needle slowly penetrates through the retina into the frontal lobe. The Optimizer injects a coolant placed around the plutonium pellet to keep it from exploding. The O.I.A forced him to accept the explosive device into his brain after being sentenced to the Cyprus rehabilitation center. The alternative was death and that is the case with every human found guilty or unworthy by the New World Sector.

After years of use the pain is still searing but David sits motionless. He has been able to control the pain threshold put against his body. It is why the S.O.G utilizes his talents repeatedly. As the needle retracts Idle comes walking into the room. He walks over and shakes David's hand in a weird fashion. The S.O.G handshake is undeniable in that the lower level Reapers turn their thumbs in to be accepted by the higher ranking warriors. It is a showing of being dominated by the higher powers. David who is a Polonium Reaper can act alone and make decisions for himself. There are roughly a hundred Polonium reapers who are all competing for the mega slot of becoming a venial hybrid reaper in 2010. The new position will be the first of its kind in the Plutocracy and the small capsule in Delicious's breast implant is the key to unlocking the Plutocracies Grandmaster power so David's being in the right place at the right time or perhaps coincidence if there is any has placed him at the head of the heard to become a Venial reaper.

"David my brother you look amazing with that long mullet." Idle says in a deep Russian accented voice.

"Well thank you mister Idle." David blurts out.

The two start laughing hysterically as David wipes away the blood speckles on the floor with a mop.

"Brother you look like some kind of faggot with that semi mullet scaling down your back. I really prefer you as Cane. At least you look manly."

David shakes his head and rubs his right eye at the same time while flipping Idle the bird.

"Shut up Idle your fucking bald and have to wear a wig when you go on runs, but hey I have to ask you something serious; does it seem like the serum isn't as strong as it used to be?"

Idle shakes his head no and reaches into his pocket. He pulls out a baggy full of little circular pieces of meat with spiral holes in the center of them. He puts it towards David and gestures for him to take a handful.

"No way, I'm not eating meat that shit flows through. You're a twisted bastard Idle.

"So what's the deal with the gook?" Idle blurts out.

"The powers to be believe that the tiny fragment that I found in her fake tit is thee God particle or something. Rumor has it that the particle is from a fallen angel and whoever possesses it can rule the world or some shit like that."

Idle shrugs his shoulders and walks over to small refrigerator. Grabs a can of Coke and chugs it down. He could care less about world politics or rulers as he just tries to live a simple life. He lets out a huge burp. Wipes his mouth and returns to David's side.

"You know Idle that burp smells just like shit. Are you sure that you cleaned your rectos properly before cooking them?" David busts out laughing.

"I could give a shit less about who rules the world as long as it doesn't affect me. I just want to eventually open a chain of seafood restaurants down in Louisiana somewhere. Preferably near the French quarter where all the whores hang out. You know, just in case I need a few ingredients."

They both erupt into laughter. Idle smacks his legs as he always does when he laughs hysterically.

David walks over and grabs the handles of the wheelchair. He spins Delicious around to face the door. "According to directive 138 you are to take her to the I.P.C.O building, give her a shot of uptime juice and send her in with this briefcase."

Idle kneels down beside the wheelchair. He rubs his fingers across Delicious's lips, "My God she is beautiful! I don't think that I would have had the will power to do this to her. And you know me I fucking hate everyone not white. David you must be one soulless fuck!"

David shakes his head no and stares up at Idle, "Orders are orders Idle!

Idle leans in and put his right hand on David's shoulder, "Hey do you remember when we met in that gay club the Rusty Pickle years ago," Idle blares out laughing as he returns to his feet.

David starts to laugh again too as he remembers. He was there to meet up with Idle to abduct Abdul Jocklestockey an eighteen year old Bangladeshi-an for a rich sheik in Dubai. During the sheiks visit he fell in love with Abdul but he would not comply with the sheiks demands.

Typically the S.O.G reapers were not informed of their purposes or ever questioned the Plutocracy of their motives. Most were all grateful to be part of such a strong brotherhood as they all would die for one another if the situation ever arose. The only reaper to go against the grain was John Adams who eventually met his demise from the hands of a young child, his own daughter Grace Adams.

"Yeah Idle I can remember that one cowboy, what was his name? Miguel I think. He was all dolled up in a light blue denim vest, white Stetson cowboy hat and a red thong with a big white star on the Johnston area.

If I remember correctly you two were dancing right?" David blurts out while laughing uncontrollably.

Idle pushes David to the floor; he goes tumbling down hitting the wheelchair holding Delicious. It takes off rolling down the hallway towards the bedroom area where Monica is supposed to be sleeping. The two jump to their feet and run down the hall after her.

Idle Vein who stands six foot six inches carries two hundred and ninety pounds of muscle on his large frame and can move like a cat despite how big he is. His entire body is covered in tattoos from the neck down. He is especially parcel to the red rooster tat driving a big rig on his right forearm. The saying right above the roosters head is" KEEP ON CLUCKIN." He always dresses in the finest suits available for his large size. Even in the scorching hot summer weather you will see Idle all suited up with no place to go but down under. Idle Jin Vein was born a four pound six ounce premature boy on October 31st 1969 in Moscow. He was shipped to the U.S when he was only twelve. Both of his parents were taken together in a tragic car accident on route 605 in California near City of Industry exit. An illegal Mexican immigrant by the name of George was driving an eighteen wheeler in the fast lane when his burrito meat fell into his lap and caused him to swerve into the carpool lane. When he swerved the big rig the

Vein's 1971 Dodge Charger plunged underneath the flatbed that was hauling chickens from Texas. When Idles father hit the brakes the car slid under the flatbed. It resulted in the decapitation of Idles parents instantaneously. When the smoke cleared Idle witnessed the most horrific site that any child of that age could witness. It was the heads of both of his parents lying on the floor staring up at him. The car was filled with big white chickens and feathers flying everywhere. All that could be heard was the screaming death of hundreds of chickens burning up underneath the fire stretching out from under the big rigs transmission area. The stench of burnt blood, feathers and burnt human flesh made Idle become something other than human. He grabbed a shard of glass from one of the broken windows, cut off the head of a crippled rooster from inside the car, rubbed its blood all over his face, stuffed the still squirming head in his jeans pocket and crawled out of the wrecked chargers window where he slumped down to the ground onto a pile of dead chickens.

There were dead chickens everywhere. Crippled one's were flying up and down and across the freeway causing other vehicles to smash into one another. Seventeen cars came to rest in the pile before it ended. A 1967 Stingray Corvette traveling about ninety miles per hour up the North side tried to stop and ended up flipping up over the top of the barrier right on top of the Vein's Charger. The rear wheels of the Corvette were spinning right above Idles head until the 427 big block engine blew up. The driver of the Corvette was killed on impact. Fire began to envelope all around Idle as he laid there still dazed from the impact.

Up on top of the car pile in the rigs cab Idle could hear George screaming to be helped. Idle pushed off from the back of his family's car, waded through the fire, jumped up onto the big rig and crawled in through the broken windshield of the rigs cab. He sat there face to face with George for a minute. George was screaming all kinds of Spanish. Idle looked down and seen the burritos all over the rig. He realized that his parents were sacrificed for a ninety-nine cent bur-rito. Idle pulled the dead roosters head from his jeans pocket, plunged the birds beak deep inside George's left eye socket and twisted it around six or so times until it gave up his eyeball. George was screaming and bucking like a wild bronco but he could do nothing as both his arms were pinned to his sides by the rigs large steering wheel and his legs were both sheared off from the dash crushing into them.

Idle stared at the dirty brown eye for a second, plopped it in his mouth, got real close to George's face and squashed the eyeball between his teeth like a grape.

He then showed George all of the meat in his teeth before swallowing it.

"Tell God that I sent you motherfucker!" Idle screamed at the top of his young lungs," Tell him. Tell him. Tell him. Tell him. Tell him."

George tried to get free but it was too late as Idle has already plucked the right eye out too. He threw it into the oncoming traffic lane. One of the free chickens grabbed the eyeball and took off running with it down the highway.

Idle held George's nose until he opened his mouth and then stuffed the roosters head down his throat. He anxiously waited for George to suffocate to death. He exited the rig, climbed back into the Dodge Charger, grabbed his Fathers billfold, his mother's purse and took off down into one of the canals before the police arrived. He used all of his father's savings and has been off the grid ever since that awful day. It wasn't until the S.O.G recruited him back in the eighties as a wheel man that Idle was ever known to exist.

David thought Monica was passed out from Brompton mixture that he spiked her whiskey with earlier. He had no idea that she got up to pee and witnessed everything that he had done and he definitely did not know that she swapped out the God particle for a piece of licorice. She learned about everything, the S.O.G, the murders, the Plutocracy and she saw Delicious all bandaged up wheeling down the hall towards the bed that she was thought to be asleep in. Hell he had no inkling that she was spying on him the whole time. And if he had known that she saw him pushing rose stems down inside his penis hole and posing with them in the second bedroom mirror he would of slit her throat. That was something special that he did just for Celeste. She loved the pictures of him posing with beautiful objects.

Monica quickly buried her head into the pillows. She listened closely to Idle and David discussing how Delicious was skinned alive and her flesh was perfectly preserved in a briefcase for her to carry into some location.

As David wrapped up the conversation with Idle, Monica laid in the bed as still as possible pretending to be fast asleep. David climbs in beside her as Idle quickly rolls Delicious to the elevator, he signals goodbye to David and graciously leaves the building.

With the past visions once again fresh in her mind Monica starts to sob uncontrollably. She is yanked back from her daydream, right back into reality, a reality that stings a lot.

"Oh delicious you aren't so anymore."

Monica pulls back the shower curtain and screams at the top of her lungs, "I'm sorry my love! IM SORRY! I know I'm a bitch sometime."

Dennis runs from the bedroom and climbs into the shower with her. He holds her tightly in his arms, "I can't believe that you are this upset with me. Please forgive me!"

He holds her tight against his chest and just loves it when she is vulnerable and needy. Monica lifts from Dennis's grasp and walks to the bathroom sink where she brushes her teeth and then briefly steps back into the shower. She looks down in horror at the One Step pregnancy stick that she urinated only moments before getting in the shower and at that very second of an instance in time Monica knows what she has to do.

CH 3
THE BIRTH OF IT (1985)

1

The horrible deaths of millions which went unnoticed for year's would come to a final resolve --or so many thought-- would start as anyone knows or could be told with a kite slapped together with moderately cheap household products flapping in the cold wind of a passing storm.

The makeshift flying device, (A.K.A the Starburst), screamed upward, then abruptly to the left, then a hard right and finally into a downward spiral toward Center St... The Starburst was twirling toward the ground like a wounded dove after being hit with a full spread from a low brass twelve-gauge shotgun shell. Starburst crashed with such a force that it sent several pine cones flying over the sun gleaming pavilion and directly into the nearby Iron creek that divided Center St. with a bridge that flowed toward Wilson St and finally came to rest in Crystal Falls Lake. The creeks were real high for this time of spring in April 1985 in Latrobe Pennsylvania. All of the snow from the harsh winter storm three months ago has now melted away and found its way into every creek abroad. Just about every piece of land contained in the town limits of Latrobe was contaminated with the overflowing hunger of melted snow.

It's 10:00 AM on April 1ˢᵗ in 1985 and a tall one leg brace ridden lanky boy in a sleeveless blue T-shirt tries to run and his tiny brother wearing a large green long sleeved shirt and toe bearing sneakers rush gleefully through the wooded lot near Wilson St rolling up string like spaghetti noodles around a white plastic fork.

The sun shines brightly like the tip of a cherry red hot sparkler on that particular Saturday in April. It was a lot less gloomy than most years the boys thought or maybe just the joy of watching their project take flight overpowered their usual sadness.

There hadn't been snow now for a month now but the rain suppressed everyone in town for weeks after. On this early morning the sun shined brightly but far to the east large black clouds were rolling towards the park at an eerier speed. The scent of the pines was starting to fill the air and echoes of crows could be heard for miles. Mating season was almost here.

A small sprinkle of light rain droplets began to pelt down with a mild fury. It trounced upon the new blue metal roof covering the park pavilion creating a melodramatic sound of echoing beats like a drum. The tears from Heaven echoed like machine gun bullets scattering over army tanks armor in one of those nine-teen fifty army flicks.

The taller of the two is Cannon Mathias Knight-(A.K.A) Freak. At least that's what his forged U.S birth certificate reads. The date on the birth certificate states June 6th, 1970 but in all actuality his creators do not recognize the birth from the womb but rather the day of creation which was exactly Sunday October 31st, 1969 at 7:13AM. Cannon was not born but created from the genes of many of the world's elite blood lines and he supposedly contains the entire DNA chain from all of those involved. The DNA had been collected for thousands of years before being mixed like J.B Weld. Some would believe that whoever made the mixture left out the hardener because Cannon seemed frail and weak. At least that was how he acted as a young boy. That was at least for now.

Life for Cannon began as a concoction in a small test tube with the initials O.I.A engraved on it. The creation known as Cannon came to life in an underground lab in England before human rights laws could catch up with his creators. He was smuggled across the oceans and implanted into Audra Ivory Knight while she lay in stirrups for one of her gynecological visits. Unsuspectingly she became pregnant and gave birth to Cannon thinking that the father was Zachary Mathis Knight, which was partially true. Even Zachary believed that he was the father and even shared in cutting the umbilical cord. When Henry Knight found out that the Knight bloodline would not go on he pulled a lot of strings throughout the world and intervened. Somehow the birth of Cannon healed Audra's womb and shortly after came Mitchel. The entire Knight family was unexpected of Mitchel and poured tremendous amounts of love to him when he arrived. So much so that Cannon was placed on the back burner. That was until Zachary met his demise and everyone parted their ways.

The five foot five one hundred and sixty pound boy was quite muscular despite his poor diet. He always sported shiny black hair, blue eyes and a great smile with no teeth exposed.

Freak got his name because when he was two he accidentally drank Drano instead of juice. The caustic cocktail burnt his vocal chords and just about burnt off his tongue. He had more than a stub but it was slightly mangled. It sometimes made his speech garbled that usually led into a long stutter. So as of age six in kindergarten school Cannon became Freak. He accepted it and now everyone calls him that but not so much to his face. Even if he heard it being whispered under people's breath it wouldn't bother him much. It was when people called him dumb or stupid that upset him. And Sir called him dumb and stupid all the time. Cannon hated sir with a just hatred because he was a horrible human being. Sir was the boys stepfather but not by their choice.

Sir's birth name is Bruce Allison Blythe, born June 6th, 1955 and raised a Canadian in the city of Windsor a crossed from city of Detroit. As a child he was almost premature and malnourished which kept his body from growing properly like all the other children. This left him frail and weak and all the other children constantly picked and beat on him profusely and from all of the years of abuse Bruce or now known to the boys as only Sir developed small man's disorder. This is a disorder with no cure. It leaves a smaller man in a position of power to treat others like assholes. Unfortunately the disease seems to run rampant in the United States because so many assholes seem to run amuck these days, especially little bastards holding a position of power.

Sir somehow became a U.S citizen, enlisted in the army but within less than a year screwed up badly by accidentally killing Cannon and Mitch's father Zachary Mathias Knight.

Zachary Mitchel Mathias Knight the boy's real father was born on October 31st 1957 through a C-section operation performed by the Sisters of the Dawn at the Knight mansion in England, Zachary who was titled as a moonchild according to the Sisters of the Dawn an English nursing society prophesized that his bloodline would conquer the world.

Zachary created from the two family blood lines of Henry Cannon Knight and Deidre Ophelia Welch both contended to have bloodlines reaching back to the mythical city of Atlantis. No one ever objected as both families all contained the signs. They were all tall with blonde hair and blue eyes which the belief system was written in history from past scholars. Whether they were descendants or not the families believed it whole heartedly. Some have said that Henry actually found a family crest which contained the blood of his Atlantis family descendants off the coast of Sohar Beach in the country of Oman while on one of his diving expeditions looking for the Ring of Lawrencium a mythical city that bore angelic beasts according to Nordic Mythology. Henry who always referred to the finding as the black pearl of lasciviousness wore it around his neck in a small titanium vinaigrette that he later named Osiris. The vinaigrette normally used for smelling salts in the nineteen-hundreds never left his body until his final demise in the seventies when it had to be surgically removed from his chest cavity after a terrible accident unexpectedly stole his life.

There is much disbelief about the old wives tales that Henry would portray but after that expedition in Oman the Knights lives changed forever. Not only did the whole family act differently but it seemed that the world around them all bowed down. Unconsciously or unknowing but everyone wanted to know them and respected them deeply.

When Lord Henry moved his family to the U.S little Zachary was just seven years of age. Henry Knight established his Engineering firm in Pittsburgh Pennsylvania where he began developing thrill rides for the amusement park industry. Knight Mechanical became world renown for the fastest roller coasters on the planet. He lived and thrived on adrenaline put forth from his creations. Lord Henry as most called him was a deeply devoted father who took young Zachary with him on all of his job assignments and he even tested every one of his creations before signing off on the certifications.

In an unfortunate accident on a cold Sunday morning of March 1975 Lord Henry Knight met his demise when a mechanical subcontractor known as Mazzo left two sections of track out of the top of the first hill after the ninety mile per hour drop in the beginning portion of the ride. It is the second largest steel roller coaster known as Mt. Vesuvius that he produced at Kenny Wood Park to this day. Despite all the sign off certs Henry climbed into the front seat of the first six cars and went for it. At the height of the first hill it was said that Henry's cars propelled him ninety-eight miles per hour over the entire park and directly into the Monongahela River running east from Pittsburgh city. At the funeral the Zachary made up his mind and went against his father wishes to lead the business into the future and became a Navy seal trainer instead.

Sir killed Zachary with supposed friendly fire from his M-16 rifle. He then somehow found the boy's mother Audra and married her out of remorse or so it is thought. Bruce Blithe is so terrible that he is to be only addressed as Sir by the boys. They are not allowed to call him Bruce, dad of father. He holds a grudge against Zachary to this day for his death and mostly takes it out on his blood children Cannon and Mitch because in Sirs mind if Zachary wasn't where he was at the time then death would not have taken Zachary.

Sir speaks through a crooked grin from the broken jaw that was given as a compliment from the boy's late father Zachary. When a bar fight erupted in the Kingdom of Bahrain at Diggers night club over a Chinese whore who spilled her White Russian drink on Sir's boots he blamed Zachary. And when he would not let it go a drunken Sir swung, Zachary ducked and responded with a sharp blow to his face. Since the altercation never got recorded from the M.P's no evidence could be put against Sir after the supposed friendly fire accident but all who were at the bar that night knew exactly what went down.

Sir was approached by General Hatchet Grounder who forced him to participate in a program only known as the letter "Z" at the time. With Sir's agreement he did not have to serve any time in the brig and was dishonorably discharged.

That spring of 1985, three months before that horrible demons birth and eight-teen years before the final resolve of its fate, Cannon Knight had awkwardly grown to the age of fifteen.

The tinier of the two wearing a hand me down long sleeved shirt in the spring time cool air is little Mitchel Knight, Cannon's younger brother. His four foot six inch weak structure is less than impressive. Mainly because of poor diet and insulin dependence. Mitch constantly struggles to maintain his weight.

Mitchel Zachary Knight was born four pounds six ounces premature on exactly 7:13 PM on a full moon Sunday night in October 31st in 1973. Based on the C-section birth delivered by the Synagogue of Saturn Sisters Mitch was deemed a moonchild. His pink eyes and red hair caused him a little grief. Mitch was close to being an albino but sported skin two shades darker. Still pale white like a ghost compared to others he was always careful in the sun as he was all too familiar with experiencing a terrible sun burn. Mitch didn't endure as much torture as Cannon but occasionally he would get the, hey red head your hair is as red as the head on the dick of a dog or hey fire crotch, do you smell smoke or his favorite, hey milk with a red fruit loop on top or the best of them all was, you look like paper on fire.

That's what the degenerates would yell from time to time just to irritate him.

Most of the time the two were inseparable! That was unless Sir had his way. Sir was so jealous of the two because they were all each other had. They were blood brothers from the same parents and this infuriated Sir with an unquenchable hatred.

Even all the cases of Rolling Rock beers didn't drown out Sir's hatred it just made it worse. But when he was drunk at least the boys could run away and hide from him and when their mother went to work at the tampon factory it happened often.

The weather seemed to fluctuate now and the boys knew that if they didn't get Starburst down the wind would surely carry it into the creek and it would be lost forever. The conquering wind seemed to peel open their clothing to take a bite of their flesh like a rabid animal. Still the boys fought the force and proceeded into the woods to retrieve Starburst. The mud from all the rain created quick sand like mud. It caked to the boys shoes some four inches thick and weighed down their feet by almost a pound per shoe but still they pressed on.

"M, m, m, Mitch my shoes weigh a ton", Cannon yells!

Mitch starts laughing uncontrollably and falls face first into the mud, "Oh shit", Mitch blurts out! "My clothes are filthy, Sir is sure to light a fire under my ass now."

Cannon kneels down to pull little Mitch's to his feet. He stares deep into Mitch's eyes like a loving brother should, "Don't worry about that asshole. Will get you cleaned up in one of the creeks before we head back."

Once at the base of the pine tree that reached out and captured Starburst the boys began contemplating how to retrieve the battered kite. Mitch seemed pretty upset. He had put so much time into this kite and really wanted it to fly high.

Mitch looks up at Cannon, "how we will get it down?"

He couldn't hold it back anymore, small droplets of saline start to pour forth from Mitch's eyes. Cannon put his head down and shakes it side to side. He knows that the skinny pine is too shabby to climb and once he makes it to the top it might fall over but still he attempts the climb anyway for Mitch's sake. Cannon hates to see Mitch frown. Usually the frown is Mitch's most worn face, especially when Sir is around. But then again Sir makes everyone sad. He doesn't even have anything nice to say about Jesus.

It seemed that the Starburst actually put a smile on his face this day. Cannon drops back down from the tree. He says in his stuttering, growling voice,"M-m-m-Mitch the tree is too tall and skinny. If I climb to-to-t-to the top I'll fall."

Mitch's eyes began to pour forth tears a little harder.

So Cannon decides to take a chance despite the horrific consequences that they both will face. He hops down from the tree, "I-I-I-I- I damn near lost my p-p-p-p-pecker on t-t- that limb" He laughs!

Mitch's frown once again becomes a smile, "Your small pecker couldn't be found with a magnifying glass!"

Cannon flicks Mitch's right ear, "O yeah, w-w-well you have a c,-c-c-c-c-c cricket dick and your p-p, president of the cricket dick s-s-s-s-s-s-s, society."

Mitch is now laughing hysterically.

Abruptly Cannon grabs Mitch's hand and heads toward Sir's garage. He always seems to stutter more as he gets excited.

Mitch pulls back from his hand, "Cannon, no we can't because Sir will surely kill one of us."

Cannon continues walking on. He lifts his hand to Mitch's face, "You s-s-smell how g-g-good that p-pine smells?"

Mitch nods in acceptance. He enjoys all of the natural smells erupting in nature.

Cannon smears the pine sap on Mitch's face and tries to run from him with his hobbled leg. Mitch runs a little behind him as to make him feel better about himself as he is the older brother. He knows that he could outrun him for sure but his love is undying for his brother.

The two make it down to Loyalhanna creek where they wash the mud from their worn sneakers. Cannon watches Mitch try to keep his foot from getting soaked, "J-j-j-j-just jump in a-a-already, and y-y-your shoes w-will be dry for s-s-school Monday."

Mitch looks up with a worried face, "Oh no, I haven't finished my report for Mrs. Hazelett my English teacher. I'm going to get an A-." Cannon jumps up and down in creek washing the mud from his holed up Converse sneakers.

"An A-, that's what you are worried about? Hell b-b-b-brother I'm just t-t-t-trying to keep my C's a f-f-f-float. C-cause we all k-k-know what D's bring, d-d-d-d-disaster from the hands of Sir!" Cannon climbs up out of the creek, "One day Mitch I'm g-g-going to s-s-settle the score with that b-b-bastard for all that he has done t-t-to us! It's because of him that I w-w-wear this God f-f-f-forsaken b-b-brace on my leg. I swear to God I am going to k-k-kill that Mother...!"

Mitch intervenes grabbing Cannon by the arms, "Calm down, calm down Cannon, anger will get you nowhere in life. You have to forgive and forget." Mitch can see the rage in Cannon's eyes,

"Think we might need an exorcist to bring you back Cannon!"

Mitch laughs as Cannon shakes his head like a dog and starts up over the hill, "Mitch, p-p-please tell m-m-me one of your s-stories. They always seem to calm me down!"

Mitch grabs Cannon's hand as the two head towards Sir's garage, "Maybe we better go to the garage so that we can oil your brace up don't want you to rust up like the tin man"

They both chuckle as the two gallop along. Mitch pulls a dirty plastic bag from the back of his pants. Slowly he opens the bag like a piece of precious candy and removes a small thick leather bound notebook. Cannon looks down and smiles, "I can't b-believe that you c-c-carry that t-t-thing with you everywhere."

He tries to smack it out of Mitch's hands. Mitch pulls back and cracks Cannon in his chops.

"Do you want to hear or not?" Mitch yells.

Cannon heads towards the big oak tree and plops down at the base, "O-o-o-ok I'm sorry! Don't have a w-w-w-wussy attack!"

Mitch kneels down beside Cannon, "Wussy attack huh?"

They both giggle and stretch back against the big oaks huge root system.

Mitch fumbles through the book and pinpoints and a folded edge on one of the papers. He looks up at Cannon with a shit eating grin, "One day Cannon I will solve all of our problems. When I publish my books we will eat like kings and there will be no Sir's in our lives anymore!"

Cannon smiles as he knows that Mitch had gotten the brains out of the two. He wasn't exactly sure what parts he got because nothing seemed to work right on his body.

"Well come on with it already if it's that good," Cannon blurts out.

2

Right then the two boys got startled by Mandy Cunningham, Grace Adams, Ricky Bishop and Emmitt Vines when they came running down from the street up above the big oak. They all attend Derry Area High School with Cannon and Mitch. The girls are both fifteen but look twenty. Grace has the better body of the two, a beautiful poor brunette with an hour glass figure and a troubled past. Mandy an extremely large breasted blonde is a bit chunky but cute. She is daddy's little rich daughter who gets everything she wants. Old man Cunningham runs the Metz tampon factory that is named from his home town in Italy. This is where Cannon and Mitch's mother Audra works and a great many of others living in the Latrobe area. Her rheumatoid arthritis has made her fingers crooked but she still works hard to feed everyone.

The plastic insert packer position is a low paying job but the conditions are comfortable.

Mandy loves to point out the fact that there mother works for her rich father any time that she can just to rub it in. It's like because of the work situation between they're parents she is somehow the boy's boss too.

Cannon and Mitch's mother now, Audra Blithe and who once was a promising Audra Ivy Knight before marrying Sir is a forties hard worker that supports the grunt of the family.

When the boy's true father Zachary Mathias Knight died Audra went into a mental meltdown and began streamlining Percocet and Adderall through a crack pipe. The burnt narcotics slightly damaged her brain. It landed her into several mental institutions and then eventually into the arms of Bruce Blithe where they both resided at Green Oaks asylum for six months. Audra and Bruce met at the drug rehab facility and quickly fell in love. It was the perfect mixture for disaster.

Ricky nudges Emmitt and points to a large bluish-green slag rock that came from the Vanadium steel plant a few miles outside of Latrobe. Emmitt swiftly kneels down and picks up the baseball sized rock. He walks a little faster to get closer to the big oak tree.

Ricky Lee Bishop is the only black Chinese person that any of the kids in Derry Area High School had ever seen. He speaks English real well but speaks Mandarin even better. The only African trait was the dark blackness of his skin. His eyes were emerald green and he had blondish brown wavy hair that curled down below his shoulders.

"You need to smack that freak right upside his fucking gourd with that rock," Ricky says.

Emmitt tosses the rock up and down as they near the big oak. "Once I get closer I'm going to hell Mary it and see if I can hit him," Emmitt blurts out as he stuffs his lower lip full of mint Skull snuff. He shoves the green can in front of Ricky so he takes a small pinch despite the fact that he had never chewed before in his life. He tries to stuff the snuff into his lower lip but it goes all through his mouth. The gritty mint taste almost makes him puke so he stops and spits all over the road.

"What's wrong with you? You are not a little panty waste like old freak show down there are you? Put the snuff down into the right side of your cheek and that way it won't go all through your mouth so bad."

Ricky shakes his head no and continues to spit out the fine grains all through his teeth.

Emmitt puts the rock into his left pocket and pulls a red can of Skull long-cut out from his right pocket, packs it against his right palm and then hands it to Ricky. Ricky takes a bigger pinch and stuffs the chew down into the right side of his cheek as Emmitt ordered.

The two laugh and continue walking but being such a light weight Ricky immediately feels the nicotine rush into his veins and he becomes dizzy. By the time they get close enough to catapult the rocks at the oak tree Ricky starts turning purple.

"Come on Ricky I hate that freak fucker and I want to see if I can kill him with this big rock. You need you to help me. To me freaks that can't talk right need to be put down. They have no purpose!" Emmitt growls out.

"I will Emmitt just give me a second so that I can get my bearings straight. I'm feeling real dizzy here." Ricky says in a sick voice.

He doesn't want to show Emmitt that he is a candy ass like when they used to all call him black peter for two years straight after he played Peter Pan in the school play. He sported the whole green leotard and all of the boys in the entire school would not leave him alone. There were always some kind of peter, pecker, pumper or penis jokes blurted out whenever he entered other kids space. But despite what everyone deduced Ricky Bishop secretly desired to be a botanist or a cross breeder in floriculture. He especially loved orchids like his mother Ann Marie Bishop who works as a florist for Flemings Garden Pot in downtown Latrobe. They both especially love the pink Paphiopedilum orchid, a clonal hybrid also known as HS Spring-water and especially because it was the same orchids used at his father funeral. Ricky's feminine side started to shine brightly after his father's death.

Ricky's father Cory Bishop was an industrial salesman for the carbide grinding industry before he met his demise in the summer of 1984. His idea to be more-green for the planet led him to trade in his big Chevy jalopy for a smaller more gas efficient 1983 Ford Escort would ultimately be his undoing. When the experimental dual revolver cement mixer truck lost control and came down over the Laurel mountain route 30 highway near Seven Springs resort Cory didn't have a chance in hell. When Ricky's father's death made the front page of the Latrobe Post newspaper, many witnessed the picture of the flattened 1983 Ford Escort underneath the cement trucks wheels. With the insurance settlement Anna Marie Bishop was able to raise her family and continue her affair with Maxwell Vines.

Mandy and Grace are ten or so feet behind Ricky and Emmitt. They can almost guess what the two evil bastards are up to. Emmitt always seemed to pick a fight with Cannon anytime that he could just to show dominance.

"Mandy what do you think that those two are up to know?" Grace says as she brushes the pollen away from her shoulder.

"There is no telling Grace. You know that Emmitt hates Cannon and enjoys hurting him. Do you remember the time that Emmitt and Donavan gave Cannon that swirly in one of the boy's restroom toilets?" Mandy asks.

"I do remember Cannon rushing out of the boy's restroom soaking wet and covered with chunks of brown stuff and toilet paper.

"Yeah rumor had it that Stanley Grounder that big fat kid took a dump in it and plugged it up right before Cannon's face went in. I'm sure that the chunks were Stanley's shit."

Grace takes a stick of cherry Chapstick out of her pocket and applies it evenly to her plump lips.

"My God Mandy that is just disgusting. Well I'll tell you what I like Cannon and if Emmitt starts any crap I'm going to knock him out."

"Oh you like Cannon do you? Do you want to kiss him?" Mandy starts laughing.

"Don't be retarded I don't like anybody like that. My asshole uncle made me that way. The piece of shit won't stop touching me when I try to sleep at night. Cannon and I have just been spending some time together at night. We are closer now because his father died too that's all."

The two are almost up to where Emmitt and Ricky are now standing on the null roughly eighty yards from the big oak tree.

"My God Grace have you told your mother bout that pervert?"

"No, Mandy my mother won't listen to it because Jackson is the only man that will even get near our house since my father's death. And after all that news coverage the world hates us."

"Well Grace I don't believe all those rumors that everyone spread about your family on T.V. Your father had hundreds of cook outs and invited the whole town and everyone ate his barbeque. It was great. There is no way that it was hum-."

Grace nudges Mandy in her side and points at Emmitt and Ricky kneeling down in the dirt.

"I don't want to talk about it anymore Mandy. That's all that I heard about for the last couple years of my life and as a matter of fact I don't ever want to talk about it ever again! Ok?"

Mandy reaches into her purse and pulls out a pack of Stripe bubblegum, eats a piece and then hands a piece to Grace. She then runs up to Emmitt and Ricky and tries to buy they're love by offering them a piece of gum too.

Emmitt pulls down his lower lip to show Mandy the Skull chew-tobacco lining his teeth, "No thanks fatty I'm trying to quit." Emmitt says.

With hurt feelings she retreats back to Grace's side. The two stand there for a second and watch the two boys contemplate their strategy and then without warning the two boys jump up and throw the rocks down at the big oak as hard as they can. Ricky grunts as he tries real hard but his strength is like that of a small girl. Emmitt's rock goes all the way down to the big oak and then they take off running in the trees direction.

Emmitt Vines a blue eyed blonde haired Irish and German mixed rich boy stands five foot eleven inches and growing is a label whore and always sports all the cool clothing and most expensive shoes. He is a complete failure despite his silver spoon fed upbringing and still resides in the same lower grade at seventeen. The two girls were sweet on Cannon and loved Mitch but Emmitt was a true little rich hateful bastard. His parents seemed to buy him out of all trouble that he got in. Emmitt's drones Donavan and Isaac weren't carrying his balls for him this day. Usually the trio were inseparable but rumor had it that Donavan and Isaac got busted spitting hockers into a cum coffin and placing it on their science teacher Mr. Ryan's door knob so that they could get out of class for a while. Just as Donavan tied the knot near the ring and Isaac stretched t over the knob Mr. Ryan grabbed the two by the ears and drug them to the office. According to Dwight Fife who sits right beside Cannon in Social Studies, he saw the whole thing go down. He said that the two were taken to the Torrance State psych ward for evaluation.

3

The whole school knew of the story about the two beautiful blonde twins Lacey and Lindsey Reed who said that there Chihuahua Duffy told them to kill their parents and plant their hearts in the flower bed outside their home on Main Street in downtown Latrobe in 1984. Both girls were found in their night gowns covered in their parent's blood lying outside making snow angels in the middle of Main Street. Lacey was first institutionalized because of her psychotic nature towards cruelty to animals when she was just five years old.

Lindsey didn't have her meltdown until the age of eight but it was worse because one night she went downstairs for milk and cookies as her nightmares woke her up so she had a tall glass of milk; three Oreo's and then put their Siamese cat Tut into the microwave, turned it on high and went to bed.

In the middle of the night the fire alarms went off and when the Latrobe Fire Department found the exploded cat remains in the microwave they had no choice but to have the Pennsylvania State Police investigate the issues. Once the DNA proved to be feline the Humane Society stepped in and pressed charges against their parents Kyle and Addie Reed.

When Kyle Reed was placed behind bars for six months he was visited by Dennis Dangle Jr. from a new company called Dangle & Beria associates. Dennis Dangle Jr. promised to prove his innocence by showing the state that his two girls possessed the extra Y chromosome that creates psychopaths before they are born. He explained that one out of every eleven girls and one out of every nine boys has the potential to become a psychopath. He swore to Kyle that he had the technology to prove it and the evidence would hold up in court. Dennis went into a little depth to explain the PAS system or the Personality Assessment System that shows three basic dimensions and two-hundred sixteen basic types of personalities. He goes on to tell Kyle that if he finds any unusual issues inside their brains that his team can perform a basic behavior modification through frontal lobe injections. During a conjugal visit with Addie the two signed the papers and Addie mailed them to Dangle & Beria associates. Within two months the court cases came and went and all charges were dropped against the Reeds as the proof was in the pudding. From then on the Reeds all seemed to live in perfect harmony up until the disaster of Thanksgiving night in November 1984. Kyle and Addie were found in their bed with their hearts ripped from their chests. The wishbone from the turkey was ripped in two and a piece was placed in each parents' mouth. According to the coroner's report they both were alive when their hearts were ripped out. The beautiful twins were detained and escorted to Torrance State Hospital and never seen until 2007 when a report surfaced about two blonde women exiting the Crackle-wood Acres apartment complex right before the Pittsburgh S.W.A.T team led by Sargent Maxwell Vines stormed the building entrance. The massacre made international news and forced agencies to combine into I.P.C.O in an effort to capture all of those involved. And still today the Crackle-wood Acres massacre is used as a training tool for new agent recruits.

Emmitt's father Maxwell Vines is a Pittsburgh S.W.A.T Sargent and his mother Autumn Snow Vines is employed as a Chief Biochemist at the Beria weapons facility in the lower city of Pittsburgh. One day Emmitt came to school bragging about how his mother was on a huge billboard in Station Square but it turned out to be more like a big poster on a building.

4

Within minutes the three were upon Cannon and Mitch. "BANG" "BANG" a loud thud came crashing down through the big oak trees limbs.

Immediately Cannon jumps up and yells," W-W-WHAT THE FUCK EMMITT"! Why would you t-t-throw r-r-rocks at m-m-me?"

Emmitt gets right up into Cannon's face. He can smell the stink of mint Skull chew tobacco on his breath, "W-w-w-w-w-w-w-w-w-what will you do FREAK?" Emmitt screams in his face.

As Cannon begins to open his mouth to speak Emmitt spits tobacco juice right inside it, "Ha-ha-ha you stupid bastard, that's all your good for! Your nothing more than a walking spittoon!"

Cannon bends over spitting and gagging.

Abruptly Grace jumps between the two. She puts her hands on both of their chests, "Just get lost Emmitt. You are such an asshole! Please leave or I'm telling your mother where your porno mags are hidden." Grace shouts loudly.

Emmitt looks at Grace with such hatred. His eyes almost tear up as she hit a nerve, "You wouldn't dare cannibal bitch."

And before any of them knew it Grace had Emmitt on the ground beating his eyes shut. She knocks him right out of his new white Nike basketball sneakers before plummeting to the ground. He yelps like a gazelle being slaughtered by a lioness before closing his mouth after biting his tongue. Blood trickles down from his freshly busted bottom lip and immediately his right eye started swelling shut.

Cannon grabs Grace around the waist and before he knows it. "SMACK" His nose explodes. Blood went everywhere as he flew into Ricky and the two of them went tumbling down over the large oak trees roots. Cannon lands on his back with a loud thud. All the air exits right out of his lungs as the loud thud and crackling leaves on the ground below echoes up through the entire wood line from his back to earth impact. Cannon crashes like an asteroid colliding with an orbiting planet in the earths' atmosphere. Despite the irony blood taste trickling down Cannon's throat he still gets a whiff of the acorns and wet dirt that lay hidden underneath the snow for several months before the thaw.

Ricky continues to tumble down into the blackberry bushes several feet from the base of tree and only inches from Byron's creek. He begins to scream as he lay there picking thorns from his arms and face. After a few stunned seconds he jumps to his feet and runs after Emmitt.

Once Grace realizes what she has done she pulls away from Emmitt's limp body, wipes the blood from her knuckles on his superman shirt, climbs down over the trees roots, leaps down three feet to the tram road and starts caressing Cannon's head.

Emmitt slowly pulls his beat ass up from the wet ground, Ricky helps him to his feet and the two run off towards home. Emmitt is crying all the way to the wood line, "Your just like your fucking cannibal father bitch"! You wait whore! Your done! Your done! I swear I'll kill you all." Emmitt screamed and yelled as he ran off through the woods. And within minutes he and Ricky disappear into the woods behind old man Clyde Strong's house.

5

Clyde Strong now at the ripe age of seventy didn't resemble his last name a bit now nor did he ever and standing just roughly four foot two inches which was not much taller than most midgets according to the town's people. Most said that his silver wolf like super mullet gave him the extra few inches he needed to keep him from being extreme vertically challenged but there wasn't a day that went by when Clyde would climb out of his modified Mustang two and someone would laugh at the two by four wood blocks duct taped to the cars gas and brake pedals. Most would snicker, stare and point but Clyde dismissed the remarks and went about his business as usual. It is believed that all the torturing he endured throughout his life had made him so cold towards others and that is why most times he and his wife live like hermits.

The hobbit looking fella just couldn't keep his nose out of everyone's business despite the fact that his wife Ingrid told him to do so and he especially liked to get Cannon and Mitch in trouble by Sir. It was probably all caused from the time Clyde went to pick wild black berries and he caught the boys picking them as well. Clyde thought that he owned all of the woods around his house despite the deed that stated he only owned an acre of land; he would still try to run anyone off the grounds by threatening to call the police.

The six hundred acres of mostly maple trees, oaks and pines that ran all the way up to the old Murphy's salt mine, down past Blairsville, Ligonier and then in an awkward boot like pattern to the city of Pittsburgh was owned by a large German conglomerate out of the Pittsburgh area. They had posted no trespassing signs all around the borders of the acreage but no one ever patrolled the land. The only initial on the signature area of the sign was D & B.

Even though Clyde's young 37 year old wife Ingrid possessed the brains of the two Strong's, household, together they weren't much smarter than a box of rocks and their conversations showed it. Tons of Rumors spread throughout the town that Clyde Strong pulled all of his pension money out of the Pot-lucky waste treatment facility and bought Ingrid as a mail order bride but no one will ever know the truth. On that April day Clyde is staring through his bottle thick glasses taking it all in and sure to tell someone at the right time to cause some kind of trouble.

Grace pulls Cannon around so she can see where the blood is pouring out from, "Oh my God Cannon I'm so-so sorry! Will you ever forgive me?"

Cannon looks up and smiles. He has blood all over his face, teeth and shirt, "Y—y-y-yes, He garbles out softly. It takes every ounce of concentration for him to speak properly around Grace because the loud thuds of his heartbeat drown out everything else.

Grace tears a piece of her blouse off and begins to clean off Cannon's nose. She turns to Mitch and says, "Run over to the creek and wet this so that we can wipe away the blood and see how bad it is."

Mitch runs there and back swiftly, and in seconds he hands her the wet muddy material. He did it quickly in fear that she would beat his eye shut next.

Mandy gets close and tries to assist but witnesses Graces stare upon her.

"What bitch? Why you giving me the evil eye? You act like he's your boyfriend or something." Mandy blurts out.

Grace spits at Mandy abruptly, "Do you want a taste of this," Grace yells while shaking her fist at her."

Mandy quickly backs down and kneels near the big oak. She slips and gets a little of the bark under her skin. She picks it out as Grace rescues Cannon.

"No, no Mam I don't I already tasted it before," Mandy whisper under her breath. Mandy remembers the time that she made the rumor that Grace wore her mother's stinky hand me down underwear. And when Grace beat her stomach black and blue with a dead possum behind her house one evening she never made up lies about Grace again. Mandy still has nightmares of being covered in the rotting carcass meat and now she won't eat hot dogs because Grace made her stick the possum's tail in her mouth. In her brain a hot dog is the same pink color and texture of a possum's tail.

Grace continues to wipe Cannon's face until it's all of the blood is removed to reveal a small cut up underneath his left nostril. But the more she wipes the more it bleeds.

"Feeling better now?" Grace asks.

At that instance of a moment in time it wouldn't have mattered if Grace had stabbed Cannon deep in his hear fifty-thousand times because he was totally in love with Grace and he was pretty sure that she knew it too. All of the time that the two spent talking was a dream come true for Cannon as Mitch was his only friend that he spoke with.

Cannon sniffs a little and swallows the metal tasting bloody boogers down his throat but he still sports a smile even though the pain is rocketing through his brain like a 351 Modified Ford motor with a thrown rod, "I-I-I-I-I'M ok. Thanks Grace."

Grace smiles and grabs Cannon's hand. He can feel the warmth emitting from her rough hands. He thinks that maybe she is so rough and tough from all the gardening and farm work that her and her siblings perform on a daily basis.

"What are you two doing down here anyway? We never see the two of you come out of the house. Hell we thought your retarded uncle Jebedia might have killed you!"

Now the three of them are all standing beside Cannon who is still lying on his side on the ground. They all bust out laughing. Cannon laughs so hard that bloody snot flies from his nose.

Mitch sits down right beside Cannon and tears off a piece of the sleeve of his already torn shirt so that he can wipe away the snot. Cannon, embarrassed quickly takes the cloth and wipes away the mess.

"What? Jeb would never hurt a fly. He only likes to buy tools from people with his social money he gets." Mitch replies.

The two girls sit down beside Cannon and Mitch on the ground as well. As Mandy starts to squat down beside Mitch she violently farts. And not just farts a little girl fart but a huge fat trucker fart that seems to spew on for eternity. The harder Mandy tries to squeeze it back up in the worse it fights her.

"Oh my God excuse me. I'm so embarrassed," she whispers as she puts her head down.

Grace gags, "Dear Lord what did you eat Mandy, pickles? I swear that I'm eating it here."

They all start looking at each other and bust out laughing hysterically. Mandy gets up and starts to leave. Mitch immediately jumps up and grabs Mandy's hand while covering his nose with the other, "Don't leave! I have a something to tell you."

Mandy stops dead in her tracks. She knows that Mitch is younger but he's a very cute boy to her and no other boys seem to be interested. As far as she's concerned any attention is better than none. Especially when you have a rich father that's only obsessed with money and tampons. She envisions her father as a big tampon. She would love to stuff him in one of the plastic applicators and shove himself right up his own ass, "Oh what is it Mitch?"

Mitch looks down and then up into her face. He pauses for what seems to be an eternity and fights real hard not to laugh, "You know Mandy, I have been thinking a lot about you and I love a woman that blows ass so freely in public!"

Mitch falls to the ground and starts rolling. He holds his stomach in pain.

Mandy stomps her feet like a little two year old, "I can't help it my doctor said I'm allergic to gluten and Grace made me eat an ice cream cone. It's all her fault."

Grace leans forward, "Hey I don't control your butthole. That's all you girl."

Mandy spins around, "Mitch," She says with a hard M," be nice or I will tell my daddy to fire your momma. So there!"

Cannon rises to his knees and pulls Mitch to his side. Mitch whispers, "The blonde is mine even though she's a bitch."

6

Cannon nods with his big freakish grin and then looks up, "M-m-m-Mandy, don't leave yet. M-M-M-Mitch was about to tell me one of his greatest stories."

Mitch softly punches him in the shoulder, "Why you putting me on the spot like this? Paybacks are a bitch brother."

Cannon grabs for the back of his pants, "Come on Mitch show them how good you are!"

Mitch couldn't believe it. Not a one stutter came out of his mouth. He must really want to hear the story or he was concentrating to impress Grace, he thought. Both girls giggle.

"Come on Mitch tell us your big story," they both taunt.

Mandy plops down right between Grace and Cannon. Mitch squirms a bit, looks at Cannon and then pulls out the notebook, "Well my brother if I read then you need to show the girls your art work."

Both girls clap like kindergartners. So Mitch thought! Cannon nods yes.

He clears his throat, "Ok so I call this Defiant-I'm Watching.

"What's it all about Mitch?" Mandy blurts out before he can utter a letter.

"Well it's about a top secret government organization called O.I.A that creates evil Hybrids out of children by injecting demons into the babies eyes through their mothers stomach before they are born. And the Hybrids eat the hearts of humans for food."

Mitch sits back and looks at all of their faces for a response and he gets it. He can see all the whites of their eyes.

"Oh my gosh," Grace screams," Where do you come up with this stuff?"

"W-w-w-what is O.I.A s-s-s-stand f-f-f-for Mitch? A-a-a-and why do t-t-they do it?"

A frustrated Mitch pulls his knees in tighter to his body and sighs, well, "Optimal Intelligence Agency is their name and-"Mitch doesn't want to tell Cannon the next part because he knows that it will most likely hurt his feelings but he goes on only because he asked, "O.I.A determines if a baby has defects or disabilities and then tries to correct them through specific surgeries before they are born."

Cannon puts his head down," W-w-w-what happens t-t-to the ones t-t-that c-c-can't be fixed?

Mitch takes a deep breath and thinks long and hard about the question, "Well Cannon they are forced to be slaves to the system or gorged with product until they are old enough to be used as food or spare body parts."

"S-s-s-so I guess I'd be food then?"

Mandy slides back against the strong oak. Her face looks on in horror, "Mitch I don't think that I want to hear anymore because you are really starting to scare me. I'm going to have nightmares tonight." I don't like demons or killing babies. I mean who kills babies?"

Mitch shrugs his shoulders and begins reading anyway.

"What shall be the most undeniable nefarious power adroitly harnessed by a mere bewitched mortal? Why it is none other than the obsessive magnitude of raw evil, imbalanced and secreted through its purest form. It is undoubtedly the bloody root of all chaotic implosions within the interior cells of a human's corrupt cerebellum. This multitude of devastation is most definitely capable of inflicting bloody blistering torments against all who uncontrollably attempt to wield its forsaken rage of aggressiveness."

Mitch looks up to witness their faces. All eyes are on him so he continues.

"With mellifluous capabilities of swiftly liquefying the sharpest of minds, It's no wonder that lucid drums of nonchalant ears rupture against the obstreperous thundering bursts, left trouncing behind from the aphasia bent mind detonating explosiveness. A mythical heart pulverizing weapon of such is not detectable by the minor five common senses known to mortal man and only slightly noticeable to the eyes of an elite few."

Mitch sits up a little to adjust his back. He cracks his neck and looks at Cannon. His hands are shaking uncontrollably as he tries to lift the notebook. Cannon looks on with concern.

"M-m-m-Mitch your sugar is low. You need to eat something quick," Cannon says.

Mandy reaches into her purse and pulls a big box of gum drops out. She starts passing them out.

"Here Mitch eat a few of these," Mandy says.

They all quickly gobble up the candy. Especially Cannon and Mitch as their meals are few and far between. Mitch pulls one of the gum drops from his teeth and goes on.

"The deluded asperity becomes subordinately indomitable to all. Legends deduce that canards accrued through time state that deities beguile humans in a conspicuous manner for the pure purpose of castigating the human soul. Knowing of the severe apocalypse to inevitably come, few adjusted. Mankind would come to know a new form of latent peril. A languishing indelible curse insinuated by millions to be nothing more than myth. As malevolent loathing transpires worldwide a manifested creature is adduced to demodulate society back against the proper mannerism and driven to force all within the laws stated by the Decalogue. Sin is inevitable to many and this seems to be a catalyst for the new circumstantial evidence in hand. Massacring all who fall prey to its abominable wrath. But the hierarchy of mankind struggled through time to devise a plan to ensure humanity would forever prosper despite what the holy rule book preached. As of this second of this instance in this unknown time mankind cleverly pieced together such a devious contraption to capture the wicked fingers that has been catapulting explicit deceitfulness a crossed the earth for centuries. Although indestructible by mortal methods the beast posed no apparent threat if detained and defused or so it was thought. The forever thinking that the ability to grasp a piece of the fountain of youth was attainable, deceitfully led millions to believe that they were allowed to mischievously propel forward and accepting not even an ounce of regards to the chaotic society that engulfed the whole of them." Mitch licks his lips and continues on. The other three could tell how involved he was in his story.

"It is unfortunately now the year Two thousand twenty. And mankind's pathetic attempt to stop the inevitable has occurred. In the past the forefathers of the country were producing unimaginable creations of destruction and on one instance a certain Professor Englestein.

The professor was a Jewish Holocaust survivor hell bent on ridding the world of sin. His creativity produced a complicated solution that secretly detected latent nefarious spiritual forces, the entities that infest every corridor of our minds with uncontrollable cravings beyond our desires."

Just then Mandy squirms a little to adjust her seating and, "swoooooooooooosh, swoooooooosh" two of the longest farts sound out, "Sorry, Mandy weeps.

Mitch looks on in terror. He wasn't so sure about the blonde now, "Oh Mandy that reeks terribly. I don't need sound effects for my story," Mitch says," my god it's like raunchy cheese with meatballs or something."

Cannon pokes Mitch. He is amazed with the writing ability of his young brother.

"C-c-c-continue p-p-p-please I want t-to hear m-more."

Mitch looks down and begins again. Grace pulls closer with full attention.

"With this new untapped form of uncertain destruction, America set forth with a new type of enforcement personnel. Born and bred with angelic blood and referred to as ELEMENTS, containing the same magnitudes of unyielding strengths as Goliath who mythically towered above David in prophetic times of Christ. Mythically was supposed to be the key word at the time. No one, I mean no one believed their eyes would witness a rehash of history. It was just not possible. So it was said, said in many different languages by billions, billions all over the globe. Mankind sought out to dazzle an abounded collection of scattered mirth, supposedly ensuring the capture of the serpent.

All of a sudden loud yelling echoes from down the street a ways.

"Grace! Grace, get your ass home now! You know what time it is girl," Jackson Mirth hollers through his cupped hands.

All four turn and see a roly-poly figure of a man walking up the street and trailing a few feet behind him are six camouflage military vehicles. Its Graces uncle Jackson Mirth, her mother's brother. He is a perverted drunk and a two bit thief who sucks like a leech from Graces mother Judy. But since the death of Graces dad he is the only father figure that would even step foot into their house after all the craziness that went down at their place back in 1982.

Just before Mitch could start again Grace stands up. "Mitch you sound like a genius," Grace says," the words your using, Uh, I never even heard before. I mean you are like a human dictionary or something."

Mitch smiles and stands up as well, "Thanks Grace that means a lot to me. It is my dream to be a writer one day so that Cannon and I can have a better life. I actually study etymology to help me with writing."

Grace blows a kiss to Cannon, "I'm really sorry Cannon! Hopefully one day I get to see some of that art work Mitch brags so much about. I'm sure it's beautiful."

Cannon pulls himself with the help of the big oak's trunk," Grace w-why are a-army m-m-men following y-y-our uncle?"

Grace turns to Mandy and then looks back at Cannon with sad eyes. Cannon can feel the warmth coming from her soul," I'm not sure Cannon but this mean old guy named Grounder or something keeps wanting to test all of us kids for some reason but my momma is fighting him.

Mandy lets go before I get in trouble. You know how my asshole for an uncle likes to start with me."

Mandy jumps to her feet and the two girls run down to the road. Jackson quickly runs up behind the two girls and pats Grace on her ass. She speeds up a little to get away from him and then looks back and waves again at Cannon. He waves back at her and stands up on his tippy toes to see her little better. The two girls, Jackson and the army vehicles disappear down the street.

Cannon follows Grace with his eyes until she is completely out of site.

"Mitch, what the hell was that? I never even heard that s-s-s-stuff before?"

Mitch reaches for Cannon's hand. He pulls him to his feet, "I can't tell you my entire secret stash brother. If I did I'd have to kill ya."

Cannon starts laughing. He lightly punches Mitch in the nut sack.

"Cannon I'm not sure how I know this stuff but I swear that I read it before or somehow lived it in a past life."

Mitch looks down at his journal.

"Cannon, do you know how some babies are born and remember every detail about coming out of the womb?"

Cannon looks up with a puzzled face, "No I never heard of that Mitch."

"Well I remember a lot of things from that day, pretty much everything and each year more reveals itself. Cannon I don't think my birth was under normal circumstances. I saw a film in school about birth and I'm pretty sure that I wasn't born that way. I mean I can still feel the pain inside me as if it were yesterday. Sometimes it's all I think about. It's getting harder to concentrate now that I'm getting older. Almost like some voice in the back of my brain speaks to me."

Cannon looks at Mitch with a distorted face. He never heard him talk this way before and the worrying look on his brothers' face scares him a little. "Well Mitch tell me s-s-some m-m-more,"

Mitch totally has his full attention now. The two head in the same direction of the girls. Mitch takes his notebook and continues to read on as they walk.

"Where did I leave off? Ok here it is, and to finally free mankind, desperately mankind became their own legends in essence. An angel, the first to be exact created in the image of God and almost as wise as he tragically manipulated many through pacifism. Necromancy proved an important role towards the future. Being bewildered with mellifluous anxiety from society the U. S. government sought out a new agency. An agency that emerged in the far past but laid to rest by orders of a past unrestricted president. Ultimately laid to rest before necrology logs tremendously increased again. The new uprising agency would surpass its ancestors with crude discoveries emitting around us all. Thus the rebirth of the Optimal Intelligence Agency ensued it was almost indomitable in the eyes of many. O. I. A'S jovial outreach program blinded the thoughts of all forcing a maelstrom of majority approbation. The agency appeared harmless with little uncertainties. That was until paranormal insanity rushed a nation. Horrific acts of human mutilation began to seize the rationality of all. Missing persons soon became a major disorder among the states and even some foreign countries reported acts of disappearance by some leaders.

Mitch stops, sucks back a mouthful of lugy and spits it on the ground.

"O. I. A was secretly granted a class clearance 10, the code data- MAXIMUM NECROMANCY boisterously setting the unwinding nefarious ball into indelible motion. Unfortunately containing no wisdom of what lied beneath the secret studies to come. O. I. A carelessly unleashed a hellish form of physically lined soul consuming entity. Determining to emit mass destructive forces as far as the mortal eye can see.

Like prophesized writings in the past. Mankind chose its own destiny, a destiny causing amplitude modulation to dwindle forever into the darkness but not a darkness committing the ever seeing eye but a darkness plaguing the soul with convulsing apostasy and deifying the one who forces mankind to pray.

Now societies' infrastructure has collapsed and eternal damnation has begun, and with no place for sinners to reside, Hell on earth has aggressively commenced."

Mitch stops and points to a symbol in the book and then points to several more with odd shapes and designs.

"Cannon did you ever see this symbol before or how about these three? The symbol looks like an s or serpent slithering around the earth. It's stuck in my brain that way. I always see it, especially on T.V when I watch it but mainly on the static channels with no picture."

Mitch points to his right eye and blinks repeatedly, "The symbols are placed on the sclera in the right eye according to my story. I want you to check my eye for me because I'm scared."

"W-w-w-what are you t-t-t-talking about Mitch? D-d-d-d-id you hit your head or s-s-s-something? Nothing like t-t-t-that could e-e-ever b-b-be real, just f-f-finish p-please." Mitsch goes on.

"I am the explicit form of byproduct created entirely from sin and the paper like shell which encases the fierce rage furiously growing deep within me is aggressively beginning to exhort decadence. All who think they have come to know me will soon be confronted with a multitude of horrific forces and the savage deceitfulness hidden deep within my labyrinth of sub consciousness. Buried for what seems to be an eternity. With a shuttering blink of an eye as your pupil begins to dilate due to immense core meltdown, your flesh will secrete fear, pure adrenaline pumping, soul scattered fear. Violently transcending through gaseous pheromones of aromatized content and latently exploding out from within the millions of pores lining your pasty flesh. Sweat pours down a brow. The heart skips beats. The sweet scent engulfing your intents slow to a halt and if the nose captures a hint of cotton candy. It's too late! Your dead! Your body just doesn't know it yet!

Then without remorseful conscious wielding ignorance I violently enter your gateway to your miserable soul, consuming and sampling all the irrational delectable thoughts created from the frightening adrenaline pumping circumstances thrashed upon your sacred chest and as the bitter sweet blood like nectar pours forward down the creases of my lips. I will stop, but only for an instant of a second to hear your aching heart pump for one last pathetic beat, but not before your fleshy pile of wasted space comes to rest atop the ground. "I cannot be contained. I am DEFIANT."

Can you see me? Cause I see you. I'm everywhere! I'm all around you. "I'm watching.

Cannon pats Mitch on the back and starts clapping wildly, "W-w-w-wow Mitch t-t-that w-w-w-w-was a great story but s-s-strange!"

Mitch stands up, grabs Cannon and pulls him to his feet. By now it is midday and getting pretty warm. Cannon can feel the sweat dripping from his pits as they walk, "Mitch I don't stink d-d-d-do I?" Y-y-you thin Grace smelled m-m-me?"

Mitch leans in and grabs a nostril full, "Not too bad for swamp trash that can't even afford deodorant. Why are you worried? You like her don't you? You have a crush on Grace."

"D-d-d-don't be s-s-silly she wouldn't l-l-like someone broken l-l-l-l-l-l-l-l-like me anyway."

Mitch could tell that it upset Cannon pretty bad and he knew that Cannon loved Grace because he watched him carve it into the big oak tree a long time ago. Cannon swears that he didn't but Mitch knew better and so did Grace.

The two hit the pavement and begin their decent down Center St. Cannon grabs Mitch's arm and spins him sideways. He has no idea that Mitch was chosen to be a prophet from the ancients and that some parts of his story will possess a true meaning in the future.

"Why didn't you tell them that s-s-story about that terrorist extraordinaire Dr. David Christopher? You know the guy with t-t-t-two first n-n-n-names. Or about Chucky Upchuck who eats all that chocolate and shits his pants or even Arcane Tact the spy artist? The one I like the most! Now that's f-f-f-funny s-s-s-stuff!"

Mitch shrugs his shoulders and continues on. The two are right in front of their run down old house. Now reality has set back in. Mitch takes a step back.

"Cannon have you ever seen such a piece of shit in all of your life? I mean I'm just a young kid but who in their right mind pulls a trailer in long ways on a hill and stacks up some twenty foot high concrete blocks to hold it up?"

Cannon looks over the run down old red 70's trailer on stilts. If a hard enough gust of wind came through the trailer would blow right over he thought. As he gazed around he realized just how poor they all really were. Still even though they were poor living in a shack, they both had each other and lived in the country area that sported lots of beautiful woods he thought. It could always be worse he though.

The pieced together place has a ten by twenty run down old makeshift garage put together with cheap wafer board on the right side and a beat up old porch made out of pallets on the left. The boy's grandparents live right above them and overlook their place. Everyone has well water in the area so Mitch often thinks he's drinking Jeb's piss so he always tries to drink juice, milk or soda if there ever is any or even mix some of that old lemonade mix in with it to make the color change from cloudy brown to yellow. Most times the boys will take jugs to school and bring back water or even drink from the clean springs up on Skin hill.

"For a minute there I was lost in my story so much that I totally forgot about Starburst up in the tree all alone."

Cannon looks up and down the street as he starts to pull the door to the side of the rickety garage; he nudges Mitch and points at a large black turkey buzzard tearing the viscera from a pile of what resembles a dead raccoon splattered on the pavement near Clyde's. The two watch in horror as Clyde's wife Ingrid comes out of the front door and chases the buzzard away with a broom. She then kneels down on one knee, grabs the coon by the tail and carries it off into the house.

The two boys look at one another in disgust and cringe.

Mitch pulls on his back pocket, "Cannon, are you for sure about this? I mean I'll just take an F in art class. It's not worth it. It's just not worth the whipping!"

Cannon pats Mitch on the head, "Come on. I-I-I-I-Its ok Mitch we c-c-can be in and out b-b-before Sir comes home. B-b-b-besides he's up at old man Weavers place cutting metal or something. Sir always w-w-works l-l-l-late w-w-when he's up there."

The two pull back the door real hard to peer inside the garage.

CH 4 ALL WRAPPED UP (2008)

1

Its 7:00 A.M now on a Monday in May 2008. The sun can be seen just barely rising above the hills peeking through the tree line in Washington PA. Monica decided to go against her better judgment and give it up to Dennis during that morning again. She gave her best ever and pulled no punches. She even let him penetrate her in places never seen by any other man. Well except David but she never viewed him as a man. As the two romped for hours they both realized how late it had become. Dennis is afraid of missing a very important conference call and Monica is just plain afraid of what is ahead of her this morning. Dennis gazes into Monica's eyes.

"I do love you with all my heart," Dennis whispers," I just want you to know that my love is eternal."

Monica just lays there staring back at Dennis. She begins to tear up as a thought of never returning to Dennis fills her mind. Even though he was a big pain in the ass sometimes she really does love him in a weird way. All the others were just play toys to satisfy the itches that Dennis just couldn't scratch. She really wanted to tell him what she had done but cant. She looks away.

"What's wrong babe," Dennis says louder," don't you feel the same about me? I know I'm old b-."

Monica puts her finger over his lips. She smiles wide with her pearly whites peering through, "SHH! I do love you. With all my heart! Please be careful at work today alright!"

Dennis gives her a puzzled look as he strokes her fiery hair, "OK. You be careful too."

Dennis wanders what all the carefulness was about. Hell he has the best security money can buy. Hell he has more security than the president of the Unites States, he thinks.

They quickly pull themselves together and go their separate ways. Dennis races off to work as usual in his 2008 canary yellow Porsche 911 and Monica in her

2009 pink H2 Hummer. Supposedly she's off to re-hearsal and the clothing stores.

2

Monica exits the Goddess Massage Body Shop around 10 AM. She doesn't dare try tanning. Her skin is just too pale white. Most importantly she doesn't want her tats to fade. But the manicures and pedicures' are the best in town and the bikini wax is to die for. She can also walk a crossed Liberty Avenue to the Cascade hotel waterfront resort which is only five blocks away. It is the perfect getaway for the elite rich in downtown Pittsburgh. Her Hummer sits in front of the spa all day incase eyes are watching. It's the perfect plan. So she thinks.

It's 10:30 AM when a stout drink of a man strides in to the pool lounge area and goes up to the bar. He is dressed in all black. His style exudes money. Lots of it! Monica peeks out from behind the long white curtains addressed over her personal bungalow by the pool. She can see the outline of the man's package from quite a distance. She even thinks that she can smell his scent of Giorgio Armani cologne that he wears. Monica thinks that he is even sexier now than when the two met that night in the Luxor casino in Vegas but she knows that she must resist his charm. The bartender points to the cabana by the pool. The handsome man muddles his way through the pile of half-naked ladies lying all around the pool area. All eyes are on him and he loves it. He slowly struts past the hot tub area when he is approached by Cassandra Gorgon, "Hello handsome" she whispers in his ear softly, "What's your name stud? I'm Cassandra, "She says as her hand slides down over his back to cups a handful of his tight ass.

David looks back to see her roaming hand, "Well then my name is Mr. Christopher, Dr. David Christopher to be exact." Cannon who is in incognito loves to tell lies to the ladies. It's what makes him such a good Reaper.

Cassandra exudes pure unadulterated sex. She is the epitome of bang me queens. Her body should be on a poster for plastic surgery though. But still she is a gorgeous woman for her age. David looks down at the huge rock on her left hand, "That's an awfully big rock on your finger Cassandra."

She looks down at her hand, "Don't worry sweetie this rock doesn't block any of my holes!"

David immediately begins to throb in his pants and he knows Cassandra can feel it when she starts to pull herself closer to him. And then abruptly as the encounter happened David is pulled from her arms by Monica, "Good day Cassandra."

Cassandra smirks, "She's married Romeo, better watch out."

She slowly walks away knowing that she is no competition for the younger singer. Her body is much tighter is more place than hers. She stops for a second to look back at that tight ass. It crosses her mind that maybe Monica would share the stud but then quickly disregards the thought as she remembers the predicament the two got in several months ago. It was all supposed to fun and sex until Monica caught feelings for the last bozo. That last bozo being Dennis Dangle one of the richest men in the world. Cassandra missed her chance and unfortunately had to settle for Jimmy Gorgon the biggest plumber company owner in Pittsburgh. Moneys money she thought.

Now Jimmies last name wasn't always Gorgon but rather Dagreah so all through his childhood life he was teased as Jimmy Diarrhea so now in his adult years and sporting a huge bank account he thought that it would be just awesome to have a name like that of the mythical Greek three headed serpent that was turned to stone by Hercules using Medusas decapitated head.

His forty-seven facilities in thirty-six states and all his rigs sport a huge three headed serpent being turned to stone by Medusas head. They explode with a bright yellow Gorgon decal in monstrous letters.

Of course Cassandra knew that Dennis wouldn't believe her but why not take a picture for possible black mail later. It couldn't hurt or so she thought. Slowly she pulls her Droid from her bra and snaps a few shots of the two standing there looking in her direction. Cassandra thought that she got away with it until David's eyes met hers. She smiles, puts the phone back in her bra and strolls into her very own cabana. Monica leads David into her cabana. She kisses him and then sits down on the bed. He knew that something was wrong because normally she is all over him like stink on shit. This was a different woman here. And not even a peep out of her. Normally she couldn't keep her trap shut. She sits there with her legs crossed, crackling her gum and admiring her manicure that Dennis's money had just paid for. The look of pure dissatisfaction lines the entire surface of her face and the way she puckers up her top lip when she scolds David makes her a lot less pretty but still with all the fuck you-s and other truck driver mouth lingo exiting her pretty mouth, she still thinks her ass is golden. David wonders why he even plays with such a bitch at times. He thought that maybe it was the closest thing that he had to a normal human relationship. But none the less he knew what had to be done so he had to put up with her bullshit until he could get her alone.

"Listen David, I've been thinking long and hard about these situations that were both in. You know that you travel so damn much with your profession and well a girl has needs. You know?" She says. Monica sits forward a little closer, "And David I seem to be having these reoccurring images of Delicious. Do you remember that little Thai girl in Vegas? What did ever happen to her, because she was gone in the morning?"

Monica really thought hard about her words. She even rehearsed it a few times in her head like an actress before they met that day. Her plan was to scare him enough with the whole Delicious incident that he would just leave in fear of being arrested.

David just sits there speechless. He can't believe what an ungrateful bitch this little twat was being. As much as he wanted to tear off her head and shit down here neck he kept his composure. And now he wasn't sure what the hell she had seen that night. Guess it was all just too good to be true he thought.

After Monica dumped the huge pile of dung in David's lap he placed his face in the palms of his hands.

Each breath that he took was like that of inhaling extreme heat from a burning forest fire. With each inhale his lungs began to quiver as if he just inhaled something toxic.

He briefly drifts into a bent reality where he could taste that same burnt toxins he endured at the Blithe residence. And then he snaps back to reality. Tears pour forth as his heart flops in his chest like a dying fish out of water. The pain takes him back to the oak tree where he sees Grace's face but then just as fast as the tears started flowing they begin to trickle down his cheeks at a slower pace. Slowly one by one they begin to dry upon his soft tan skin leaving nothing behind but a small trace of salt sediment barely allowing you to know that a tear once ran there. Within minutes of the painstaking arguments about sleeping with other people David begins to change. He can feel something pushing through his skin. It becomes rather uncomfortable forcing him to crack his jaw by opening his mouth. It seems as though someone else or something is beginning to take him over. Slowly the tears come to a halt and his pupils begin to reflect that of an unquenchable fire. Now the once intense pain of heartbreak is manifesting into an undying hatred. Even in the midst of David's peril, Monica giggles and sighs as she sends text messages through her phone to an unknown individual that she only refers to as Oregon. David never paid much attention to all her innuendos about this Oregon fellow and he truly disregarded all the jive talk about all the boyfriends she could get for each day of the week but know he knew for sure. He can see straight into her soulless vessel. He can even taste the sweat on her lips from the other man now that he has evolved closer to the beast that resides within him. Monica always puts David down. She always plays head games with him like most immature woman but no more. On this day Monica is going to experience the most devastating occurrences of her short life and no longer will David be the bitch.

David takes Monica's hand noticing the ring band mark, "Monica lets at least have one last evening together. Would you agree to that?"

Monica nods her head cautiously. She can't believe that David is being this calm. She thinks that maybe she dreamt the whole Delicious incident. Hell she did suck down quite a few Mai-tis that evening before the bedroom romp.

David takes Monica's hand as he leads her to the back of the hotel. She is hesitant at first but then succumbs like a lamb to a wanton. They both walk out to the parking garage where David points to a brand new

2008 black ZX8 Jeep. He brushes his hand across the hood, "This baby has a Hemi in it. 475 horsepower will rocket you anywhere, anytime fast."

Monica's jaw drops," You bought this for me?"

David leads her over to the driver's side door. He pushes the unlock switch and helps her into the Jeep. David gets in the back behind Monica. He reaches in to an old camouflage backpack. Monica looks in the rearview, "What are you doing sweet heart?"

David smiles back at her, "Oh my love"! You aren't married are you?"

Monica looks down at the band of faded skin around her finger on her left hand. She tried to cover it up with cream but it still showed through. She looks back into the rearview to witness David holding a little suede black box with a huge ten carat diamond ring in it. "Oh my God," she cries, out.

Immediately she thinks that maybe her marriage was to the wrong guy but just maybe she could play them both to get both of their money, just like what she had been doing for nearly a year or so. So many thoughts are racing through her tiny brain. Unfortunately none of them were good thoughts and David was listening to them all. Monica is a label whore bred for greed.

David let her hold the box and admire its contents for a while as he fumbled around in his bag.

Just as she looks at the ring and David one last time she feels a little pinch in the left side of her neck. "Ouch," she screams," David what are you do-?"

Before all the words could exit her mouth she was out. David grabs Monica's little lap purse. He finds her wedding band inside. Inscribed on the inside is "D.B Forever and Always will thee love". How corny. He thinks. Inside a hidden compartment he finds her license.

"Monica fucking Dangle, Dangle and Beria", he shouts. "

He looks down at the syringe in his hand, "Wow that Brompton mixture has a little too much chloroform in it!"

He pulls Monica into the back seat, opens up the gold butterfly locket around her neck, takes the God particle out and puts it in his pocket. He stares at her beautiful face for a second and then covers up her body with a blanket and some plastic bags from a store.

David then takes her pass to get back into the hotel, all her security passes for the D&B building and her condo key. He then locks the Jeep and heads back inside to the lounge area near the pool. There he slithers through the glass doors like a snail just moving fast enough to collect women's attention and then darts straight to Cassandra's cabana. When David enters the curtains he sees Cassandra masturbating profusely. Embarrassed she jumps from the bed trying to hide it, adjusts her thong while wrapping him right up, "I knew that you couldn't resist big boy. What's in the backpack, Toys?" She whispers right before gorging his ear full of tongue," What's your name again sexy?"

He pulls her close, kisses her hard and then bends her over the bed, "My name is Cane," He says," Cane like pain you know?" Cannon who has multiple personalities shifts to each situation. The doctors believe that he is such a good chameleon because when he gets into certain places the other entities in his body seem to take over leaving Cannon to take a back seat to his surroundings. It is explained like committing a sin, like when people say,' I can't believe I just did that or I don't know what had come over me. Well Cannon knows what comes over him, it is the entities residing in the same body as him and unfortunately for Cassandra she is meeting one of the vilest of Cannon's multiple monsters lurking just beneath his flesh, Cane. She will never forget him as she burns in hell.

Cassandra is moaning already and the fun hasn't even begun. She repeatedly backs up against his groin area as she pulls her thong to the side to reveal an area of hot dripping wetness, "I don't care what the fuck your name is just smack that ass please! Give it to me Cane. Give it to me like you hate me baby. Show me the pain that you are promising."

Cane aggressively rips her bikini bottoms all the way over to one side, spits on his hand, applies the saliva and forcefully enters Cassandra. She bucks, moans and hollers like a wild pig. Her moans and screams can be heard all through the hotel pool area and clean out into the lobby. One guest covers the ears of her young boy sitting by the pool when he asks,' mommy is than a wolf howling like that? I'm scared!"

No one cares though because this isn't Cassandra's first rodeo. And Cane isn't the first stud to make her holler but he sure will be her last. The more he thrusts the louder she screams. Slowly he pulls a diamond tipped cutting wire used for cutting granite form his pocket. He lays it out on across her naked back wondering if it will work since he has never tried it before. He got the idea after watching an episode on one of those learning channels. In his mind he thinks that the wire will cut flesh like butter but never tested his theory.

Slowly he takes each end of the wire in his hands and wraps it around Cassandra's neck. He is surprised when she pulls it tight herself and begins screaming, "CHOKE ME! CHOKE ME! I fucking love it. I love. Oh yeah right there. RIGHT THERE! IM CUMMING! IM CUMMING!"

David delivers vaginal destruction. He bangs her ass like the pistons slamming is a locomotives diesel engine, the sounds of ass smacking thighs is evident. Cassandras lust scent is overpowering. The way she milks his loins is incredible and he even puts down the wire for a few minutes. He figures that the least he can do for this goofy bitch is giving her a few hundred orgasms that she will never forget. And then as he pumps he pulls on the wire, one, two and three. "Holy shit," he mumbles.

He can't believe that it only took three pulls for her head to come right off. David continues to pound Cassandra's twitching body. The death seems to turn him on even more. His mind can't help drifting off to that tomb of Juniper Savage. She was his first piece of ass after all. She popped his cherry at a tender young age of 11. It was cold but enjoyable. Although the 30 weight motor oil from Sir's garage made his pecker break out in a rash it was none the less worth it, more than worth it, he thought. A loud crash brinks him back to reality. He stops for a second, looks around, pulls the covers over Cassandra's severed head and continues thrusting.

Not paying attention a set of hands begins to rub down over his chest. He can smell the scent of rum exiting from a woman's hot breath. "I'm Jasmine. I' next, she says in a sexy but drunk voice."

Cane stares back into the face of a beautiful African American female. Several more pumps and he pulls from Cassandra's lifeless body spilling his seed everywhere. It is one of the most powerful orgasms that he has experienced in years. The mess is spewed all over Cassandra's ass like hot wax melted down from an overflowing candle. Jasmine kneels down and takes in every drop. He thought for a moment that he was busted until she bends over top Cassandra's lifeless body and guides him into her. Canes mind is about to detonate. He is living one of his wildest fantasies ever. It just can't be real he thinks. He knows that the others won't believe him. How can he be banging this sexy black chick over top a corpse, he thinks? Hell he couldn't even get the stock in the mine to do these kinds of things. Not without drugs or force of course. After a short while this beauty erupts like a volcano all over Canes Johnston. Her orgasm is so immense that it drips all down over his balls to his legs. A squirter, 'he thinks,' how lucky I am. He even has one more in him for her as he pulls from her love glove erupting again. She passes out right on top of Cassandra's dead body.

It couldn't have been any more perfect he thinks. Cane stands there for a second taking in all the scents of sex, sweat and death as sweat rolls down the crack of his ass causing a little chill.

He quickly pulls a cloth napkin from room service's cart, cleans himself, Cassandra and Jasmines body. He sprays them down with the DNA remover Gone, then takes all the napkins, puts them in a sealed bag and stashes them in his backpack. Then he pulls a few of Dennis's used dinky condoms from his back pack and begins dripping the contents all over jasmines back and into both women's crevices. He pulls Cassandra's severed head from under the covers and puts it into a garbage bag, stuffs it into his backpack and then pulls her phone from her bra where places it in his pants pocket. He rummages through her purse to takes all of her jewelry and cash. The Reapers loot every victim that they destroy. Each of them has a different addiction; some collect driver's licenses while others collect jewelry and some even go to the extreme like Cannon who collects the heads. While digging inside he pulls out her husband's business car and reads it, "Jimmy Gorgon Plumbing."

How ironic he thinks, as Jimmies card shows a picture of a decapitated Medusa on his business card, now here lays his old lady looking the same way. Cane decides to put a cherry on top of it all but he feels somewhat bad about it but he just can't resist the temptation so he wraps the cutting wire around Jasmines right wrist. He knows that he has to get rid of the pictures off Cassandras phone because Monica is the only woman that he doesn't shift into disguise for. He just lies to her about his name. Quickly He throws the pack over his shoulder and exits the hotel to the parking garage. He jumps in the Jeep and drives off into the city of Pittsburgh towards the airport.

2

Now 4:30 Pm a distraught Cannon is quickly traveling west bound on route 376 leaving Pittsburgh. The weather is beautiful on a Pennsylvania evening despite the dark clouds rolling in. He is utterly destroyed from the conversation with Uriel. His body is week from the God particle impact, so week that his mind is unclear and his driving lacks a bit. It can clearly be seen that the east bound traffic is backed up clean to the Squirrel Hill tunnels. Sirens can be heard coming from all directions. Police cars, swat trucks, ambulances and even several military vehicles were screaming down the east side into Pittsburgh. Cannon looks in his rearview where he can see smoke rising up from the middle of the city. He leans down and turns on the radio to see if someone is reporting on the incident. Again he looks in the rearview, wipes his mouth over and over. He can't believe that the sick sadistic bitch didn't even try to hide the stank of another man on her breath. Oh how fucking sick. He thought. The sweat! The cheese!

"Damn that bitch Monica," He screams."

Cannon is despised by homosexuality. His past afflictions ensured that. Just the thought of another man being in the same place he was minutes before he got there was enough to make him puke. All at once the rage bottled up from the past broke through. He started to think of the Faggot Big-T and begins punching the roof and dash of the jeep. In his hysterical fit of rage his eyes catch a glimpse of sexiness. Before his brain is able to execute orders his right foot is already braking, the jeep as he rolls right in behind a yellow V- Bug. The super fine piece of ass hanging out from under the hood is totally bone-fiable, Cannon thinks. Bone-fiable is his term for any woman worthy enough to perch atop his Johnston of pleasure. Slowly the sweet piece of meat strolled toward the Jeep. Her posture looks good, probably had a few good parts left in her so he thought or maybe even make a good wall mount if she has all her teeth.

She points to herself and then towards the Jeep. Cannon is mesmerized by her long legs that run all the way up to her pussy belt. It is most definitely a pussy belt, he thinks, because that is just too damn short to be a skirt. And when she leans in the drivers' side of the Bug to get her purse he captures a shot of a perfectly shaved little beaver. She is a perfect spinner for sure. Cannon prefers the little types. He can't believe how lucky he is on this day. He starts to drift off into a daydream of pounding this little bitches face for hours but just as fast as he is gone the cold steel of a small pistol reels him right back into reality. Slowly his right eye glances over to catch a skinny black male in the passenger seat. It was the hand attached to the pistol.

"Yo, motherfucker. Put your boner away and get this Hoop D rolling," the man says.

The sexy blonde crawls into the back seat, puts his backpack under her head and lies down across the back seat. Cannon hesitates for a second as he watches her enter the Jeep. Even in this situation he is still trying to catch another glimpse of that little beaver. It is Cannon's weakness or sickness that some may call it but he embraces at every moment.

"Get movin now biotch," the man yells.

The skinny black man looks back at the girl, "You believe this sick motherfucker Rhonda? I have a gun to this motherfuckers head and he still is trying to see your pussy. Sick mother fucker."

The blonde girl reaches into her bag and pulls out a one hitter, "Calm down Reggie! The man has good taste in woman that's all. He thinks your woman's sexy. A sexy little vixen", she mumbles."

Reggie gets right up in Cannon's face where he stares into his eyes, "Move the car now, MOTHERFUCKER! You don't want none of the baddest fucker in town do ya?"

Cannon knows that he is serious so he puts the Jeep in drive and slowly pulls back out onto 376 west bound toward Cyprus. The Hemi rumbles as he brings it up to the speed limit.

"Calm down man. I don't want any trouble. I'll give you anything you want," Cannon assures.

Reggie seems to relax a little now that they are moving. He sits back in the passenger seat. "Damn right you will! Anything I want. Cause I'll fucking take it if I choose whitey." He keeps the gun pointed at Cane from his lap.

Just then a woman with a whiney voice blurts out from the radio,

"This is your traffic update and news with Tracey Butler your local channels 1.007 mediators. East bound traffic is backed up to the Monroeville exit. Drivers should be looking for alternate routes away from the Pittsburgh city so that emergency personnel can get to the disaster area. It is believed that a terrorist attack was launched on the city of Pittsburgh around lunch time today. Anybody with information regarding this matter should contact the Pennsylvania state police immediately. Now back to your eighties hits at noon. Def-Leopard blares through the speakers. "Stand inside, walk this way. It's you and me babe. HEY! HEY"!

Reggie looks back at Rhonda, "You don't think tha-?"

Rhonda cuts off Reggie immediately, "Shut your mouth Reggie. We don't know this guy from Adam."

Cannon looks back in the rearview. Rhonda is sitting in the middle of the back seat with legs spread wide open. It's all hanging out. She starts to sing the tune on the radio. Cannon is cool, calm and collective. He knows that she can smell the Alpha male in him. And he couldn't understand why this hot little piece of ass was with a skinny little crack nigger like Reggie and hopes to ask her after he kills him. Reggie wasn't the first to threaten Cannon in his new advanced state of being and he is sure that it won't be the last. Cannon glances down to see where the gun is pointed. Reggie sees Cannon's eyes wander so he rocks the gun back and forth against his thigh. Once again the whiney voice cones out from within the dash;

"This just in, There are two leading suspects being sought for the robbery and death of a Shaler man at the Seven Eleven mini mart on seventh and tenth street in Pittsburgh this morning. An African American male and female were seen leaving in a yellow Volkswagen Bug with the plate number HP-"

Just then Reggie turns the radio to XM 90. The speakers are spitting out some kind of rap sounds. Reggie begins singing along making spitting sounds with his lips.

Rhonda leans up over the back seat and hands Reggie a crack pipe. He sucks gags and chokes in between his power ballads. His eyes immediately become bloodshot dripping tears, the haze across his pupil's show that he is almost there. "Oh that's good shit man, good shit", he mumbles under his smoke laden breath as the meth kicks in.

Cannon rolls down the driver side window a few inches, "That shit stinks like burnt plastic!" It is the same burnt plastic stink that would rise up through the Blithe residence when Sir burnt it.

Reggie jumps up from his stoned state. He puts the gun to Cannon's face again, "Someone tell you to put the window down you honkey motherfucker? HUH!"

Cannon pushes the gun into his cheek as he turns to look at Reggie, "Listen I don't like drugs. My body is a temple." Cannon is totally bullshitting now. He just smoked one of the fattest hog legs anyone had ever seen just hours before this incident, hence his inability to react in time to the individual now holding his life in his hands.

Reggie chokes on the crack. BANG! The twenty-two shorty goes off. The driver's side window shatters from Cannon's head smacking against it. Cannon feels the hot lead burn through his face at a racing speed.

The enveloping scent of gunpowder emits into the air from the gun as the Jeep swerves into the medium. The U-Haul cart being towed behind jumps around erratically. Rhonda is screaming hysterically," WHAT DID YOU DO? WHAT DID YOU DO REGGIE?"

Cannon's head slumps down into the steering wheel. The explosion of pain in his face sends him rifling to the past. He begins to think of his brother Mitch. He wonders if this is the type of pain that he felt before he died. Tears pour forth from both eyes but not from pain. From sadness in what he had left for a heart which wasn't much after Monica's escapade and all Cutlass's bullshit but the pain felt good he thought so he embraced it. He fights hard to keep the others in his head at bay, especially the Dragon. Cannon is pulled back to reality when he hears the Jeeps tires grinding against the concrete medium. Reggie puts the gun down on the Jeeps center console and grabs the steering wheel. He hurries up and sets the speed on the cruise control to keep them rolling, "Damn I'm sorry man. That was totally an accident man." When Reggie looks over he sees the blood spewing from Cannon's cheek. It makes him hungry for strawberry pie at Eat-N-Park as that is what the blood looks like dripping down through the eyes of a drug addict. The drugs make the colors so vivid.

Cannon pulls his hands to his face. Reggie can't seem to help from laughing. "See bitch he aint dead I just grazed him", Reggie pleads to Rhonda.

Rhonda leans forward again to inspect the situation, "Reggie it's always an accident with you. How many people have to die by your hands? Huh Reggie? I'm so done with this shit."

Reggie gives Rhonda the evil eye, "He aint dead bitch. I told you. But counting, if he dies. This cracker would be number five. That right five, five mother-fuckers, slain by the maddest motherfucker in the land. And I aint been caught by the Popo neider."

After all his bragging he guides the Jeep to the side of the road onto the largest pull off right before the Irwin exit. He takes off the cruise control and feathers the emergency brake to come to a complete stop. Cannon spits two of his back teeth into his hand. He rolls his tongue around and feels the twenty-two bullet lodged in the upper part of his mouth.

"Damn you are bleeding out dude. You got blood everywhere," Reggie blurts out.

Cannon's head is throbbing. It's hard to concentrate. For a brief second he swears that he sees Mitch standing in front of the jeep. He blinks repeatedly but he's still there. When he starts to get out of the jeep

Reggie reacts, "Whoa you fucking pig. Get your cracker ass back in here."

Cannon slumps back down into the seat. He stares out the windshield but now his little brother is gone.

Rhonda takes the pipe from Reggie. She starts lighting up. The sound of her sucking on the pipe in the back seat gives Cannon wood. Pain and sex are his specialties. After a moment or two he gains his composure and reaches into the center console past his modified Judge where he pulls out a handful of napkins. He stuffs them into his mouth to stop the bleeding. Reggie grabs the pistol and points it at Cannon again, "Listen man I said I was sorry. No hard feelings right?"

Cannon nods in displeasure as he pats the blood away from his right cheek. He looks up in the rearview mirror to inspect the damage. He sees that his face is already ballooned up with fluids and his right eye is completely bloodshot. Rhonda laughs, "HA! HA! Man you look like a chipmunk with all them napkins stuffed in your mouth."

She is completely stoned now. Crack cocaine, gunpowder and burnt flesh linger inside the Jeeps interior. Reggie looks at Cane completely different. He can sense a little that he has changed to a different person. He swears that he sees a creature try to push through

Cannon's face. He rubs both of his eyes trying to make the meth calm down a little as he thinks that he is tripping really badly like he did a few weeks ago when he accidentally shot a circus clown while he and Rhonda were at the state fair in Mt. Pleasant.

"Hey man put down the window now cause your burnt stank white ass is making me sick over here."

Cannon pulls the big wad of napkins out of his mouth and tosses it down on the driver's side floor. He reaches down on the side of his seat and pulls out a pouch of Redman Golden Blend. Reggie looks at him in disgust, "What, no you aint gonna! You really gonna stuff that shit in your mouth man?"

Cannon never says a word. He takes a big pinch of the chew and places it into his right cheek tight against the bullet hole entrance. He cringes a little from the sour taste as it bites back against his tongue. Like a mentally handicapped person Reggie bounces back and forth like a in his seat pointing, "Rhonda! Rhonda wake up will ya? Look at this sick fuck."

Rhonda rolls her heavy head around to see Cannon. She bursts laughing again. Her eyes are rolling back in her head, "OOOHHHH!"

"There's tobacco juice and blood dripping out of that small hole in your cheek man." Reggie yells.

Cannon presses against the wad of tobacco in his jaw with his tongue. Juice sprays out of the hole like a humpback whale taking a breath after a long dive below the ocean.

"Ho! Ho! Ho! motherfucker. Watch where your spraying that shit," Reggie bitches.

Cannon starts to laugh and laugh. Tears are dripping down his cheeks and the harder he laughs the more Rhonda and Reggie laugh too. And then as abruptly as he started he stops dead. Slowly he puts the Jeep in drive and heads towards Johnstown. The two criminals are still laughing wildly. Rhonda passes out from all the drugs. Cannon looks at Reggie, pulls the chew in with his tongue and spits a mouthful of bloody chew saliva right into his face. Reggie gags as he can taste the Redman entering his mouth. It burns both of his eyes profusely. And quickly as you can on crack he points the gun at Cannon's head as he begins wiping his eyes with the other hand. Cannon rips the gun from Reggie's hand and throws it out the window. Then in the blink of an eye he smashes in Reggie's face with his right fist. The explosive force makes Reggie's nose explode all over the passenger side window and dash. Reggie slouches down in the passenger seat falling into an unconscious state as he pukes out blood and teeth. Cannon knocked him clean out, "You stupid fucking porch monkey! Only my luck, what the fuck is going on?"

Cannon shakes his head and spits the wad of chew out the window. He looks down at his crotch. "Gotta stop thinking with my dick it almost got me killed. DAMN IT! DAMN IT," He shouts as he smacks the steering wheel wildly. He pulls a cell phone from his right blood soaked pocket and dials Idle. He puts it on speaker phone hoping to hear him since both eardrums are both ringing form the blast. Idle picks up. A Russian accented deep voice answers," Ellen's doughnut shop how can I help you?"

Cannon laughs a little with the searing pain shooting through his mouth.

"What do you want bitch? " Idle says jokingly over the phone.

He spits a mouthful of warm blood out the window, "I need a pint of A positive and get the table ready. Also don't alert Cutlass on this because I have something big to discuss with all of you ok?"

He can hear Idle gobbling down something," For sure Hoss! Is all ok cause you don't sound like yourself brother?"

Cannon spits out the window again, "All is good, bringing in two," He looks over at Reggie, "Make that one and a half. Oh and get Freckle down there immediately!"

He spits another mouthful out the window again. Rhonda leaps forward, "You motherfucker", Rhonda screams, "You motherfucker! "

She starts kicking wildly and smacks Cane in the face.

Idle yells, "Who is that?"

Cannon pushes Rhonda back into the back seat, "Sit the fuck down you crazy bitch. This is our new toy. Make it happen. C- out."

Rhonda stares at him. She pulls an ink pen from her purse and tries to stab him in the side of the neck. He grabs her around the neck and chokes her until she almost stops breathing. Instantly her body falls onto the floor as she gasps for air.

Immediately he pulls to the side of the road. Pops the hatch and grabs a backpack from the trunk. He zip ties Reggie's hands and feet and then throws him in the back. Rhonda tries to exit the back door and run but Cannon grabs her stoned ass before she got too far, "Where do you think your little ass is going? HUH?"

She kicks and bites his hand like a caged animal.

"Oh I love me a feisty bitch," He smacks her head off the roof of the car. She goes limp. He puts her in the passenger side and seat belts her into place. Rhonda comes to and spits blood in his face.

"MORE! MORE! MORE," Cannon screams as he spits a mouthful of blood back at her. The blood splatters all up over one side of her head. She thrashes while rubbing her face on her dress like the blood is poison. He pulls both her arms behind the passenger seat and restrains her with zip ties. And then secures both her feet to the rail of the seat. He shuts the trunk, enters the driver's side door, puts on his seat belt and continues driving. Rhonda is screaming at the top of her lungs, "Oh oh oh oh my God you killed Reggie. Oh Reggie no. NO!"

Cannon laughs in her face. He reaches around the back of his seat where he pulls a bag from the backpack. Rhonda is watching anxiously. He pulls Cassandras head from the bag and perches it atop the shifter. Her beautiful face never changed. Not even in death. Good Botox, Cannon thinks.

"Here bitch talk to Cassandra, she's lonely," He takes his pointer finger and makes Cassandras cold lips move, "Rhonda I really want to kiss you with tongue." Cane says in a low deep evil voice.

Rhonda goes ape shit. She starts jumping up and down wildly, "YOU FUCK, YOU FUCK, Your that sick bastard that everyone is talking about aren't you? You cut up all those people didn't you?"

Cannon turns and blows her a kiss, "You are not going to lose your head over me too are you?"

Cannon busts out laughing again in Rhonda's face as he plays with the hole in the side of his cheek. He puts his finger in the inside of his mouth and pushes it out through his cheek. He then wiggles it like a worm at Rhonda. He loves to torment. It's his forte.

Rhonda screams uncontrollably and so does Cane. Back and forth the two yell for miles and miles down the highway while he races at 140 MPH banging the Jeep off the medium. Several times the Jeep swerves and almost loses control when the tires bite into the concrete.

"OH! OH! OH! FUCK! FUCK, "They both scream," OH! OH! OH! FUCK! FUCK, OH! OH! OH! FUCK! FUCK!"

Rhonda is now losing her voice. She has little red dots starting to appear on her cheeks from screaming and crying so hard. Cannon almost feels a little sorrow for her. Because he used to sport those same red dots most of his childhood. Once off the highway exit they are up a few hills and then down a couple to the old lake bed. He looks at Rhonda," Hold on bitch."

She sees the building coming up fast. With the fear of death before her she mumbles under her breath, "Our Father who art In Heaven hallowed be thy name, thy-."

Cannon cuts her off and looks down in her face, "You for real asshole? He's not listening to you."

"SMASH" The jeep plows into the building at 110 MPH, the speedometer sticks in place.

"Damn it I missed the one hundred twelve miles per hour record," He looks at Rhonda and smiles with bloody teeth covered in cheek meat.

Then after a few seconds both airbags deploy into their faces. The gas radiates into both of their lungs causing them to choke. Cannon inhales the gas and blows little smoke rings. He reaches down and pulls a little black box from the center console. He pushes a blinking red button on a remote. A loud ruckus comes from underneath the Jeep as they feel the ground beneath them shutter. Slowly the floor begins to drop. Instantly everything goes black. Rhonda can't even see her hands in front of her. And then a huge plunge downward tickles her belly. It will be the last pleasure that she will ever feel.

"Oh God please, she begs, "Please let me go. What is this? Where are you taking me you sick bastard?"

Cannon reaches into the back seat. He pulls Rhonda's purse to the front. The stink of antifreeze oil and gasoline are filling the interior of the Jeep. The odors are making Rhonda's eyes drip. He roots around in her purse until he finds an eighth of weed, pulls the pineapple blunts form what's left of the center console and rolls up a fatty. He lights it up with the Zippo that he found in Cassandra's purse and sucks in long drags. He then blows it in Rhonda's direction.

"You make me sick you fuck."

Cannon just smiles and takes another hit, "Reggie's right you know. This is some good shit."

Just then the Jeep hits bottom with a loud clang against metal. The doors rip open. Light eats up the dark in the Jeep. Rhonda's eyes never opened this wide before in her life. She can't believe what she was seeing, "Where are we?" She screams with her frog like voice.

Cannon puts the blunt out on her forehead before losing consciousness, "YOUR IN HELL BITCH, YOUR IN HELL!"

CH 5 THE CRYPT CLUB
A BRIEF GLIMPSE IN THE PAST
(1996)

1

No one could believe the clothes or lack thereof that people were dressed in to enter the **CRYPT***; writes reporter Danielle Coitous news editor of the Greensburg Review Paper.*

Grand opening flashed across two big iron doors that thwarted off many waiting for a peek at the newest talent that this world had to offer. These gateways were part of the old Ferrell factory, now known as the CRYPT club is located just two miles on the outskirts of Latrobe city limits and directly above one of the main salt veins 2000 feet below the earth that connect to the underground City of Cyprus. The old factory building lays dead center of an old industrial complex that once employed several hundred people back in the early seventies. Many of the older city folks built their nest eggs from these factories. When the U.S government agreed to overseas trade agreements the rich bastards who controlled these big corporations got a little hungrier for wealth and started using slave labor in low income countries to produce a lower grade mass product. Unfortunately the motto became quantity over quality and thus these big wigs crashed and burned.

Hundreds of people waited outside on the black carpet waiting for a glimpse of world renowned artist and sculpture extraordinaire Centaur who became an overnight success with his Reality line of paintings and the never unforgettable Flesh art. His paintings are so in demand that most customers wait on a list for several months before delivery and at a whopping twenty-five thousand dollars per piece and higher for some larger sculptures does not persuade clients. The majority of the lines revolve around dark masochistic roots which allures some of the weirdest people to flock around these events. A big bald man only known as Tim was a martinet himself who dabbled in the explicit art of pain as well and it was most evident in his work. The last event, two months ago in L.A resulted in a four million dollar profit for the artist and hundreds of customers were even turned away. The majority of the pieces were sold within three hours on the first night. Centaur told reporters that the Crypt which would house an art gallery by day and a night club for weekends was going to be his home base in the states. He said that the serene country side would allow his mind to be clear in order to produce some new fantastic pieces of art.

All over the outside of the club were posters advertising positions at the club. There were bartender positions, dancer positions, waitress slots, cooks and even a couple of janitor spots.

Jessica Hickey and Amanda Joule were two of the first girls applying for jobs at the night club. Jessica a beautiful big chesty student of art was seeking the dancing position and Amanda was applying for dancing or waitressing but any position would be fine by her because she just wanted to get inside the hottest new nightclub to hit the scene. With not much around for miles everyone knew that the Crypt would go off without a hitch. Most watering holes were nothing more than just that. They were stagnant cesspools that contained a bunch of old farts sitting around talking about old times and shitting their pants. Nothing existed for fresh young people to enjoy. The majority of that age kids would travel over an hour just to party for a couple of short hours.

Jessica grabbed two applications posted next to the missing person's poster from the front door billboard and then headed back to Amanda's dads Beemer. Amanda just got done tonguing a fresh blunt and offered Jessica the honors. Amanda smiled giving visual access to a huge ten gauge tongue ring. "Fire it up bitch," Amanda shouted. Jessica laughed while she shoved a Blink 182 CD into the dash. The music pounded through the twenty-thousand dollar sound system. Jessica placed the blunt into her soft lips and began to puff as Amanda lit the tip. As Jessica took a deep drag the cherry blazed like a set of acetylene torches turning steel into molten metal. After what seemed to be a lifetime Jessica finally passed the hog leg. The exhaled smoke rifled out of her hot mouth like the exhaust from a passing 747. The inside of the car was layered in a fog of cannabis. Just then the girls heard a loud rumble approaching. Jessica wiped the haze from the passenger window to reveal a bright yellow sixty-eight Mustang approaching. Too stoned to talk she just nudged Amanda and pointed. Little groans erupted into a," holy shit Amanda some-one's coming. Put that damn thing out." By now the muscle machine had pulled right beside them. The black tint kept them from seeing who was inside but they knew that the driver of this car was close enough to smell the marijuana smoke. Hell the residue on the windows could have been scraped off with a credit card and smoked again.   The Mustang revved then finally shut off. Out from within emerged one of the sexiest guys these two infidels had ever seen. Instantly they both were creaming their jeans and Jessica's would soak clean through because she never wore underwear even to church. The man was Centaur. They knew him from TV and the entire newspaper clippings. He sported a tight black wife beater which flowed into a pair of faded snugly fit Levi jeans. His jet black hair accented the warmest pair of blue eyes ever encountered. Several tattoos rolled around a set of huge Lox balls for biceps. Arcane peered into the girl's car, smiled and then entered to the club doors. Jessica and Amanda vigorously sprayed themselves with vanilla musk and proceeded after him. "Excuse me sir, excuse me," Jessica screamed. Centaur turned and leaned against the door. Jessica almost fell into him as she trotted in a pair of six inch pumps. The stench of pot lingered over both of the girls. Centaur sprouted one of those model type smiles that screamed," I'm hot and you all know it." But the attitude did not follow. This man was a real charmer. Amanda stumbled in a close second to Jessica.

The frown she sported evaporated a kind of jealousy. Jessica was always the center of attention when the two hung out. Amanda felt that it was Jessica's big tits that landed most men because her brains, the little she had were in her ass. Unfortunately for Amanda she only erected small B-cup breasts that were just mediocre to her. Fortunately Amanda had her own sugar daddy which would buy her anything as long as she blew him every once in a while. Her mother would never come to find out about her and Michael Vincent, a married sugar daddy to young ladies because no one was to ever speak of it. Michael's Johnston was the first and only Johnston she would ever wrap her lips around, unfortunately because she became quite good at it.

Centaur reached down and grabbed Jessica's left wrist. His hot lips mashed against her pale flesh exposing a little tongue as her body quivered like that of a convulsive seizure attack. Orgasmic tickles seemed to ricochet throughout her loins and Centaur could tell. For as long as he knew, that was the effect he gave all the ladies, especially human ones. Of course it could quite possibly be that the bedroom eyes exuding, 'I'm gonna make you cum like a race horse,' had something to do with it too. Jessica moaned a little as Centaur came back up for air. Amanda forced her hand out to be kissed as well but only received a comfortable handshake. The freckles splattered all over her face diminished her looks a little bit but she was still pretty. Centaur's eyes x-rayed her lean athletic body and pulled her close to him. His hot breath mildly scorched her ear tip as his lips gently kissed her cheek. Centaur could feel Amanda's body melt into his arms like hot wax. Instantly a mild sweat erupted through her pours. Delighted with the ladies attention leaped right into conversation, "So ladies how can I be of assistance to you?" The words he uttered rolled off his tongue like a finely orchestrated melody. Both girls giggled like kindergartners. Amanda started but was cut off by Jessica. "We are here for the club positions Mr. Centaur," Jessica whispered softly in her sexy voice. It is a voice that you know every woman on earth possesses and powerfully wields with several of their alter egos. There are bone me voices, I'm a bitch voices, its rag time voices, I'm a dirty whore voice and last but least I love you voice which Centaur was yet to encounter. Ultimately Centaur had only experienced one time before and it never came from his parents. No not once! All the rest he had encountered numerous times. Amanda spoke up in a squeaky bone me voice," are you still looking to fill positions Mr. Centaur?"

Cannon never stopped smiling and he was almost tempted to say hell yeah how about doggy style, could you fill that one but he didn't. He said, "I'm always looking to fill positions." All the attention was flattering and he loved it. Ever since the melt down women flocked to him like magnets. And after several months of this kind of playful pleasure he became immune to the come on's but never passed up a piece of beautiful strange ass. And Jessica was just that.

Centaur exclaimed to the two girls just how busy he was. He reached out and grabbed both of the girl's hands and said," Jessica why don't you come over tomorrow evening and Amanda you come down the following evening. How does that sound?"

Both the girls looked mesmerized, they were star struck as all young girls become.

Amanda spoke up," were sorry Centaur but we have never met anyone famous before."

Centaur chuckled, "Girls, girls I assure you I am not anybody special. I'm just an artist trying to make my impact in this crazy world. That's all." He went on to tell the girls how demanding the art side of the business was and how it rarely left him with time for pleasure. Then Jessica reached over and kissed Centaur's cheek. She whispered in his ear, "tomorrow night then. I will be panty-less." The heat from her mellifluous lips almost made Centaur bend her over right in front of the club doors and he may very well had if Amanda wasn't cock blocking that day. Centaur almost became uncontrollably intoxicated by her lust but resisted for other latish purposes that needed much attention. He knew that his Johnston could wait a little later. Amanda kissed the other cheek. Her shit breath curled Centaur's toes but still he reacted politely. He thought, 'Jessica was at least kind enough to eat a Certs mint to cover up that reefer stench.' He could tell by Amanda's actions that she had a lot of growing up to do. Before the girls departed Centaur gently cupped Jessica's cheeks into his large hands, "Girl, have you ever thought of getting into art?"

Jessica replied, "why no. Why do you ask?"

Centaur caressed her face a little more, "I think your face would fit beautifully into a couple of pieces I'm working on."

Jessica's face turned a deep plum red despite her stoned state, "I would love to be in some of your art work Centaur."

Amanda grunted in a litigating burst of intrusion. Her jealousy now poured through her bones. Centaur looked directly into Amanda's eyes, "I think that I may have just the spot on my wall for you as well Amanda."

Amanda stepped back. It was almost as if she peered into Centaur's dark soulless vessel for an instance. Centaur, catching these facial expressions abruptly smoothed them over with big teeth bearing smile and then a tight hug. The physical touching seemed to make all Amanda's fears disappear immediately. Centaur patted both of their asses and sent them packing.

The girls waved and smiled as they walked back across the dark parking lot to their car. Centaur hated to see them go but loved to watch them walk away. He especially liked how Jessica's long legs came up and made an ass out of themselves. Unfortunately there was no time for play that night. He knew that there were greater matters at hand. All of his works of art needed some addressing and his new pieces needed finished. Centaur entered the club and got right to work.

2

Cannon, who shifted his face to become Centaur kidnapped his mother a few days ago, woke her with smelling salts and once she awoke from her slumber he wheeled her through his building of flesh art 2000 feet below the Crypt club. People were still alive on feeding tubes and dangling from the ceiling. They appeared bolted to the walls. Big T was the first on exhibit. Cannon pulled a paint ball gun from his pocket and fired several shots at him to bring him to life. The rotting corpse like being began to dance a bit until finally the head moved and it screamed," Please kill me you bastard. Please! Haven't I suffered enough?" The man coughed and spit up bloody mucus that flowed down off his chapped chin. Cannon shot him two more times in the face. Yellow and red paint trickled down over the man's dirty half eaten cheeks full of crawling maggots. Terry's body dangled by some kind of meat hooks ripped into his back and arms. His legs were almost rotted off by gangrene and fat feasting maggots. Terry was the actor on the DVD's that would be distributed to law enforcement. The exhibit in front of him stated, (FAGGOT MOLESTING BASTARD). The stench of ammonia brought tears to Audra's eyes. She struggled to get loose from the wheelchair but her wrists were zip tied almost cutting off the blood circulation. She screamed and cried as Terry began to piss and shit himself adding to the already five or six foot high pile of waste residing beneath his half eaten stubs for legs. She could no longer bear to look at him. Her heart almost stops beating. The sadness in the man's eye and the constant begging destroyed her as a human being. She knew right from that second of eye contact that she would no longer be the evil bitch to her new sons if she lived to see the light of day. The ammonia from the urine was so potent that her eyes burned. The man begged again," please kill me. Please I can't take much more."

Cannon smacked his hands together, "Shut up you piece of shit. You've been dying for five years now but I'm still waiting."

Audra started crying profusely. Tears poured forth from both sockets like an erupting spring. She Screamed," why would you do this Cannon? Why?"

Cannon stared into his mother's face," don't you dare cry for this bag of wasted space mom. Hell you never cried for Mitch or I did you? Ask old shit pants here why he hangs on this wall today. Go ahead ask him."

Audra turned her head away. She couldn't look at this destroyed man anymore. Cannon started to get angry. He grabbed her chin and pushed her face in Terry's direction. The stink of rot is thick in the air. She flapped her jaws as she tried to make it leave her mouth.

"Ask him mom now!"

Audra pulled away again and then turned back to Terry. Her instincts told her to obey because she knew that she would be worthless if she was dead or put on the wall too, "Why are you on the wall?"

Cannon grabbed her face again, "Speak up mother. That piece of shit can't hear past his on groaning."

Audra shook her head. She still couldn't believe what she was witnessing, "WHY ARE YOU ON THE WALL?"

Terry's body shook awhile until he gained the strength to lift his head rotten off his chest again. And then that one sad crying eye stared in her direction. His hair seemed to rip away from the scalp as he moved. Out from within Terry's cracked phlegm covered lips came," I raped young boys."

Cannon pointed his finger at Terry and yelled," Louder asshole!"

Terry dangled his stubs in anger. The left meatless bone smashed into the cesspool of crusty excrement at the top of the pile. The stench rolled right into the direction of Audra and Cannon. Audra instantly gagged. Saliva dripped all down her clothes. Cannon was not phased whatsoever. It was like he enjoyed the stink. He wiped off her face. Then whispered into her ear," mom don't ever judge me or you will be joining these pieces of shit on the wall.

She looked straight into his eyes. The pain and affliction seemed to exacerbate as he spoke to Terry. You could tell that Cannon contained a just hatred for this man.

Cannon spoke again," Now Terry I'm going give old mom here all the facts and you correct me if I get out of line. First off Jerry is a molesting faggot. Let's get that straight. He has probably molested young boys for twenty or so years now, right Terry?"

Terry let out a fluid drowning whimper. The fragment of a man appeared to be losing energy just from talking. Cannon lit a blunt and started again," Terry had two of the older boys from the boot camp beat me into a pulp and then put a pillow case over my head so I couldn't see who they were. Oh but don't worry I found out their names. Mom I'll introduce you to them later. Anyway these two fucks dragged me to the bathroom where yours truly up there handcuffed me to the handicap shower rails. Then that lump of shit tried to stuff his dick in my ass. He tried profusely but I kept clenching my legs and ass to keep him out so the two assholes each grabbed a leg and spread me wide open. Once again two pint Terry up there got the bright idea to cut my asshole open with a dull razorblade. After he slit my asshole to my balls he shoved shampoo in the wound and he and the other two older assholes fucked me six ways from Sunday. This went on for two months until I broke a piece of glass from a window and slit both my wrists and jugular. I wanted to die but the staff put me into a mental institution for the rest of my time to heal."

He then wheeled her through his building of flesh art. People were still alive on feeding tubes and dangling from the ceiling and bolted to the walls. There were thousands of heads in canisters lining the long walls. There was a machine grinding up the remains of the dead in a corner. People screamed for hours upon hours. The place in which Audra was taken to was like that of the myths about hell. Cannon took his mom to a special spot on the wall where he decided that she would hang for a while.

CH 6 THE RETURN (2008)

1

Grace Adams is racing up 376 W towards the little town of Latrobe. The early snow laden morning in May 2008 makes it difficult for her to navigate the Jeep Grand Cherokee she's pushing forward in. Snow in May was not unheard of in the parts. The state of Pennsylvania has odd weather conditions throughout the year. Many that live through the four seasons can attest to it. Grace is now thirty-eight years of age and it's been years since her return to see her mother. Just then her cell phone rings. Mandy Cunningham's face appears on the screen, "Mandy hey how are you? It's been awhile."

Mandy can be heard crackling her gum over the line, "Hey your mom told me that you were coming into town so I took down your number and decided what the hell I miles well give you a jingle."

Graces Jeep swerves near the medium where it almost does a 360 in the middle of the highway.

"Jesus Christ what the hell, Grace blurts out.

Mandy yells, "Grace don't you dare take the Lords name in vein."

Grace pulls the Jeep straight. She looks up and sees the Monroeville exit so she knows that it won't be long now, "Mandy do you really believe in that superstitious shit anyway? I mean hell look at the outcome of my life does it seem like Jesus cares?"

Mandy slurps down some soda and burps. Grace thinks it's same old Mandy from the days at the big oak tree burping and farting as usual. Mandy coughs to clear her throat and starts again, "Yes I believe Grace. All I have is faith. Once I got diagnosed with Krone's disease a few years back and they took out ten feet of my fucking intestines and installed a fucking colostomy bag and that's when I found it." Mandy starts crying. She can't believe that she is actually talking about her feelings over the phone. Master Psychiatrist Sheridan Ozark insists that speaking your feelings out loud helps to alleviate the internal pain that we are all plagued with since birth.

Grace cannot believe her ears. This is a whole different Mandy for sure because the old one was a self-centered little rich bitch fed with a silver spoon.

"I didn't know Mandy."

"I'm sorry Grace. I know it's a sore subject for the both of us. Especially after the Blithe residence incident years ago. I mean I really liked Mitch and Cannon. Anyway I called because they just reopened the Crypt club from the 90's and an art expo up here. The Centaur is supposed to make an appearance in town. My God I just have to meet him!"

Grace slows her speed, puts on her right turn signal and rolls off the Irwin exit. She pulls up to the toll booth counter, "Mandy what the hell is a centaur? I mean I know what but who what?"

Mandy can be heard clicking her buttons as she texts someone, "Centaur is the artist from the 1990's that paints with blood. It's sick but oh so cool". My father was a huge fan back then, God rest his soul! I have two of his paintings in my house. I'll show you when you come over this week."

Grace hands her money out the window to the toll booth attendant, "Receipt please."

Mandy blurts out," What did you say Grace?"

Grace pulls the receipt from the attendant, "Thanks she says." Slowly she pulls out onto the slick route 30 and heads west again.

"No Mandy I was getting a toll receipt for this trip. Now that the agencies have all combined my asshole for a boss requires every nickel to be accounted for. Hell I haven't even met him yet. I think his name is Johnson or Johnston, who knows"

Mandy flicks her phone back up, "I thought you were released after the accident. I mean how do you uh work as an agent with one arm? Oh shit! I'm sorry. I'm not being to insensitive am I? I'm really sorry!"

Grace pulls into the left lane and speeds forward. The thought of Mandy's words pissed her off sorely but she doesn't let it get to her, "Mandy its ok I'm fine. Let's just talk-"

"Grace did they ever catch the guys who took your arm?"

Grace slowly puts on the brakes and pulls to the inner barrier. She knows that everyone will be inquiring about how she lost her arm.

"Has anyone been arrested?"

Grace starts to choke up. She just can't take any more of the questions, "Mandy let's just talk tonight and I'll fill you in so that you can pass it along to all your pals. Ok?"

Mandy speaks right up in a soft voice, "No Grace that's not it at all. I really do care. I do. I did come up and visit you at Green Oaks when you were in there didn't I?"

Grace lets off the brake and starts driving again. She's now passing the mall in Greensburg, "Listen Mandy I'm in Greensburg right now. I'm going to visit my mom for as long as I can stand it and then will talk tonight."

"Ok Grace take care and I'll-"

Grace ends the call and starts to cry. Tears pour forth hard. She had never encountered anything so terrible in here entire life like that night. Even when her father took her hunting at night was not that frightening but she was never on the business end before. She looks down at her left prosthetic arm, wipes her tears and floors it.

She drifts off into the memory of that night. That haunting night seemed to never let go and it was always in the back of her head just like an old horror flick playing over and over again. The pain made it feel like it happened yesterday. Grace recalls the silhouette standing right there in front of her and then finally seeing the flash from the barrel rocketing right in her direction. Abruptly the hot lead penetrated her flesh. The smell of gun powder and scorched human flesh rushed into her nostrils. Tears poured forth from both sockets as the indomitable pain seared through her lung. Within seconds Grace can see herself lying with her face against the dirty wet street. She started drowning on her own fluids as blood began flooding into her lung. Grace knew that if she didn't get moving she would surely die a painful death and that was not acceptable to her. Slowly she crawled towards her squad car stopping every five feet or so to dump the blood from her lung. The irony taste still lines the inner parts of her mouth. After pouring the blood out of her throat she was capable of another few feet until she finally made it to her car. The dispatcher could barely understand Grace's gargling cries for help. Grace knew better than to meander off down an unknown street by herself. She recalls not even being on duty that night but when she rounded Fifth Avenue onto Mordant Street she witnessed a perpetrator standing over a young woman. He was clothed in a normal fashion but his actions alerted her sense. Graces instincts were right on the money. She hit the lights on her squad car and assisted the victim. Unfortunately the young woman was already dead. The woman was decapitated. Then immediately after checking the victim's vital signs she rounded the corner into a dark alley way where she met her doom. The strangest thing happened; as time persists on she remembers more bits and pieces of that unforgettable night.

The mundane streets of Latrobe seemed to give Grace too much time to think. She knew that the exhilarating chase after lunatics was long gone and most likely she would do nothing more than collect dust atop her badge, but to her now that was ok. The adrenaline kick was no longer feasible by any means anymore.

As the Jeep starts to swerve again Grace comes back to reality. She doesn't even realize how she had gotten so far down the highway without knowing it.

2

The next day was another cool early morning in Pennsylvania as a wrecked red Mitsubishi 3000 GT races towards Green Meadows high security prison. Grace had to borrow Mandy's car since her battery went dead in her jeep that morning. Once there agent Grace Adams will come face to face with some of the purest evil vomited out by the planet. Green Meadows houses some of the most notorious serial killers from through-out the world. On this day Grace will speak with Larry Feather or professionally known as MANGE, a lunatic ice cream man from Detroit. This psycho would lure young children to his ice cream truck with the simple sounds of his soft melody jingles. All the children would run to the vehicle in hopes of feeding their sweet tooth but would only come up short when they entered the vehicle to choose their flavor of Popsicle. Larry is quite the genius. Top agents from I.P.C.O organization have chased MANGE for twenty plus years.

3

The red Mitsubishi reaches the asylum parking lot around three in the evening. Grace pulls into the clos-est spot to the side entrance. An entrance she knows all too well. She takes a long drag from her Newport and smashes in into the cars ashtray. It's such a dirty habit, she thinks but returning to a place like this definitely called for one. The stale burnt nicotine seemed to line the inner parts of her mouth, leaving her breath not so pleasant. She rolls her tongue around the front of her teeth to chase away any debris left behind by today's earlier lunch date. After several minutes of snooping through her rather larger purse she comes across a pack of old Tic-Tac's. She pops two in her mouth, exits the car and heads for the two security doors on the left side of the building. As she approaches the doors her nose catches the slightest hint of the chicken gravy drifting in the wind. She remembers that smell of that slimy shit all too well and it seems to make her stomach a little queasy, hell just the thought of Green Meadows was enough to make any ex-patient nauseous. Once at the doors Grace places her I.P.C.O badge against the security monitor. The door buzzer alarms and she is granted access. Only a select few have permission to enter the new facility and that is governed by Juniper Savage. Green Meadows is now the front line in the fight against serial killing rehabilitation. If the work shop can't fix the broken parts then they are shipped off to Cyprus which is the last resort of rehabilitation. When all the other government agencies combined because of government over expenditures I.P.C.O was created. There is a consistency of several types of board members that operate the agency. Not all of the founders have the best interests either. Many of the donators to the agency have their hands in other government agencies pockets despite I.P.C.O's claim to fame of being self-reliant. Everything still operates on a chain of command just like any other agency and that's why some cases come and some go. On the case of Mange it has become personal to the world. Despite the efforts of the agency to hold back press releases of the incidents and crimes posed by this character it has become unstoppable like always. Money talks, somehow, some way pictures leaked to the media about Mange's unsatisfying craving for young children's flesh. And unfortunately for Grace that was her specialty. She was a specialist on why humans eat other humans flesh. That's why the organization approached her personally and reinstated all her past credentials despite the fact that she was once a Green Meadows resident in a past time. And also there is the fact that Horsehead was asking for her personally," He said that she was the only one that he would talk to." Even though Grace is deemed handicapped by O.I.A, the I.P.C.O agency kept her in service for her intelligence on the taboo subject matter. But it was mainly because her father ate a few people back in the eighties.

4

Grace goes to interview Horse head Horace before Mange to see if he is the one who hacked off her left arm. She tells doctors to examine the DNA she tore from the perpetrators lip the night of her encounter. Grace walks into the interrogation room where Hogs head is sitting. His unusually large head sporting what could only be considered a greasy lion's mane to some just isn't given justice by the Newspaper photographs. After the two stare at one another for a few seconds Grace sits down in front of him. He points and laughs at her prosthetic arm. She makes the joint bend with her right hand and places it on her lap. She is so embarrassed of it that it makes her sick. Sometimes it's all that she can think about. Driving, showering, taking a shit, it is all more difficult now with one hand. Just trying to open a peanut butter jar has become a chore. Horace slams his cuffed hands on the table," Hey bitch, you ever eat the anus of a young child before?"

Grace just stares into his cold dark eyes. Horace leans in a little closer," It's the most tender part of a human body. Doesn't taste like shit neither like you would think!" He smiles showing broken black teeth. Grace still doesn't move a muscle. She can see that something is wrong with his body as he constantly convulses like he has a tic or something. He blows his breath in her face when his stank nearly knocks her off her chair. She coughs a little, wipes her face and then turns back in his direction, "Listen asshole why don't we cut the chit chat and get straight to the point. You called for me to come down here because I sure as hell wouldn't come to visit a piece of shit like you on my own time!"

Horace picks a booger out of his nose, looks at it, rolls it around on the table until it's not so stick, gets it up on his pointer finger and flicks it into Graces face. The sticky booger lands right on her bottom lip. She spits and wipes her mouth. Thoughts of diseases from the beast before her bounce around in her mind as she quickly reacts to the foreign substance. Horace cracks up laughing and falls off his chair. The chains around his neck are choking off his airway but he can't stop laughing. Then abruptly he stops laughing crawls up on his chair and looks at grace,   "No really in all seriousness," He pauses for a second," You ever pick the corn out of your shit? I just wandered if I was the only one who did that." He starts laughing like a hyena. The more pissed off Grace looked the louder he laughs. Grace stands up, walks over to the door, locks it and then walks right up to Horace. Horace smiles at her again," What, what will you do cripple?"

Before Horace can react Grace removes her Prosthetic arm, swings it like a baseball bat smashing in his face. The stunned Horace with tears pouring out of his eyes now spits blood and teeth all over the white table. Grace puts back on her arm, sits back down and looks at Horace," Now that I have your attention you ugly motherfucker. Why don't you tell me something useful?

Horace isn't smiling anymore. He looks at her with the death ray eyes.

"Aw what's wrong little baby? Not so funny anymore is it asshole?"

Horace jumps to his feet but the chains keep him in position. He swings his arms in a roundabout fashion while screaming," You fucking cunt I'll eat your heart, I'll rip out your eye and skull fuck the socket you whore." He stands there panting like a lazy dog.

"Sit down you fat tub of shit before you have a heart attack. I want some answers before you kill over. See that diet of assholes has made you obese." Grace is laughing now. Horace doesn't find it funny. He hates women with a terrible hatred. Young girls were mainly his targets. He didn't discriminate races but only killed boys or men if they got in his way. He sets back down in his chair, catches his breath and starts again," When my Lord gets ahold of you he is going to eat you."

Grace isn't sure how to take what he said because he says such off the wall shit. She taps her finger on the table trying to figure how to respond. "So you are telling me that Jesus Christ is going to come down and eat me, is that it?"

Horace plays with his bloody teeth on the table," No you silly Cunt what are you talking about?"

"Well then what Lord are you referring too?"

"The Shining one, he is the one that had me cut off your arm so that he could eat it."

Grace moves around in her chair. The conversation has just got a little bit uncomfortable. Horace is still moving around his bloody teeth on the table.

"What does the shining one look like Horace?"

Horace looks up from his new toys," Not shiny like you think jackass. Shiny as in intelligent, brilliant, genius, do you get it cunt?"

Grace can't believe that she even allowed herself to be talked into the interview. She feels that it is just too soon. Some nights she wakes up from wetting the bed while dreaming of being attacked. Horace points at her prosthetic arm," Can you feel the serrated blade sawing through your flesh? How about the sounds of the knife cutting the bone or when I cracked the ulna and ripped it from the rest of your body? You remember cunt? Do you cunt, cunt, cunt?"

Grace looks away from Horace. She doesn't want him to see the tears forming in her eyes.

Horace puts his face down on the table and starts licking up his blood. He chases his knocked out teeth around with his scaly tongue. "He's a Plutarch you know! I didn't kill you because of that tattoo on your neck. You know that right cunt?"

Grace reaches back to her neck where she feels what she though was a birth mark. Horace sees her touching it.

"That where your daddy put it little Gracey? To hide it from them so they didn't get it?"

Just then Horace starts screaming in agonizing pain. A loud shrilling sound can be heard coming out from inside his head. A man wearing a doctor's jacket barges in pushing a wheelchair. He nods at Grace as he puts a type of helmet over Horace's head. She can see that his eyes were rolled all the way back in his head and bloody drool is dripping all down over his green jumpsuit. The shrilling sound continued to sound even through the helmet. She could tell from the Foxfire military issued boots that he wasn't a real doctor.

5

Graces third morning in PA couldn't get any worse or so she thought. On this day the sun gazes through a decaled window onto an old walnut coffee table. The coffee pot can be heard percolating for its second time that morning. The aroma of fresh coffee and banana walnut muffins linger throughout the small house. Grace sits there moving her toes in the warmth as she sips her coffee and Amaretto. Her face is sunken in and her body hangs towards anorexia. The coffee keeps her awake while the Amaretto gives her the buzz she needs to keep her sanity. She sits there the same way as every other morning. Only this day was Sunday, wash day. Her clothes were fresh smelling of Gain rather than stinking of B.O and booze. Her .40 Caliber Glock lays there cocked as always, ready to fire. Tears pour forth from both eye sockets as she slowly pushes the weapon into her mouth. The taste of the Remington gun oil makes her lips curl a bit but it does not slow her for an instance but then she hears her mother enter the house again. She is still in shock by what Hogs head had told her and she wonders if it was all bullshit. What the hell was a Plutarch anyway? Some kind of made up kids bologna she thought. Still though she wonders why someone would take the time to blow up his head if it all wasn't true.

The mailbox hangs overflowing with mounds of letters. The house looks abandoned. But it was Sunday and her mother Lydia was already in the works of getting her daughters house straightened out for the week. If it weren't for Graces mother helping her get over her horrific ordeal, Grace would probably still be in Green Acres Asylum for the mentally disturbed or worse be sent through the Cyprus program run by O.I.A. Her six month recovery finally shed some light when Argot Crypt was apprehended, Crypt who is believed to be the serial killer "Road Kill who killed and dismembered hundreds throughout the U.S and scattered their limbs all over the highways was captured on August 26th 2007. This was several weeks after Grace encountered her assailant. A man with no face, an unknown perpetrator to this day or so she thinks. Her time spent in the institution made her feel safe. It was a place of solitude, a place where no one could harm her again or that's the bullshit that she was fed from Dr. Francis Dix.

For days on end she would lay on the blue padded floor of the rubber room attempting to forget the past but the doctors and detectives constantly harassed her for evidence to capture the psycho at large only brought back rancid memories of that late July night of 2007.

Unfortunately for Grace the past was about to revisit her at a speeding pace. Either Grace would accept and move on with life or she would plummet into a downward spiral into the catacombs of insanity. The F.B.I didn't care about the feelings of agents. Especially know that all of the agencies combined into the conglomerate I.P.C.O. As far as I.P.C.O was concerned the training was supposed to help their agents deal with the pain. The men and women of the new organization were supposed to be made from the stuff Wolverines skeleton was made of, ademantium, tough as nails, strong as hell and unbreakable.

Grace could hear her mothers' footsteps approaching quickly so she puts the safety back on the Glock and tucks it under the pillows next to the Blithe residence police report.

"Grace honey. Gracey honey someone is here to see you," she says in a soft voice," Grace come on now." She walks by and throws a letter onto her lap as she opens the curtain to allow a little more sunshine to come through.

Lydia's voice always seems to soothe the pain. For at least awhile, that was until the images squirmed their way back into her head from that night.

Grace looks at the front to see that it is from Cannon Knight," What the hell," she hollers.

"Grace you ok in there?" Lydia says.

She can't stop staring at the front of the envelope and thinking about what Horse head had told her or the fact that he was forcefully shut up after saying something that he shouldn't have.

"Yes mom I'm fine," she says as she rubs the birthmark on the back of her neck.

Quickly she rips into the letter. The first page is from Dr. Francis, " It reads," Grace inside this envelope is a holographic card that will grant you access into the Viper program operated by I.P.C.O but you must go with the agents that should be arriving at your door at any minute because there is no way into the building without their assistance. Use the holographic card to lead you through the long hallways to a special machine. Climb inside, put the card into the slot near the chair and sit back. I am not promising anything except the truth and a lot of physical pain but I know you personally. You will be able to handle it. God speed Grace!

P.S

Cannon is most definitely alive but he has something inside of his body that may alter his thoughts. If you love him as much as you told me in our sessions then you can save him from damnation. I have included a letter written by him when he was in the exact rubber room as you.

Innards part 1: The forgotten files.,

"A creature stirs within"

The facts stated on this page and the rest of the Innards Fractions are findings drawn from the conclusions derived from the minds of past psychopaths. These are unpublished thoughts from the diverse minds of several specialists who were involved in the design and set up by the I.C.D or International Criminal Database. These findings read almost like a personal journal entry. The author classifies these findings as illegal probing of the human psych and refers to these findings several times within the journal as "Innards: A GLIMPSE INTO THE EYES OF A MONSTER.

None believe that these words were to ever been read by the eyes of a non-believer and should of never exited Dr. Crackle's mind.

June 5th, 1986

How can man created in the image of God be so psychotic?

Created from the purest form like pure forms are to be?

No not just a single man but a whole multitude of men, women and even children possess the capabilities of inflicting explicit fragments of torment against their fellow brothers or sisters.

How could this be?

Hear this:

Psychopath: A person with an antisocial personality disorder, especially one manifested in aggressive, perverted or criminal behavior. "Crank and Puff dictionary"

Psycho: Mind; mental: A disturbed individual not possessing normal human capabilities. "Font, Puff and Do-Do"

Psychopathology: The studies of the origins, growth and symptoms that cause behavioral and mental disorder

And last but not least and by far the most disturbing to me, a predator with unimaginable powers of the mind or a being that lacks remorse for anyone but itself and an unusual appetite for pain and suffering. Sounds just like me, whoever me is.

Just like the predator that fed from all those victims in the abandoned motel.

Like the beast that strewn the carcass's all the way from the U.S to Canada.

Who are these predators? Why are they feeding so frequently these days? Are they human?

It's sort of amazing to feel the kind of fear residing within the bowels of my body. I mean a man of my caliber and a witness to the most bizarre. Although after witnessing the kind of chaos that was wielded against those poor innocent victims in the motel it's no wonder that it's hard not to be frightened by such a thing. This feels like I have been sucked into a novel and most believe that you are not to possess fear until the ending unfolds, when the beast lurking below the fog rips your beating heart from your chest.

And if this were a story, it isn't written like any of those superficial horror novels. Believe me, I know you think you have it all figured out but not everything is as it seems.

This didn't just happen yesterday. My documentation began when people began disappearing sometime in the early 1980's. In my mind I believe that this is when I have truly awakened to the facts around me. I became aware that I was above all of those pathetic sons of bitches that pranced atop this God forsaken planet. All those doctors and psych-wards thought that they had an ounce of a clue to what the hell was going on.

All the tests they performed on my brain were useless. You see I was the one in control the whole time. I would allow them to see only what I wanted. That's how it is when you are one of the elite chosen by God himself. That's right. A son of God!

The biggest misconception doctors make about psychopaths is that they are single minded and have only one vision a vision of destruction. Although destruction is most definitely my forte, it is not the only agenda on my schedule. You could say that death and devious torments are a mere hobby for me but I have a bigger plan in action a plan to rid the world of weak mother-fucking assholes especially the stuck up ignorant kind. And oh last but not least stuck up user cunts. Yes that is the proper term for them, cunts. Now there is no specific detail in the dictionary regarding this term. There is only slang that has passed down from generation to generation. Many would say that it was a woman's genitals or even a sissy boy of a man but my definition goes into much greater form. And I know what your thinking, all of this coming from the mind of a psychopath. Well I'll have you know that one in every three men is a psycho and one in every ten women is a psycho. And that's a fact so I guess were all fucking psychos in this world and everyone else is equivalent to naught equal to that of a dung pile.

Cunt: anyone who crosses me. A female that thinks her shit does not stink and uses men for the pure purpose of her gain or men who don't have the balls to stand up for themselves or anybody else or women who disregard the feelings of men who love them to no end and rip their hearts from their chests and stomp on them or assholes in the purest forms. The mentioned above seem to rule the world. There are many more classifications than this. The public classifies all others not identical to them as outcasts or psychos. How convenient.

In my world we are to get into the mind of the psychopath. This is a place unimaginable by any normal human being. It is a corridor of many compartments that contain mainly devious thoughts. I was the first of my kind to slip past all the enforcements placed before me. In doing so I knew that I would be able to train others to be identical to myself. I figured that if I could take a blank and implant all my ideals and beliefs into their minds the world would be thinned out appropriately. These super beings will be my children. They all will possess the powers beyond the normal human capabilities but not just any will be accepted. All blanks have to be tested to see if they possess any psychic or paranormal skills. It is written in the lost scrolls of Babylon that there will be a time when the Sons of God will reign upon mankind. The S.O.G. will seek out and devour any unclean beast that gets in their way. They will seek out destroy and reign for eternity.

Osiris

6

The future has now come and more maniacs than ever have emerged through time. The academy at Quantico has long been forgotten and the cobwebs along the window seals could tell stories of less suicidal times. The majority of the baby boomers now run a newly funded organization. V.I.C.A.P has discontinued and grown into I.P.C.O. This new government agency combines all the countries throughout the world. N.C.A.V.C, The National Center for the Analyses Of Violent Crime, B.A.U, The Behavioral Analysis Unit, C.A.S.M.I.R.C, The Child Abduction Serial Murder Investigation Resources Center and V.I.C.A.P, Violent Criminal Apprehension Program have all combined. Serial killing has now become an international issue and now I.P.C.O has gone global. The International Psychological Containment Organization is funded by every continent and its agents are trained extensively. The coming about of this agency was fueled by the New World Order. An order proposed by a stricter more inhumane American government. Now that all nations are in the process of committing to one world government and one world currency, containment and labeling of possible liabilities has become much easier.

The agents programmed for this agency carry almost as much gear as S.W.A.T units and they are trained with even higher classifications. They're whole intent is to seek out and destroy. Killers are no longer tolerated; mostly they are disposed of immediately to Cyprus.

The I.P.C.O division that studies, contains and disposes of the criminally insane is on the basement level of the research center in Pittsburgh. It is an eighth mile below the city. Grace Chaplin is being dragged by two agents after being cuffed and removed from her suburban home. She has bloody knuckles and blood stains on both knees from attempting to defend herself against the two brutes who now have her in custody. Tom Brody, the agent on her left sports a bloody nose and a fat lip while agent Roger Cashmire wears a black eye and blood covered shirt sleeves.

The elevator reeks of Gone a cleaning substance used by high classed agencies to dispose of D.N.A. Grace knows the smell all too well. She looks at her bloody reflection in the shiny metal of the elevator doors. Her nose is still bleeding and her lips are swollen. She smiles at her reflection as if she is happy to be beaten. When she looks at her left stump of an arm her blood begins to boil. She told herself that no man would ever hurt her again and here she is being beat down by two thugs.

The music in the elevator is scratchy enough to make the most insane individual go beyond the limits of insanity. An eighth mile depth on a tin can for an elevator seemed to take an eternity. Within exactly five minutes they reached the destination. Grace knows exactly how long it took because she timed weird instances like that. She didn't know why, she just did.

As the two agents took their first two steps Grace drops to her ass and pulls her legs through her cuffed arms in the time it took the two agents to blink. First she kicks Tom's legs out from under him and then leaps like a lion into the air and flips Roger to the ground with her cuffs. Toms head hits the concrete floor with a shuttering thud. Rodger is gasping for air as Grace is pulling harder on the cuffs around his neck. Grace can hear large thuds coming from down the hall. She recognizes the sounds as the military issued Foxfire boots that she used to wear when she was in the Special Forces. As she attempts to get to her feet to take a stance she feels a sharp pain enter into her neck and then she hears the crackling. Instantly twenty-five-thousand volts pass into her body. Within seconds her body slumps to the ground motionless.

7

Grace comes back to reality. She looks around quickly realizing that she is in an interrogation room. The two way mirrors give it away. Tom and Rodger come barreling in through the door.

"Do you know why you are here Miss Adams?" Rodger asks.

Grace tilts her head up from the table," I think that I'm here to teach you how to suck Toms cock."

Tom walks over to Grace. He smiles and then abruptly plows his right fist right into the side of her head. With a melon smashing sound her head slams against the table leaving a huge blood stain behind when she lifts it back up. He flips his hand up sloshing blood all over the mirrors. She can feel the warm blood spewing from the gash in her noggin.

Just then after witnessing the event from the other side of the mirror Juniper Savage walks through the door. She kneels down, removes Graces cuff and hands her back her prosthetic arm. Grace pulls the fake arm from her and holds it tightly. She feels naked without it now. Tom and Rodger both look at one another and smile.

"If you two assholes lay one more finger on this woman, "Juniper yells," I'll cut your fucking balls off and make a purse out of them. Am I clear here?"

Both tom and Rodger reply simultaneously," Crystal clear mam."

Juniper sits down beside Grace, wipes away the blood from her head with a wet handkerchief and looks into her eyes. She points to the screen up on the wall, "Grace Two days after the arrival of these movies the crime lab has ran every test possible and there are no prints or evidence connecting anyone except for your uncle and brother. Which both have been dead now for many years but somehow their remains showed up in an envelope with the DVD's and according to your interrogation of Horse Head yesterday you are somehow connected whether you want to be or not."

Juniper now has Graces undivided attention. "What does that all mean and what does that have to do with me?" Grace asks.

"Well were not sure Grace," Juniper says," but we wanted to bring you in just in case your life was in danger. I mean you witnessed the Hog almost blow apart, we just want to analyze you and make sure that you are safe."

Grace throws her prosthetic arm up on the table. "Does it fucking look like it could get much worse than this Juniper? Who gives a shit if someone kills me? I would embrace it at this point!"

Rodger pulls his Taurus 44 Magnum from the holster. He spins the cylinder, clasps it back into place and points it at Grace's head. "I would sure love to help you out with that," Rodger says.

Juniper pulls her titanium Smith & Wesson 500 Magnum from its holster and sits it on the table, "Just start the DVD already asshole before I throw you a can of whip ass Rodger."

Tom and Rodger sit down to view the material. At the beginning the camera zooms into a faceless man. They can't distinguish that the face at all and then within seconds the camera moves in to action. They all witness a dark figure beating a woman with a cane. Gut wrenching screams echo throughout the video, the agent's watch in horror as they witness the figure binding the woman into a kneeling position. He uses hand controls to zoom into the woman's mouth. Grace puts her head down in disgust. Tom Brody one of IPCO's top field agents grabs Grace's hair and jerks her head back into place to see the event unfolding. Grace forcefully watches as the dark figure uses a razor blade to remove the eyelids of the woman. He neatly places the blade over the left eye and begins slicing. His hands are steady like a surgeon. He then examines the film like flesh. Playing with it like a child playing with his veggies on his plate. Abruptly the figure runs up to the camera and inserts the woman's eyelid skin into his mouth. Grace begins gagging and hunches over the chair. Within seconds that mornings coffee and muffin spew from her lips. Agent Brody jumps to his feet, "You stupid bitch you ruined my new shoes."

Grace pulls herself back up. Agent Brody kicks the chair beside Grace, "Rodger, would you please replay that scene for Miss Adams here?" Tom says.

Grace peers up at Agent Brody to see his pearly whites tearing through his lips. He seems to get off on this stuff. Once again she sees the figure insert the meat into his mouth and the camera zooms into his mouth. They all watch in horror as the meat is chewed over and over again until finally he swallows. The figure makes sure that the camera captures his now empty mouth. Pieces of meat and eyelashes line the outside of his lips. Agent Brody clears his throat. Despite his cool cock the walk attitude he shows some signs of disgust. He puts his hand on Grace's shoulders, "Does this shit make you wet Grace? I'll bet your mouth is watering right now isn't it?"

Grace looks up at him with tears streaming from both eyes.

"Come on Grace, you tasted this before," He wickedly spits out.

Rodger, who seems to have a conscious pushes pause on the DVD, "I think she has had enough Tom," Rodger says.

Agent Brody turns on the lights, "You have enough little Gracey? Is it true that you pissed your pants when the big bad man sawed your arm off?"

Grace leaps like a gazelle to her feet and before the two agents can blink she slams agent Brody's throat with her prosthetic arm. He cripples up and falls to the floor holding his throat. A loud thud from the carbon fiber limb connecting with soft fleshy tissue echoes in the little room. Grace wipes the slop from her lips with her good hand and sits back down. Agent Brody lies squirming on the floor gasping for air. His eyes bulge as he chokes. A shock of surprises satisfaction comes across Juniper's face.

"Shall we continue agent Adams" Juniper says," You just saved me a shit ton effort of putting that young asshole in his place."

Grace says nothing. She just nods continuing to watch. Agent Brody musters up enough energy to pull himself back into the seat. He stares forward keeping his silence as he massages his throat with his tiny hands. The three continue forward watching the videos.

The woman on the tape screams while gargling on her own blood. The camera zooms in to witness the man trying to grab the woman's tongue with a pair of pliers. When she resists he turns on a head lamp and begins knocking out her front teeth. He then places a device in her mouth that jacks her jaws apart. Finally with her tongue exposed the man grabs it with a pair of pliers and begins to pull on it. The amount of force pulling on her tongue could be seen by the amount of stress the chains were pulling on the woman's restrained body. The figure taunts and probes for several minutes. The woman's screams are ear piercing. And then finally the figure pulls what looks to be pruning shears from his pocket and snips the tongue off. He then places the tongue into a wooden box and sets it aside. Then without hesitation the man stands up and does a little dance. He kicks his feet and screams like an animal. After several minutes he kneels back down and pulls a flare from his pocket. The woman begs in a bloody garbled voice as any woman would with no tongue. Her gargling and groans makes the hair on Grace's neck stand straight up. The movie is completely disturbing and she knows that the images will haunt her for the rest of her life. She thought some time ago that her father was the sickest creature on earth but now she realizes that her thoughts were wrong. Grace begins to cry as the figure ignites the flare. The man shoves the red hot flare into the ladies mouth and then instantly pulls it out. Her head lights up like a jack-o-lantern during Halloween. Agent Brody gags. "I don't think he is done," Rodger says," He's cauterizing the wound for the big finale. The smoke fills the lens of the camera. Everything is glowing red. The woman could be heard gagging and gasping for air. When the camera clears up they witness the figure putting an oxygen mask on her and providing her with air. "He doesn't want her to die just yet," agent Brody whispers.

"You're a great commentator Rodger," Juniper says sarcastically," Don't quit your day job kid. No scratch that quit your day job so that I don't have to deal with you anymore."

Within a few minutes the figure drags the woman over to a nearby wall. This time a different camera zooms in from a side view. The three watch as the man removes the mask and metal device from the woman's mouth. He then covers her lips with super glue and inserts a flexible plastic clear pipe into her mouth. The poor woman squeals with what little life she has left. After a few seconds the man grabs the hose glued to her mouth and pretends he is jacking off with it. He then slides the hose over a black one half inch pipe protruding through the wall. Abruptly a third camera zooms in. This angle reveals two holes in the wall that show a bathroom on the other side of the wall. Within minutes the camera picks up a man coming into the bathroom. He stands on the opposite side of the wall of the woman and man. He spits tobacco juice into a urinal and begins urinating. The camera zooms back to the woman. She begins bucking and convulsing as the tobacco juice and urine rush into her throat. They witness the woman throwing up into the pipe and then drinking it repeatedly until finally she doesn't squirm anymore. The camera then zooms into the smile on the figures face and then shuts off.

All three agents stand and stretch their limbs. As Grace stretches her arm agent Brody flinches. Grace smiles at him and the sits back down. Rodger ejects the DVD and puts in the one marked FAGGOT MOLESTING BASTARD.

"Do you two want a break before we go any further?" Grace nods yes and exits to the rest room. She looks around to make sure no one else is inside and then runs into the stall. She starts crying hysterically. She kept her hard outer shell intact in front of the two other male agents but in the stall she could no longer contain herself. She pulls a bottle out from her pocket and shoots down three pills dry. After several minutes Juniper is beating on the door. "Grace are you alright in there?" Grace flushes the toilet and comes out of the stall. She stands in front of the sink starring into the mirror. By now the drugs are kicking in and she stumbles back into a past time of remembrance. A place she vowed never to go a place of haunting, violent memories of her father. A.K.A Mutilator.

She starts to remember the road trips her daddy took her on. But one in particular seems to stick. It was summer time. She can remember the beautiful fragrances of the flowers in a nearby field close to home. And then like lightning striking the visions change to a cold dreary day in the same nearby field. She sees her daddy sharpening his favorite Rapala fillet knife. Her ears capture his haunting voice, "Oh yeah, we are gonna eat well tonight honey. I'm gonna cook fillet humogn."

Grace cried out, "NO DADDY, NO don't do it please Daddy. PLEASE!" Her daddy smiled and licked his chops as he pulled a black bag from the bed of his Ford pickup truck. The bag was squirming and grunting. She closed her eyes tightly but her daddy made her open them wide. He placed the knife in her hand.

BANG! The door to the ladies room slams shut. And just as fast as she entered the past she came back. Grace drops to the ground unconscious.

Juniper gets Rodger to carry Grace to the infirmary. Evelyn a fortyish nurse cracks smelling salts under Grace's nose. Within seconds she revives in a groggy state. She whimpers out," what, what happened?"

Juniper holds her hand," You must of fainted Grace. Maybe we will continue viewing the other videos tomorrow." Juniper knows that as hard as it is to show a human compassion she must do so in order to find the other God particle that Graces father hid. When general Grounder couldn't find it in 1985 after the mans' death an all-out search commenced.

Grace shakes her head no. She didn't want the agency to think she was week and she has wanted to work for IPCO since it came into service. There was no way she was letting go of this opportunity despite of her past. She knew it was going to be difficult and she had nothing to lose, hell just earlier that morning she was sucking on the end of a Glock P eleven.

8

"Grace all of us here at I.P.C.O wan the best for you," Juniper says," try to get some sleep tonight and we will hit it first thing in the morning. The beds are comfy as the private investors don't spare any expenses to keep their new world sector free from degenerates." Juniper smiles, turns and exits one of the thousands of the cadet rooms that Grace is staying in. Grace thinks that Juniper is strange. She moves like a robot or puppet, she thinks. And the stink of sauerkraut or bad cabbage seems to flow over her.

Grace realizes that Juniper did not lock the door. As she sits there on the edge of the bed the sorrow turns to rage. The anger fuels her thoughts of ripping agent Brody's larynx open. When the warm blood flows onto the floor from her fingernails breaking through the skin on her right hand she pulls from her delusional state. She looks down at her hand and immediately reaches up inside her prosthetic arm to pull out the holographic card mailed to her by Freckle or whomever. After a second she pulls a Kershaw snap blade knife form it as well. She throws the fake arm on the bed, pulls a water bottle from the little college refrigerator, downs it while quietly sneaking out into the hallway.

Grace presses her thumb against the holographic card, a small blue hologram of the entire structure lights up above the card. The locations are marked A to B where she is and has to go. Fortunately the journey is a short one. Grace pushes her long hair back from her eyes as she slowly creeps down the hall with the wall to her back being cautious with every step that she takes.

"Where is she off to," Juniper says," and where did that hologram come from?"

Juniper and agent Cashmire are watching Grace on a monitor on the third level control room. "I'm not sure mam," Rodger says," she was clean before we brought her underground. Maybe she smuggled it one of her orifices. We didn't go that far mam!"

Juniper's eyebrows invert in an evil fashion. "One of her orifices you say," Juniper sighs," Rodger are you sure that O.I.A didn't find you and Tom a little semi?"

"Semi mam," Rodger asks with a puzzled look.

"Semi restarted you twit. What is wrong with the god damn new societies evolving?

Juniper looks down at the screen to see Grace make a right and head down towards the human imprinting lab. Juniper sits in the office chair beside Rodger, "Son can I ask you what it is that you do in your past time?"

Rodger perks up a bit. He sits up in his chair sporting a big smile. Finally he feels that he can speak without being beat down from the queen bitch. Queen bitch is what all the new recruits call her but most of the older agents just call her cunt. Rodger would never utter either of the names to her face because a painful punishment would surely ensure. He knows this for sure because his roommate smacked her ass during a training exercise. Jacques Lacroix who was called Jacques the cock by just about everyone at the academy banged just about everything he could get his Johnston into. A few of his college buddies swore that he banged a chicken on YouTube for a dollar but no one could ever find the video. It's possible that bestiality type videos are forbidden on the site.

The next morning after the small love tap on Juniper's ass Jacques the cock was strung up in front of fire training maze. His odds of survival were pretty good until the A93 Raptor drones were sent in to thin the herd of failing cadets. When the massacre ended three recruits were dead and all the rest had pieces of meat and blood spatter dripping down over their faces. None the less Juniper proved that the new Viper program was no joke. It was a make or die program. No one was allowed to quit or leave regardless of the outcome and if your wound couldn't be repaired by Petunia the artificial intelligence operator running the Viper program then you were sent to the Cyprus rehabilitation clinic. That is what was bred into every cadet and new recruits head. Not one soul on the planet without the proper security clearance ever knew that Cyprus was actually the City of Cyprus 2000 feet under the earth run by the Plutocracy that consumed humans for food. The unknowing would just wave good bye to their fellow cadets, get on a bus and never be seen again. It can only be thought that many of the failures of the Viper program had learned to become good slaves or ended up becoming a pile of Plutarch dung.

"Mam, I play Call of Duty- Black Ops with my roommate mainly but we also fancy Dead Island and Zombie Apocalypse."

Juniper looks straight up at the ceiling in disgust." Son aren't you in your late twenties?"

"Why yes mam I am. Mam look she is lowering down through the floor near the imprinting bay facility."

Juniper looks closer at the monitor," Alert Garvin's squad of man haters," Juniper growls out," I think that they came in last night for refueling per Zhang's orders. Also get general Grounder on the line and tell him to get down here because he may want to see the outcome."

"I'm on it mam," Rodger says as he multitasks.

Juniper puts her finger on the monitor. She pulls up the buildings schematics on the second screen and puts her other hand on the same spot, "Rodger that mini elevator is not recorded on the schematics. Where is she going? We need to know before we lose her."

Rodger quickly puts down the phone receiver. "Mam the general cannot make it at this time he said that he may need the entire Viper army."

"What, that's more than 200,000 troops for dispersal. Has he gone mad? What the hell is going on here?"

"Mam we are going to lose her position once her head passes below the floor."

"Well you better figure something out Rodger or it's your ass son. If we lose her it's to the Cyprus rehabilitation for the both of us. Do you want that?"

Rodger takes a deep breath. It's hard for him to swallow his saliva.

"I understand but mam she left her prosthetic arm in the room. That's where we put the tracking device locator beacon."

Juniper abruptly stands up. She puts both of her hands on her head. "Shit," she yells. "Did she drink anything in the room? See if you can track any of the nano's in her blood stream yet."

Rodger configures the band width on the scanner system, "Mam we barely have a reading on her. She is not lighting up like the rest of the cadets. I'm not sure what is happening maybe the equipment is malfunctioning, should I call a tech mam?"

Juniper rubs her hands through her hair. She gains her composure, takes a sip of her pumpkin spice coffee and sits back down. Freckle is the cause of this I know it, she thinks, "its ok Rodger just do your best. Don't sound any alarms, I will go down there personally to see where she went." She throws her empty paper cup in the trash and exits the control room.

9

Grace is lowering down underneath the floor in which she came down. From a distance she can see a multitude of mechanical machines operating in a frenzied fashion. She squints to make sure that what she is viewing is actually real. "What the fuck," she blurts out," Those can't be people, can they?" She drops onto a lower platform that is 200 feet below the floor. The holographic card shows her to get in a sphere like chair. She sits in the chair and sees a slot for the card. She inserts the card into the slot and immediately the chair comes to life. A glass dome wraps all the way around the sphere to completely enclose her. A big green go button flashes on the center of the screen. She hesitates for a minute but then pushes it. A few clangs, clunks and then a roaring sound like an engine can be heard. Smoke pours out of the back side of the sphere. Grace catches a hint of something like diesel and then within the blink of an eye the entire sphere rotates west and rockets towards the frenzied machines. As she passes the robots performing some kind of assembly she can see thousands of people being plucked like grapes from the walls. They are being stuffed into a type of armor. It's almost comical to her to see the arms and legs flying as the people are being thrown around at break neck speed. When she realizes that her whole ordeal will be much more painful than what she is seeing she will not be smiling. Her mind is about to explode. Grace has never seen anything like this before. She has only read about things of this sort in sci-fi or fantasy novels but to witness it first hand in reality is sickening. As the sphere moves on she sees people on an assembly line being created by robotic arms moving in a weaving motion back and forth. She witnesses the process from start to finish and watches in amazement as a full grown adult human walks off the last platform of the line.

When the sphere rounds a corner Garvin's Siren squad opens fire at her. She puts her hands up to protect her face. The bullets deflect from the protective glass surrounding her. But still they reload magazine after magazine trying to stop the sphere.

"What are we supposed to do Garvin," Viola hollers," the glass is bullet proof. She flips her Colt AR-15 over her back and adjusts the sling. Garvin launches a tracking device from his 40 mm grenade launcher under his AR onto the spheres engine frame. "Will just wait until it stops and intercept her there," Garvin says," How bad can it be?"

Uriah grabs Garvin by the lips," This place goes on for miles," Uriah says," at least get us a sphere or wheels of some sort."

Garvin pulls away from her grip," Are you girls ragging it this month or what?"

Ruthenia buts in," Viola and Uriah are. That's all I have been listening to is, cramps this and cramps that. You bitches are supposed to be elite warriors, come off it already."

Eunice loads another magazine into her modified AK-47. Her Russian upbringing has always made her fond of the weapon. It is her kind of way of honoring her countries heritage. Abigail kneels down, picks up a .308 casing and inhales the smoke, "I love the scent of gunpowder in the morning, "she says," It makes my nipples hard." She looks up from her orgasmic rush to see everyone staring back at her," What, what did I say?"

Garvin shakes his head at her. The radio blares off, it's Juniper," You stupid assholes don't be shooting down there. If you pierce one of the reactor walls we will all be turned to ash."

They all start laughing. Garvin turns down the radio." That bitch sounds hostile, huh?"

Drusilla pulls Garvin around to face the incinerator. "Garvin are they burning people alive over there?" He puts his hand on her shoulder, "Yes Drusilla. This is the generals cloning facility but don't worry because those things you see aren't really people, they are just like pieces of meat with directives to kill. It's something to do with operation Zeitgeist but that is only rumor so don't mention to anyone!"

Abigail stands right up," What the hell are you talking about Garvin? Why does the general need to make an army of meat bots?"

Garvin walks over to Abigail. He slides on the empty casings almost falling off the ledge into a blast furnace full of molten metal. "Oh shit", he yells. Abigail grabs him by his gun sling and pulls him back against her body. She looks deeply into his eyes. A bright smile sweeps across her face. He sweeps the casings into a passing by ladle. Sparks fly from the casings hitting the molten metal. Garvin puts his hand over his face to block the heat and smoke rising up from the ladle, "Listen ladies we are not even supposed to be down here. The clearances that we have will expire in," He looks down at his watch," 27 minutes. After that we will be decimated by those enormous drones hanging up there above us like buzzards. We only jumped on the call because we were the only squad in town so just pretend that you didn't see any of this happening down here. Are we clear?'

All the ladies turn towards Garvin and scream," HOORAH."

10

The sphere transporting Grace comes to rest in another sphere ten times larger than the one she's in. A robotic voice tells her to exit the chair and stand.

When she gets to her feet the chair drops below the platform. Two robotic arms come out of the walls and guide her to the center of the platform where she places both of her feet in grooves. Once her feet are locked into place the two robotic arms grab her right arm and her left stub. The machines stretch her a little. Two smaller arms come up from the floor and rip off all of her clothes. She looks around to see if anyone can see her standing there buck ass naked. As she looks down she realizes that her winter bush has grown out of control. Thoughts of trimming herself up quickly fade when a helmet like device with a tube attached drop from the ceiling. Laser beams from the spheres walls paint her body in red. Arms from the helmet lock onto her head to center her face. A mouthpiece type device slowly opens her mouth. When this happens she starts to question her motives. She thinks, 'what have I done, this is not going to be good in any way.' She tries to free her arm to see if she has a possibility of getting out. Once the machine identifies her mouth location it shoots a KY substance inside her mouth. Grace can taste the rather bland sloppy substance dripping down her throat. She starts to gag a little when the machine aggressively shoves a tube down her throat as a pincher squeezes her nose. She starts screaming and bucking but it makes no difference. As she jerks around a blinking red light flashes like when you get your blood pressure checked at one of the monitoring stations. The red light blinks don't move. The cold air entering her lungs smells like mint. And as aggressively as the tube is shoved down her throat one is put up her rectum and another in her vagina and one in each ear. She yells even louder but no one is around to hear her screams. She is in the special warrior's room designed by Dr. Freckle and hidden from everyone else's eyes. Last but not least a type of goggles is placed over her eyes. The platform rotates sideways as an egg like structure seals Grace up inside of it. A blue substance pours in from the top of the egg. The cold slimy fluid sends chills down her spine. The fluid fills the entire egg to the top. The feet restraints keep grace grounded so that she doesn't float to the top. And all in one coordinated motion the egg is lifted by a large crane and dropped into a type of incubator.

Garvin presses the button on the radio," Juniper, do you copy?" He says. A garbled sound comes in but can't be understood, "Listen Juniper our security pass has 7 minutes left on it so we are hitching a ride on the monorail. Pick us up at the Cyprus rehabilitation center if you copy." Juniper never receives the message and if she had she would have warned the Siren's to not go to the Cyprus location under no circumstances.

Garvin waves to the girls to get on the bus with twenty other damaged recruits. He waves his clearance to the guard as they enter. They all pile up in the back two seats together.

"How did all these kids get so beat up Garvin?" Viola asks.

He leans up over the seat. "The programs aren't what they used to be like back when we trained. We are elite but the Vipers are supposed to be even better."

"Shit, these little kids better than the Siren's," Drusilla chimes in. Drusilla Hussey who went against the family business of being a stripper in Derry PA joined the Marines at age 17 and has been in the one of a kind Siren squadron ever since. She decided rather than be prodded by drunk men like her twin sister Holley at the strip club she could rip off their heads and shit down their necks and that's exactly what she did to Casper Dorcus when she tried to dance like Holley at the Lake Lounge in Derry. After the incident Drusilla had the choice of do time or sever your country, the judge said. She quickly chose the latter.

Garvin reaches into his pack and hands out MRE's to each of the girls.

"Do we really have to eat this shit Garvin," Uriah says," I'm tired of slimy chicken pot pie. Don't you think that this Cyprus place will have something good to eat?"

Viola throws her MRE back at Garvin," Yeah we want steak or Lobster not this shit."

"Suit yourself girls but don't be bitching that you're hungry." Garvin flips the chemical reactor on the bottom of the bag. He digs in to the chicken pot pie and finishes licking out the contents," Also aren't you all happy now that we decided to put on these new nifty SPEAR suits? I mean I never even felt any of the heat from that furnace until I lifted my visor."

"Anyone ever tell you what a pig you are Garvin," Eunice says," and yes to ask your question the suits are extremely well balanced and comfortable." The other girls agree as well.

Garvin throws the empty bag down on the floor. As he peers down he sees blood all over the floor. He thinks that it is strange that the transport is so filthy when the rest of the entire facility is spotless. A strange gut feeling starts to come over him as he squashes his boots in what looks like a huge pile shit under the seat in front of him. He temporarily dismisses the feeling, looks up and points at Eunice," You know girls I bet that I am the only C.O that lets his squad talk to him this way." He looks around to catch a glimpse of each of their faces.

"Listen boy," Ruthenia says as she pets her AR," if you spoke to us like the rest of those assholes in the other units you might receive a little friendly fire in your ass." All of the girls start laughing and pointing at Garvin.

"Ok come on girls if someone sees us acting like this on camera they may take you all away from me and I'm not sure if that would be bad or a blessing." Gavin starts laughing but quickly stops as six sets of evil eyes stare back at him, "I'm just kidding girls I couldn't live without any one of you!" Abigail who is sitting directly beside Garvin puts her hand on his thigh. Garvin looks at her and smiles. She quickly pulls away before any of the other girls can see. She knows that if any of them would see the jealousy would rock the squad as they all compete for Garvin's approval. Most times he is the only man that any of them get attention from. They all look out the window as the monorail swiftly transports them to the Cyprus rehabilitation center.

11

After six hours the egg containing Grace spits out of the incubator. It rolls down a set of rails like those used at bowling allies for the ball returns. At the end of the rails the egg smacks a sharp stop that forces it to crack all the way around. The end section of rail shifts right sending the egg down a small hill onto a large soft pad and once there the egg cracks open it pukes out all of its slimy contents that include a reborn Grace. Her slimy naked body rolls near the edge of the pad. When she finally gains consciousness she rips the tubes from her orifices. As she stands there wondering what the hell just happened, she pushes the slime away from her face with her left hand. When she realizes what she just did the facility that recently cooked her explodes behind her. The hot blast makes the slime on her body sizzle. She looks at her left hand in wonder. She wiggles her fingers and swings it around. At one point she tries to pull it off thinking it is a prosthetic. After a few minutes a great hunger takes over her rational thinking. She falls to her knees holding her stomach when she sees someone walking towards her carrying a drawn weapon.

"Grace Adams, don't be alarmed I am Autumn Duke, "she says," I'm here to help you evolve."

Grace walks up to Autumn who has an odd weapon pointed directly at her forehead. She tries to talk but starts puking up blue slime. "What did you do to me?" Grace asks.

Autumn puts her weapon in the holster. She pushes Graces blue hair out of her face and looks into her emerald eyes, "I made you a goddess Grace. Just look at how your arm has grown back. No one will ever be able to hurt you ever again. We had to mutate you into your true form before Juniper got her hands on the God particle."

Grace looks at her hair. She can't believe her hairs blue. "Will I be able to die my hair back to its original color?"

"My god, what a typical human, you have so much more going on here than just blue hair my girl," Autumn says in a cocky voice.

Autumn hands Grace a robe and walks over to a large metal box. She quickly covers up her naked body and realizes that her skin is sparkling in the light. The metallic shade makes her look almost robotic she thinks, "What God particle are you talking about? I never had anything like that on me."

Autumn points to her neck," Your father planted it right there when you were a little girl. He knew that one day someone pure would come for it."

Grace remembers back when her father handed her the blue pearl. He told her that it was a special vitamin. "So why did he have it in the first place Autumn?"

"Grace your father was not who they said he was. First off anyone that is injected with the Plutarch blood will crave human flesh hence all the cannibal psychos that eat other humans. The government created several ravenous humans, your father included to force the world to allow I.P.C.O's laws to be put in place and to allow O.I.A to finally implement the long awaited eugenics program. Unfortunately he was a statistic like the rest."

Grace's mind is spinning towards a downward spiral," I'm not sure that I can handle all of this Autumn. This sounds all so crazy right now."

Autumn walks over to a large shipyard cargo container where loud thuds can be heard coming from the inside.

"Grace inside this container is the one who sawed off your arm. Would you like to meet-."

Before Autumn can finish Grace has already drifted beside her. She witnesses Grace sniffing the air and licking her lips like a snake searching for a heat signature.

"You can smell that goodness can't you Grace? I know how it feels because I smell that Delicious aroma as well."

Autumn depresses a switch that lifts the door on the container. And there standing before them is Grackle a huge Praetorian Plutarch. At first Grace is taken back by the sheer size of the Plutarch but when she realizes that the being standing before her is alien to her nature she steps way back. She almost runs in the other direction. Viciously Grackle grabs Grace by the neck and runs out onto the pad. "Where the fuck am I," Grackle hollers," You bitch I was promised fresh babies."

Autumn walks over in front of Grackle. "Look over there Grackle. The one you have in your hand just hatched out of that large egg. She's a big baby that's all."

Grace is trying to pull Grackle's large hand from her neck. He slowly continues to squeeze.

Grackle shakes Grace, looks at her, sniffs her and then takes a lick like she's a lollipop. He then whips her body towards Autumn. "I only eat human meat Autumn. You most of all know that."

Autumn lifts Grace to her feet. "She's not human Grackle; she is a Xenite like me."

Grackle's face expression turns to a look of fear instantly. He takes two steps back away from the women. "That's impossible! All of the Xenite's were exterminated on planet Galion by my personal armada over a thousand years ago. Ha, a Xenite? Please!" Grackle spits on his fingers and parts his bushy eyebrows. He stands there erect with his massive chest protruding out. When he sees Grace sniffing at him in the air he takes a few more steps back. He looks down over the edge of the pad and sees that there is no way out but through the two women standing before him. The thousand foot drop would most definitely kill him. Grackle realizes that if she is telling the truth there will be no fight but a slaughter.

"Grackle what do Xenite's eat?" Autumn asks

He points at her and then shakes his fist. "I'm not scared of you. I'm well aware of what Xenite's eat but if it were true you would have already killed me. A Xenite's hunger is ten times worse than that of a Plutarch's." Grackle almost has to force out the words through his big tooth filled mouth. He is only the second largest Plutarch on planet earth but by far the strongest. His ancient blood ties have put him in one of the high council chairs.

Grace starts to walk towards Grackle. Her hunger is taking over her rational thinking. She can hear Grackle's hearts beating faster by the second. She licks the air. She can taste his fear.

"Better be careful Grackle she looks hungry," Autumn says," I myself have been gorging on Plutarch the whole time you invalid. Your ruler Cutlass has been feeding a few of us this whole time."

Grackle cracks his knuckles. He drops to a lower stance awaiting Graces next move. "I'll kill this little bitch if you don't call her off Autumn."

Autumn walks over to join Grace in front of Grackle. "You can't kill a Xenite, Plutarch. Nothing can kill us."

Before Grackle can spit out another word Grace is already climbing all over his large body like a speeding spider. He swings wildly trying to get her off him but she is so fast. Autumn is shocked at how fast Grace moves. Grace's fingers elongate on her right hand like serrated knives and her left arm morphs into a sharp spear. As Grackle tries to holler she plunges the spear up through his jaw into his brain. She licks the brain matter from the spear as Grackle's body meets pavement. Autumn rips up through Grackle's asshole like a possum does a dead deer along a highway. She eats her way from the inside out. Grackle's body hits the ground like a ton of bricks. His stomach puffs out as Autumn roots around inside devouring all of his viscera. Big old Grackle never stood a chance and neither would five of his kind would have stood a chance either.

All that was left of Grackle were his large bones and his head. The women gorged on his meat for hours before coming to rest on the pad.

Grace wipes the blood from her mouth, "Autumn, are you serious about not being able to be killed?"

Autumn, tweaking like a drug addict licks up and down Grackles severed tongue. She then takes a huge bite allowing her fangs to protrude from her lips. She chews and chews as her eyes roll around in their sockets. Pure ecstasy comes across her face. She opens her eyes turning her head towards Grace, "No I was totally bullshitting but he surely bought it didn't he," She starts laughing; "I mean it's pretty hard to kill a Xenite, especially the women. I fought a girl by the name of Deidre Ophelia Welch for days it seemed like over a human man, can you believe that? It seems like it was hundreds of years ago or more now. I'll never forget that bitch because she damn near ripped my eye out."

"So why go to these great extremes Autumn? Why not just take over the world and be rulers?"

Autumn gets up to her feet. She walks over to Grace and pulls her to her feet.

"Why would we want to rule such animals? No offense Grace but humans are idiots. You all hate one another, no one can live in harmony and I even watched one dumb son of a bitch kill a poor elderly lady for fifty cents. But in all reality only a few of us exist, Grackle wasn't lying when he said that he destroyed our planet cause well he really did and that's why it was satisfying to rip him apart."

Grace takes off her bloody robe. She wipes off her body with the cleaner inside area, "So tell me then when did these Plutarch aliens get here because I have never seen anything like that in my entire life and I'm pretty sure that no one else has either."

Autumn rotates her index finger back and forth, "I wouldn't say that sister. The boy who popped your cherry back in the eighties sure does frequent with them!"

Grace throws the robe onto the ground. Her face expression shows more shock than when she saw the alien, "What are you saying Autumn that Cannon is an alien too?"

"Not exactly Grace but here is the hard part to swallow so brace yourself, the Plutarch colonies live thousands of feet under the ground right below everyone's feet in the City of Cyprus but mostly right under your house, the big oak tree mainly, Latrobe you feeling me?" Grace nods her head in agreement. Autumn continues, "Your father," Grace looks at her in fear if what's coming next," Yes your father worked as a Reaper for the Plutarch's but don't hate him for it because he was only protecting you and your mother. When he realized that Cutlass was going to take over the planet with intent to kill all humans he hid one of four God particles in you."

Grace drops to her knees and busts out crying, "I killed my father to save Juniper Savage. What the fuck is a Cutlass?" Her head starts to throb as sadness feels her heart.

Autumn kneels down beside," Listen kid you didn't know but now you do and you can change it. You got played, we all do, even people from different worlds. Its life but we must move forward and fix those things that are broken and Cutlass, well he is a wanna be dictator asshole who should be number one on your menu now and not as an appetizer but a main course. You feeling me sister?"

Grace puts her head on Autumns chest. She tries to suck up the pain but it's tough. The Xenite in her makes her tough but the human side still has emotions, "So where does Juniper come into all of this?"

Autumn rubs her hand down over Graces face then pulls her face up to see hers, "Grace, Juniper was going to gut you until she found the God particle in your body. She is general Grounder's queen bitch do all drone. Hell she has so many different strands of DNA floating around in her body that none of us are even sure what she is anymore. We are almost certain that she was once human but that has not been proven. She is the upfront puppet like your president. She tells all of the generals lies and takes fault for his wrong doing and Gentry, he's like the silent partner in all of this but what the world doesn't know is that he is about to take rule of it all. He has manipulated everyone to gain total power."

Autumn takes Grace by the hand where she leads her to a small room. It is lightly furnished and there is a set of clothes lying on the bed. "Get a shower; wash off that Grackle scum," Autumn snickers," get dressed and I will show you how to motor around in your new body."

Grace buck naked covered in Plutarch goo quickly obliges. She washes, gets dressed and the two Jump on a two person elevator. "Grace have you ever ridden a crotch rocket," Autumn asks," I need to know because there are two of the sweetest bikes that your eyes will ever lay upon at the top of this elevator. Grace flashes her thumbs up," I was in the 200 MPH club long before nitrous was installed on vehicles honey."

When they reach the top a small door opens and they step down into a parking garage. When Grace looks back she realizes that they just rode up through a large water pipe. She catches up to Autumn where she is already putting on her helmet," Grace these are not your average bikes. They have been built with Xenite technology and burn hydrogen for fuel so the government can kiss our asses with their bullshit $5.00 a gallon fuel costs."

Grace Chuckles," Amen to that sister."

Autumn can see the new bounce in her walk. Hours before she witnessed the same dreary Grace dragging her ass along just getting by but who wouldn't after they lose a limb she thought. Autumn straddles a fluorescent green Hayabusa while Grace jumps on a pearl black one all decked out in air brushed skulls. "Once you put on your helmet you will see a heads up display flash on the screen and once it recognizes your face your bike can then only be driven by you or a Xenite as it will automatically recognize your DNA.

Your guns hidden in the compartments below operate the same way."

Grace nods. She puts on her helmet and sees the heads up display. They both fire up the bikes. The engines roar like an F-18 hornet turbine engine. Autumn does a wheelie down through the parking garage and Grace follows suit. They hit route 376 heading towards the underground City of Cyprus to Find Cannon and eviscerate Cutlass.

CH 7 ECHOE VALLEY (1985)

1

It's a beautiful Pennsylvania May summer day in 1985. The wind crests above Zaijdel's orchard causing the swift gusts to taste like a breath of candy. With all of the apples ripe and hanging low on the limbs the sweet aroma carries for miles.

The hot sun glistens across Mirror Lake. That day couldn't have been more perfect and the memories will linger in Cannon's brain forever. He couldn't stop thinking of Grace and wished he had mind powers to summon her to his location. This type of goofy thought always bounces around in his brain, especially when he wanted to vaporize Sir for being an asshole.

On this morning Cannon and Mitch are wondering along Albert's creek less than a mile from the big oak catching salamanders and crawfish to feed a baby raccoon that Mitch named Bandit. Now according to Mitch Bandit was no ordinary pet. He was the smartest creature these two boys ever encountered.

Three months ago to this date Cannon and Mitch were heading back home after a long journey atop the ridge searching for morels and sheep head mushrooms when they came a crossed a baby raccoon. Immediately Mitch grasped the little bugger and started cradling it like a baby.

It must have been his feminine instincts instilled by his mother Audra from birth that made him love and care so much for others. Cannon on the other hand would have much rather dissected and killed the coon for shits and giggles. Cannon grabs Mitch's arm. "P-p-p-put it down so I can s-s-s-step on its head and put it out of its m-m-m-misery," he says with his stumbling tongue.

Mitch quickly pulls away. Sometimes he swears that Cannon has a demon inside of him because he just doesn't know where he comes from sometimes. "No, I will not," he screams.

Cannon insisted again to give him the coon," Mitch that l-l-little guy will d-d-die without its m-m-m-mother. Just let it go t-t-t-then."

Mitch looks at Cannon with neon death-ray eyes. If they would have worked Cannon's ass would've been smoked for sure. He looks up with a shit eaten grin, "I'm gonna take care of him since his momma left him."

"N-n-no d-d-d-damn it," Cannon yells, "You know that S-S-S-Sir will surely K-K-K-kill us if we take a s-s-s-stray home. Hell that piece of shit b-b-b-bastard can't even afford to f-f-f-feed us let alone another stray."

By now you could see Mitch getting a little teary eyed and nothing hurt Cannon more than to see his baby brother cry. Hell he had seen it more often than not when Sir came around. Sir loved to make them cry, especially Mitch because he looked like their father the most.

2

Just then Grace Adams dragging Mandy Cunningham came trotting down the creek. Grace looked more gorgeous than ever. She had matured way before her time. Her plump rounded size D breasts bobbled and bounced as she jumps through the creek and when the cool water splashes against her bra-less chest her nipples emerge like little monsters attempting to chew through her cotton shirt. These nipples reminded Cannon of oversized tootsie rolls. He could not stop starring at her and immediately sported a throbbing boner as his dripping deformed tongue seemed to crawl out of his mouth like a dragon emerging from its cave after a long warm snooze. He started tugging at his shirt and crossing his legs in an attempt to hide it from seeing eyes. Cannon knew about Gracie and how she loved all the boys. At least that was the rumors floating around high school. He especially loved the fact that she was so direct in what she wanted and he knew she had her sights aimed right at him.

Within seconds the girls were right on top of the boys. Instantly Graces breasts were pressed against Cannon's chest. His heart was pounding so loud that he feared she could hear it. She stood there rocking here hips from side to side as if dancing to the drum like sounds of his heartbeat. Her nipples were like erect pencil erasers rubbing against his flesh.

She smiled and said, "hey boys whatta you two doin out here?"

Cannon was still tongue tied. Well a little tied more than usual. He thought Grace was not this direct with him last time at the big oak. He could tell that something had changed in her. It didn't seem good but he could not complain with such excitement.

Mitch stepped up and said in a soft polite voice, "We are saving Bandit here. This cute baby raccoon was left by his momma."

Immediately Mandy kneeled down beside Mitch to pet Bandit, "Aw, what a cute little baby.

Gracie never looked away from Cannon's eyes. She just kept rocking back and forth against his body. The swaying motion began to gyrate into Cannon's loins as well. Now they were both swaying and starring at each other in a trance like state. Mandy and Mitch looked at the two with strange faces. Gracie slowly reaches down and grabs Cannon's hand. Her hands felt like fresh untainted silk right from the worm's ass. Or more like a semi-strong current of water slipping against the finger tips. She pulls slightly leading him up the hill. She looks down into his face again, "Come on Cannon I want to show you something."

Cannon was so mesmerized by her beauty that his words seemed nonexistent. He just wandered up the hill in an awkward stride like a lamb to its slaughter.

This day would forever change Cannon's life forever and he kind of knew it because two weeks ago John Riddle the class clown came to school on a Friday and told everyone how he made out with Grace and fondled her tits for a few minutes under the schools' gym bleachers during a pep rally. He said that he was so close to getting a stink finger but a couple teachers caught them. Gracie never denied it. She would always smile and say," boys always tell stories."

By now Cannon could smell the sex on her at least that is what he thought it would smell like. She was exuding the most toxic pheromones he had ever encountered. Cannon was astonished at the fact that she was interested in him but even if she wasn't maybe he'd get a glimpse of a real set of breasts, he thought. Or maybe she was so kind to him because of the craziness that happened at her house with her father back in 1982 when her father was going to kill him. It seemed that the two got pretty close that year before it all went down.

She looked again with a smile from ear to ear. Cannon knew that she took great pleasure in tempting boys. Mandy abruptly jumps to her feet and shouts," Not again Grace, I'm not waitin for you to bump uglies. And this is the last time I lie to your brother for you."

Her voice seemed to echo a distressed plethora of jealousy. Gracie just waved her hand with an unpleasant gesture. She knew what she wanted and her whiny little friend wasn't going to stop her. Once they crested the top of the hill Cannon yelled back in a nervous stutter-y voice to Mitch," M-m-m-Mitch s-s-s-stay right there and I-l-l-l-I'll b-b-b-b-be r-r-r-r-right b-b-b-b-b-back in a m-m-m-m-m-minute."

Mitch was so enthused about taking care of his own pet that he barely lingered in anybody's world let alone Cannon's. Mandy jumped and splashed as she angrily bounced down the creek.

By now Gracie is once again pressed up against Cannon. She is smiling and starring into his eyes. He knows that she feels his Johnston protruding through his shorts. Cannon has an erection like a heat seeking missile chasing an F-16 fighter jet to its death. He is embarrassed of his big member. All the boys in gym class told him he was deformed. And then it happened. Gracie slid her hand down his shorts and began to slowly stroke him. When she couldn't get her hand around it she looked up at him as if she found buried treasure.

She said," oh my God Cannon! I would have never guessed. Your like a half man, half horse, holy shit!"

Cannon's eyes roll way back in his head. He couldn't talk. Hell no one has ever touched him in that way. Well except for old Grandma Blithe when she would yell at him and smack his pecker with a metal ruler while she made Jeb stand there naked and watch. But those were nightmares. This was a heavenly dream come true.

His breathing sounded like a locomotive on steroids. When Gracie heard him gasping she started plucking away harder. Then with bold intentions and no idea what he was doing Cannon slowly slipped two fingers into the waistband of her shorts. When she didn't pull away he pushed a little deeper. Now he could feel some of her soft hairs and the heat was like the oven back home when his Grandmother opened the door after making cookies. Grace pulled herself closer and kept on stroking. Cannon started again going deeper but he was afraid that she would stop him so he inched downward at a slow pace. Just then Gracie grabs Cannon's hand and shoves it all the way down into her panties. All Cannon could think was, 'I'm getting a stink finger; I'm getting a stink finger."

He had no clue about the bigger picture. As he scuffled his hand around in her soaking wet sticky panties he located the source. Once there he entered the tip of his finger slowly. Gracie gasped with immeasurable pleasure so Cannon went a little deeper. The hot sticky goo was all over his hands as he inserted even deeper. Soon he didn't have to move his hand at all because Gracie kind of had her own rhythm going. As she slid up and down on his finger she stroked him up and down as well. Cannon's brain was heaping mounds of mind detonating hallucinations. He still couldn't believe what was happening and then as if it couldn't get any better Gracie unbuttons his jean shorts, pulls down the zipper and then pulls his Johnston out. Cannon's mind is about to explode. Gracie pulls close and kisses Cannon hard. When she tries to put her tongue in his mouth he resists. Grace opens her eyes to see Cannon's closed. She wonders why he doesn't want to kiss her. The late nights the two had been spending together made her begin to love him. She didn't know why the special attraction existed or why he turned her on so much, she just knew what she wanted.

Cannon is embarrassed of his tongue. It looks and feels like a dead snake that was run over by a car fifty times. Still Gracie persists. Once inside Cannon's mouth she caresses and licks his stiff dead tongue with hers. There was no hesitation whatsoever. It seemed as if she liked the broken tongue. Then again another surprise as she kisses him more aggressively now she starts pulling her shorts and undies down together. Then like an expert she drops his shorts too and pulls him on top of her as they fall to the ground all in one motion. And she never stopped kissing him for an instant, not once. Slowly she slid her other hand down to grab hold of his erect package. She gently glides it up into the front of her love glove. She spreads her legs a little wider rocking her hips until finally it slides up inside her, Cannon quivers and bucks like a wild colt as she gyrates her hips to make the missile go deeper. Cannon's mind explodes that very instance. He was in Heaven he thought. She kisses him deeply and then whispers into Cannon's ear," I wanted you to be the first before I didn't have a choice."

He couldn't understand what she meant but the warm wetness milking his loins rendered it too difficult to understand anything. Her hips were rotating like a tilt-a-whirl tickling the bellies of a hundred people. The feeling of pure nirvana engulfs the whole of him. Grace begins to gyrate harder and thrust a little like when they were standing by the creek but with a more aggressive intention. Cannon's Johnston was throbbing like a ringing bell. He had never felt anything like this before. The hot, wet and sticky hole surrounding and massaging his genitals had complete control of him. He can feel her warm milk flowing all over his balls. As much as he was loving this very second in time he knew that this encounter would be the death of him. Grace was moaning and huffing like a fan. She kisses him harder and harder as her eyes roll way back in her head. By now all of Cannon was deep inside her, clean to the trunk of the tree. As he penetrates her, he can feel her internal muscles milking every inch of his Johnston. Soon Cannon knew what to do and began pumping back. Now he was like a jackhammer busting up concrete. As he drives it deeper each time it seems like Graces heart skips a few beats but she never stops. Within seconds they both reach the point of no return. Gracie's derriere is smacking against the leaves as Cannon drives her body across the ground with every powerful thrust. Grace groans with every pump. Both of their bodies are slapping together liken two fish out of water until finally Cannon erupts inside of Gracie. He lets out a kind of wild animal roar, a sound that he has never made until that day. Grace starts quivering and shaking with ecstasy as she feels the hot fluid pouring forth from her body all over Cannon. They both lay there together for a few seconds. Their young minds can't comprehend all that just happened. It seems as though the heat of the moment turned them into two different individuals. As they lay there Cannon begins to think about health class and how the teacher told them all to use protection if they had sex or they would have babies at a young age. But it didn't matter because right then Cannon would have married Gracie in a heartbeat.

CH 8 I.P.C.O VIPER PROGRAM (2007)

1

The future has now come and more maniacs than ever have emerged through time. The academy at Quantico has long been forgotten and the cobwebs along the window seals could tell stories of less suicidal times. The majority of the baby boomers now run the newly funded organization. V.I.C.A.P has discontinued and grown into I.P.C.O. This new government agency combines all the countries throughout the world. N.C.A.V.C, The National Center for the Analyses of Violent Crime, B.A.U, The Behavioral Analysis Unit, C.A.S.M.I.R.C, The Child Abduction Serial Murder Investigation Resources Center and V.I.C.A.P have all combined. Serial killing has now become an international issue and now I.P.C.O has gone global. The International Psychological Containment Organization is funded by every continent and its agents are trained in every language and fighting style known to man. This new type of training was an ingenious design that came out of O.I.A or the Optimal Intelligence Agency which stemmed from its German eugenics program known as T-4. The coming about of this agency was fueled by the New World Sect. Now that all nations are committing to one world government and one world currency, containment and labeling of possible liabilities has become easier. The agents carry as much gear as an S.W.A.T unit and they are trained with even higher classifications. These types of security passes would have been inhumane to most in the past years but now immediate death somehow became mandatory.

The top dog of this new operation is late forties Juniper Savage. Her hair is jet black with the gray starting to shine through mildly. She feels that it shows her wisdom as it states in the Bible. The lines on her face travel from ear to ear showing years of abuse and intersect with the quarter inch thick scar running from her right ear and down to the right side of her neck.

Juniper's eyes are a beautiful emerald green mixed with hazel in the center that gives her the appearance of a cat. Her stature stands five foot eight inches, (tall for a woman) so she thinks, but she is a total mesomorph and has been her whole life. She took up track and ju-jitsu at age six and fell absolutely fond of it. It was her father's idea and she was glad that he had pushed her in that direction because if it were up to her mother she would have been one of those no brain pageant beauties that dress up like dolls. Her father Michael Savage was also in the Federal Bureau of Investigations which led her to be just like daddy. His name proceeded him and he was one of nine that helped transform the entire network into the now I.P.C.O. Michael was all of his daughter and more except for one little flaw. His tender heart for young woman and that ultimately was his undoing in the end.

The lean muscle striations that protrude through her tan skin seem to put off the most buff of men that she has encountered in the years. She is equipped with a nicely defined eight pack that most people on earth dream about. And with fifteen inch guns on a woman, it's pretty impressive. The thought process in Juniper's mind is, your body is your temple, what you put in you get out so her diet and exercise regime is so rigorous or maybe even extreme depending on who's judging. Six meals a day, three major and three protein shakes in between followed by jujitsu early AM and power lifting in the mid-evening concentrating on one major body part per day six times a week with mostly Sunday's off for Scientology church if it fits in her busy schedule. But lately with the new position and all the brutal protocols for international captures she has been lacking. The French crueler doughnuts and pumpkin spice coffee in the mornings have been taking their tolls as the dimples on her ass cheeks tell her.

Juniper is a Harvard grad that has been with the F.B.I right out of college for 20 plus years. Her skills have surpassed many of her predecessors, even her late fathers. If it was not for her insight on the profiling of serial killers many of the top murderers of the new millennium would still be at large. The Mutilator was her biggest case and solving it catapulted her to the top level in her agency.

It's Thursday, December twenty-second, two thousand seven, just three days before Christmas at 7 AM. It's a very cold morning in Windsor Canada on this particular day of winter. The harsh spray of wet snow came in from the Detroit side and wrecked all the streets. Thousands have come from all over the world to mark the first day of the International Psychological Containment Organization start up. It has been in effect but on this day the rules change for judgment on those who commit harm to others.

Juniper stands behind the D&B recycled plastic podium at the head of the room barely containing all the attendees. The auditorium was built for the queen some forty years ago and was supposed to house two-thousand for parliament voting purposes but it must have been before fast food took the world over with its obesity reign as most were stuffed together like sardines in a can.

Colleen Edwards the General Representative for Dangle & Beria approaches the podium and hands Juniper a hot cup of pumpkin spice coffee. Colleen is built like a brick shit house too. At five foot six inches and a thirty-six inch D chest she demands attention with her body and she knows it. She is quite the label whore as all her clothes scream big name labels. Her cherry Armani dress sported a price tag of six grand and her Choo stiletto hills were double that.

"Good luck Juniper, she whispers.

Juniper pulls the cup to her mouth and takes a nostril full of the pumpkin spice coffee. The warmth seems to dull the ache of the arthritis in her right hand. She looks down at the cup and thinks, 'Maybe it's time to reduce my caliber from a fifty to maybe a forty-five or

even a forty but then my reputation may be tarnished.'
She was the only woman on the force sporting the big
gun issued by the department. And this made her feel
good and confident in a man's world. Most men would
quiver when she asked them if they wanted to rack off
a few rounds from her piece and most couldn't even
hold the grip due to its large clip capacity and weight.
That was except for Jax Jakovich who went by the nickname Cadillac Jack. He also carries the same Israeli
made fifty caliber automatic pistol with the exception
that he always uses a much hotter load. He would run
past the manufacturers recommended load using sixty
grains of powder infused with a titanium cobalt mix
that always made the gun reach up about forty-five degrees and no one could hold onto it except Jax. But
then he upgraded to a Smith & Wesson .500 magnum.
Now by far the most powerful hand gun used on any
force. Juniper always thought Jax did it for bragging
rights but his rather large hands accepts the grip quite
well and he shoots a perfect score every time. She never
collaborated with any of her colleagues in the rumor
mill about Jax being some sort of half man half robot and that's why his hands could hold on to such a
powerful boom stick. Despite all of the bullshit being
tossed around the different bureaus she thought that
his hands felt just fine. Maybe even more than fine!

She nods in respect to Colleen and then turns to the crowd and begins, "First off let me start by introducing myself and all of you to each other. I know that there is a lot of talent and big egos in this room today but I hope that you all have left that at the front door as we have a ton of work to do and a shit ton of training to take down the newest opposing threat."

She looks down at the piles of papers and stacks of thumb drives spilling off the podium, "For all of you that do not know who I am and for the few that do I'm Juniper Savage, a First Mark Lieutenant with I.P.C.O. Our Admiral position is yet to be determined as the abrupt death of Admiral Walters took everyone by surprise. Many of you probably knew my father or even worked side by side with him in the field. He didn't take any shit and neither do I so let's get that out of the way. My purpose here today is to inform you all that I will be heading the new International Psychological Containment Organization or we all know as I.P.C.O. Any objections, she sternly announces?"

She would love nothing more than to say listen up assholes, the P in I.P.C.O really means Plutarch as in an alien race under your feet just to watch the entire groups' eyes bulge from their heads but she also knows that a humans mind is so fragile so she resists the temptation on the tip of her tongue. She looks around at all the pale faces staring back at her.

The crowd begins to make a lot of chatter. Most of the older agents are coughing, choking and throwing around lewd remarks. Mike Evans a fifty-two year old fat slap dick doughnut hurling thirty year veteran looks at Arty Gibbons and nudges him in the gut. Arty spills his Rage energy drink all down over his neatly pressed baby blue cotton shirt. Arty Gibbons is a fifteen year field operative who was assigned to I.P.C.O from his meat pipe challenged mentor Christopher Lee Johnson who mainly went by Johnson. No one knew why but everyone joked that it was for his love of Johnson's in his rectum. He would always come into the locker rooms and stare at all the new recruits and sometimes try to shower with them despite the fact that all the officers had their own shower rooms and quarters They would all wash real quick and get out, sometimes not even all the way shaved or clean, that was all but Arty. In all of Johnsons forty years on the force he managed to get a more stylish agent issued boot, softer toilet seats and cherry scented air fresheners for the office. And despite all the rumors Arty had no issues at all polishing Johnson's boots.

"You believe this shit," Mike whispers," I work thirty God damn years with the agency and now a cunt is going to be my boss." As the words exit Mike's mouth his eyes lock on to Juniper's. She smiles back at him as if she hears every word that he is saying. He thinks in his mind, 'It's not possible because that crazy bitch is easily 50 yards from us. Mike roots around under his chair to see if it's bugged or something. He looks back at Arty wiping off his shirt.

Arty snickers and nods in agreement to Mike's comment. He takes the stylish silk yellow handkerchief and slowly pats the wetness from his shirt. The fruity substance from the can is now his perfume, he thinks."

Mike Evans was a great agent in his prime but after he reached the ripe age of forty it was all downhill from there. His hair fell out, lost all his teeth which resulted in getting dentures and the testicular cancer completely removed any trace of testosterone in his body. The once stout man now resembled a more like fat woman appearance. He even had to buy a Bro, a man bra to contain his rather large man tits.

Juniper smacks the podium with her fist. The sound echoes through the microphone. It grabs every ones attention. With all the egos in the room it's tough to navigate but Juniper's balls seem to be a little bigger than her male counterparts in the room. The scars on the left side of her face prove it. And just about all knew it too except for maybe some of the foreigners. Juniper clears her throat and sips the coffee. All attention is back in her direction, "You all know why you are here. I'm sure that your department heads have informed you of the situations at hand. With the latest massacre at the Reynolds truck stop across from Crackle-wood Acres on route twenty-two it shows that it is time to step up the game immediately!"

Juniper takes another sip of her coffee and looks down at the graphs that she prepared for the projector. She prefers the old projectors rather than Power point presentations on the laptops as she can write right on the graphs while in place.

"Hit the lights," She yells at Colleen in the back of the room, "First off these two graphs show the rise in crime in just the last two years. We are up twenty-seven percent from just last year alone. And gentleman, (she pauses to catch herself while she looks at the next slide) and ladies this is not just crime but rather a twisted sickness that must be stopped. Apparently someone out there is trying to get our attention and well they sure as hell have gotten it!"

She removes the graphs and begins with one of the most disturbing sights encountered by a set of human eyes. Sue Kim sitting out in the front row looks away from the rancid photo. Her best friend Vicky was one of the victims as well as Dick Schroeder's daughter Jessica taken down by the hands of Hogs head Horace.

The picture showing across all the 152 TV screens in the large convention center show decapitated bodies strewn all over the truck stop bathroom on route twenty-two. The two body's laying right in the center is Dick's daughter Jessica and Sue's friend Vicky. They both were identified by their love of tattoos. Jessica had a series of butterflies along her right hip and Vicky sported the Zodiac sign on the left side of her neck.

Dick stares at the screen with anger and stands up, "Why are you showing this shit Juniper?"

Juniper wipes the sweat from her brow. Her stomach is churning uncontrollably. She knows that the irritable bowel syndrome introduced from the Mutilators dirty blade piercing her intestines harasses her when she doesn't eat in the morning. All those grueling hours of surveillance have taken their toll on her body and it is especially revealing itself on this day. And If being a bit nervous wasn't enough in this testosterone infested room her bowels weren't helping the matters at hand, "Dick I know that you are angry but this is no time to get pissed off at me."

Dick pushes his seat back and starts heading to the front of the room. Dick steps in and he is quickly greeted by two field Cell Viper agents, Ted and Desmond. They are both dressed in full out infiltration urban warfare gear. They both tower over Dick at six feet tall thick as a three foot wall. Neither of the two have a last name nor a past as they are experimental test combat drones introduced to I.P.C.O from Dangle & Beria Research and Development Corporation. No one really knows their true origin or what they are really made of but they interact well with everyone and take orders until their death.

Dick shouts, "What are you going to do Juniper kill your own kind with your zombies here? That's my daughters naked corpse that you are promoting up there for everyone to see. TAKE IT THE FUCK DOWN NOW OR ELSE!"

Juniper abruptly pulls the picture from the projector, "I'm really sorry Dick but I had to make an example to show everyone else in this room exactly what we all should be feeling right now. Seventeen students from all over the world died that day from the hands of several assailants."

Dick jumps to his feet and exits out one of the side doors.

Before Juniper could continue Jax Jakovich stands up, "What do you mean several assailants? You have Horace Escobar in custody? The Hogs head Horace, the hermaphrodite from Hermosillo, right? How can there be anymore?"

The whole room is stirring. Juniper puts a picture of Horace up on the projector, "Hogs head

Horace the cannibal is an obese immigrant from Mexico with an extremely large head that quickly gained his nickname at an early age. With his long brown hair, extremely deformed nose and big blusterous cheeks, his face did very much resemble that of a hog. Rumor has it that all of the toxic waste being dumped down in Hermosillo led to a lot of children being born with deformities. He always evaded authorities and was very difficult to capture because he did not own anything. This man never applied for a green card or legitimately worked and paid taxes a day in his life but he lived like all the rest of us enjoying the American way. He even had several drivers' licenses from different states. We believe that he killed and consumed hundreds of people over the years of his miserable life but for one man to slay seventeen kids at one time and remove each of their heads I think not!"

Juniper takes another sip of her coffee despite the acid reflux torturing her bowels. She places another slide on the projector. People in the audience start to gasp for air as they turn away from the madness on the screen.

"It's highly unlikely that he was alone Jax!"

Jax sits back down. He can't believe that she remembered his name. Hell it's been at least fifteen years since the two had met and the only reason he stood up was to see if she recognized him. And he knew that she was on to him. Jax hoped that their last encounter didn't ruin his chances of a repeat encounter on this day.

Colleen brings Juniper a stool to sit on. She plops down and begins again, "People we have a real issue here. As you can see from the above slide there are students severed heads placed in each of the urinals with their genitals precisely placed into their mouths. All their tongues have been removed and eight of them had their rectums cored by some type of deer hunting tool we believe and ten of the heads are nowhere to be found. All of their clothes and belongings are gone as well."

She flips to another slide and has to look away for a second herself. Gagging noises and heavy breathing can be heard echoing off the walls of the large convention center.

Abruptly two female agents in the farther back area getup and rush out the door spilling their breakfast all the way to the bathroom.

Slowly Juniper regains composure and starts again, "As you can see here we found Horace sitting inside a type of hut built out of the bodies of the seventeen students and the remainders of the heads were placed in an orderly fashion around his body in a planet Pluto type sign lined with peach scented candles. Odd symbols were drawn in blood and fecal matter all over the restroom which is normal for most psychopaths but one symbol alone stuck out. And that symbol was the Greek sign for Pluto the ruler of Hades."

Juniper moves to the next slide while struggling to swallow her own saliva because now the symbols on the wall struck a nerve. With an epiphany she begins to drift off into a confused state and starts to relieve that exact night in 1982 when she was brought on to investigate the case of the Mutilator from Latrobe. It was that same place where she received the deep embedded purple scar on her right cheek. But just as soon as she drifts Colleen grabs her by her left arm, "Juniper you ok?" Colleen asks.

Colleen runs down off the stage and returns with a bottle of water. She hands it to Juniper. Juniper takes a long gulp and then stands closer to the podium. She decides to use the past to fuel the feelings. She grabs the microphone form the holder and begins again, "I'm sure that many of you know but for the one's that do not, I obtained this beauty mark on my right cheek from none other than John Adams A.K.A The Mutilator. And the reason I bring up this very sore subject is that John used the same symbols as we found at the truck stop. Now this is twenty-five years later and his teachings have resurfaced. It was always believed that he had disciples but none ever surfaced until now. The circle above the cauldron like radius represents the earth and the straight line down represents the underworld. Pluto in earlier Greek mythology was believed to be the ruler of the underground which was known as Hades or Hell. He was believed to be the rich god because of metals being mined underground. The only two people that possessed an even close resemblance of this mark was John and his daughter Grace Adams who is being sought for questioning at this very second."

The crowd is at awe as Juniper zooms in a camera showing her thick purple scar running from her right ear down across her neck. Everyone can see it all over the big flat screens all around the convention center.

She looks up at the biggest screen and wonders how she even survived that night. She mumbles under breath, 'Grace.

The visions of torment enter her mind, once there she can see a young twelve year old Grace picking up her large fifty caliber pistol and putting it to her father's head as he begins to carve her right cheek. She could feel the cold steel lay open her face as the warm blood spurt forward all down over her neck and around her blouse as the stink of rotten flesh and Brute aftershave woofed in the air as he precisely moved his large arms to cut. John pushed the gun deeper into the side of his temple as he turned to look into Graces eyes. And as he went to swipe the sharp blade down across Juniper's neck again-. "BOOM" The gun fired and it does a complete forty five straight into the air as Grace flew back against the old barn wall. Juniper looked on in horror as the top of Johns head exploded erupting brain matter all over her face. She pushed John off her and grabbed Grace to make sure that she was ok. Grace broke two fingers on her right hand from the pistols recoil. She sat there crying hysterically in Juniper's arms until back up arrived.

As Juniper pulls back to reality she witnesses Colleen waving her hands. Apparently in her daydream she turned on the weapons slide show on the laptop and it was fast forwarding through sounding like one of those chipmunk's songs. Giggles can be heard resonating from the upper back areas of the convention center. She quickly recollects her thoughts while adjusting the screen, pulls off the Greek symbols slide and once again places another picture of Horace.

"As you can see in the photo Horace was sitting in his own urine and fecal matter for possibly several days. The forensics team estimated the children's time of death two days before our arrival and an unusual large trace amount of weapons grade Uranium-238 was littered throughout the bathroom. Horace read hot at 64 REM. The least traveled highway route twenty-two between Derry and Blairsville Pennsylvania did not receive much traffic because of the Steeler game that weekend. Ramesh an Indian immigrant from India strolled right past the bodies, Horace and everything to use the toilet in one of the ten stalls. It was when he climbed up on top of the toilet to place his feet on the seat he noticed something was wrong. When he saw Horace sitting in his human temple he ran out screaming into the highway and a local woman called the police on her cell phone. And now because Horace had never been caught for all these years and now for a grown man to sit in one spot for two days covered in his own filth, well that leads me to believe that something big is on the rise. The I.P.C.O think tank believes that there is now an army of twisted sickies who have banned together to ensure their survival. And somehow they are all communicating together for some grand plan."

Jax tries to but in again but Juniper cuts him off as she has to show him who has the bigger penis.

"I know there are questions but we have many grueling hours ahead of us that need to be crammed in, in these two days. So listen up or you all will be here into the holiday vacation. And if you piss me off or interrupt again I will be sure to make this happen. So if you want to see your families for the holidays, mouths shut please."

Fifteen minutes later Dick overwhelmingly stinking of booze and cigar smoke staggers to the front stage where Juniper stands behind the podium. He stands erect in front of Juniper and gestures that he is reaching for his field revolver. Within three tenths of a second or the blink of an eye to some Ted points his ten gauge street sweeper with a thirteen round drum and lets one off. Asses scatter as Dick is engulfed in a prototype casing called Hades Dander. The recipe is like that of the sixties napalm mix used in Nam but the extreme temperatures reach a million degrees within a small confined area in milliseconds.

A scream was heard and then Dick was dust.

Now the room is stirring. People have scattered to the edges of the convention center walls. The intense heat from the blast could be felt throughout the entire room. A few people ten feet or so from Dick had their shoes melt to the floor.

Most stare in disbelief as they have just watched one of their own scorched to death. Many are staring in Juniper's direction with looks to kill. Most of the men have more time than her and wonder who she blew to get her lead position. Thousands applied for the position but she was the triumphant one who landed it. Her reputation preceded her but even she wandered why she was chosen. There was so much talent in the room that it could barely be contained. Many of the people have contributed their philosophies and ideas to come up with the standards used by all enforcement agencies today.

Juniper pulls her jaw up to look around at everyone in the room. She is dumbfounded form the incident, she almost runs off the stage. Ted lowers his piece. He steps back beside Desmond. Before a sound could be uttered Two Optimal Intelligence Agency technicians rush removing Ted and Desmond from the room before a mob begins. They are loaded into an armored van and rushed away.

Juniper gets a grip, she announces into the microphone, "Listen up everyone. Dick was a good agent but when the life of another agent is threatened it's a no holds barred situation, everything goes so think twice before engaging anyone of your own kind. A threat to the life of another agent results in death. This is the new I.P.C.O way to operate!"

At least a hundred agents throw in their badges while exiting the building. The rest return to their seats a little more attentively. A few of the cleaning technicians in the building come in to sweep Dick into a box where his ashes are toted off to the back. All that remained was a six foot circle of black stained ash embedded a few inches down into the wooden floor.

"Ok group let's take a fifteen minute break," Juniper announces.

Almost immediately the entire group gets up and heads to the refreshment area and restrooms. Conversations can be heard going on all throughout the entire area. The voices sound like that of many waters.

Juniper knows that it was wrong to kill a fellow agent but she had to use it, she though. If she had shown fear the others would panic and a mob would most certainly have ensued so she embraced the moment and used Dick as an example of what would happen to anyone that crossed the hierarchy of the new organization. And so it appeared that her tactic worked as all but a few returned to their seats without a peep.

Juniper waves her hand at Colleen in the back. She and ten others take several carts. They begin distributing packets to everyone in attendance. Juniper exits the stage and quickly scurries to the ladies room. She quickly enters the stall and drops her drawers but from the shit stain staring back at her from her granny panties she clearly wasn't fast enough. Abruptly she pulls back her underwear from her skirt to see if it went through. 'Thank God, 'she thought.

She pulls a tanto blade from her bra and cuts off her panties. She turns up her nose as the stench begins to curl her toes. She looks up to witness some of the thoughtful shit house poetry and begins to read. "For good dick call Tim Shaftron. He's the biggest in

Windsor." I shit, I farted but I called Tim and now I'm not broken hearted."

Juniper chuckles a little. And despite the stench she can still smell the burnt smell of Dick all over her clothes. A tear starts to form in her right eye but she holds back. She shakes her head and looks on the left side of the stall. There is a pentagram carved into the metal with the words Satan on it. She sees a large paragraph and begins to read under her breath again,

"All day long I wander with such a strain and Its not long before I'm off running towards the stall with bowels full of pain. My cheeks begin to flutter so I swiftly run cross legged trying to avoid a stain. The door slams, my knees begin to buckle as the guy beside me begins to chuckle.

Funny noises blurt out with such a shutter, my whole body shivers as my ass turns to butter.

Hours seem to pass though it's worth the relief but the stink tears my eyes, imagine the other guys belief. The cold porcelain caresses my derriere as fragments of fecal matter explode within the air. The green cloud hovers as my asshole begins to pucker and my body convulses as the toilet begins to buckle. One more squirt forms sweat across the brow and three large plops echo throughout the stall as air forcefully begins to howl. I cuff my nose with such a frown and can't believe that I just plopped down. Ass gaskets, huh I forgot, there was no time, couldn't react my pants would've drowned. But now I know that all the chuckles weren't because of me, It seems that someone stole all the damn TP."

She laughs again out loud this time but then quickly reaches up under the roll dispenser to make sure that the poem wasn't going to get her too. With a relief she pulls her hand away as there are two full rolls. She thinks how ironic I just shit my own pants.

After quickly relieving herself she drops the soiled clothing into the trash can, washes her hands and face and then returns to the podium. She grabs her own packet and plops down on the stool. The majority of the people there are reviewing the thick detailed reports.

"Ok ladies and gentlemen we are going to go over some old routines just as a refresher. The material before you is old school but it is and has been the basis for all of our operations since the conception of V.I.C.A.P and the B.A.U. First page starts off with the certain types of Psychos. The four subtypes are Primary Psychopaths who usually suffer from a term known as semantic aphasia which means that they do not grasp any type of life plan and use anything for what suits their own purpose at any given time The Secondary

Psychopaths are adventurous risk taker who continuously worry about the stress in their own lives. Due to their abnormal obsessions for a particular person or object their anxiety increases and so does the attraction to have it. This type of condition makes their kind extremely vulnerable as they are tempted by the lure of their own desires. With being a secondary means that they are not fully considered a total psychopath and possess the ability to be rehabilitated. The Distempered Psychopaths are similar to the most notorious serial, murderer rapist the Boston strangler in that they have unreal sex drives with abilities to perform astonishing feats of sexual energy and their obsessive sexual urges seem to creep up on them at an early age. They are mostly men who fly off into a frenzy or rage easier than the other subtypes. Their characteristics resemble drug addicts, pedophiles, kleptomaniacs and any illicit or illegal indulgence. The constant need for the adrenaline high or endorphin rush makes this kind of individual very difficult to transform but it has been done in several occurrences through the new technology produced by O.I.A. And last but not least the Charismatic Psychopaths are the worst kind as they come on strong with their attractive lies and charming personalities. They are so irresistible that thousands have literally been talked out of their own lives. The abilities are demonic like and people are persuaded for the gain of the psychopath only. Many of them possess such an egocentric personality that only allows them to use humans for pleasure and nothing more. This type lacks any sympathy for anyone but them-selves and they are unable to feel sorry for anyone else in an unfortunate situation with no feeling of remorse or guilt. However, the Charismatic Psychopath usually possess the most noblest of human qualities. He or she will be a fast talker who uses words to get out of trouble and makes a lot of friends easily. This manipulative subtype believes in their own fiction, love to bask in the adulation of many and seek admiration above all."

Juniper lifts up off her stool stretching her arms and legs. All eyes are in her direction. She loves that everyone is cooperating quietly so that she can wrap it up moving on.

"Let's face it people these are not normal individuals that we are talking about here. As a matter of fact they don't even appear to be human once they reach these levels. And quite frankly and this is my own opinion, and I know they're like assholes, we all have one but when a person becomes a monster of this sort it's time to be put down. What do you all think?" She yells.

The entire room stands and applauses.

"Fortunately we now do not have to abide by the humane laws that were put into effect by the bleeding liberals from the past. And unfortunately for the perpetrators they are no longer considered equally human. This allows all I.P.C.O agents the free will to apprehend, subdue and obtain any information pertinent to end the onslaught that has plagued our planet for so long and you all are now Judge, jury and sometimes executioners. As you all have witnessed from today's demonstrations! Guess will save some tax money."

Juniper's face shows a sense of ease despite what had just transpired minutes ago. Hours upon hours passes rather quickly as she went down the long list of objectives set out before them all by the hierarchy. Their demands are strict but justified.

Hands are raised all across the room, "Please take the packets back to your rooms and study them in depth. Tomorrow we will go in depth into the new weaponry program that Dangle and Beria has so generously supplied to our agency and how to use them properly. Ok all, tomorrow we will touch base on the fetishes and all the new apprehension procedures as well. And I will be sure to answer all your questions if they are not answered by the packets that I provided. Thank you and I will see all of you tomorrow. The same time and place tomorrow. Good night.

Juniper exits the stage; she grabs Colleen's hand and pulls her into the ladies room with her, "Colleen what the hell just happened in there?" Juniper shouts.

Colleen runs her hands through her long beautiful blonde hair as she peers into the mirror. She tries to block out Juniper's comments but here squeaky voice continues to penetrate. Juniper spins her around putting the two face to face now, "I think you need to tell Poyang that his pet science projects need a little tweaking."

Colleen pulls her arms back from Juniper, spins back to the mirror, pulls her apple red lipstick from her purse and begins to apply a precise pattern around her juicy lips. Juniper looks on in horror as she paces, "Hey don't you give a shit that a life was just taken minutes ago by one of your mutants? Well ok then what if the secret gets out about the Plutocracy?"

Colleen pauses from her stroke on her bottom lip to look at Juniper but then continues to apply her lipstick as if she didn't hear her and after just enough is covered to her liking she turns to Juniper, "Listen you adapted well we hazed you and you did what needed to be done. Now there is not one person in that room that will ever fuck with you for a thousand lifetimes! Any you weeded out the weak which is exactly what this department needs. I mean you know that big fat Dick would have never made it through the Viper program so no loss."

Juniper can't believe what she is hearing. She rolls her head forcing creeks out from her neck to sound off. She stares into the mirror teary eyed. She thinks, 'what have I become?'

"Dick was a good man Colleen! He just lost his only daughter a few weeks ago."

Colleen licks her lips, she puckers them in the mirror checking for imperfections and heads for the bathroom exit, "Listen Juniper, Dick sacrificed himself to ensure that your empowerment would take a strong effect and it really did. Embrace it!"

Colleen exits the ladies room, crosses the large parking lot and heads for the Caesars Casino right next door to the auditorium. Juniper is right behind her. She enters the casino, blows right through the cigarette smoke clouds, gets into the elevator and rises to the fifth floor.

Once inside Juniper disrobes, puts her back up Springfield .38 + P revolver into the night stand drawer beside the bed. She then heads for the large oval tub. She starts to draw a nice hot bath but runs back into the other room to call in some room service. She almost forgot about eating. It was because the site of Dick being destroyed still plagued her mind. Juniper sits on the edge of the bed, pulls a menu from the lower nightstand drawer and scans it for the most efficient meal as she always does. Her shaky hand grabs for the phone receiver, dials five and givers her order to Rebecca the hostess in the hotel restaurant on the other end of the line. "How can I help you mam?" Rebecca asks.

"I'll have the grilled salmon minus the dill sauce and what are the side dishes today? "Juniper replies.

Pots can be heard clanging in the background as multiple voices echo to and from, sounds of papers being scuffled, a sigh is heard and then crackling of gum. Rebecca is leafing through the menu as well. She is a new hire at the casino and doesn't know the menu by heart yet.

"We have fresh steamed broccoli, mixed vegetables, mashed potatoes, baked potatoes, corn-."

Juniper cuts her off. "I'll take the steamed broccoli."

The steamed broccoli is what she always orders as she does every night she has to stay in a hotel but tonight she decides to cheat a little.

"I'll also take a piece of the French silk chocolate pie as well."

Rebecca quickly jots down the order.

"Is that all Miss Savage? Will there be anything to drink with your order?"

Juniper quickly rescans the menu. She contemplates having a glass of red merlot to dull her thoughts a little but quickly drops it onto the stand and replies, "No mam that will be all."

"And that will be a room charge or cash," the loud voice replies back.

Just then Juniper's cell phone vibrates a cross the other nightstand. She glances over and quickly returns to the conversation. The text was from general Hatchet telling her not to scare the recruits as they need more platforms for the Viper grafting program.

"Yes mam that will be room five eleven please."

Rebecca nods on the other end of the line.

"Ok Miss Savage you can expect your order in forty-five minutes."

Juniper quickly drops the receiver and returns to her bath before the water overflows. She gently slips in. The warmth engulfs the whole of her body. As her breasts protrude out of the bath farther she realizes that her flesh has just absorbed a quarter of the water so she adds a little more hot. The heat almost takes away the previous mornings thoughts. She enjoys the bath for as long as it takes room service to deliver and gets fifty pages absorbed of Kings newest scary novel. Once the order arrives she gorges the food in what seems to be three bites and quickly turns in for the night.

2

It was another cold winter day in Windsor, Ontario Canada, the wind plowing past the buildings near the convention center seemed to permanently apply a frost lining atop the flesh of people passing by. This evening was a special evening if any. On this day the world of crime will change forever.

It is seven twenty-five AM on a Friday and Juniper Savage is once again approaching her eight o'clock deadline for her second presentation on the new outbreak of serial killings throughout the world. She can't decide whether to start with the McNaughton Rule, Paraphilia, weapons training, the Plutonius symbols popping up or the slaughter at Crackle-wood Acres. As she clears the piles of eraser dust from her hotel room desk she jots down Crackle-wood. Although everyone was familiar with the other technical terms she realized that the Crackle-wood massacre was still extremely fresh and she wanted her presentation to go off in the proper direction. Not like yesterday's fiasco where a dick got mutilated. She was sure that if another day occurred like it, it couldn't be endured by any of their puny human brains.

Juniper walks up to the podium. She sits her pumpkin spice coffee down beside her papers. She looks out at everyone, grabs the microphone in her right hand and decides last minute to show the grand finale with the weapons testing. She hasn't observed the video herself yet but she is eager to see what the new age field operatives will be utilizing for their protection.

"Ok everyone let's start this day off as simple as possible. We are going to sign off on all this paperwork. Submit all our DNA samples and get out of here for the holiday but first let me show you all Dangle and Beria's weaponry training video so that we all have an understanding of what we are all dealing with here. Oh and be alarmed as live test subjects were used in the testing video. This is not Hollywood special effects either so I'm told. And most of you will not engage with this type of power unless you enlist in the Viper program."

Colleen hits play on the laptop. She and Juniper sit down in the back of the stage area sipping Starbucks coffee. The film shows operatives that have a similar appearance to Ted and Desmond. Big Chartreuse letters come over the screen. It flashes the word. "WHISTLER"

The operative resembling Desmond takes a rather large modified looking shotgun and places an odd shaped shell into the weapon, chambers the shell and aims at Joe Vicarious, A.K.A Turd Burglar, a known sex offender from the local Youngstown area.

Joe Vicarious is a sociopath who frequents the porno club scenes. He rolls around in sperm and feces on the floor of a local porno store called Lackey's. He licks the stains off the floors and glass encasements and then masturbates himself while watching dirty videos according to the dancers. When he started to cut himself and threaten the dancers he was kicked out. But apparently Joe's true undoing would be performing his grandest scheme of all. At some point in the mentally unstable brain of Joe he concocted this idea to sneak down underneath one of the old outhouses in Legion Keener Park. In his greatest plan ever he purchased a small supply of products at the local sporting store and suited up for his big night. Joe put on bib overall waders, a rain parka, a fisherman's cap with a light strapped to it and goggles. And he pulled a six foot step ladder along with him to get close. He decided to leave out the gloves so that he could feel with his fingers. And in the middle of the late night when the park was closed Joe snuck down to the large sewage drain running into Loyal Hanna creek that runs straight through downtown Latrobe and walked up the pipe a hundred yards where he set up his step ladder right in between two of the outhouse toilet seats down under the ladies room and patiently waited. At some time around eight AM a call came in about a man being down inside the women's outhouse in the park. Janice Dixon explained to the two officers on site that when she sat down to perform a number two she felt something touch her rectum so she jumped from the seat in fear that it was a snake only to find a hand reaching up through the seat. When she looked closer that hand was attached to Joe Vicarious who at that very second earned the name "Turd Burglar." A.K.A the Turd Burglar was sprayed off with a fire hose, arrested, detained and placed in the back of one of the squad cars. Apparently when Janice flipped out and threw her flip flop at him before running out the door screaming he fell from the step ladder in to the dirty blue pudding. The blue goo stained Joe so bad that when he was arraigned the picture wouldn't take properly as the blue color was fading into the blue background. He was stained blue for a week before fading back to a normal color. When officer Madden asked Joe what he was thinking his response was, "I just wanted to see how it comes out but I didn't get to see because I was so excited that I touched it and it sucked it right back up inside before I got a good glimpse."

After Joes prints came through the agencies database he became connected to several cases in question. Joe was let go on a misdemeanor purposely to hopefully lead the agency to a much bigger fish. Juniper was the first to be placed on the case and she tracked down Joes stomping grounds. She found useful information by speaking to Emily one of the dancers and she told Juniper that Joe brags about not working anywhere but has cash in the bank to fuel his desires. Slowly she links Joe to John Adams with close surveillance. Apparently all sickies know each other or maybe it's the new web page Death Book where crazies can sample one another's twisted stories. Joe used to set up the kill times and dates of strippers arrivals and departures since he was such a regular. He also used to be the guy who would drink your spunk for five dollars just to see a peep show for five minutes. That was until the Mutilator set him up with heft payments. The store was a pervert's candy land and Joe was the best type of customer.

Joe's final admission after weeks of grueling torment led the agency to the old abandoned motel known as Crackle-wood Acres on route twenty-two near Blairsville where the agents seen some of the sickest, demented things any human could ever imagine.

After a few seconds Desmond pulls the trigger and what appears to be a missile like projectile rockets out the end of the barrel. Immediately a thunderous whistling sound can be heard coming from the Thorium-232 fueled X-9 mini turbine used for sidewinders on the F-16 fighter jet.

Just about everyone in the audience puts their hands over their ears. Juniper and Colleen follow suit as well as they both witness a great horror. The speed of the projectile was purposely slowed down to show the full effect of the load.

Within nanoseconds the projectile plunged deep into Joe's chest and began to whistle or more like scream like a rocket. The camera zooms in closer to show the inside of the projectile start to fire up and once the four inch gadget reached full speed all of Joes organs were expelled through a small port at the end. Joe was immediately drained of all his blood and viscera in seconds. With the camera pan ramming around Joe's body it could be seen that his tongue, brain and eyeballs were even sucked from their sockets out through the whistler.

The screen goes black and words once again begin to form a sequence in bright orange letters.

Midget Plunder- Can your enemy, Hades Dander-Burnt out, Mighty Thunder-Boisterous and Bucks tears-Melt it down are listed on the screen. These and other tactical weaponry brought to you by Dangel and Beria research and development Corporation.

Juniper stands up, approaches the podium, rolls her head around to loosen up her shoulders and looks down at her list of things to cover. She takes a mouthful of water and grabs the microphone, "Ok everyone I'm going to run through this rather quickly and then we are all out of here. The Whistler is standard issue to all field operatives with specialized Viper training as well is the rest of the specialty items. All others who pass on the training will be issued standard AR-15'with .308 calibers with extended magazine capacity, your choice of side arm, E-phone technology that interacts with your every move, a special formulated body armor that moves with your body, its thinner and more agile with the same amount of protection, frag grenades and night vision contacts. There is a plethora of other neat items that you all will be exposed to in the next few weeks. Ok so hand in your DNA samples and exit slowly through the east wing please."

Juniper hands over the remotes to Colleen and follows the rest of the crowd out to the parking lot. Most of them jumped in their cars and headed towards Detroit for the early flight home for the Christmas holiday. Jax Jakovich and Juniper head to the casino where they get into the elevator together. They both stand beside one another quietly. The sexual tension between the two was thick in the air. As the elevator approaches the fifth floor Jax grabs Juniper's hand, "Juniper I really miss you.

She looks at Jax and smiles. Even though he fought real hard with the erectile dysfunction problem on their last embrace he still fought hard she thought. "Ok stud I'm going to rest awhile and then I'll meet you downstairs to tie one on like old times. I think we both need it after the last couple of days. What do you think?" Juniper whispers.

The look in Jax's face is total amazement. He can't believe that she even acknowledges his existence and this time would be different he thought as his little blue pills would overcome any issues. "Sure what time do you want to meet?"

"How's eight-thirty sound? It will give me a few hours to get caught up on emails and relax."

Jax lets go of her hand and cracks his knuckles. "Of course eight-thirty sounds great. I'll see you then."

Juniper walks off to her room. The elevator carrying Jax rises to the sixth floor.

CH 9 ASCENSION COMPLETE (1985)

1

Mitch once again warns Cannon not to go into the garage. He grabs Cannon's back pocket roughly pulling him back away from the door. " Don't touch any of Sir's things or there will be repercussions for the both of us," Mitch says in a low whispering voice.

Cannon steps back a little, he begins to reminisce to why they were in the predicament anyway He envisions the two of them days earlier with their backs against the cheap moldy plywood covering the old rickety shed attached to the run down old building Sir called a garage. Rain poured through the so called patched roof that Sir said he fixed three weeks ago. It was difficult to write on damp paper and a dry place to write seemed nowhere to be found. The house was off limits when momma was at work and especially off limits when Sir was trying to sleep so the boys had no choice but to use the shed as their creation station. They had to rearrange old lawnmower motors and bags of beer cans in order to have a small space to work.

Cannon was the designer of the kite that Mitch was going to pilot. They both put their heads together to construct the sleek design. Both of the boys wished they had access to Sir's precious tools in the garage to make life easier but their bruises reminded them that it was off limits. Even the signs on the front door were intimidating. They stated, 'STAY OUT OR DIE', and Sir meant business. The boy's only hope was that they could find enough left over junk in the old shed to complete the project. Two days ago their mother Audra picked up some discarded string out of a garbage can at the tampon factory. She knew about Mitch's project and figured that the boys could put the string to use. She wanted nothing more than to buy Mitch new products to create his school project but Sir prohibited her from doing so and she didn't get paid until the following week.

First Cannon laid the blueprints out on cardboard paper while Mitch made a list of supplies. Cannon's artistic drawing skills really proved impressive on the design of Starburst. After a final decision on the design they both rooted through the old shed out back to obtain all the materials. Cannon used an old linoleum knife to crop the wings out of an old wax covered corrugated cardboard poster of Mario that Sir picked up two years ago in the garbage and tried to pass off as a present to Mitch for his birthday but the food stains on the back gave it away. Cannon cut as much as he could down through the red sections in order to give Starburst some color. The body structure was molded out of old straws that Mitch had packed with Styrofoam to give them strength and stability during flight. With the impressive two by two foot Starburst all assembled they decided on one last important element, waterproofing.

Cannon told Mitch to wait in the shed while he snuck into the house to get something and like a thief in the night Cannon had snuck into the house, down into the basement and returned with a quart of Sir's shellac that he used to coat over little paper baggies of substance that he sold out of his car to people.

"Why do we need to cover Starburst in that stuff Cannon? It stinks like bleach or something." Mitch said in an excited voice.

Cannon held up Starburst and began to paint all long the connection points from the wings to the

cockpit area and especially all over the four string connection points on the bottom.

"T-t-this is t-t-to strengthen and waterproof it
M-M-Mitch." Cannon replied in his usual deep stuttering voice.

The two took turns applying the shellac until Sir's
shellac was all used up. Cannon put the lid on the empty can and handed it to Mitch, "Make sure t-t-that you
h-h-hide this g-g-good or our asses are g-grass. Got it?"

Mitch took the empty quart can and stuffed it deep
into one of the bags of aluminum cans. He was almost
sure that Sir would never check in the bag. The two put
Starburst into a black garbage bag. Rested it on one of
the sheds shelves and turned in for the night.

2

Now it is 11:30 AM on that same April 1st morning
in 1985 and Mitch has Starburst flying sky high. The
bird can barely be seen by mortal eyes. He runs as fast
as his little bow-legged limbs will carry him but the
wind at Starbursts height is picking up fast and when
he can't keep pace he starts to lose control. Mitch is

now running almost out of Cannon's sight. He trots up over a little null rounding further towards the tree line. Starburst is screaming towards the biggest tree in the park. A hundred some year old oak tree named Ben that towers approximately one-hundred feet high or at least that's how all the kids in town viewed it. Dixie Delores Denton or 3-D as everyone nicknamed her was the only tenth grader daring enough to climb its thick limbs. Dixie made it all the way to the top but then had to be rescued by Latrobe Cities rescue fire patrol. Her dad spanked her ass six ways from Sunday so 3-D wasn't so daring anymore. She told everyone in school that her dad had to pay a five hundred dollar fine for her shenanigan. Before anyone could get to know Dixie her dad was deployed to Iraq for operation Morning Star and her mother and she moved to Germany in order to be closer to him.

The trees bark radiated years of abusive torture. The withered lines of abuse scattered all around the truck and up as high as you could see. The veins looked like a series of scattered dead end roads on a map. All over the base were carvings from probably everyone in town. Benny loves Jenny. Mikes a fag or Robs a queer but the worst was Knights are poor white scum. Cannon tried to scratch that carving away but it was just too deep. He often thought that Sir carved it in there with a power tool but it seemed pathetic even for a degenerate of his caliber.

Then from the corner of Cannon's eyes he sees it. "OH NO!" Cannon screamed like a terrified child in a haunted house. His heart skipped several beats as he looks up the road," Oh s-s-s-shit Mitch, o-o-o-oh shit we have to go. M-M-M-Mitch, Mitch come on, "Cannon yells in his grumbling stuttering voice as loud as possible. Cannon grabs Sir's bow saw as he heads towards Mitch. Once Cannon is thirty or so feet from Mitch he points in the direction of Sumner road. And there barely rolling to the stop sign is a muddy primer black colored 1965 Ford Thunderbird. Sir's Thunder Bird. The old 390 big block sounds like shit at idle but once the spark plugs get hot enough the old girl can put power to pavement quick but Sir doesn't take real good care of her. The old boat sounds like a bucket of bolts dropping on pavement as it bounces into several of the two feet deep potholes. Sumner road is the most treacherous stretch of pavement flowing onto Center Street below old man Clyde's house. It stretches all the way up into the ridge for several miles. The rickety road was an old tram road back in the old coal mining era. At the other end of Sumner is Kingston club road that passed through skin hill. Now skin hill is an eerie location that has scattered patches of dead trees and farms all around it. Skin hill is the ultimate party hang-out. Its name tells it all. Young teens and some adultery bound grownups would park in the area to get their rocks off. But that's not all the desecrated place erupted with. One time in June of 1986 local authorities found a rotting corpse of a newborn baby girl in a trash bag. It is believed that the aborted baby suffocated to death in the trash bag. Still to this day her body has not been identified.

Mitch screams," Oh shit Cannon". We have to get the saw back before Sir finds out it is missing". Cannon panting like a dog puts his hand on Mitch's shoulder," ho-ho-hopefully he's too-tot-too drunk to realize it wa-wa- was missing.

Mitch starts to sob a little," I don't want"… He pauses. Wipes away the dripping snot and wipes both eyes on his sleeve, "I don't want a beaten Cannon. I still can't pee right from last week's beaten. You know Sir really has it in for me and I'm afraid that one day he is going to kill one of us. He is an evil bastard."

Cannon lightly smacks Mitch in the back of the head," don't swear damn It. Your gonna to go to Hell on a freight train. You hear me?"

The words came out straight. Cannon never even knew it. When Cannon spoke with passion the stuttering seemed to disappear. Mitch while chewing the fleshy cuticle material above his fingernails shakes his head yes. Cannon in an attempt to contain all composure for Mitch kneels down to keep his knees from chattering together. The brace on Cannon's left leg is almost rattling the screws right out of it. He is kicking all kinds of ideas around in his mind. He knows that if the bow saw isn't returned before Sir sees that it is missing the two of them won't be able to piss for a week and when Sir gets angry he doesn't just give a spanking. Oh no. He delivers an ass whipping like no other. He would pull out his three feet by-one-by twelve inch paddle drilled full of holes and start swinging. It didn't matter where the wood landed as long as hot splintery wood met flesh. Most of the time when he wound up like a professional batter and let it fly the boy's bodies would launch some several feet and then finally after traveling through the air for what seemed to be eternity come to rest into the opposite wall of the room. To this day Cannon still believes that when he was just a tiny baby Sir beat him so bad that his bones grew crooked. The doctors called it Perth-ease disease. This was an abnormality in his hip bone. The x-rays showed a grapefruit like hole in Cannon's left hip bone.

This unfortunate disease landed him in a hideous brace which required a God awful boot to be attached to and it made Cannon feel like a retard and that is just what all the other kids in school called him except Rosalind Banks, Cannon's second love after Grace. Rosalind a beautiful Italian girl with long brunette hair streaming down her back was accepted by Cannon because she too sported an unfortunate handicap as well. As life would have it Rosalind was born with only part of her right arm. From the elbow down was gone and only a stub remained. Cannon was the first boy to ever touch her stub and in return she left him fill up her breast under the bleachers at school. Rosalind was the first alive girl that Cannon ever touched but he often didn't count his encounter with Juniper at the cemetery as being with a real girl because after all she was dead.

Rosalind's family was poor like Cannon's and the only prosthetic they could afford was an oversized adult's prosthetic arm. The fake arm made her look ridiculous but despite her handicap she pressed forward with high spirits and even tried out for the cheerleading squad where she landed the top spot as the fly girl who climbs all the way to the top of the human pyramid and then drops down into the squads arms. The popularity went to her head and she never looked back at Cannon again.

Mitch drops the string from Starbursts forward controls and starts running down into the woods. He didn't care about getting a bad grade in school for not having completed his project on time anymore because a whooping was far worse than bad grades anyway, he thought.

At last Cannon catches up with Mitch in the woods. His body comes to a skidding halt after sliding a few feet down the slick muddy hill.

"Cannon what are we going to do?"

Cannon is gasping for his breath. He can't run like Mitch because the brace holds him back. The doctors told him to keep the metal brackets locked straight but sometimes Cannon would break the rules and release the latch to free the bending abilities of his leg. And once he lets loose the leg will carry him like a gazelle in the wild plains of Africa. He looks at the bow saw and then back at Mitch, "What if we hide the saw?"

Mitch shakes his head. "No way, "he blurts out," Remember the time Sir misplaced the fingernail clippers and blamed the two of us?"

Cannon nodded, "Y-y-yes! My thighs were b-b-b-black and b-b-b-blue for t-t-t- three days."

The fear radiates out of both boys profusely. Cannon's stutter seems to be worse than ever and Mitch knows it no matter how cool Cannon plays it off.

Mitch stands there chewing a different finger than before. His bad habit plagues him with sore fingers constantly. Even to the point that it becomes hard to write sometimes and that is what he enjoys doing. Cannon is biting the numb tip of his tongue. It makes an awkward sound like a toilet being plunged. He always does this when he is nervous. Once he looks up and sees Mitch listening to what he is doing he stops immediately. Cannon doesn't want Mitch to see his fear getting the best of him.

As the dark eats up the light the boys sneak down the wood line closer to the house where they witness Sir pulling his jalopy beside the garage. He exits he car and staggers inside the house as usual.

Cannon looks at Mitch, "M-M-Mitch I think we- we- we- were home f- f- free. Sir J-J-J-just pulled the C-Car up and went I-inside. He is probably trashed as usual."

Mitch is still biting on that same finger. Trickles of blood begin to pour out of one nail so Cannon pulls Mitch's hand away from his mouth.

"Stop chewing your nails Mitch, we are gonna B-B-be ok."

Mitch starts to put his hand back to his mouth until he sees Cannon's face light up.

"Cannon let's stay in the woods tonight."

Cannon grabs Mitch's arm and pulls him up to his feet. They both begin walking towards the house.

3

Cannon pulls up the makeshift garage door as high as the old chains locking it down will let him and then Mitch slides a cinder block underneath it. They make sure that the door will hold as the two find the lowest dip in the ground to slide in through. They push the cinder block out from under the door as they can exit out the side door and lock it when they leave. It slams down with an ear ringing thus. Cannon swiftly puts the bow saw back in its place and heads towards the side door where he sees Sir's big red floor safe with the door hanging wide open. When he leaves the side door and heads to it Mitch grabs his arm, "Don't do it Cannon. We need to get the hell out of here fast before Sir comes down here."

A determined Cannon goes forward pulling Mitch with him until he lets go of his arm.

"Just w-w-watch out the d-d-d-door for Sir M-M-Mitch while I take a l-l-look in here. I see something g-g-glowing that c-c-caught my eye in there.

Cannon wasn't sure what was drawing him towards the safe but it felt right. It felt just as right as a nice warm bath engulfing your body on a cold winter day. That was the same feeling coming over Cannon's body at that moment. He gently opens the safe door wider. He starts to fumble around in it and there in a clear plastic container, he finds a blue glowing titanium vinaigrette with strange engravings all over it with his left hand. He holds it up by the chain to show Mitch, and within a second Mitch was at Cannon's side staring in awe, "What do you think that is Cannon?"

Cannon shrugs his shoulders, opens the vinaigrette and pours the contents into his right hand. A little soft black marble plops out. The two boys look at it in amazement as the glow dissipates. The small ball seemed to roll over to the center of Cannon's palm where just hours ago a crab apple thorn once protruded out from there when he fell to the ground off of the big oak tree after Grace accidentally busted his nose.

Just then a loud crash comes echoing in from outside. It is Sir putting out the trash cans for the garbage. The two twist their heads towards the side door at neck breaking speed to see if Sir is coming in. But after they hear the kitchen screen door slam shut they know that their ok for the time being.

"Put that thing back you numbskull, Mitch says as he turns back to Cannon's hand.

The two boys look back to Cannon's palm to observe what they found and are surprised at the site.

"M-M-Mitch, did you see where that ball rolled t-t-too? It was just h-h-here a second ago."

Mitch shakes his head no and starts to look on the ground for it. Cannon puts the small canister around his neck, gets down on his hand and knees and looks under the 1978 Ford Bronco that Sir has covered with tarps. He pushes back a set of headers and slides an oil pan out of the way to see if it rolled there but it was to no avail. The little black marble was gone.

"Ok Mitch I have an idea. Get me that tube of from Sir's workbench."

Mitch leaps up, grabs the grease and returns to Cannon's position. The grease is slimy and hard to maneuver but as the dirt takes to it the molding process became easier. Mitch watches as Cannon takes a small dab of grease and mixes it with some dirt from the floor to make a perfect little ball. He admires his brother very much.

"I don't know if that will work Cannon. Sir is pretty dumb but that looks nothing like the little marble that you found. And it doesn't glow."

Cannon shrugs again, puts the grease marble back in the vinaigrette, puts it into the clear plastic container and then puts it back in the safe. As Cannon is putting the assembly back to the way it was Mitch grabs a few folders out of the safe and reads the contents. Mitch opens the folder and shows Cannon a picture of their late father Zachary Knight. The two haven't seen a picture of him for years because Sir made their mother burn all of her past memories. Sir told her that the old memories would just force her back into her old suicidal ways.

Mitch pulls a few more papers from the folders and begins to read. He learns how Sir was dishonorably discharged from the Army for accidentally killing their Father and didn't do any time in the brig because he was awarded amnesty for participating in a program known as "Z" a program run by General Hatchet Grounder and funded by D&B corporation..

Mitch looks up at Cannon with tears in his eyes, drops the folders and slides his back up against the old Bronco, leans his head back and closes his eyes. He begins to think about the time a few years back when he was just ten years old when Sir was trying to change the steering box on the old Bronco that the two are leaning against. The weight of the truck over powered the jack and fell onto Sir's skull and when Mitch came around the side of the garage to feed Brutus Sir's dog some table scraps, he found the front pumpkin of the Bronco sitting directly on top of Sir's forehead. The old jack that Clyde next door let him use gave out from the excessive weight as it was under rated and should have only been used on cars not 4 x 4's. It never dawned on Mitch to let someone die because he doesn't have a hateful bone in his body and when he seen the blood coming out from Sir's ears he ran to Clyde's house where they called 911. But after reading the material in the folders on this day he wished that he had left his brains squash out from the weight of the Bronco. He even closed his eyes and could see himself jumping up and down on the Broncos hood until Sirs skull threw up its tiny contents.

Cannon elbows Mitch. He comes back to reality. Cannon could tell by the smile on his face that he was somewhere pleasant.

"W-W-What Mitch, what did you read?"

Cannon grabs the folders to look for himself and the disbelief begins to line his face. An emotion of sadness and hatred takes him completely over as tears begin to form in his eyes. When he gets to the last folder he looks at Mitch with a face of disgust.

"M-M-Mitch we have to pack some clothes and leave this place quick because we are not safe here anymore."

Mitch grabs the folder from Cannon; he looks at the contents inside, "Cannon these are life insurance papers on us aren't they?"

Cannon shakes his head yes, takes the folders from Mitch, stuffs them in the safe, grabs Mitch and drags him out the side door to the house with him

Despite their age difference the two boys are forced to sleep in a bunk bed which takes up three-quarters of their room. The boys stayed in their bedroom until bedtime. Dinner was nowhere to be found as usual since their momma was in the hospital with Sir's demon spawn. Food was a rare commodity around the Blithe residence. All Sir worried about was his beer and drugs. And as long as he kept getting high the boys knew that if they stayed out of his way they were safe. Around eight o'clock or so that night the boys washed their hands and brushed their teeth with their five year old decaying toothbrushes as they always did every night. As they headed to bed Mitch began falling over. Cannon had almost forgotten about Mitch's insulin. Quickly Cannon helps Mitch through the small hallway where he puts him in his bottom bunk, "W-W-Wait here M-M-Mitch I'll see if I can s-scarf up some f-f-f-food and get y-your insulin shot." Cannon heads down the crooked steps trying not to make them squeak and as he gently steps off the bottom step he passes through the hall into the kitchen near the living room. He peaks in and sees Sir pulling a yellow colored substance from a baggy and placing it into a green lizard looking pipe. As he starts rooting around for his zippo lighter Cannon moves on before being seen.

The living room looks like a tornado swept through it. The best words to describe it would be that a landfill through up all over itself repeatedly.

Sir who believes that he is some kind of inventor would get stoned out of his gourd and try to create games or tools that he believed he could sell for a fortune. In his mind he believes that one day he will make it big and get rich quick. His greasy tools are all over the living room floor, a playing card pyramid in the left corner that he, Ralph, Craig and Bob had built on one of their drug infused nights. There are old broken model airplanes on top of an old kerosene heater near the window and piles of shoes that constantly pour out of the coat closet. Sirs old aqua blue stained recliner with silver duct taped arm rests sits in the corner near the crooked dirty steps. The book shelves along the far wall are full of comic books, nonsense fiction and Star Wars figurines. The three horror novels are all King's books.

Sir collected the toys as a boy and always believed that he was a Jedi warrior of some sort. As he and his cronies got drunk they would act out scenes from the movies.

The boys believe that he placed the recliner near the steps so that he could catch them coming down the steps. The puke green carpet is all stained from motor oil when Sir stored his Husky 250 race dirt bike in the living room so the hoodlums up the street wouldn't steal it. Audra the boy's mother opened her mouth about it just once and got told twice to shut up. Her two black and blue eyes proved it. The carpet all around Sirs recliner has cigarette holes burnt in it, food droppings all over and skin clippings from his fingers, hands and feet that looks like snow fell.

The coffee table in the center of the living room and the two matching end stand tables were gifts from Sir's parents Everett and Betsy Blithe. The beautifully constructed stands were constructed with the grainy wood from Myrtle trees out of Jerusalem by a poor carpenter.

And when Everett and Betsy were in Israel they saw the man on his knees in one of the cobble stone roads leading into the city begging for some money to feed his family. Betsy who is like one of King Solomon's daughters out of the Bible that would say, "Bring, Bring," reacted the same way and said," Take, Take," so Everett connived the man out of his hard work, took the stands for next to nothing and then had them shipped to the U.S. When Betsy got tired of them collecting dust in their mansion as she gets tired of everything in the same manner after a short time she had their maid wrap them, ship them to Pennsylvania and then gave them as a wedding present to her son and new daughter in law.

The old T.V that sits upon a plywood shelf against the wall was built by the hands of Sir. After the T.V fell twice he propped it up with two old two by fours and screwed them down with four inch lag bolts. It is an eye sore but it works and that's Sir's motto. "It's ugly but it works," that's what he always says or just plainly uses as an excuse because he is too lazy to do things right. The stands are stacked high in old newspapers and car magazines that will just flow over with the slightest bump.

As Cannon gets closer to the kitchen he hears Sir stirring again so he climbs into the broom closet in the small hallway. Just as he shuts the door Sir comes stampeding down the hall talking to his self. The words are coming out muffled but Cannon still hears what is saying. "Tomorrow is the day boys. Pay day is here. Oh yeah tomorrow has come. Ha-Ha-Ha-Ha," Sir says in a hateful low growl. He beats feet through the small hall, went into the kitchen grabs another six-pack of beer and then staggers back to his stained recliner.

Slowly Cannon opens the broom closet door and peeks out. He can hear Sir cracking open the top of a Keystone Ice beer and guzzling it down. Sir lets out a tremendous burp and then shit his pants while watching Woody wood pecker on the cartoon network. Cannon hears the nagging squeals of Woody talking, "he-h-he, ha-ha-ha," are heard echoing throughout the house. Sir imitates the cartoon and starts hollering like Woody.

Watching T.V was a luxury that the boys are not allowed to join in on unless they hide on the steps and watch the reflection off one of Sir's buck hunting pictures hanging on the wall.

Cannon exits the closet swiftly making his way into the kitchen.

The 60's era lime green tea pot paneling lining the walls is stained with nicotine residue, the matching puke green linoleum is so warn through that the compressed sawdust wood used in all cheap trailers in that day is peeking through. The old kitchen cabinets are constructed out of the same cheap wafer board plywood that Sir used for the T.V entertainment stand. Most of the hinges were used mismatched junk that Sir collected from the local Junk yard. The old electric pink stove covered in food droppings has one burner that actually works when it wants too and the old green refrigerator with the broken freezer door handle is always over freezing leaking water all over the floor.

As Cannon opens the refrigerator door the stench of mildew rushes out nearly crippling his legs. The cold water leaking out of the freezer rolls out wetting his dirty socks. He takes a step back wiggling his toes to regain the warmth in them. The stink of rotting lettuce, moldy fruit and old hot dogs bellows out from underneath several saturated paper plates containing an unknown red oily substance. Between gags Cannon hears the grill lighter clicking again behind him in the living room and then within seconds a scent of burnt plastic infused with kerosene lingers through the air. It invades his nostrils making him choke. He grabs a dirty dishrag from the sink wrapping it around his face twice. He looks like one of those afghan warriors now. The intoxicating fumes make him choke harder as his eyes tear up making it hard to navigate. At that point he knew how hard it was for firefighters to navigate in burning homes.

Cannon can hear Sir taking big gasps from his crack pipe over and over. He remembered that exact smell all too well from the past, a nasty past that he tries to forget often.

A year or so ago he witnessed Sir, Ralph, Craig and Bob smoking the same stinking crack cocaine. He knew what it was because the four idiots told him what it was and how it was made. Ralph, one of the dumbest of Sir's friends got the stuff for doing some mechanical work on one of the local drug dealer's 1968 Mustangs. Every one of Sir's friends is idiots as far as the boys are concerned. That day the four of them got totally stoned and proved it. Ralph grabbed Mitch and Craig grabbed Cannon while the two were coming through the yard after collecting blackberries up on the ridge that day. The men all grabbed handfuls of the berries and gorged them down their throats. The juice was smashed all over their faces. They looked like monsters that ate the viscera of humans out of a horror movie, Cannon thought. The boys screamed kicked trying to get away from the assholes. And unfortunately on that day their mother was down at the grocery store picking up groceries with her WIC card for Sir's demon spawn little Nicky Blithe. They held the boys down while Sir heated his skull ring cherry red with a pair of pliers over the flame of his Zippo lighter and then proceeded to brand them both on their back sides. Sir took the glowing ring and plunged in into Mitch's left ass cheek. The stink of burnt flesh and hair filled the air. Mitch let out a shrieking squeal and then fell to the ground convulsing. Ralph kicked him in his guts laughing hysterically while Mitch curled up on the ground convulsing. When Sir reheated the ring to brand Cannon he abruptly twisted, bit his hand and then pushed Craig down onto the ground. He then jumped to his feet punching Sir square in the balls. Sir crippled up and fell to the ground like a folded up dove shot with a 12 gauge low brass load. He chokes and gasped for air. Ralph let Mitch go and then the three of them kicked Cannon to a bloody pulp.

After a few minutes of rooting around in the refrigerator looking in all of the fridges compartments he finds Mitch's insulin underneath some bad cheese and old bologna. He rinses the slime off of his fingers and insulin vials in the sink, dries off the little vials and puts them in his pants pocket. The food stains made the labels on the vials hard to read so Cannon takes an ink pen from the junk drawers beside the sink and labels the two vials accordingly. He places an L and an R on the faded insulin bottle labels. There are bags in the left kitchen sink drawer beside the junk drawer that are supposed to contain Mitch's insulin syringes but they are empty so Cannon goes outside to look through the trash to see if he can find a used one that can be recycled. He can't understand why there aren't any left because the state welfare pays for all their medical needs. Then he begins to think," Unless that stupid bastard sold them for drug money," Cannon mumbles under his breath.

He is disgustingly overcome with a sickness deep in his stomach. He cramps up feeling like he may need to pinch a loaf. A nasty hot SBD fart slips through his pants. The stench is so ripe that it overcomes the mildew stinking dish rag around his face. He knows that Sir is an asshole but to jeopardize a kid's life is beyond him, or so he thought. He slips outside the kitchen do where rummages through some old spaghetti noodles in the trash where he finds three old syringes that still have the caps over the needle end so he takes them into the kitchen. He cleans the sauce off of them in the sink, dries them and then places them in his back left pants pocket.

He then quietly creeps down the hall to the living room where he peeks in on Sir to see him clipping the skin from his feet with a pair of nail clippers. This is something weird that Sir does when he gets too high on drugs. Even his friends look at it as strange. Thy all freak out when he spits the skin at them. Both of Sir's hands and forearms are pink because of the clipping and both entire feet up to the ankles are the same way. He puts the skin in his mouth, chews it for s bit and then spits it in all directions. The shards of skin are all over his clothes, the floor and his stinking duct taped rabbit slippers. After a few last trimmings Sir's head begins to weave and bob. Then he passes right out on his cigarette burnt infested recliner. His fat peter belly hangs down over his torn green jogging pants. Cannon cringes as he sees his belly button filled with a yellow puss looking substance.

Cannon sneaks in puts out Sir's burning Basic Lights that is hanging out of his left hand about to burn through the duct tape arm rest on his dirty recliner. In the process he finds a half-eaten Twinkie lying in some stale potato chips for Mitch but as he starts to smile darkness comes over him. And as the electrons begin to pop in his brain he begins to think inside his head how easy it would be to kill the dirty fucker right there in his nasty recliner and no one not even his sadistic fucked up mother would miss him. Cannon smiles wide as he looks right up into Sir's face eye to eye with his face. He can see the dirty blue crusty teeth of an asshole that he hates more than anything on the planet. He starts to count the erupting pimples on Sirs face when the pig shits his pants. He literally shits his pants from taking in so many drugs. Cannon's smile reaches from ear to ear showing a glimpse of his mangled tongue lurking behind his sharp teeth as he envisions ripping out Sir's teeth with the same needle nose pliers that he branded his ass cheek with. This feeling of hate feels awesome to Cannon. The power to kill was something that crossed his mind repeatedly when he thought of Sir but right then and there he knew that something has changed inside of him. He tilts his head sideways in a strange fashion rolling it around like trying to pick up a signal from space. And as he tries to fight the urges a voice comes into his mind. It tells him that he is Osiris and that he is in there with a few others waiting to get free. Osiris says that he is now part of him and would always be there to protect him, even unto death. All of this talking in his mind continues as he seems to sit back witnessing his right hand reaching into the end stand drawer beside Sir's recliner to reveal a stainless steel 357 magnum revolver.

Cannon tries to resist by ordering his legs to step back away from Sir but his body is moving forward without his consent. As the adrenaline erupts into his veins he feels unbelievable. For once in his life he feels more powerful than ever. Before he knows what is happening, his thumb pulls back the hammer. The clicking sound seems to echo inside his ears for a second or two. Sweat begins to trickle down his brow as he wiggles the barrel of the gun back and forth into Sir's dirty mouth. The clanking of his rotten teeth against the cold steel almost makes him get an erection. The stink of rot is flowing out around the barrel from Sir's mouth up into Cannon's nostrils as warm saliva is dripping all down over the gun barrel onto his right hand. Sir starts to suck on the barrel. In his passed out state he is trying to take a hit from the barrel. The fluid from Sir's mouth makes him cringe. And then the voice speaks up," Pull the trigger already, end your pain or you will surely die tomorrow. Do it he's sucking for it."

As Cannon starts to pull feeling the pressure from the trigger on his forefinger he hears Mitch calling his name. And abruptly as fast as he went into the madness he returns to his true self.

When he pulls the revolver back out of Sirs mouth a little his eyes open. He stares up at him. Tears begin to pour forth as Sir slowly shakes his head no. His teeth are chattering against the gun barrel. Cannon slowly slides the gun all the way out of his mouth, drops it into his lap and runs upstairs without looking back.

He hopes that Sir is just opening his eyes in a drugged out state as he usually does and won't remember what has just transpired. Hell Cannon hopes that he can forgot as he has never felt that kind of evil come over him before. Then as quietly as possible Cannon tip toes to the upstairs bathroom, roots through the cabinet under the sink to find some alcohol. He sterilizes the inside of one of the syringes, wipes off the top of the type R vial, injects it with air and pulls 3 CC's out to inject into Mitch. He then goes into the boys room, rolls over Mitch, plunges the needle into his left ass cheek, depresses the needle, pats the spot with toilet paper soaked in alcohol and rolls him over to see him, "M-Mitch here eat this T-T-Twinkie and chips so that you don't go into shock."

Mitch scarfs down the food and passes out. He never even flinched from the pinch of the shot as Cannon over time became a great nurse to Mitch. And as he always does Mitch lays there with his eyes wide open. It is a spooky habit that Mitch does but not uncommon.

As Cannon leans closer to Mitch he can see something weird on the white side of his right eye near the pupil. And when he can't get a clear idea of what it is he pulls a magnifying glass from one of Mitch's drawers under his bunk and begins to examine but when he hears clanging downstairs he quickly dismisses it and rolls over. He knows that if Mitch has any kind of pain he will have told him because Mitch is not a person that can tolerate pain well.

Cannon sits there with his back against his sleeping brother. Mitch squirms up against him snoring loudly. He begins reliving the moments in his mind that occurred in the garage earlier and starts to get scared at what has transpired in the living room just minutes ago. He isn't sure why he is hearing voices in his head because it has never happened before. He could remember having thoughts of his own but never heard an actual voice before. And the voice made chills race up his spine. It felt like the reverse of the warmth that he felt while praying in church. Then it dawned on him. The little vinaigrette that they found in Sir's garage had a soft black marble in it. He remembered how the two had though that they dropped it onto the floor.

Cannon puts his right hand up in front of his face to examine it. He can see a small red dot right in the center, as he looks closer a blinking red eyeball appears. Viciously Cannon jumps from Mitch's bunk to his feet in shock but when he looks again the eye is gone. Immediately he dismisses the weird instance, jumps in bed with Mitch falling fast asleep. Cannon's eyes peel open to reveal 3:13 AM on the alarm clock. A warm sensation has overtaken his groin area. Quickly he lifts from the bed thinking that maybe Mitch pissed the bed again but when he feels his underwear are dry he quickly runs into the bathroom. He turns on the light. After all the previous thoughts about the black marble he is afraid to look into his under drawers. Fear takes over. He is scared that his penis will fall off. As he fondles his groin he believes that it has shrunk so he slowly peeks inside. The site that he takes in is horrifying. There staring back at him is a black oily fluid all through his underwear. It's black like motor oil but not stagnant, alive, crawling, moving around in his underwear like some kind of eel or leach. Chills race up and down his spine. He tries to scream but only air comes out. The thought of something alive inside his body makes him feel dirty, infected. Cannon lets the waist band fall back on his stained tight white's. Scared to look again he prays, "Please dear God don't let this be real! Please dear God I'm sorry about the dirty thoughts of Miss. Canary my art teacher, please just let it be gone and I'll-."

He is cut off by the movement in his underwear. Right in this instance he can feel that it is real. The slimy coldness rolled all around his Johnston. And then he thinks about where he and Mitch had been. The pond, the pond where they always catch bullfrogs becomes stagnant but usually not until summer. And then he pulls back his underwear again to take another peek and as fast as he seen the odd black fluid it abruptly crawls back up inside his pee hole. Cannon falls to the floor, pulling, stroking; trying to stop the pain but it is to no effect. It continues. Continues strong, like a glowing sparkler being shoved up inside his penis repeatedly. Like a jagged 20 mm kidney stone trying to pass through your urethra tube eighty mile per hour. But then as fast as it occurs a cool feeling comes over his body. The pain subsides in his groin area but now his brain is throbbing. Apparently as he fell backwards his head smacked against the electric heater mounted to the bathroom floor boards. He pulls on the sink to get to his feet. The mirror reveals a small cut on his forehead. As he inspects closer it appears that a large black hair is protruding from the cut, a wild black hair like that in a big puss filled pimple but before the investigation can resume Cannon's ears capture the loud thuds of feet climbing the upstairs steps. He swiftly darts down the hall, climbs back into bed with Mitch, says his now I lay me down to sleep prayer and doses off.

4

Seven o'clock the next morning the boys awake to the sounds of wrenches clanging with Pink Floyd blasting through the entire neighborhood. The scent of bacon, eggs and toast lingers through the air. It is a strange smell that rarely exists in the Blithe residence. Mitch wonders if it is the boys last supper like how Jesus had his last supper before being crucified by Pilot. For a few seconds he lays there envisioning Cannon and himself being crucified by Sir or his cronies but then he starts to chuckle when he can see Sir dressed in a leather skirt. As he breaks from the thought he pushes Cannon's body out of the way, climbs out of his lower bunk bed and races to the window to see what all of the commotion outside is about. He feels down between his legs realizing that for the first time in weeks he hasn't pissed his pants at all through the night. It makes him fill well for a moment.

He twists his head far to the right to capture a glimpse of the wood line near the park across the street from their house trying to capture a glimpse of the tree that they cut down.

Mitch's crooked red crop cut sticks up in the air like a woodpecker or some type of Indian Mohawk. He seems excited to get up and back to the field where he left Starburst pilot less.

Sir, Ralph, Craig and Bob are all over the old Bronco like ants on an ant hill scurrying for food. They have the hood pulled off from the rest of the body revealing the old blue pray painted 351 Modified that had been rebuilt by Ralph a year ago or so. The entire truck is resting atop cinder blocks as Bob and Craig are working on the brake system lines. Sir or Bruce to his friends is sitting in the front driver's seat of the bronco wiring up his newly purchased stereo system. The stink of burnt plastic rises into the wind as Bruce heats the shrink tube over the speaker wires with his zippo. He is obviously the boss of the gang as it can be seen clearly the way that he barks orders to the other three "Ralph, spray some either down into the carburetor so that we can get this bitch fired up, "Bruce commands," as he pumps the throttle while pulling in on the choke.

"Ok but get ready because this beast is going to scream with those new Holly headers on there," Ralph replies.

The 351 Modified, spits, sputters, and blows flames through the carb from the either. Upon its first initial start the starter can be heard whining for miles but then the beast knocks a little as it awakes from its long dormant slumber, slowly it mellows out to a rough rumble. Clouds of white smoke bellow out from the sides of its exhaust like a dragon right before it catapults fire from its throat. Ralph almost falls off the bumper as he steps back with both hands over his ears.

Bruce continues to throttle the gas pedal to keep the beast from stalling as Ralph jumps back in to tweak the carbs adjustment screws with a flat head screw driver. The motor comes to life at 1300 RPM with a sweet purr. Bruce shuts down the motor. He waves to the other three to come into the garage with him. "Guys let's have a beer or six to celebrate. Hell I couldn't have done any of this without you three," Bruce," states in an excited manner."

Ralph takes a Rolling Rock from the old refrigerator in the garage, cracks the tab, chugs it down in three seconds. "Damn that is good beer," he says. He almost gets a brain freeze.

Bob cracks his can, takes three sips and leans against the old work bench.

"Bruce what is the celebration about here," Bob says," You never splurge on the good beer?"

Craig pounds beer after beer, one by one until he gets a brain freeze as usual. He slips down on top of a 5 gallon bucket awaiting Bruce's reply. If the bucket could talk it would scream from the entire fat sweaty ass forcing it to collapse.

Bruce opens the old safe door, pulls out three folders and holds them up for the guys to see, "Do you three see all these black finger prints all over these folders? The two little bastards defied my rules for the last time. Apparently the two little assholes snuck up in here sometime last night while I was busy. They rummaged all through my shit!"

Bob walks over. Grabs the folders and reads the contents, "These are insurance papers for the boys so what is the big deal if they looked at them? Looks like what, a hundred thousand dollars on each of them if they accidentally kill over?"

Bruce kneels down, accidentally hell,' Sir thinks,' those little fuckers are gonna suffer.' His lazy eye rolls around in its socket trying to find due north.

Craig drags his drunken ass up off the upside down bucket. As he approaches Bob he abruptly falls to the ground face first. On his speeding decent his skull impacts the base of an old drill press. The vice, spindle and bits fall all down over his head in a loud crash. From the ground a pain stricken Craig looks up laughing to reveal a nasty cut atop his right eye. Ralph grabs Craig under the armpits. He lifts Craig to his feet while inspecting the nasty gash above his eye.

"Holy shit man. You might need some stiches man," Ralph says," or possibly a hand job from old Lucy down at that queer bar, the Male-Box club."

Bruce starts laughing hysterically. "Are you alright brother?" Bruce says.

"Holy shit that sounded like a pumpkin smashing into the ground," Bob inserts, "oh yeah, by the way, Lucy's a tranny Craig. Hope that helps your head."

All of them bust out laughing. Craig laughs as well but with a little hesitation. He takes the bottom of his T-shirt, wipes away the blood from his eyebrow. He heads to the fridge. Takes out another beer, plops onto the bucket and starts the process all over again. He begins to think about the whole tranny thing. The way Lucy walks all square, broad shouldered, her neck and how she always wanted anal sex rather than the other. "Oh my God," Craig yelps," say it aint so."

Cannon rolls over, licks his chops to taste the nasty morning paste that lines his mouth then smiles at Mitch with his crooked grin. He pulls himself from the lower bunk as well, looks down at his right palm after thinking about what happened last night and walks to their small bedroom window near Mitch. As he leans on the broken wooden window seal the duct tape holding the window in place cracks putting dust all over his feet. He shakes his feet off and then looks down from the window to see Sir, Ralph, Bob and Craig frantically working on the Red 1978 Bronco. The two boys look on in amazement as Ralph climbs under the hood and Sir fires up the Bronco again. And Just as their excitement for Sir actually completing a project raises they see their neighbor Mr. Fletcher who lives caddy corner from their house and right beside Clyde Strong's run across the street. He hands Sir a piece of paper, says something and points to the wood line near the park just behind the big oak tree. The blaring rock tunes engulfed Mr. Fletcher's voice entirely but Cannon had a pretty good idea that Mr. Fletcher was telling Sir how they cut down the skinny pine tree. Cannon knew that gay bastard couldn't keep his mouth shut. It was like the pervert loved to see the boys get in trouble and Marvin his partner was no better. The two gays were just as bad as Clyde with not being able to keep their noses out of everyone's business or maybe it was just the fact that their house was an eyesore on the street and just about all the other residents wanted Sir gone. His constant neglect from cutting the grass and the trailer falling apart made him an easy target and not to mention that he treated everyone that he met like an asshole.

Cannon's cheeks curl up with a facial expression of eating something rancid, "Mitch I-I- think We-We-were in trouble."

The pasty stench in Cannon's mouth made it difficult to spurt out the words. Mitch's eyes protruded like eggs emerging from a ducks ass, "Do you think Mr. Fletcher told on us?"

Cannon shakes his head, "O-O-oh for sure M-Mitch. Mr. Fletcher is one of the bi-biggest trouble-making as-assholes on this -planet. Re-re-remember the time that our baseball went on his lawn and we saw his partner Marvin hanging upside down naked from the chandelier and Mr. Fletcher was doing something strange to his pecker with a black rubber glove?"

Mitch nods and starts busting out laughing.

Cannon begins again, "that pi-piece of s-shit called the co-cops, which in turn made Sir irate and landed you in the hospital for a day."

Mitch reaches over hugging Cannon with a tight grip. Cannon didn't realize that his stutter was barley acting up despite their potential trouble. The tears in Mitch's eyes showed how sorry he was for coaxing Cannon into getting Starburst down. He knew that Mitch must be scared.

As the boys went to jump into their old duds they find two piles of brand new clothes piled up on their old dresser. There are a few pairs of new Levi's jeans, socks, underwear, and cotton t-shirts. Both boys took turns taking a shower in their old rotted out tub, brushed their teeth, combed their hair, jumped in their new duds and scampered downstairs to see if they hit the lottery or something.

When they get down to the kitchen their momma has two plates full of breakfast and two full glasses of orange juice waiting for them. The two boys wonder what the occasion is but quickly disregarded the thoughts, scarf down their food like two vultures and scamper outside still stuffing they're faces with the warm salty bacon. Cannon savors the honey maple bacon as it has been a long time that his tongue tasted something that delicious. And the sunny sides up eggs were prepared perfectly he thought. To die for even but he never would have entertained that thought in his brain if he knew what was going to happen next. The way the yellow goo sopped up on the perfectly toasted bread almost made him ask for seconds. He wasn't sure why but the food tasted really good, way better than usual.

The volume died down outside as Sir pulls the Bronco into the garage. And as the garage door closes the boy's move faster trying to scram. The two of them aren't sure if Sir knows about the bow saw but they don't want to take any chances anyway.

As Mitch walks through the door he is fiercely ripped to the side of the house by Sir. Before the two of them can comprehend what is happening it is already too late, Sir has a strong hold on Mitch and is in the hot pursuit of delivering some major whoop-ass. Sir covered in oily grease turns his head to show Cannon what the face of a madman looks like as he drags Mitch into the garage.

Abruptly Cannon hobbles to the garage door where Sir has drug Mitch by his neck. The taste of burnt Ford exhaust races into his throat. He chokes for clean air when the sounds of Mitch's head being slammed off the garage walls penetrate his ears. Cannon knows that if he doesn't intervene Mitch will be hurt really bad because the last beaten Sir threw upon them he almost killed Mitch. The doctor said that Mitch's kidneys were bruised after examining his bloody urine sample but of course Sir and their momma falsely accused the livid bruises to a sled riding accident. Guess the doctor thought that snow actually fell in hell. Not in July it doesn't.

Both of the boys knew better than to ever really tell the truth because it backfired one time before. As Cannon sported two black eyes and Mitch sported double hot dog sized fat lips they sat in front of their guidance counselor Mr. Roper and reported the abuse from Sir's hands. The little pamphlet's given out to them in school stated that If you are abused report it to your teachers. You will be protected! Unfortunately the pamphlet did not state in fine print that if your drug addict parents are drug buddies with the teachers your ass is grass. The whole experience was terrible for Mitch and Cannon. The beatings that day after school were the worst in the history of Sir's abuse. Sir's wooden paddle lay busted in three pieces when the punishment ended. The boy's Mother Audra even got a bitch slap to the mouth for trying to interfere. Both boys laid on the tear soaked carpet curled up in the fetal position.

Mitch cried himself unconscious and since Cannon was older he got the man beaten. He was punched profusely in the side of the head, neck and ribs. As the clock struck seven, an hour into the beaten the boy's bruises began to take color. Cannon can remember it as if being there in real time. The boy's momma Audra once again screamed at Sir.

"If you send the boys to school like this we will both go to jail. You shouldn't have gotten so carried away damn it. They are only children."

Sir began swearing uncontrollably," these fucking afterbirths should have been put to death. If you wouldn't have slept with that faggot piece of shit of a man ex-husband of yours and had these two bastards life would be much smoother for us right now."

Audra cried in a hoarse voice, "but they are my blood and tissue Bruce. Why do you hate them so much? They are also part of me."

Sir punched holes in the walls. He freaked out again and threw a coffee table in her direction. The wood smashed and splintered just above her head. "You goofy bitch there not my blood and I told you in the beginning to send them packing with their asshole grandmother."

Cannon sobbed and sobbed on that day in history as he overheard Sir's remarks about him and his father. That was the only time his mother stuck up for him and Mitch and because of that she too would become one of the thousands to die a horrible painful death from the hands of a monster but her time wouldn't come just yet.

Cannon hobbles into the garage doorway where inevitably his face meets the backside of a spade shovel. SMASH!

Cannon's nose explodes worse than when Grace smacked it up at the big oak tree. Blood splatters three feet to each side of him as he plummets to the cold concrete floor. Cannon's sight slowly comes out of blurriness. He witnesses Sir's indomitable actions eradicate Mitch's skull into the concrete. He can see Mitch's eyes rolling into the back of his head. He knows that if he doesn't act now Mitch will surely die or become a vegetable. Cannon pulls his body to his feet. He grabs the shovel from the floor with two hands and swings with every ounce of strength his body contains. The spade slams into the side of Sir's head with a thunderous sound like a cantaloupe squashing against pavement. Meat peeks out from under Sir's scalp. Blood trickles down over his cheek as the immediate sounds of a hundred little drummer boys echo in his ears.

Sir instantly drops to his knees, rolls to his side clasping his hands on one side of his head. Adrenaline sears through Cannon's arteries. It felt so good to finally get this bastard back. It felt just like last night when he put the .357 Magnum into Sirs mouth and now at this very moment in time he wished that he had pulled the trigger. "Come on motherfucker, get up and get some more," Cannon yells. He spins the spade shovel to get a good angle to Sir's neck. He has all intentions of placing the point over his Adams apple and jumping on the shovel head to decapitate Sir but before Cannon can get the spade placed just right Sir Screams like a little girl, "stop him."

Abruptly Cannon's neck explodes with pain. His body twists in a downward spiral toward blackness. As he comes in and out of consciousness he hears the old Ford Bronco start up. Despite all the pain he thinks that the 351 Modified sounds good when he tastes more of the stale burnt exhaust fumes as the engine roars louder.

He begs for his eye lids to open but they fail him miserably. And then as his body is pulled backwards to the Broncos driver side door his right eye peels open ever so slightly against the concrete to reveal only more pain. There on the cold dank floor he watches in horror as Mitch's head is placed under the back tire of the Bronco. Cannon tries to scream but only forces out bloody bubbles of air. As the horror continues his view is blocked by a muddy boot. He tries desperately to raise the eyelid a little farther to capture a full glimpse of these boots. The word Lackey is engraved on a little leather tag above the sole. Cannon can hear Sir barking out orders to Ralph, Craig and Bob. "Ralph put Mitch's head under the right tire, and depress the jack under the rear pumpkin as I hit the throttle a little," Bruce says, "and Bob make sure that the radiator hoses hold."

Ralph drags Mitch's body entirely under the Bronco where he places his head right in front of the Broncos right snow studded tire. He then goes back to start lowering the jack as Sir gives the Bronco a few more RPM's.

Bob walks over to the front of the Bronco waving his hands back and forth repeatedly so Sir lets off the throttle, hits the brakes, puts the Bronco in park and turns off the engine.

"What the fuck Bob? Are we going to do this or what? Do you assholes want to get paid?" Sir yells.

Bob walks over to the driver's side door pointing to the floor. "Bruce if you keep going were all going to die. That shitty rubber fuel line that you clamped on to the existing line is leaking gas all down over those new headers," Bob says, "I'm concerned for my own life now."

Bruce jumps down out of the Bronco's driver seat, runs over to his work bench, grabs a straight screwdriver, stops near Cannon, kicks him in the mouth and then climbs under the Bronco where he quickly fixes the gas leak. He then climbs back up into the Bronco and as he starts the truck Craig walks over and hands him a brown paper bag. Bruce reaches into the bag and pulls out two bottles of cheap whiskey. He hands one to Craig and lays the other beside him on the seat.

"Go back with Ralph and pour this all over Mitch's body, we will douse Cannon when we put him in the seat."

Craig nods. "Bruce are you absolutely sure that this will work because I am not going to do anymore time. I already did two years and I will not go back. I'll die first." Craig says.

"Craig just get it done and then go home. When the cops come none of you will be here. And anyway Sherriff Hunt who is my best friend from a long time ago is going to drive past here in roughly thirty minutes so come on man get your asses moving." Bruce Hollers.

Craig takes the whisky doing exactly what Bruce wants. He wipes his prints off the bottle and smashes it under the wheel near Mitch's limp body. He then exits the side door of the garage sneaking up through the wooded hill to his house.

Bruce starts the Bronco's engine once again, begins pushing on the throttle as Ralph starts lowering the Broncos rear end. Then the boot that had walked off was back in front of Cannon eyesight again. He knows that he will never forget the boot with the tag Lackey on it and the person in them was now on his list. Cannon twists his head to find Mitch but it's difficult to move because his head is pounding, "M-M-Mitch, where's Mitch? I can't see you Mitch. Someone help Mitch. Please help Mitch." Cannon cries out loud but only God can hear him.

Without any warning Bob grabs Cannon by the back of his new shirt. He drags him closer to the Bronco's driver's side door. He sprawls out Cannon's body, places his head in Mitch's direction, wipes the blood out of his eyes and holds open both eyelids for him with his thumb and forefinger to reveal the Bronco rocking back and forth trying to pull over Mitch's head. Cannon smells his Brute cologne all over his fingers. It is a smell he will never forget.

He tries to scream again but only puffs of bubbly air come out through his nose. His consciousness is drifting in and out at a rapid pace. As Cannon's eye wonders he catches a glimpse of Mitch's body quivering as the engine of the Bronco roars erratically and then just as fast as the eyes are opened they slam shut as Bob runs over to put Mitch's body back in place. The visions are cut off and only fragments of sounds can be heard over the revving engine. The tires sound like they were spinning in mud or oil Cannon thinks. Seconds later Cannon is falling into an unconscious state again. He thinks to himself, "It feels like I am floating" and then he is out cold.

When Bruce opened up the throttle too wide Mitch's little body rocketed to the backside of the front wheels of the Bronco. He got wedged up under the radiator shroud. Bob pries his little bloody body out from under the truck with a rake. When he sees Mitch's face he nearly throws up the squirrel stew that his momma prepared that evening. When sour taste rises he quickly forces it back down with a Rolling Rock.

"Hurry up and get him back under there." Bruce yells

"What the fuck do you think I'm doing asshole? It's not easy he's wedged." Bob yells back.

Bob drags Mitch by his left ankle; he places his bloody head back under the tire. He then grabs a piece of the old tarp that was covering the Bronco, wraps it around himself like a raincoat and then sits down on top of Mitch's legs to hold him in place. Mitch doesn't feel anymore. He is not gone but not in his little body either. Some say that he was standing there the whole time with the taker angel Gabriel watching the horror envelope his little body. He is not sad so don't be so for him as he is just a few steps away from eternal happiness.

Cannon can unconsciously hear Mitch letting out blood curdling mumbles but he cannot help his brother this time. He thinks he hears Gabriel or something sounding out. Someone hit him in the head way too hard this time.

Bruce continues to rev the engine as Ralph once again lowers the jack. But this time Bruce put the Bronco tranny into reverse so when the studded tires meet Mitch's face it flips his head into the opposite direction throwing his skin and teeth all over Ralph's clothes. And when Ralph yells, Bruce shut down the Bronco. He then goes into his safe, pulls out the vinaigrette, dumps the makeshift grease marble that Cannon and Mitch made into his left hand and stares at it for a minute. He then walks back to Mitch's body and shoves the little grease marble into Mitch's bloody toothless mouth. He waits for something to happen but it doesn't.

Ralph and Bob join Bruce at his side and watch Mitch's body as well. They all watch like Mitch is going rise like Jesus did or something. They all acted as if a miracle was about to unfold.

"Bruce, are you sure that he is the right one?" Ralph asks.

"Yes of course I think that he has the mark on his right eye like the papers said. Go check Cannon and see what went wrong. Hell who knows how long it's supposed takes anyway." Bruce says.

Bob takes off the tarp and runs over to check Cannon's right eye. "He has no mark on his eye guys. I don't know what's going on here but I'm outta here. You and Ralph can figure it out since he is covered in blood anyway. "Bob blares out.

He checks his leather boots for blood walks out the garages side door and takes the same preplanned path of Craig. Bob reaches Craig's house, jumps in his El-Camino and races to his mother's home in Blairsville. When he sees through the window that his elderly mother is asleep in her rocking chair he peels off all of his clothes out in the back yard, puts them in his burn barrel and lights them on fire. Immediately he runs into the house naked wearing nothing but his boots, showers off the blood spatter on his face, eats a hot pocket and then goes to bed.

Bruce opens Mitch's right eye and sees the mark. He feels it with his finger realizing that it is some kind of metal implant. He then checks Mitch's pulse and realizes that he is dead. The entire episode was a waste, he knows that not only will he not get paid but he will now be tortured and put to death in Cyprus. He sits there in Mitch's blood pondering on what to do next. And then it dawns on him, "Ralph grab me the needle nosed pliers out from the drawer on my work bench quickly." He figures that no one will know the difference. He even kind of thought it would be funny for the assholes underground to try and make something out of old freak show here. It was his duty he thought, after all they had to pay for making him shit his pants when he seen their faces!

Ralph grabs the pliers hands them to Bruce. He dabs Mitch's right eye with an old rag to find the metal mark when he does he grabs it with the pliers and yanks it out. Almost immediately a loud shrilling sound comes out from the metal piece as it begins to glow red hot so he swiftly runs over to Cannon, pulls back his right eye lid and shoves the metal piece into the white part of his eye. The barbed end seemed to accept the flesh sliding right in place. A sizzling sound erupts as the stink of burnt flesh reaches out capturing Bruce's nose. He cringes a little, runs over to Mitch's body and roots through his bloody mouth for the black marble. Once he has the marble in hand he runs back over to Cannon and shoves it down his throat.

Bruce looks at the time on his cheap watch. He motions for Ralph, "Ralph, help me get Cannon into the Driver seat and then you get the hell out of here quick because Harry will be here within the next ten minutes."

The two load Cannon into the driver's side of the Bronco. Sir unscrews the bottle of cheap whiskey dousing Cannon's body with it. He leans back Cannon's head and dumps half down his throat, wipes his prints off the bottle and then throws it onto the passenger side floor of the Bronco. Ralph took off in the same direction as Bob and Craig but made a left up through the woods to his house on High Street. It is a perfect name for a street where Ralph lives because he is always high. Bruce starts the Bronco, drops the tranny into drive, wedges Cannon's foot against the gas pedal, shuts the driver's side door and then goes to the rear of the Bronco where he flat out drops the jack.

The spinning wheel crushes Mitch's chest on impact, it sends his body flying up against the old rickety garage door. And when both wheels hit the concrete the Bronco launches out through the opposite end of the garage wall where it races up through the yard coming to rest when it smashes into a large pine tree that breaks in half and comes down crashing on top of the Bronco's roof. Bruce throws some gasoline on the garage door, lights it with his Zippo and heads into the house to clean up before Harry Hunt the Sherriff arrives. First he stops at the door strips naked, puts all of his clothes and shoes in the wood burner in the corner of the dining room and lights them on fire, he showers real good, jumps in clean clothes and waits for Harry to arrive. And fortunately he does arrive before the whole place burns to the ground.

CH 10 I SEE YOUR BONES (2008)

1

Two-thousand feet below the earth the air is warm pleasant as long as the fans are circulating but the smell is always a bit dank with a hint of saltiness. That is as long as the East corridor waste fans are blowing at full capacity, blowing the stink of rotten corpses out the stack to the top out.

When the skip slams down onto the salt mine floor the Praetorian guards come running from all corridors to investigate the ruckus before them. The sixteen men and women dressed in full Kevlar body armor are armed with the new AR-19's that are designed to fire the plutonium tipped incendiary rounds. They are the same sixteen who surrounded Cannon in the asylum when he was fifteen. The rounds were discontinued by the U.S when NATO signed the treaty for humanitarian rules of warfare that expressed only steel bullets could be used in all warfare.

The Plutocracy in which all of these warriors belong to, live for one true purpose, a code instilled deep within their souls from years of programming and intense training that forces them to succeed in all missions put before them or die trying. You do not join the Plutocracy you are born into it. You are programmed before your body exits the womb. Most are created through a series of experiments through parthenogenesis but those that sometimes are conceived naturally by the elite bloodline are altered before birth by having a series of needle injections into their bodies through their mother's belly to ensure a perfect creation enters the world. These moon children as they are referred to are born premature, weak and able to be programmed the easiest.

As the doors to the skip elevator open a battered U-Haul trailer smashes down onto the mine floor. They can only see the taillights of a jeep. Celeste the top Lupine, a Praetorian guard of the sixth degree starts to verify the license plate through her helmet visor. When the tailgate flips open, Reggie jumps out starts hopping down the south corridor. As he bebop's farther down the corridor like a crippled rabbit all the guards take aim at Reggie. The impact of the Jeep into the skip elevator broke the zip ties on his left wrist when the skip hit the floor he came to it enough to open the Jeep's tailgate and took off trying to run but his extra-large pants fall down around his ankles. And then abruptly Rhonda breaks free, climbs out through the hatch takes off towards the North corridor running full tilt into the darkness.

Half of the Praetorian guards split aim in Rhonda's direction waiting for an order to come from their leader Celeste but as she waits for the control room to provide her with an answer she lowers the boom on Reggie's skinny ass squeezing off a round, a thunderous burst of green smoke exits from her rifle barrel as the green glowing shell rockets towards Reggie. The powerful burst from the rifle pushes Celeste into two other guards. In nanoseconds the powerful round enters into Reggie's back. The round jettisoned like a firefly juiced up on coke screaming through the air at Mach speeds. And before anyone could blink the round detonates in a brilliant bright reddish yellow light that ends in a small mushroom cloud. Reggie looks like a jack-o-lantern as he starts to light up inside he turns to face the guards. They all witness the destruction of the rounds as fire starts spewing out from his nose, eyes and mouth. The aftermath leaves Reggie's body severed into several piles of burning mush. As the REMS start to rise in the corridor an alarm sounds near the elevator as an exhaust fan unleashes a fury of wind that nearly knocks all of the guards to the ground. They all lock their arms together and tighten their stances until the fan shuts down.

Celeste spins to put a bead down on Rhonda as well but the control room chimes in through her helmet and tells her to stand down immediately, that the vehicle belongs to a Reaper in the S.O.G a Plutocracy special intelligence division but to proceed with caution investigating as the vehicle was not to be returned until the next day. So Celeste orders two guards to look inside the Jeep where they find an unconscious Cannon Knight or as he is known to them as Arcane Tact sometimes depending on his time of the month. When they scan his face his identity is confirmed. As they probe his body he goes into cardiac arrest. The blood dripping from his jaw turns black. It rolls all the way down his right arm where it drips into the mouth of Cassandra's decapitated head. The head starts to vibrate. The once pale eyes take a deep green hue. They roll around looking at the guards and when Celeste makes eye contact it takes her back. She grabs the medic T and pulls him away from Cannon's body. "Something is not right her

T," Celeste says," call Dr. Freckle on the radio and get him down here quick."

T is just one of hundreds of thousands of dwellers who live in the mine below normal civilization. T which could be short for Terry, Tommy, Tony or Teddy doesn't matter because the letters or numbers are just slaves to the system of the mine. They all know it. Accept it and don't fight it because the alternative is much worse.

"Control room says that Dr. Freckle is nowhere to be found," T says," His retinal scanner is not responding and the thermal imaging system show no trace of his body down here."

Celeste quickly pulls up the Cyprus entry prioritizing log. It blinks on her screen that an unknown vehicle transporting two unidentified individual life forms traveled up the monorail roughly the same time that Cannon left to retrieve the God particle.

"T something is really wrong here I can feel it. No one enters or exits the City of Cyprus without the control room knowing of it beforehand but here is Cannon's Jeep. Why didn't an alarm sound?"

T takes a sample of Cannon's blood as he jump starts his hear with a deregulator device," Celeste what do you want to do with the moving head? It's looking up at me Celeste."

When she reaches in to grab it by the hair the head tries to bite her. She reacts quickly by pulling back and knocking it on the floor.

Cannon comes back to consciousness. He reaches out to Celeste and drops a little glowing pellet into her hand," Here give this to Cutlass."

But before she can even contemplate her next move Cutlass is already at her side staring down at Cannon. "Give me that damn thing," Cutlass yells as he grabs the small BB sized pellet from Celeste's hand. He holds it up to the light peering through its contents. He turns back to Celeste and T to reveal his dirty smile. He places the particle into his shirt pocket, pulls his radio from his side and begins," This is Cutlass your leader. We are enacting reformation Akathartos 676. The entire city of Cyprus is to be put on lockdown as of 1600 hours. Call all reapers abroad for back to the city for cerebral cleansing, "He puts the radio back into its holster, "Celeste you are to take Cannon to cell 19 with the rest of the Reapers until further notice. And quarantine this vehicle and the hauling container immediately!"

Before she can utter a word the rest of the guards load Cannon onto the conveyor system leading to the prison section of the city. As Cannon is raced away he lifts his head to see Celeste one last time. She sees the movement of his head and realizes that he is ok. He gives her a thumb up gesture. She looks on wondering what exactly he is up to.

2

Nuke the warden of the prison system in Cyprus rips Cannon from the conveyor system and throws him into cell 19 by himself. Cannon sits up; he sees Idle, Melee, Sullen, Crass, Hail, and Roach in the cell beside him," Melee come here please, "Cannon whispers," Melee hurry."

When she kneels down on the opposite side of the bars next to Cannon he reaches through, grabs her face and kisses her hard. As he sucks on her tongue a blue glow can be seen passing from her face to his.

Idle kneels down beside Melee, "Your really going to do this right now while we are all trapped in a cage?" Ivan says.

Cannon opens one eye to see Idle staring at him with his big arms crossed tightly. He tries to pull away but Melee keeps kissing him shoving her little hot tongue in his mouth. He can taste the wasabi on her breath. He speaks to Idle while still kissing Melee. Everyone in the cells around them can hear their lips smacking. Cannon's words come out jumbled but Idle understands them as," Wow your arms look huge. Have you been working out a little harder?"

Idle pulls Melee away from Cannon's face," Yes I have been working out but what the hell is going on here? One minute I'm preparing anal soufflé and the next I'm out cold waking up in this stinking cell with these other twits."

Roach kicks dirt at Idle," Hey who you calling twit?"

Cannon looks up at Roach," Hey your stoma is gone."

Roach points at Cannon," Yeah my voice sounds much sexier now, don't it?"

Cannon and Roach start laughing. Idle shakes his head in disgust as he stands back up to his feet. Melee kneels back down near Cannon," I'm sorry Cannon but they made me do it. I didn't have a choice."

Idle pulls on her shoulder a little bit to see her face. He can tell that something is not right," What are you talking about Melee? Do what? And who made you do what?"

Abruptly Crick walks over to the cells carrying a fire hose. He pulls back the lever blasting Cannon right in the face. The force from the water pushes him into the back of the cell. Crick then turns the hose on the rest of them. Roach being the biggest of them all at 400 pounds takes all of the water force keeping the rest dry. He covers his face to keep his eyes from being ripped out by the waters force. The skin on his face begins to bleed through as Crick rushes in closer.

"Wait," Cannon screams," Crick I have something for you but you better take it before Cutlass kills me or he will take it for himself."

Crick closes the nozzle, he drops the hose on the ground and approaches Cannon's cell," What could you possibly have that I don't? You fool Cutlass has decided to make me a Master Reaper. I am taking my turn in the Graviton in just a few minutes."

Cannon pulls himself to his feet. He wipes the water from his face and walks over to Crick. His wet boots sound like a dying duck. He holds out his right arm.

Crick spits in his face," I already have a watch dick bag."

Cannon depresses a little switch on his watch and the Guardian comes alive swirling around his body," Can your watch do this?"

All the others in the next cell step back. Crick looks on in awe," Why would you give that to me? What's the catch here?"

"No catch here Crick," Cannon says," I just want my last meal before my death in the arena that's all?" The others look at Cannon in disbelief. He can see their face expressions and when Crick turns around to think for a minute Cannon waves at the others to be quiet.

"Well Crick what will it be, food for an unimaginable power or what?"

Crick walks over to Cannon's cell," If it's so powerful than why don't you just escape then?"

"You know that we all have that deuterium based plutonium round lodged in our brains. If any of us try to flee were all dead. Why do you think that every Reaper is on their way back here right now? None of us could ever run and we will always be slaves to the Plutarch's."

Crick strokes the bars on Cannon's cage," Well all of you assholes might but mine was removed when I vowed allegiance to Cutlass."

"That's great Crick! You truly are the best of all of us. I always knew it. So what do you say? Do we have a deal or not?"

"Give it to me and I will bring you whatever you need."

"Now do you think I'm an idiot Crick?" Cannon spins around; he looks at the others with a big smile across his face. He knows that Crick is a dumbass.

Crick looks down at his new boots supplied by Cutlass.

"The answers not down there Crick," Cannon says.

"Hold on a minute I'm thinking here."

Roach lunges at Crick trying to grab him," You little fucker if I get free I'm going to rip your head off and wipe my ass with it after I shit."

Crick pulls his judge from its holster and blasts Roach in the chest. The disks peel up under his flesh. Roach hollers in agony as he falls to the cell floor.

"I have the power out here assholes. No one tells me what to do. Got it," Crick yells.

"Wait, wait Crick please calm down. Please stop," Cannon says.

The anger in Crick's face slowly evaporates. He holsters his Judge," You better get those disks out of your meat Roach because if they detonate it will blow you all to bits."

"Crick, do we have deal or not?" Cannon asks.

"Yes god damn it what the fuck do you want to eat already!"

Cannon uses his mind to guide the guardian around his body at Mach speed," We all want to eat Crick not just me so I'm going to need the turkeys out of the back of that U-Haul I towed down here."

Crick looks on in amazement. The sounds emitting from the sphere are mesmerizing. The others in the cell beside him are amazed as well. Roach even forgets about the pain for a few seconds as the guardian puts off a pink array of light while it is in flight. And then as fast as Cannon launched the guardian in motion he stops it right above his palm. It turns back into a watch on his forearm.

"Ok I want it. I'll be right back." Crick says as he storms off towards the bay area.

Roach hollers again in agony as Idle moves in front of Cannon in the other cell," Why don't you just use that thing to get us out of here?"

"You'll see my pretty!"

"What? Did you hit your damn head?" Idle asks.

3

Crick returns on a six wheeled buggy carrying seven midsized metal cases, 'You must take me for fool Cannon. If there's a turkey in this case I'll shove it right up my ass in front of all of you!"

"That's not necessary Crick," Cannon says," I don't think that any of us would get any pleasure out of that. Would we guys?" He turns to the others. They all say no in unison.

Crick pulls and prods trying to break open one of the cases. When he pulls out his Judge Cannon intervenes," Crick stop. I have the key right here." He holds up a little gold key. He shakes it at Crick as he walks to the front of the cell. When Crick reaches for the key Cannon rips his body into the bars. He then kisses Crick just like he kissed Melee and as Crick shoots three rounds into his chest cavity he still holds on to his face. Melee screams.

After a few seconds they both fall to the ground. Crick is choking holding his throat while Cannon lies on the floor bleeding out. Idle can see the three large holes in Cannon's chest.

Crick pulls himself to his feet. Bloody snot is dripping all down over his Armenian suit. The crew in the cell next to Cannon can see that his eyes are hazed over. Crick turns and walks away in a zombie like state.

"What the hell did you do Cannon, you dumb son of a bitch? Have you gone mad?" Idle says.

Melee reaches for Cannon's hand," You are going to die Cannon unless we get you help. Why did you do this?"

Cannon smiles, he clicks the watch. The Guardian immediately races to and from cutting the cell bars with a laser. Melee runs over to Cannon to try and stop the bleeding. Cannon takes her blood soaked hand and cuts it with a piece of the cell bar metal. She pulls back from the pain but he doesn't let go. When she looks down she sees Cannon's blood now turning a black color entering into her body. Melee falls to the ground convulsing.

Idle rushes to Melee," What is happening here," Idle says," what did you do Cannon?"

Cannon reaches for Idles hand but he pulls away.

"Idle I would never steer you wrong my brother," Cannon says," Now if you want to live you have to lie down in my blood my brother."

Melee stops convulsing and sits straight up. She roots around in her mouth with her tongue for a second and then spits out a capsule into her hand," My God Cannon is this?"

He cuts her off," Yes it is the explosive device but if we don't move quickly none of us will get a moment to enjoy our freedom. And get that thing in some water before it explodes."

Hail, Sullen and Crass both kneel down beside Cannon. They both cut open their hands the same way and the same thing happens to them. When Roach does it the discs expel from his chest and his wounds heal.

"Idle you are the last one my brother." Cannon says.

Idle hesitates for a second but then kneels beside Cannon," What will happen to me? I don't want to become like one of those vampire things like in the movies."

Cannon laughs as he shakes hands with Idle, "You will become number one on the food chain again my brother," Cannon says as they squeeze one another's hands!"

Melee looks on in disbelief as Cannon's wounds are healing. They all watch in horror as his blood crawls back to his body.

"What has happened to you Cannon?" Sullen asks.

"Take this key and open all those cases," Cannon says," I will tell you everything as we prepare for the arena battle."

I have believed, therefore have spoken;
I have been humbled exceedingly.
I said in my excess: Every man is a liar.

PSALM 115: 10-11

CH 11 CYCLOTRON

1

A little ways down the street sirens echoed against the old run down steel buildings in the small town of Latrobe. Latrobe fire rescue arrived to assist Sherriff Hunt. At five o'clock that night the blood from the Blithe residence flowed around thirty or so beer cans, out from the garage, then all the way down the drive-way to finally come to rest at Sheriff Hunts boots. Mitch was pronounced dead at 5:12 PM but then re-vived thirty minutes down the highway. A faint pulse echoed across the cardiac monitor in the ambulance.

The Sheriff explained to Latrobe Post reporters that the boys were in an unfortunate accident while fre-quenting in a binge drinking frenzy. Both parents were at work during the time. There were no witnesses only evidence that points to the older brother Cannon as the culprit as he was behind the wheel while intoxicated.

Mitch's Starburst picked up a gust of wind and tugged at the string holding it back. For a short time the kite swung back and forth between two trees and then finally the glue let loose and Starburst rocketed to Heaven like an angel seeking God. Starburst climbed to the height of an incoming V-shaped flock of geese but somehow miraculously slung past them without a bruise.

2

The next morning the boy's momma went into labor. Sir decided not to tell her about the boy's accident until after her pregnancy was over. He fakes a couple of sobbed tears as he explains to the police about Cannon's violent behaviors. Sherriff Hunt concurred.

Cannon lay unconscious strapped to the rails in a hospital bed secured by police handcuffs. As he slowly comes out of his dream state he faintly hears a doctor tell someone that Mitch's face had been burnt off from the Broncos spinning tires. Most of the bones in his upper torso had been broken and all his guts had shot through his rectum. Mitch could only be identified by his teeth which had to be pulled from the treads on the tires of the car but somehow the EMT's put everything into a bag and was able to get a pulse later down the road.

Cannon partially wakes. His eyes barely peel open to once again peer into the world of reality. He hears a terrifying voice emitting form somewhere but he doesn't see anyone. The voice is strong. It is very dominant. It keeps repeating over and over like a broken record.

"Kill everyone, eat their souls, fuck their eye sockets, "the voice inside his head yells," fuck them all to death." Immediately Cannon lifts his head to see who it is but no one is there. And then it dawns on him. Rushes right in like a bad dream. That voice oh no! It is the same voice that haunted him before he fell asleep last night. It's the same voice that forced his hand to put the .357 Magnum into Sir's mouth. As he squirms to get away from it he feels the cold steel of the handcuffs binding his wrists to the hospital bed that he lies in. The jingles of the cuffs alert Sir who is standing right outside the door with Sherriff Hunt and two Latrobe deputies. Sir stares in at Cannon with hateful eyes, rubs his dirty, steps out of Cannon's site and pulls the door closed on the room.

Cannon's head is in the direction of the bed beside him. As his eyes become clear he sees Mitch's big toes. Those big toes he would notice anywhere," he thinks", only because he was the only one that would clip the toenails for him so that he didn't get ingrown toenails. Cannon always seemed to be the mechanical one while Mitch was the brains of the operations. And it worked. Not all the time, especially when they were younger but now at their ages it worked like a well-oiled machine. Most likely because they were all that each other had. That was until today!

The two brothers are both in the critical condition section of Westmoreland hospital. Cannon can hear Mitch being kept alive by the respiratory breathing machine. He cries. Turns away, tries to remember but his head is cloudy. The evil voice descends to the back of his subconscious mind. He thinks that the voice existed because of his concussion or over powering imagination but it wasn't because it kept lingering inside the corridors of his mind like a nasty cheese laden fart in a hot car. It just keeps annoying. Not as powerful as it once was when it exited the sphincter but raunchy enough to tear up the eyes.

Just then he hears Sir discussing the so called accident in false detail with a doctor. Loud foot stomps can be heard outside the door.

There are police holding back crowds of reporters. Channel 4 news station is trying to catch a glimpse of the action with they're big cameras.

Just then a nurse comes in. She gracefully walks over to Mitch's bed and inspects his monitors. Cannon can see Sir posing, smiling and pointing into his room as he throws down lie after lie. The lies burn his ears. He can feel the blood rushing into his face. The intense heat cooking his brain is almost unbearable. Bright flashy lights begin to drift in and out of his eyesight. In his mind he sees that night when he put the .357 Magnum in Sirs mouth. "Oh dear God why didn't I pull the trigger, "He says," That bastard needed to die, die, die." He lifts from the bed again and tries to glimpse around the curtain blocking his view from Mitch. He can see Sir's brains exploding out from his skull all over their bullshit family portrait on the wall.

"If only my eyes could see through stuff like superman or around corners." He mumbles.

Tears pour forth like two open faucets, "Oh Mitch I'm so sorry my brother. Will you ever forgive me?" As the words slip from Cannon's mouth Sir plops down in the chair beside the bed. He just sits there starring at Cannon. A large smile pulls back his blistered lips to reveal little rotten swords. The front choppers are stained black as all the rest are margarine yellow dripping with some type of food. Sir leans closer. The stink of Copenhagen chew infused with beer on his breath gags Cannon. He immediately turns his head to escape the awful odor. This was the closest that Cannon has ever been to Sirs face. They were never close. Sir hated Mitch and Cannon because they were not created from his loins.

He couldn't understand why his mother was even remotely attracted to such a piece of shit. The man was a waste of air, nothing more than a slump of shit taking up space.

Sir lifts over top of Cannon's face, grabs his head with both hands starring deep into his eyes. "You little motherfucker how did you live, "Sir asks," If you say one word I'll gut your precious momma next. You hear me you little fuck?"

Cannon abruptly pulls his head away. Gains some balls, rises up, head butts Sir in his nose as hard as he can screaming to the top of his lungs without so much as a hint of a stutter.

"Fuck you! You motherfucking piece of no good shit, I will fucking kill you, you killed Mitch motherfucker! You killed Mitch and I will kill you for it." This obviously was not good for the position that Cannon was in. Sir a devious bastard laid out his plan good because now Cannon is just confirming all the lies that Sir told the police. How Cannon was so violent.

Sir flies back against the chair. Blood spews out from both of his nostrils. It pours like an open faucet all down over his shirt. He has never experienced such aggression in either of the boys the entire time that he knew them both.

Cannon can see the fear in his eyes. He likes it the taste in the air evokes an unnatural rage in him.

He lifts, bucks like a wild bronco trying to get free. All he wants to do is get his hands around Sir's neck. He envisions Sir's eyes popping out of their sockets as he squeezes.

When the police rush through the door they witness Cannon going spastic. It seems as if his body levitates off the bed. His arms are convulsing wildly. His legs whip erratically. The monitor above Cannon's head explodes. A surge of sparks fly as glass goes flying several feet out into the hallway. The lights flicker off and on repeatedly. The saline bag begins to boil; another plastic bag melts into a liquid dripping down all over the floor. Sir put his hands over his face as if to block something. The heat turns the palms of his hands beat red. A surge of heat waves begin to melt the hairs on Sir's scruffy goatee. An invisible force forces his body backwards into Mitch's bed. The plug for the respiratory machine keeping Mitch alive is ripped out of the wall. Mitch's bed drifts into the other side of the room. The cardiac monitor goes from a slow bleep to a dead silence. Alarms are echoing all throughout the hospital halls. Within minutes three nurses and Dr. Francis rush in. They swiftly put Mitch's monitors back on but the pulse bleep does not return. As they work frantically to revive Mitch, Dr. Francis peers into Cannon's black fluid filled eyes. What he witnesses is absolute evil at its purest form. Something vomited up from the bowels of the earth. And he knows it as he has witnessed a similar explosive nature from Todd Church a patient that he once treated years ago.

"Doctor, doctor what do we do here," Nurse Betty yells," What's next?" Her voice shrills like a poltergeist hell bent for souls.

Dr. Francis pulls his embedded gaze away from Cannon but not before he sees what he has been searching for his entire career, a search that has haunted him for many years. He quickly puts all attention on Mitch, charges the defibrillator and jump starts Mitch's heart.

When Cannon hears the bleeps of Mitch's heart on the monitor he stops screaming. Dr. Hathaway quickly runs in, shoves a syringe full of Propofol and runs back out of the room as the heat being emitted is too intense to stay but a few moments. At this point Cannon's bed has flipped over onto the floor. The wallpaper in the room has bubbled up, the nurses hair has curled, the two deputies back out of the room from the intense heat emitting from Cannon's body and Dr. Francis smiles.

3

The next morning around 8:00 AM a groggy feeling Cannon wakes inside a ten by ten foot room covered in blue padding. The entire room is padded from the floor to the roof. As he pulls his heavy head from the floor he notices four cameras in each corner, two skylights in the roof that allow a ray of sunshine to peek in. It is the only openings in the room. Even the door is covered in pads. He tries to lift his hand into the rays of the sunshine but quickly realizes that he is restrained. The illusive straight jacket worn by all nut cases," he thinks" and then he begins to remember what happened to Mitch. Cannon pulls up to his knees but then rolls back over. The narcotics coursing through his veins are still keeping him incapacitated. He can hear the lock on the door being disengaged.

In walks Dr. Francis Dix. He is a mid-fifties man that has aged very well. Not too many lines run across his face but he is covered in big red freckles. Looks like thousands of them. His rather large paint brush mustache hides his thin cracked lips. The large mounds of bright red hair around his ears accenting a bald top makes him look like a clown, Cannon thinks," as he begins to chuckle. All he needs is the big red nose.

When Dr. Francis sees Cannon's grin he approaches and kneels right down beside him.

"Do you think I'm funny looking?" Dr. Francis says," Its ok all of my patients think that I look like a circus clown. I am Dr. Francis but if we can be friends you can call me by my nickname." Dr. Francis laughs with him.

Cannon looks down in shame. He fears that Dr. Francis is one of those psychic types that can read minds or see into the future.

"What's your n-n-nickname?" Cannon says.

"You can call me Dr. Freckle."

Cannon starts busting out laughing hysterically. It's difficult to laugh with all the pain bouncing in his mind but it rolls out uncontrolled.

"Call you Dr. F-F-Freckle huh?"

"Why yes. If that is ok with you or you can call me whatever you want." Dr. Freckle moves from a kneeling to a sitting position to get comfortable.

Cannon lifts up to his knees again, peers down with steely cold eyes at the doctor with all seriousness. His stature appears like that of a predator about to destroy its prey.

Cannon can hear the loud thuds of the doctors' heart. He raises his nose if to take in a full nostril of the fear exiting the Freckle's body. He then turns his head in an awkward fashion as if he is listening to someone telling him something.

"What if I call you motherfucker," Cannon says with a deep terrifying voice coming from a dark place," what if I eat your fucking soul doctor?"

Dr. Freckle just sits in the same spot. He tries to keep from showing that his asshole just puckered up. Chills race across his spine as a little pee escapes into his underpants. The heat that Cannon's body emitted the night before has returned but not as intense.

Abruptly Cannon leaps like a cheetah on a gazelle. Freckle falls against the soft padded floor as Cannon's body follows it to the floor. Freckle can tell that he doesn't move like a human but something else. Despite the softness of the blue padding the wind is till shoved from Freckle's lungs immediately. He is dazed, confused to what has just occurred. Freckle chokes, coughs, gags and gaps for air. Cannon is on his chest with his face just centimeters from Freckle's face.

Freckle with both eyes closed shut tries to back crawl away slowly but Cannon moves as he moves. As he opens ones eye he sees that Cannon's face has changed. Both eyes are black now, soulless and empty inside. Both of Freckles eyes pour forth tears.

The doctor's nostrils catch a hint of an ungodly stench of rotten decomposed meat. He can only compare it to stink of his babies decomposing corpse that was found many years ago. Ore his six month old baby was found in the oven. Authorities believed that she had been in there for three weeks. Olivia his wife was found unconscious in the bedroom face down in a pile of her own waste. Their oldest daughter Ivy who was supposed to be taking care of the two disappeared while Freckle was chasing the dream of the Plutocracy. No charges were pressed as nothing could be proved except that the baby was dead. Ivy is still missing. Freckle blames himself for their deaths. He even blames the Plutocracy a little. It was Cutlass's idea to experiment on Ivy even though her blood plasma showed no acceptance to the parasite based serum. And Freckle refused to leave with his daughter in that state but refusal of a direct order is death in the Plutocracy. Freedom is a façade.

As the horrible thoughts enter his mind he falls into a delusional state. The sadness hurts inside. He welcomes death at this point.

Saliva drips from Cannon's mouth as his hot tongue licks across Freckle's cheeks.

"I can taste your fear doctor." Cannon says. He moves his tongue around his teeth," I'm going to eat your fucking pathetic soul Francis Dickhead."

4

"Well it's definitely in him," Cutlass Rush says," better get in there before freckle goes to pieces on us." Cutlass, the Ascended Master controls every move of the Plutocracy. He sees and knows all at all times or so he believes. Cutlass's' big fat ass rarely leaves the emperors quarters but with all the rumors of the beast swirling around the underground he had to come see for himself. Cutlass has seven wives, one for each day of the week and fourteen children.

His chambers are the largest in the underground next to the Livid Mother. The rooms are all lined with gold, jewels, and finest tapestries from Egypt and decorated with skulls from those that lost their lives for the cause of the Plutocracy.

Graham Croaker pushes back away from his desk. "Did you see that thing move sir?" Graham says," It was a blur on the screen and then the doctor was on the ground."

Graham Croaker who has been teased his whole life for his name has never let it beat him down. And in an ironic twist of fate he fell in love because of it. When Lee young a big Sumo who now goes by the alias Hung Young, according to all the people that he ever dated approached Graham with unpleasant remarks Graham fought back. In an unexpected twist of sarcasm Graham told Lee that if he was a graham cracker well then, "just eat me", he said. And well Hung Young did. He gobbled up every ounce of load that Graham could offer. The two have been inseparable ever since and live happily among the thousands of other Plutarch's beneath the surface of the earth. In the Plutocracy religion same sex marriage is accepted. Just about everything is accepted, except not dying for the Plutocracy. All that accept the mark of Pluto will eventually die for the cause.

The Plutocracy religion created by the Greek philosopher Plutarch has led to the development of an underground civilization that has lived parallel to the surface dwellers for thousands of years. The majority of the humans on planet Earth do not know that the Plutarch's exist and the one's that do turn a blind eye to it. And now with the O.I.A "T-4" eugenics program being put into full effect by the governments around the world, the Plutarch's civilization has grown sevenfold. Babies and small children pour into the underground like sewage into the drains. These undesirables bear some type of side effect or disease that the O.I.A scientists could not fix and are disposed of like trash. They are all implanted with a plutonium based explosive compound meant to detonate if they come above ground but mostly used to shorten their life spans.

The Plutarch's have been forced to stay thousands of feet beneath the earth's surface. They use humans for spare organs, blood, meat and slave labor. And that all went on for thousands of years until a recent breakthrough balanced the power, a breakthrough that threatened all of mankind with an unimaginable biblical plague known as Operation Hierarchy. The

Plutocracy has evolved into the beast or also known as big brother like the controllers above on the surface of the planet. The underground council operates within a set of rules like all governments but with a hint of unforeseen corruption to most. On the face it appears to be democracy but in all reality it is a dictatorship ruled by a hint of socialism just like the government on the surface of the planet. There is a leader or referred to as the Livid Mother, who also goes by alias's such as dark whore, black soul eater or wicked bitch by the lower class but it is never said aloud or in public because blasphemy against your leaders is punishable by a term in the true Hell which is the lower catacombs thousands of feet below the mine floor where all of the waste from the Plutarch colonies goes. There is also rumor of thousands of drums of nuclear waste in those same catacombs that supposedly mutilate all of those who get close to them. Mutilation of your family members occurs on camera for all of the Plutarch's to see or they will be killed in your place for your crimes so that you can suffer in eternal agony from their deaths. The Livid Mother has the final say. There is a council that votes and politicians who run for office each year giving the citizens a false hope like the ones on the surface above ground. The Livid Mother sits atop a throne passed down to here through royalty. Corruption is abroad just like every government on the planet. Much of it is fueled by greed. The Plutarch's have their own currency regulated by the high council. The lower class is paid with promise notes while the high council and special organizations are paid with precious gems and gold and of course whatever they keep from their victims on the surface.

There is even a corrupt lottery like the one on the surface, except you do not win currency you win freedom to roam on the surface. If you make it out alive you are awarded a new career, a home and a fresh beginning but you are not allowed to take a surface dweller for a bride or speak of the world below. That is the rules punishable by death! Some love the underground life and embrace it but they have nothing to compare it to as they have never seen real sunshine. The U.V light keeps them alive but vitamin B has to be administered in large doses. There are thousands of interconnecting cities throughout the world thousands of feet below the surface. Most surface dwellers and bottom dwellers refer to the cities below ground as Hell.

But now after all the years of being controlled as a second class citizenship a select few are allowed to roam the surface for small amounts of time and some are even permitted to stay atop indefinitely depending on their actions. Dr. Francis Dix or as all who know him below ground as Dr. Freckle is one of the elite few allowed to roam around above ground but not for pleasure but rather to find the ones who possess the black pearl as it has been classified. Mythical lure shows that some humans for an unknown reason produce a dark matter in the center of the diencephalon, right below the corpus callosum in the brain. It is believed that the spinal fluid constructs the black pearl almost like a clam creates a rare pearl over time.

5

Dr. Freckle has been in exactly the same position before, well not exactly in the same position on the floor but most definitely cornered by one of the most evil creatures ever created but he was a lot younger then, twenty years younger to be exact. He wasn't sure if his heart could handle this kind of stress anymore. In the past he was built for it, even trained to handle anything but now being older he wasn't sure anymore. He even contemplated coaxing Cannon or whatever demon lurked inside him to just take his life.

Cannon pulls up, looks away from Freckle towards the door. Four loud sounds echo out and then all four walls slam to the ground. Dust flies out from under the heavy walls. Cannon's eyes burn. Salt lines both of his lips. And there beneath the swinging padded roof and dust laden fallen walls twenty people stand armed to the hilt with a plethora of strange weapons.

The doctor blinks repeatedly as his eyes start to dry out. He knows exactly what lingers directly in front of him. They all do, especially the ones monitoring the cameras. They have come close before but the readings were never this high. The magnificent specimen before them all has been off the grid for some time. They all have searched for years, even Freckle as he devoted his entire life to finding the one. The one that could bring it all down and here he was locked away in a padded room. And the vessel in which it resided hadn't even the smallest clue.

Freckle musters up the nerve to speak, "Well Cannon if you work with me I will promise on my life to fix Mitch."

Instantly Cannon's face changes, the darkness in his eyes rescind and a smile emits. The heat dissipates immediately. The evil entity that temporarily took control slid back into its hiding place. "Mitch isn't d-d-d-dead?" Cannon speaks in a gentle voice.

From the past incidents with other test subjects Freckle knows that Cannon doesn't even have an inkling of what just occurred. It was told to him by the others that they experience a lapse in time. Even the longest lapses seem to only last seconds to the vessel being controlled and Cannon is no exception. It is like their conversation never missed a beat. Or at least the doctor thought, "No Cannon. He is not. And if we act fast we can save him. But you must keep quiet. Just pretend that he has ascended to Heaven."

Cannon abruptly pulls back away from Freckle's position, "Y-y-your full of s-s-shit, I heard the other doctor's; they said that his g-g-guts came out through h-h-h-his asshole. Nobody lives a-a-a-after that! I know because I've seen it when our dog Thunder got run over."

Cannon drops from his knees, curls up in the fetal position and begins to sob. He begins to remember how Mitch accidentally left the porch screen door open. How Thunder their three year old female German shepherd ran out onto the road after Clyde's black cat Spank.

Cannon squeezes his fists hard. Pain bounces through his head like the chrome ball in a pinball machine. He bucks back and forth; as he looks across the room, he swears that Thunder is standing there. He sees her just as he remembers. She is dragging both legs behind her body. Her entire one side is missing the hide. He can see her ribcage. All her viscera hang out through her asshole. Both eyes are sunk in. Maggots are dripping from her mouth like a small waterfall.

Dr. Freckle scoots closer to Cannon's boy. He puts his hand on his side. Cannon immediately snaps back to reality.

The doctor speaks with a kind voice, a voice with empathy. His words reached Cannon's ears like a finely tuned orchestra, like gold apples strewn over a bed of silver but his lips smack together hard when using the letters T, E, and D like he is mad at them or more like a hater of those particular letters.

"You know Cannon I'm not just your average doctor. I'm a special-"

Cannon immediately cuts him off," What kind of s-s-specialist a-are you?"

"I'm the kind that performs miracles. You know like the stories of Jesus?"

"Y-y-yes I know about J-J-Jesus. You are trying to say that you are God?"

Cannon stirs a little to pull his arms up from the uncomfortable position of the straight jacket limiting his movements. He knows all about false prophets trying to be God. He knows it well because before he came under Sir's rule his momma would drag him to church three days a week after his father's death. Mitch was too young to understand but Cannon absorbed everything. He loved the fact that a God could love everyone. But over time he lost his faith and wondered why such a loving God would allow such an evil bastard like Sir to destroy everything that he loves.

"I can help Mitch but I can't do it without your help. And if you want I can even make that stutter disappear forever. Hell Cannon I can make you a god."

Cannon rolls over. Stares at the doctor and shakes his head, "You can? What d-d-d-do I have to do?"

Now Dr. Freckle has Cannon's undivided attention. He knows that all he has to do is delicately reel the young boy in. Just like leading a lamb to a wonton.

Not only did Cannon want his brother back but he always hated the stutter. Dr. Freckle rolls Cannon over. He loosens the straps on the straight jacket to free Cannon's arms. This gesture alone warms Cannon's feelings towards the doctor but he trusts no one. The one person that he trusted now lies on a bed sucking for life through a plastic tube.

"All you have to do is cooperate with everyone in this institution Cannon and in a short amount of time I will get you released into my personal care."

Cannon shakes his head yes as he pulls his body out of the straightjacket. He moves his arms around in circular motions to lubricate the joints. He looks around to see that the room no longer has walls and there are twenty individuals pointing weapons at him. Cannon can see them all dressed in black, they are all wearing helmets with lit up writing going across the glass face part.

"Can you do this for me Cannon?" Freckle asks.

Cannon stands straight up, wipes the drool from his face, the drool from his awful tongue that always fights him. He knows that there is no hope inside the rubber room. Suicide haunts his every thought. Without Mitch he feels all alone.

"Yes I will do it," Cannon says," but are all those people surrounding us going to kill me?"

Dr. Freckle takes the straightjacket and folds it into a neat pile.

"You have to understand something Cannon. You are destined for great things! You don't know it but you possess a magnificent power inside you. We just have to refine it a little or purify it."

"There's a monster in me isn't there?" Cannon asks," I hear it from time to time. I know that it took over my body for a moment because I couldn't hear myself talking. I could only see myself moving."

Concern comes over Freckles face. He tries to conjure up his words precisely in order to keep Cannon from becoming too frightened. He can see the fear in Cannon's eyes and he knows that if Cannon catches an inkling of what really lies dormant inside his body he may try to kill himself.

Freckle pulls himself to his feet to face Cannon. His knees are clicking and popping as they often do in men of his age. He seems to move stiff like a puppet on strings. All of those aches and pains came from the similar incident to the one that he faces on this day. Accept that incident in the past left hundreds dead. His once promising research facility turned to rubble and the love of his life Olivia paralyzed from the waist down.

He places his palm against Cannon's face. It's hard to show a monster love, especially one that looks at you like food. Slowly his mind pulls up some philosophical bullshit combined with music and Bible quotes.

"Listen my son, follow me and I will give you the power to sit on the throne of the world. I will illuminate your mind!"

Cannon smiles at the doctor. They shake hands like true friends that trust one another. The armed guards stand down and Dr. Freckle escorts Cannon to a dorm like room. As they walk the halls Freckle tells him about the Plutocracy, the S.O.G in which he will lead if he can pass all the tests and training and most importantly the Graviton a particle accelerator known to create the God particle by millions on the planet. Freckle tells Cannon that the machine is of great importance, a machine known as the sword of God that can alter a persons' body to be immortal, as the doctor put it. But first Cannon is told by the doctor that his body must be able to adhere to the molecules graphed to his body by the Cyclotron before even getting close to the Graviton or it won't work.

Dr. Freckle however did not tell Cannon that the reverse side effects would either result in death or worse. And worse is being a steaming pile of flesh incapable of normal living that still thinks and breaths and only takes up space. Almost like ninety percent of the world today.

A glimmer of hope seems to fill Cannon's soul, at least for the moment at hand but that all changes when he meets Big T.

6

Almost a full year has passed. Cannon has become a different person, stronger, more confident, his leg brace is no longer needed and his stutter is gone, except for when he sometimes sees a pretty girl. The entities inside of him are at bay with the frontal lobe inductions. The food is plentiful, he is almost force fed to eat six square meals a day and all the training exercises made him so hungry but the food just didn't seem to hit the spot just right, it didn't seem to satisfy his internal craving, it is a craving that he will come to understand later and maybe even enjoy a little.

Dr. Freckle comes and goes to check on him periodically to ensure that he is on the right path. His brain is injected repeatedly every day throughout the day and his blood is taken constantly to be analyzed. He doesn't understand why. Sometimes so much blood is taken that it leaves him dizzy, almost mentally impaired for a minute. Cannon promised the doctor not to tell anyone about how he will fix Mitch or repair his stutter. He has been through a multitude of classes and different forms of mind control training to cope with the loss of his brother but according to Dr. Freckle the worst is yet to come. But according to the doctor it will make him superior to all others on the planet so Cannon goes on with it. And now it is Sunday April 1986. With all the activities programming his mind he barley thinks of Mitch or that awful night that Sir tried to kill them. Now he is being transferred to a boy's military based academy per the order of Dr. Freckle. The doctor has held up every promise so far and Cannon expected the same with the new training academy but he is scared a little of what to expect.

The mini bus stinks of rotten leather. Cannon sits in the front of the bus behind the driver. He is a really large man with rolls fat spilling down over his belt onto his thighs. All but three teeth remain in his head. Cannon swore that each one of the drivers' eyes pointed in a different direction when he looked at his face but then how could the bus drive straight, Cannon thought. Cannon tries to pull his shirt over his nose because the armpit stink spewing from the bus driver is overwhelming; it is a stink like cooked green peppers mixed with ripe dog shit. It lingers and seems to drift like a cloud throughout the seats. There are three other boys on the left side of the bus and five boys and a girl on the right side with Cannon. On the left side is a little ten year old native Indian boy named Walking Pooch, a very fat Chinese boy named Otis and a big kid named Roach. No one knows his real name because he doesn't talk much. But when he does he sounds like a hoarse robot gagging on oil. Roach is ashamed of his stoma in his neck. When he talks sputum flies everywhere. He is the biggest boy on the bus. Rumor has it that Roach was so insanely crazy about getting high that he huffed a can of gasoline, lit up a cigarette right after and his throat exploded. On the right side behind Cannon is Melee Fracas a thin 15 year old Asian girl, Crick Tingle a 17 year old white Irish boy, Sullen Lascivious a 15 year old weighing at least 250 pounds or more, Crass Swagger a 16 year old boy with a skeleton for a body and Hail Nefarious an African American with a normal body but no age. All of the children on the bus were chosen by the elite bloodlines for training to become S.O.G Reapers. That is if their minds could handle the training.

The drive seemed to go on for a thousand miles or more. Cannon could not stop thinking about Mitch. Where he was or if he was alive or if Freckle was even for real but he had to take a chance. Just a small chance could reunite the two brothers.

After two hours they reach the Elite Kaiser Militarized Reformatory Academy for boys.

It is the home of the legendary cyclotron reactor. Dr. Gordon Bevin who first designed the reactor with the help of several other scientists used it for breeding uranium -238 into weapons grade plutonium -239. The first design the Bevatron named after Dr. Gordon Bevin detonated on three- mile Island years ago but now with all the safety factors implemented into the newest design the Cyclotron and its new purpose the machine operates without a glitch.

When the bus pulls to the front parking lot he sees around fifty boys standing at attention saluting a superior. He did not even have a bit of inkling that this particular day would change his entire being for the rest of his existence on planet earth.

7

Dr. Freckle slipped in through the back door of the boy's reformatory academy undetected by the red bloods watching across the way. He strides into Terry Witt's office. Terry Witt who is a vertically challenged 4'2" excuse for a man is the head of the boy's physical education program. His body is thick, stout and his rather large head rests atop his shoulders with barely a neck holding it. All of his clothes come from the children's sections of stores like Osh Gosh and his shoes have to be special ordered because of his fat webbed toes. He thinks that he runs the entire system with an iron fist but most just laugh at his ridiculous ways. His small man disorder almost entirely rules the way he operates. But despite being a tiny asshole on steroids Terry has produced some of the most talented reapers in history according to the Plutocracy school's history books. Exceptional beasts like Bran Bane.

"Dr. Francis Harry Dix or Freckle dick, which is it these days?" Terry says," What do I owe this pleasure for?"

He speaks with a lisp that almost sounds homosexual. It is hard for his small mouth to push out big words, words longer than three letters. It could be because of his rather large front tooth that only allows him to open his mouth half the distance of a normal person. He is always referred to as buck tooth or dirty tooth behind his back. Terry tries to hide behind his newly created persona known as Big T but all that know Terry realize rather quickly that he is merely a pussy with a high powered position like Johnston. A position unfortunately granted to him by the Livid

Mother for his intelligence gathering on the I.P.C.O. agency taking full sweep across the countries.

In 1981 Terry worked undercover at the Tiny Tosser café In Nevada for a small stint as a midget tossing ball. He lifted a floppy disk from a military general only known as Hatchet at the time while he was being tossed into wooden bowling pins. There were no prizes. It was just a place to get drunk and show off your masculinity.

Dr. Freckle stares through the little man sitting before him. If Freckle could he would kill him right there and end all the dirty rumors.

"Well are you a deaf mute now? What do I owe the gods for this?" Terry says," Hope you have good news for me."

Terry leans back, throws both feet up on his desk and puts his hands behind his head.

"Well get on with it man, tell me what you need."

Dr. Freckle throws an envelope down on Terry's desk. He scrunches his nose as Terry's Stetson cologne overpowers his nostrils then steps back away.

"The name Freckle is only used by my friends underground. And you are not a friend but merely a tool, a disturbing one at that I might add."

Terry puts his right hand down his pants. He strokes himself real quick then sniffs his fingers.

"Oh how I love that smell of sweet ass! We all do what we must Francis. It's just that some of us actually enjoy what we do."

Dr. Freckle shakes his head. He heads for the door. Turns around and points at Terry.

"The instructions are in the envelope. This is the one, the only one that has ever emitted these types of REMS. Don't fuck this up like you did in 1973. The Graviton still bears the scars."

Terry opens the big white letter. He nods his head as he reads down through. He pulls a lighter from his desk drawer, lights the papers on fire and watches them burn slowly before throwing them into his trash can. Freckle waves and walks out the door.

"I got this Francis freckle dick," Terry yells," It's all good.

Terry jumps to his feet and runs out to the front window in the schools hallway to catch a glimpse of the newbies. He rubs his groin again and whispers under his breath," I got this! Oh boy I got this. Look at that fresh meat ooh wee!"

8

One by one the children march off the bus. They all step up to a blue line painted on the pavement near the sidewalk curb. In front of them are small booths with each of their names put on them except Cannon's Name.

They all see a short man wearing a military type uniform approach with four older boys as his entourage. He screams, "get in the booths now pussy's." The other kids run into the booths with their names on them. Cannon stands on the blue line as he does not have a booth to go into. Instead there is a red 55 gallon drum in front of him. "The small man is none other than Terry Wit a red blood degenerate who gets his kicks by bullying young kids. He walks right up in front of Cannon. "Are you deaf son," Terry yells, "Do you need a brail book?"

Cannon shakes his head no as he looks down to see the little man's beady eyes.

"Well which is it bitch you deaf or not because I can't hear the rocks shaking in your skull."

"I'm sorry sir but there is no booth for me to sit in." Cannon replies. Cannon gets a little nervous. He wants to pass the S.O.G test to become a Reaper.

The other kids turn around and snicker. Everyone but Melee, she looks sad with remorse. Crick flips Cannon off as he laughs.

"Turn around, put your face into the viewer headset and listen to what it says you little assholes. Now! And you will all refer to me as Big T not sir or anything else. Got it assholes?"

The viewer starts with a series of flashing lights like on top of a police patrol car and then pictures of bees appear. Then the words don't move flash on and off and then more pictures of bees and so on. This goes on for several minutes

Big T walks to the curb, takes a cane with a serpent's head on one end from the hands of Sean Glass the leader of his four minions and walks back to Cannon's location. Big T nods to Sean and he tips over the 55 gallon drum. Big T swings the cane against the back of Cannon's knees. Cannon's legs buckle and he falls face first to the ground with a loud thud. Swiftly as fast as a sawed off man can leap he perches atop Cannon's back and begins smacking his ass with the cane. "Giddy up, giddy up", he yells. The other kids turn around to see Big T riding Cannon like a horse. When Cannon's head enters the drum Big T whacks him one last time, the four boys pull the drum back to right side up and put the lid on top.

Cannon can hear the older boys screwing down the top of the drum with the locking clamp while Big T beats on the sides of it with the cane. Cannon puts his fingers in his ears to drown out the loud thuds. The ringing in his ears makes him want to scream. And before he can control his mouth it happens. "You fucking midget stop beating the can." Cannon screams.

Instantly a pin could be heard dropping. The four minions and the other kids in the booths chuckle a little. Big T pulls a little remote form his pocket, clicks a button and a glass enclosure confines the kids in the booths. Within a few seconds the kids feel a vibration under their feet. And abruptly their confined space is filled with African killer bees. Melee is the only one to sit still, the rest of the boys jump around screaming like little girls. They are stung hundreds of times all over their entire bodies.

After about five minutes Big T pushes another button on the remote and the entire bee colony drops to the ground dead. The boys are all crying in agony from the bee stings. The glass encasing opens and all the boys fall out onto the sidewalk where a dozen paramedics greet them to cool their wounds and inject them with anti-venom.

Just then Big T instructs the four minions to open the drum holding Cannon. They spill him out onto the parking lot.

"All of you were punished because of this piece of shit lying here before you", Big T yells," now if you want this one time revenge you better get it."

One by one all of the boys run over to Cannon and stomp him into the ground. Big T turns around with his back to the beating going on. He looks at the four minions, laughs and gestures for a smoke from Sean, "When this cigarette is gone you will have to stop."

Seven boys beat Cannon to a mushy banana state. There is blood exiting every orifice of his body. Crick drags Cannon over to the curb behind Big T; he opens his mouth and places it onto the edge of the curb. Cannon can feel the cement scratch against his teeth when Crick pushes down a little on the back of his skull. He wants to run but the beating is the worst that he has ever encountered. The pain is explicit. None of his limbs will work and he can barely open his eyes. The parking lot area looks like someone has just drug a gutted whitetail deer over it.

When Cringe climbs up behind Big T and leaps through the air to jump on Cannon's head Melee catches him by his neck in midstream slamming his head into the pavement. Cringe's head thwarts out a sound like an empty coconut being smacked with a hammer. He lays there with his eyes rolling around in their sockets. Blood spews out from the large crack now residing in the back of his head. Cringe does not make a noise.

Big T spins around to see that his plan only partially worked as all but one took a hatred to Cannon. Melee kneels down and pulls Cannon's face off the curb. Big T steps off the curb onto Cricks' chest. A swoosh sound exits Cricks' mouth as blood forcefully shoots out of his mouth. He then steps onto the parking lot pavement, shoves Melee away from Cannon and points his finger in her face. "Get this little slant eyed twat out of here," Big T screamed," take her to the kill box now."

9

Cannon and Melee are side by side in two small metal spheres hoisted twenty feet in the air by a mobile crane out in the middle of a large muddy field. They both are able see one another and their surroundings as the spheres are constructed of a series of welded metal bands all intertwined to form a precise ball. The field looks like a cross between an X games stadium and a monster truck track. The field appears to be like an obstacle course with high dirt ramps', whip tee do's and mud pits. At each end of the field are two goal nets like the ones used for soccer games.

"What's your name?" Melee asks. Her Asian and broken English voice is like the sound of an angels trumpet, Cannon thinks.

Cannon still dazed from the beating pulls himself up higher in the small sphere so that he can see her face. Her loving actions made him think of Grace. His eyes are damn near beat shut so he uses his fingers to pull back his eyelids to see. Her face is beautiful, dark black hair accents her cheeks, she is thin but toned.

"My birth name is Cannon Knight," he says," but after today I'm not so sure anymore."

Melee reaches through the spaces in her sphere and touches Cannon's hand. He looks up trying to smile with his battered lips.

"Do you believe in God Cannon?"

He tightens his grip on her fingers and she replies back with a little squeeze.

"I believe that every man is a liar and I-"

Cannon is cut off with the loud sounds of engines revving. Both kids look on in horror as they see two monster truck like vehicles racing towards them.

Despite the situation Cannon starts to sprout a Johnston. He doesn't know if it's her face, her voice her touch or the sense of death about to engulf the two or what. He thought at one point that maybe sporting a boner was his type of radar or something.

As the trucks rapidly approach the mechanism keeping the balls hoisted in the air releases. Melee starts to hyperventilate.

"Don't worry Melee it's all a trick," Cannon yells," You will see. His voice trails off as he rolls farther away from Melees location. He can see her bouncing around inside her sphere.

When Melee sees that Cannon has gripped the steel bands with his hands to hold his body in place as he rolls down the hill she follows suit.

The two small spheres containing the two kids drop to the ground. Both Melee and Cannon bounce several feet into the air. They scream as there spheres are rolling down the hill towards the monster trucks. The whites of their eyes can be seen from an orbiting satellite revolving around earth. Mud flies into both of their faces. It was the first time that either of them ate grass.

10

"Hey Ryan get your ass over here," Felicia Rose hollers," there about to drop in on us."

Felicia Rose is the lead technician supervising the Cyclotron program.

The Cyclotron machine is a twenty foot round sphere constructed from heavy grade nuclear grade stainless steel with aircraft titanium support columns anchoring it to the floor. The center of the machine is designed to accept the little banded spheres that Cannon and Melee are encased in.   The Cyclotron is powered with a non-unity rare earth magnet power generator.

According to Dr. Bevin the original creator of the Cyclotron, the machine spins to Mach-3, sends a magnetic field through its patients and that wave washes the brain instantly.

The encephalin released in the body from the brain helps to center the black pearl above the spinal column.

And the encephalin is released from pain being induced to the body.

Ryan runs over to the control monitor. He depresses the switch for the wash unit; a loud shrilling echo can be heard throughout the big room housing the Cyclotron. Two clear tubs full of water lift up forty feet right below two large holes below the ceiling. A red flashing light spins out on the wall near the Cyclotron as an alarm buzzes with loud pulses. The hole on the right opens and the sphere containing Cannon drops out of the ceiling into the water tub.

"How long does he soak before we release?" Ryan asks.

Felicia walks over, depresses the drop button and turns to look back out the control room window facing the Cyclotron. "Just dunk and release," Felicia says," if you overdo it they drown." She pushes the big red run button on the control panel forcing the Cyclotron non-unity reactor to fire up. Two F-16 fighter jet turbines facing opposite directions from each other fire their afterburners forcing a piston controlled mechanism to launch the huge rare earth magnets in a clockwise spin around an extremely large magneto with additional rare earth magnets that face out with the same polar force to repel one another. In theory the magnets are like a maglev-train that spins against one another riding on charged air. Arcs of electricity being generated can be seen fluttering out from within millions of strands of four inch round copper cables wrapping around the rectifier rolling around the center rotor of the unit. Two large twelve inch cables running from the positive and negative side of the magneto run across the floor to the Cyclotron to feed its hungry appetite. Once the magnets take off spinning around on their own magnetic waves the jet turbines reduce their speed and eventually shut down. The non-unity reactor is racing around making sound like worn out brake pads screeching against warped rotors.

Cannon's sphere drops out of the liquid falling right into the center of the Cyclotron. He sees Melee's sphere drop into a holding position right above him. She screams as her eyes capture the Cyclotron firing up. Her ear drums ring as her hair stands straight up from the static electricity rushing through the atmosphere.

"Cannon, Cannon I'm scared." Melee screams.

The kids see six alternating metallic bands around the sphere spinning faster and faster in all directions. The perfectly balanced bands rotate so fast that they look like a solid sphere.

As the Cyclotron reaches full Mach speeds around Cannon's sphere a wave of energy rushes through his body. A bright blue flash explodes all throughout the area around the machine.

Felicia and Ryan put on dark U.V goggles to protect their eyes. Melee looks away from the light. She can feel the energy resonating all around her. She can taste a metallic taste in her mouth as the feelings in her teeth seem to loose. Instantly a feeling of nirvana takes over Cannon's mind. He feels numb, tingly and then nothing. Cannon passes into a bent reality where he knows no one, not even himself or the past in which he lives.

"Ryan, don't stop the Cyclotron yet, "Felicia says," Big T wants to take this reaper to the next level.

"But Felicia we all were told to never go past Mach -3."

Felicia walks over to Ryan. She stares him in the eyes just inches from his face. He can smell her blush painted on her cheeks. The scent reminds him of his mother as she wore the same type of makeup. Felicia gently pushes Ryan out of the way with little resistance, then pushes the lever on the Cyclotron speed to Mach-4 and then onto Mach-5 the max setting. The entire building starts shaking. The Cyclotron feels like it is coming apart. Rivets from the structure back themselves out of their homes. The once bright blue flash turns to a fiery red, a bright green and then black.

"Oh my god Felicia I think that you opened a wormhole of some type."

Cannon's body seems to disappear and reappear repeatedly.

"Your right Ryan I have never seen this before. We better stop."

"Has this ever been done before Felicia?" Ryan reacts," I don't want to get in trouble. And I definitely am not going to Hell, I will kill myself first!"

Felicia tries to pull the lever back to the zero setting but it doesn't budge.

"Help me Ryan it's jammed."

Ryan grabs the lever with Felicia as they both try to pull it down but it won't budge.

"Listen you better get Big T on the phone because if we lose another kid today we both are in deep shit."

Felicia runs across the room, she dials Big T's office. "Terry we need you down here in the Cyclotron room fast. I did what you told-."

Felicia looks at Ryan with a face of disgust. Ryan can see that something is wrong.

"Well what did he say Felicia? Well come on with it before we all die here."

"Asshole hung up on me."

"Well dial him back. We need help because this thing is coming apart."

Melee shakes in here sphere cage; she has never seen anything as frightening in her life. There is nowhere to go but into the light. She realizes that her life is about to end, she intertwines her fingers like two crabs, just like she had been taught by her mother for fifteen years and begins to pray," please Plutonius with your mighty fire rise up and save us. May the fire of Hades reach into my soul and illuminate me."

Melee looks down to see Cannon's body morphing into something but she can't tell what as the light flashing blinds her eyes repeatedly.

What the technicians do not realize is that Cannon was never a chosen one. It was supposed to be Mitch all along. They haven't a clue that Cannon opened the vinaigrette absorbing its contents a little over a year before arriving to their installation. An evil content so feared by the ancients that it was placed in a sarcophagus with an 80 ton lid and then dropped into the deepest darkest depths of the ocean. Somehow over the thousands of years throughout time the sarcophagus washed into the shores off of the coast of Oman or Sohar beach to be exact. The exact spot where Cannon's grandfather used an underwater charge to break open the lid and smuggle its contents back to the states where it now lives within the brain of a young Cannon. An identical sarcophagus was found in the old Murphy salt mine near Pittsburgh PA where the majority of the Plutarch's reside. It was encased in a wall of the purest crystal salt. Not even a quarter of its contents survived but what was found was injected into the Livid Mother.

All of the other children were run through the Cyclotron several hours before Melee and Cannon. One by one they all were tortured and then exposed to the Cyclotron for brain washing. When the Cyclotron reached Mach 2 the Indian boy known as Little Pooch started to glow a fiery red and then his head exploded. Little Pooch is no more.

11

An hour has passed and the Cyclotron is still cranking at Mach-5. It is the longest that the machine has ever been run in the entire history of the Monarch program. Maintenance workers in aluminum heat suits from are inside the machine room trying to cool the entire unit down with fire houses. Everything is wet. Steam is pouring into every corridor throughout the facility. The heat intensity is extreme.

In the control room every warning light on the board is blinking like a Christmas tree during light up night at one of those, drive through winter attractions in one of the colder states. Abruptly a thirteen inch chunk of rare earth magnet smashes into the control room windows. Big T, Ryan and Felicia jump back.

"What the fuck are you two idiots doing," Big T yells," why did you leave it on for so long?"

Felicia puts her hand on Big T's shoulder. He spins, knocks her hand away and smashes her foot with one of his thick healed Harley boots. Felicia falls on to the ground sobbing.

"You dumb twat I told you to turn it up and back It off quick not make the kid into tapioca."

Ryan walks over to Felicia and helps her off the floor. Big T pulls and pulls on the speed control but it will not budge. His little fingers can barely wrap around the adult sized lever.

Cannon wakes from the voice Osiris in his head. He looks above and sees Melee staring back at him. She puts her shaking hand against the metal sphere containing her body. Cannon can feel that it is a loving gesture. She is crying profusely. He sees the fear in her eyes so he smiles and puts his finger to his lips with a gesture of be quiet, it's a secret. She is put at ease a little and returns a no teeth smile.

The heat intensity of the area around the Cyclotron is reaching extreme temperatures. Two maintenance workers pass out, fall onto the floor engulfing in flames before anyone can rescue them their bodies. The six inch thick bullet proof windows wrapping around the control room start melting. Big T looks out through the scorched windows to see Cannon starring right back at him. He sees Cannon's eyes glowing a bright red. Big T grabs at his throat. He feels a hot liquid dripping down his face. When he wipes his face while looking at it his fingers he sees them covered in blood. He looks back out to see Cannon but it's no longer Cannon it is a black creature with a lot of teeth. It smiles wide for Big T. Licks its chops and starts to tear apart the small sphere that once contained Cannon's body.

"Whatever that thing is or if it's still Cannon Knight I don't care but I'm gone," Big T says," that abomination is what's keeping the Cyclotron in motion not us."

"What do you mean," Ryan replies," Let me see."

They all stare out the burned windows. It's now almost impossible to see.

"The heat must be affecting your eyes Terry, Felicia says," because I see the same sixteen year old kid that came into the shop."

Big T seems to dig up a little compassion as he pulls Felicia and Ryan to the door and pushes them through it. He turns back for the last time and again sees the beast starring back at him. It is gnashing its huge jaws at the metal sphere trying to break free. As it pulls the metal sparks fly from the rings connecting with its flesh. They all hear noises like chalk scraping against a chalk board only magnified 10,000 times. The sounds make them grit their teeth.

Cannon changes back raising his hand in the air with his palm towards Melee. He makes a push gesture in the air. The round gate above her sphere opens and she catapults up through the drain pipe in which she first came. The sphere seemed to fly through the air like it was being piloted. It comes to rest on the merry go round in Legion keener Park near downtown Latrobe. The metal banded sphere sparks all around Melee, it splits in two and she exits out of it. She falls to her knees crying; starts gagging and a type of cable falls out of her mouth. Blood, phlegm and spaghetti could be tasted in her throat as it comes out. She pulls on the cable until about two feet came up from here stomach and with a loud pop sound the device attached to the end of it comes out. It wiggles crawling across the ground as if it is alive. Melee rolls on the ground gasping, trying to gain her breath. She can hear a voice telling her to get up and run. And with all she can muster she does. She runs as fast as her battered legs will carry her and within a few minutes a loud explosion sweeps through the kids swing area sending chunks of treated wood clean to Main Street. A sliding board crashes into a tree two feet from her position. She turns to see an enormous blue glow erupting up into the sky a few miles from where she now stands. Melee sees a dark creature appear, disappear and reappear over and over again as she waits to die. When the thoughts of what it really is enters her mind she remembers the fairy tales that her grandmother told her about a soul eating demon named Deciduae she quickly dismisses the nonsense and run never looking back.

12

Monday morning at 10:00 AM Mitch's cardiac monitor reveals a straight line. There is no more pulse in Mitch's chest. Cutlass Rush is standing beside the bed with the respirator chord in his hand. Dr. Freckle tries to plead with him to plug it back in because Mitch is the only leverage that they have to keep Cannon in control. The doctor knows that without Mitch all of their lives are in danger. "Cutlass you have to plug the machine back in", Freckle pleads," or we are all dead.

Cutlass throws the chord on the floor and points at the doctor.

"You dumb son of a bitch did you watch the video from last night's catastrophe? Do you want two of these fucking monsters running around?" Cutlass screams.

Cutlass rants and raves throwing his hands in the air. As he stomps around his boots squeak against the tile floor. It sounds like a baby duck begging for food.

"I did not see the video Cutlass. I don't have any free time while running around for the Plutocracy." Freckle says.

"Are you speaking blasphemy against your government doctor? I can have you join your project here if you like!"

"What I meant was that I'm so busy sir, that's all."

Dr. Freckle hates this bastard with a fiery hatred. If he could he would dispose of him. Just like he sent Freckle's brother to Hell a few years ago for disagreeing what beer had the best taste. The doctor thinks of his brother often and feels that if the Plutocracy could ever be overthrown than he would enter the lower catacombs himself and bring back his brother. That was if he was still alive. His brother Alex wasn't built for fighting and he knew that there were beasts of men down there in the pit of no return. He knew because he had put some of them down there himself when he was a guard before becoming a doctor.

A particular beast by the name of Daryl Bass was the one most feared by the entire underworld. At six foot eight 396 pounds it took six normal guys to stop him. The whole incident sparked the genetic enhancement program for the Praetorian guards and the development of the special weapons unit known as the S.O.G. Daryl was the only man to come back from the catacombs known to the Plutarch's as Hell thousands of feet under the City of Cyprus floor where all the degenerates reside.

"Freckle this is the second lab that you destroyed and the last one. The Cyclotron took years to construct. And the last time we made a special arrangement with the surface dwellers so that they could utilize the machine as well. Your special warrior program is now dead in the water."

"There was no reason for this to happen. Felicia said that Terry told her to ramp it up to Mach-5. My god man that's unheard of-"

"Don't blame Terry for your fucking mistakes Freckle. This was all you! The fucking explosion measured on the Richter scale. Thank Plutonius that the machine was partially underground and miles away from everything."

Cutlass pulls an envelope full of photos from his pocket. He shoves them in Freckle's face.

"Do you know how hard this is to cover up? And now a monster runs free!"

"How many people have to die by your hands Freckle, hundreds last time, maybe more this time?" When will it be enough?"

Dr. Freckle fumbles through the photos. His face of disgust paints a crystal clear picture.

"Are all of their hearts missing Cutlass?" Freckle asks softly.

"Yes doctor. What does it matter?"

The doctor holds up two of the photos to show Cutlass.

"Well Cutlass we didn't even get Cannon into the Graviton and the beast has already emerged so you better call upon every favor at your disposal to find this kid or mankind as we know it will be wiped out. And not only mankind but everything with a soul."

"What do you mean wiped out Freckle?"

"As it reads in biblical times the hybrids were bred from demons by ancient druids to rid the world of undesirables."

Cutlass rips the photos out of Freckle's hands and heads towards the door.

"Biblical smiblical, your old wives tales are bullshit! My grandmother told me the same shit when I was a little boy to scare me into being good. The Dragon can never come back I was there when they all died off of the surface thousands of years ago."

Cutlass had no idea that in a short amount of time, he would have to eat those exact words.

Dr. Freckle walks over to Mitch's bedside. As Cutlass turns his back and instructs the guards at the door to destroy the boy's body. Swiftly Freckle injects Mitch's neck with 10 CC's of Cannon's blood.

Mitch is gasping for air, barely breathing without assistance. His face has been sewn back together with skin grafts from his thighs and buttocks. His guts were put back together as best as they could be with a few parts missing. Just like when you built projects with the old erector sets, it looked good and functioned ok but a few parts were always left over. That's how Mitch was put back together but at least he wasn't completely helpless like humpty dumpty.

He looks nothing like the once cute kid that ran the hills behind Wilson Street. And as Freckle was escorted out of the room by the guards Mitch stopped breathing.

13

Starburst sliced through the sky and then dived like an arctic drop of freezing rain towards Latrobe's outer limits. Once the kite steadied itself several hundred feet above the city limit's a half hour after takeoff, a slight glimpse of the moons radiant rays peered upon earth. Mitch's pain had ended.

Starburst thrust upward, then rocketed to the left, then fiercely to the right and then finally through the thick black clouds floating abroad on that April night. The kite did not crash again: the two boys designed it flawless. No one knows what had ever become of Starburst, if anything at all. It's possible that Starburst is still up there flying around the skies and may fly around there for eternity, like a magic carpet from an old fable. The only thing for certain is that Starburst was still flying perfectly as it descended passed the limits of Latrobe, Pennsylvania, and out of this novel indefinitely.

CH 12 ILLUMINATION CONFIRMED

1

The time is 10:13AM on Monday morning. The Plutocracy has every Reaper on the missing boy case. They have even shared the search with local authorities to speed up the process. Not one person has come forth to reveal Cannon's position. The S.O.G could not use the Monarch protocol to force him back in as the system network deployment protocol was destroyed before the programs could be installed into Cannon's brain and his heat signature couldn't be picked up by their satellite Zeus to detect his heat signature because all of Cannon's test results were destroyed in the explosion as well.

Sherriff Hunter immediately drives to Sir's place. He tells him about Cannon missing but reveals nothing about how it came to be. Sir agreed to keep Cannon occupied until he or the S.O.G came to collect him.

2

Saturday nights weren't much to brag about in the town of Latrobe, especially on Laveen Street where a small church resides amongst the many small houses on the outskirts of the city. Outside the red brick church was a lit up sign that said,' **from invisible things, visible things might be made**: Romans 1:20

Cannon crawls around in the dark on the basement floor of the church. Unconsciously he wondered all the way from the experimental site to the church. He rolls over to stare up at the ceiling. A multitude of visions torment his mind. The taste in his mouth is rancid. He can feel a thick crust lining the outside of his lips. Slowly he pulls up and crawls through the dark trying to navigate through the unknown room. As he crawls towards an exit side illuminating the wall he falls five feet down over a set of stairs and onto a tile floor. The thud sounded like steak being softened by a tenderizing hammer before being fried. Cannon moaned as pain seared through his chest. He gasps for air but it evades him. The darkness below seems to swallow up the little bit of red light that is illuminating his path. When he rolls to his left to assess the damage a motion light illuminates above a door that displays janitor's closet on a small placard. Cannon pulls himself to his feet, opens the door and goes inside. Once inside he falls down to his knees again, he crawls to a toilet behind a shelf of cleaning supplies where he places his face in the bull and begins gorging himself like a dog. His stomach starts roaring. His ribs began to crack, bulging from the inside out. Cannon screams from the pain erupting through his body as his joints spin in their sockets. He heaves repeatedly until vomit expels out from inside him. Cannon projectile vomits all over the entire little room. The stench is awful as it burns his nose tremendously. He can see blood all over his arms as he looks down into the piles of puke. As he moves his hands around he can see teeth, eyes, pieces of flesh and hair all through the substance that just exited his body. When he pulls a gold tooth from the pile of stench he examines it closer and then upchucks again. He thinks that the entire fiasco is a dream or trick from Freckle. Exhausted beyond belief Cannon falls into the mess passing back out. For the moment the world is safe from the monster lurking within.

3

Sunday morning at 5:00 AM Richard Tickle's phone blares out a beautiful melody. He rolls to the empty side of his bed where his once beloved wife Becky used to sleep. He slowly picks up the receiver. "Hello, He says.

On the other end an old but sweet southern voice comes across," Dick, hey its Delores have you prepared the monologue for Pastor Branch this morning?" This always came out of Delores's mouth but sounding more like smorning.

Richard rolls back over. The phone slides off the nightstand crashing to the floor.

"Yes Delores the writing is all done," Richard says," It is always done the night before like I have been doing for the last five years." He rolls his tongue to reveal no teeth. Quickly he reaches over to the other nightstand, pulls his false teeth from a little glass of water and plops them in. The taste of lemon Alka-Seltzer bubbles on the roof of his mouth.

"What did you say Dick? I couldn't understand you. Let me turn up my hearing aid"

Richard pulls the phone away from his ear as a blaring buzz comes through the receiver. This was the same old routine that Delores put Richard through every morning for the last five years. He thought at one point that he was living a life like that Groundhog Day movie because every Sunday it's the same. Dick this and Dick that. Oh how he hated being called Dick. He often times wondered if his parents were trying to pull an evil prank on him for calling him Richard. Everyone knew that the nickname for Richard was Dick and his own fathers name was George. The only person that he ever addressed by that name was the mail man that delivered mail to his parents address on Saturdays. Mr. Brown who occasionally attends the very same church makes it a point to shake his hand. Who in their right mind would allow their kid to be called Dick Tickle?

"I said it is all done Delores. The writing is done I said. Did you hear me this time?"

Delores pulls the phone away from her ear; she readjusts the hearing aid and then proceeds.

"Ok Dick I heard you that time. Well that's really good. Good indeed! I hear that the pastor has something special in store for us all today. Do you know what it is?

"No Delores I don't know." Richard tries to be sweet with the old lady but sometimes she makes it so difficult.

He had no inkling that when he volunteered through the church group to help her by driving her to get groceries that it would be a trip but he needed to get out of the house before he started to think about putting extension cord around his neck again. He closes his eyes for a second. The sixth bottle of Robitussin really put him down he thought but it still didn't do the trick. As he ponders the idea about putting the cord around Delores's neck the receiver blurts out again.

"Dick are you there?"

"Yes Delores what can I do for you?"

Delores takes a sip of her coffee. She swashes the warm liquid around her mouth for a second and spits out a little white object that looks like a maggot in her hand. When she realizes that Tookey her cockatiel was just perched nearby she starts to think.

"Oh my God Dick hold on Tookey pooped in my coffee mug again."

"Are you ok Delores?"

Dolores starts gagging. Her top false teeth fly out from her mouth right into her famous fruit bowl salad that she makes every Sunday for the congregation.

"Evertin awk k Duck me teefs frew ot my moth agan. Gimme tan seconts plez."

Even though the sounds came out all twisted Richard understood her. The same occurrence happened just about every Sunday, everything except the Tookey poop. He knew that she said," Everything is ok Dick, my teeth flew from my mouth again, give me ten seconds please." It was pretty close to the same phrase all the other times before. All but one, the time when Scratch her Siamese cat defecated in her Cheerios Delores accidentally said the word shit. But when Richard joked about it she just looked on with a stern face and ignored what he said. She quickly changed the subject all together. Despite everything he liked Delores somewhat. He supposed that she went to church every day to pray for her gay son Sherry. The only part that irked him a little was that she would only put change or maybe even a dollar into the donation basket when she had hundreds of thousands in the bank. Sherry who was once called Vincent Hooper wrote a few books on proper makeup application. Once he became a millionaire he and his boyfriend Rufus Adcock moved to California where they run a medical marijuana clinic and raise Tulips in L.A somewhere. Delores thought that everyone in the congregation was blind to her son's actions but when Chad Hussey told everyone that he and Vincent sword fought with boners in the boys showers after gym class word spread like wildfire.

And everyone knew that Chad was as gay as a three dollar bill because Nurse Eloise Cohen was on duty when Chad's mother brought him into the ER to get Smurfette removed from his rectum, Doctor Francis who was on duty at the time asked Chad if he should look for Poppa Smurf up there too. Chad explained to the entire hospital that he slipped and fell onto his Smurf collection when he came out of the shower in the nude and that's how it got lodged in his anus.

"Ok Dick I'm back. That dang Tookey pooped all over the kitchen again."

Richard puts his hand over his mouth. He holds back the laughter. He thinks at least Delores makes him smile but it's hard to smile after you've lost someone that you love more than your own life. And when the O.I.A came to them with a glimpse of hope they believed in hope. That glimpse of hope turned to a nightmare when Becky's body turned completely blue and she lost her mind. Sure her heart condition disappeared but she rapidly lost her mind. And after three months of screaming at the top of her lungs she died from a brain aneurism. Richard unfortunately had to settle for a measly eyed hundred thousand dollars to cover all the hospital bills that his shitty insurance carrier wouldn't cover. And then because Becky tried the experimental treatment her life insurance refused to pay for her death so instead of a beautiful burial arrangement he had to stuff his beloved wife in a jar. What a fucked up bullshit system, 'Richard thought as he stared at the red vase on the nightstand on her side of the bed, 'all your life you pay these asshole scam artists and when you need it most they all fail you. And then as all the hatred built up inside him again a darker thought entered his mind. An evil thought of revenge began to unravel as he lay there listening to Delores breath out from her mucus filled lungs and while staring at his now dead wife's remains stuffed in a jar.

"Delores I have to go. I'll pick you up at 7:30 AM.

Before Delores could respond Richard hung up the phone.

4

At 8:00 AM it's the same ritual as every Sunday. Pastor Branch starts with a sermon on how Jesus Christ will one day rise again and then all the dead will rise from their graves to be judged as well. He then proceeds on to light fancy candles while the congregation and choir sing.

Richard thinks,' How the fuck does someone who is now a pile of ashes rise to be judged. Give me a fucking break false prophet.' He reaches inside of his jacket and flips a switch that starts blinking. He can still smell the diesel fuel lingering past the twenty peach tree air fresheners that he taped to the three inch pipes underneath his jacket. Richard looks around to see if the executives from the O.I.A and Dangle buildings are there. He notices that most were present except General Grounder. Damn it he says under his breath. Grounder is who he wanted the most. But then he see Poyang sitting there dangling his little legs over the edge of the pew. An evil smile comes across Richards face.

"God bless each and every one of you sitting here this morning," Pastor Branch says through his microphone," does anyone wish to come up, kneel down and pray with me?

Delores nudges Richard in the side. A loud metallic clanging sound echoed out. She rubs her elbow with her other hand. He looks at her with a mean look, gets up, walks down to the knee rest below the alter where he kneels before the pastor. Pastor Branch looks down at Richard quickly realizing that something is not right but he proceeds.

"My lambs Jesus will once again rise. Be aware of your sins and repent."

The pastor thought that it was extremely warm out to be wearing a heavy trench coat and most times Richard always checked his coat at the door but before the pastor could say anything Cannon comes walking up from the steps completely nude. Richard looks up, quickly puts the detonator back in his pocket and stands up. The whole congregation just sits there in silence. No one can believe their eyes. A pin could be heard dropping. When Cannon's eyes meet Richards his mind unconsciously activates. It was like he could smell something not right and all in one swift motion Cannon grabs Richard, rips his beating heart from his chest and throws him like a rag doll forty feet up towards the ceiling. Cannon moves like lightning. Some aren't even sure if they believe what they are seeing. It's like a dream or something. Cannon unknowingly drifts into the confession booth door blasting it into splinters. The congregation doesn't even realize what has just happened until Richard explodes above their heads. Everyone is covered in Richard's thick bloody viscera. The once bright white church walls are painted a dripping crimson red. Pastor Branch's once white robe looks like one of those splatter artist's paintings. When he picks one of Richard's eyelids off his cheek he throws it down and runs into the other side of the confession booth that Cannon is in. And once in there he witnesses Cannon watching everyone run out the door while he's eating Richard's cold heart until it is gone. He then regurgitates the meat back up all over his body like a snake does after they absorb their prey contents. Cannon growls like a hungry dog over his bowl. After the purge he licks the blood from his fingers. He screams like a gobbler being screwed by a poltergeist. The sounds are so ear piercing that everyone covers their ears as they swiftly exit the church. Pastor Branch covers his ears as he urinates a little in his underwear. When the screaming ends he reaches to his chest to feel the scars from a similar encounter that has forever haunted him for all of these years. The little girl's fingers burnt right through his robe and into his chest.

Delores tries to pull herself down the walkway between the pews but big fat ass Wendy Whipple plows her down knocking poor Delores to the floor. Sixty-five people had trampled upon Delores like an old piece of worn out carpet that day before she was found by authorities. Her hazy left eyeball had to be removed from Wendy's shoe. She was the only one to die on that dreadful day other than Richard, the rest survived. Some were peppered with PVC from the shrapnel coming from the bomb. Others were embedded with fragments of Richards bones and teeth. That morning Richard downloaded the Anarchists cookbook that taught him how to make explosives. The first two attempts failed when he tried to boil bleach to make C-4 but on this day the recipe all came together for him but left his body in pieces.

5

The next day Pastor Branch met with all the news agencies and authorities but he couldn't wait to get back to the enigma sleeping in one of the spare rooms in the church. When he is asked about a naked boy running through the church he tells the authorities that everyone must have been hallucinating from the explosion. That he was just preaching about Jesus's return when the bomb went off and how could a boy throw a man some forty feet in the air,' he replied to them all. Pastor Branch knew that telling a lie was a sin but he knew that God would forgive him. He knew that he must investigate what had just happened in his church. Especially because this was not the first kid to wonder into his church naked all covered in blood. He knew that right around the time of the Crackle-wood acres massacre a young girl with the last name of Dix came in the same way but on that day he was alone. The church sermon was cancelled because of a bomb threat.

6

Cannon steps out of the shower. He stares into the mirror above the sink. "Who am I," He says. And before he can blink his face contorts his eyes glow green and a voice echoes in his skull, "As soon as I am freed all will bow down," the voice says," many will die." Cannon backs away from the sink. The glow in his eyes reduces leaving him temporarily blinded. His hands are shaking. It's the same voce he heard in his head and the same voice screaming when they strapped him in the machine.

He tries to keep his hands from shaking while putting some toothpaste on an Oral B toothbrush that the pastor gave him. When he tries to screw the cap back on the fingernail on his right hand index finger pulls off. It is hanging there by a thread of flesh so he pulls it all the way off to reveal another dark colored nail beneath it. His mind begins to race. He starts to hyperventilate as he drops to his knees. The toothbrush goes flying near the toilet. His eyes get hazy all over again.

And then all his memories come racing back. Cannon remembers what happened to Mitch, the hatefulness of Sir and the lies of Dr. Freckle. He cries in the palms of his hands. The sadness hurts his heart but then he gets angry smashing his fist up through the porcelain sink. Three more of his fingernails tear loose so he rips them away too. One by one he rips all of his nails off. He starts to remember the experiment. The Cyclotron as the technicians called it. Melee he says in his head. Where did she go I wonder? He pulls himself to the mirror again and begins rubbing his eye to see if something is in it. When he rubs back and forth his right retina peels off in his fingers pulling a small metal device with it. Cannon trembles in horror as he looks down at the piece of his right eye in the sink base. His mind detonates into fragments of wonder. He doesn't understand what is happening to his body. As he starts to rub the left eye a sharp pain resonates up through the center of his body. He arches over top the sink trying not to puke. As the pain subsides he pulls the flesh from the left eye. His vision is extremely clear now. It seems to have become more vividly colorful from what he remembers it from. When he turns and looks down he can see an outline of people through the wood floor. Cannon blinks repeatedly trying to understand what is happening to him and then it dawns on him. It hits him in the face like a freight train on steroids. The doctors words he thought, oh yes doctor Freckle. "I will make you a god," the doctor said. The words seem to give him a slight understanding. When he runs a small comb through his hair the sharp edges dig in and as he pulls down half of his scalp rips off. He stands there staring down at the bloody piece of flesh with his hair attached. It looked just like the scalps that the Indians used to take from cowboys on those old western films he thought. Fear shoots through his mind. He thinks about cancer or viruses. He doesn't know what to do because no one is around to help. And it's not entirely painful which is really strange. It feels kind of good, almost like scratching an itch or rubbing off peeling skin from bad sunburn but the smell is horrendous he thinks. He picks up a small mirror from the back of the toilet to inspect the back of his head. The mirror reveals bloody blond hair just beneath the flesh that he ripped from the top of his head. He jumps back in the shower and this time he sheds his flesh like a snake. He scrubs his face with a washrag. Huge hunks of bloody flesh peel from his face. All of the skin lies in a pile at the back of the tub. Cannon stares down at the pile in awe wondering what the hell has just happened to him. He dries off and jumps out of the shower for a second time. When he stares into the mirror this time he sees a new person looking back at him. One eye is green and the other is all black with no retina, his hair is blond and his skin is flawless.

Cannon smiles at the mirror and sees that blackness has also invaded his teeth. He sticks out his tongue to reveal a black mark right in the center. He quickly picks the toothbrush up off the floor and starts trying to brush away the blackness form his tongue but it will not go away. He realizes that his tongue looks normal now to except for the black stuff on it. Cannon scrubs repeatedly and on the fourth attempt he knocks out one of his front teeth. "Oh my God," he says," just what the hell is happening to me?" When he bites down to see just how bad it looks four more teeth fall into the sink. He spits blood out by the mouthfuls. His tongue seemed to shed its flesh as well. One by one he pulls out all of his teeth just like his fingernails. Cannon washes his mouth until the blood is gone. He gathers all of the teeth and fingernails stuffing them into the jeans pocket that the pastor went out and purchased for him at Wally World. The cheap Chinese slave labored jeans fit pretty well. He throws on his shirt, socks, sneakers and walks down the back way to the pastor's quarters where he waits until Pastor Branch is done being interrogated.

Abruptly two O.I.A agents barge through the door. Cannon turns around to see them. They flip out their badges. The taller of the two kneels down pulls out a small device the size of a cell phone and scans Cannon's right eye. He looks up at the other agent and says," It is not the boy we are looking for." His voice sounds like a robot Cannon thinks. The two agents spin around, exit the pastors' quarters and leave the church.

Just then Pastor Branch comes in. "Are you ok my son," he says," I'm sorry about those two men I didn't have any choice. They are the new ordained law around these parts now."

"Yes I am fine Sir. The men did nothing to me," Cannon says," but after we are through here would you be so kind to give me a ride home?"

Pastor Branch puts his left hand on Cannon's shoulder and reads out of the bible from the left hand. A few words in and the heat from Cannon's shoulder becomes unbearable to touch so the pastor quickly pulls away. The bible starts to smolder so he drops it to the ground and jumps on it. "Oh my Lord, please forgive me for defiling the great book." Pastor Branch says.

The pastor looks over Cannon. He is trying to rationalize what exactly is sitting in his office.

"What is your name son?"

"My name," Cannon says," I have so many, little horn, Beelzebub, anointed cherub, Illuminated one, Legion, Serpent, Gentry Faust, I could go on forever."

Pastor Branch steps back against the wall. The heat coming off Cannon's body is overwhelming. He reaches behind his back to find the exit in case he has to run. His hands are trembling. Even though the being in front of him just mumbled a few ordinary words he can feel pure evil exuding from within it. The pastor felt the same kind of evil ten years ago when he helped two Catholic priests perform an exorcism on an infant. It was an exorcism that left one priest blind and an infant deformed.

Pastor Branch notices that the boy doesn't blink. His cold eyes just stare at him like a piece of meat. Cannon hears the pastor's heart beating irregular. He smells the air and starts to twirl his head in an odd fashion, "Listen priest I'm just kidding, would you relax before you have a heart attack? Let us go out into the confession booth and do this the right way."

Pastor Branch still stands stiff against the wall.

"Seriously I'm not the devil. Just joking but you should have seen your face when I said that though. It was priceless!" God it would make a great MasterCard moment, he thought.

Pastor Branch nods in acceptance. Cannon nods back.

"So how about that ride home priest?"

The two exit the church, enter Pastor Branch's Prius and head to Wilson Street to the Blithe residence

7

When the two reach Cannon's house he can't believe his eyes. The shitty run down trailer that once wobbled on stilts is no longer there. Now a $250,000 dollar mansion has been erected in its place. A mansion to redneck hill folk that live in Pennsylvania! An extremely large garage is attached where the old one used to be. Cannon looks at Pastor Branch, "Forget any of this ever happened and never speak of it priest. Do you understand what I'm saying?" Cannon looks at the priest and the beast tries to stretch through the skin on his face.

Pastor Branch pulls all the way away from Cannon up against the driver's side door. He feels a little bit of warm urine exit his private area like before, "Wait, before you go take these. And God bless you son" He hands him a set of black and red rosary beads with a small cross attached to it and a small travel bible. He feels that he may have just come face to face with the devil itself. Cannon takes the gifts, exits the car and heads to the newly constructed house.

8

Sir never knew that Cannon was standing there watching his every move like a predator waiting to attack. After Sir sucks in a long drag from his crack pipe like a cock slobbering whore in an alley way for a dollar Cannon creeps into the living room where he stabs about twelve CCS's of a Brompton concoction that he created out of household products. The mixture contains some of Mitch's left over insulin, Drano and windshield washer fluid. Well the concoction wasn't supposed to contain Drano but Cannon wanted to put his own twist on it. Besides he wanted this bastard to feel some of the pain that he and Mitch had felt for the years under his dictatorship. Almost instantly Sir is convulsing. Cannon hopes that he doesn't kill him too soon. He wasn't sure if he did until Sir's eyes crack open a little and he begins swearing, "You little motherfucker what did you do to me? I'll kill you, you little son of a bitch. When my legs wake up I'm gonna beat you like I used to beat that little bitch brother of yours."

And then he burst out laughing uncontrollably from the drugs that he smoked earlier. Cannon can smell the same burnt plastic scent coming off his breath from the cooked crack cocaine. That was enough for Cannon. He went to the bathroom and painted his face like a demon on a playing card that Mitch gave him before he died. Mitch loved the angels and demon cards when they played because he seemed to always win with it when a grueling game of war ensued. With the grayish blue face paint and the blood red tears painted on Cannon heads back to the living room. The new luxurious living room contains all the amenities that anyone could ever dream of. He stared at the monstrous television wishing life could have been normal for them all.

Sir is still lying incapacitated on the floor. It seems like all Sir had control of was his big mouth now. When Sir spins his neck around seeing Cannon painted as a demon he starts laughing again. He laughs so hard that he cries until Cannon kneels down and looks him right in the eyes. Sir spits in Cannon's face. He laughs even harder. "What are you gonna do now little bitch, aye?" he rumbles with his French, Canadian hillbilly accent.

Cannon never says a word. He just grabs Sir by one foot and drags him to the garage where he plans to eviscerate the bastard. Sir is screaming again, "Where the fuck are you taking me? What are you doin you little asshole. You better stop this shit now and I mean it."

Cannon pulls Sir all the way down the hallway to the garage side door. There wasn't always a door on this part of the house and there definitely wasn't much of a garage attached until Mitch died. It seemed while Cannon was at boot camp Sir and his momma ran out to put a lot more insurance on Mitch while he lay in the hospital comatose and knowing this bullshit just fuels Cannon's anger that much more. As Cannon drags Sir through the door down a couple of steps he hears Sir's head pounding against the steps as he pulls him all the way down to the garage floor. The sounds are like a bat smashing against a pumpkin. Still despite the slamming of Sir's brain it didn't shut his mouth. He keeps cussing all the way to his doom. He has no idea that this night is the last night he will physically be on planet earth or the fact that his once scared step son will wear his tongue as a necklace. There are a lot of I'm gonna kill you's and Fuck you slurs but Cannon has heard it for almost twelve years now. At this point every sound is drowned out by his thought of how he can make this motherfucker suffer the most in the shortest amount of time. He knows that it is only a matter of time before the Plutocracy comes looking for him. Once in the garage Cannon walks over putting power to Sir's CD player. Quiet Riot comes on echoing throughout, "were not gonna take it, oh no we aint gonna take, were not gonna take it anymore." Cannon who is now engulfed in the lyrics bobs his head to the tunes, 'he thinks,' how ironic; Oh no he isn't going to take it anymore after tonight. Sir tries screaming over the music, "shut that shit off you little dickhead. That's not music. It's just noise, garbage to my ears. I don't want to hear anymore."

Without a blink of an eye Cannon pulls a slender but short Craftsman screwdriver from Sir's tool box and shoves it right into his right ear. It makes a popping sound like when you pop a blown up balloon under your foot. Sir lets out a yelp like Bruno when Cannon fixed him. And by fixing him he shoved an air hose down the dogs' throat, turned on the air compressor and watched him pop. He got beat for the Alpo being blasted on the Thunderbird.

Sir's eyes bug out of his head with his face turning beat red. He lies their like a constipated baby stuck on its back. Cannon leaves the screwdriver in his ear while watching the blood pour from his ruptured ear drum. He chose a shorter screwdriver because he didn't want to penetrate Sir's puny brain. And besides he wanted him fully capable of feeling all the pain he was going to inflict. By now Sir begins quivering and twisting a bit. Cannon knows that he doesn't have much time to restrain him so he pushes everything off the work bench and throws Sir's body atop it. First he goes around the table and opens up all the vices in each corner real wide. Sir tries shaking his head to remove the screwdriver from his ear but fails miserably. First Cannon pulls Sir's left wrist into the left vice. He bends his fingers forward arching the wrist so the teeth on the vice will get a good bite. He then tightens them down. The handle on the vice flips around squeaking a she turns it repeatedly. Sir is now screaming nonstop. It seems a little louder this time. It might be because the screwdriver muffles his hearing a bit or maybe because when Cannon puts the final twist on the vice Sir's wrist cracks taking the shape of the vice jaws. Shortly after the first hand is restrained Cannon places Sirs other hand into the second vice. This time he twists Sir's four fingers into an awkward position while cranking them down tightly. Once steel teeth hits flesh Sir is off again whining like a dying siren on an ambulance. Two, three then finally four cranks extra, Cannon had to make sure Sir wouldn't get free because once the fun began he knew that Sir's body would starts viciously twisting. It would almost have too for what he was about to do. The fourth turn on the vise may have been too much because midway through Sir's pointer finger pukes out all its contents like a squashed grape onto the vice jaws. Cannon wipes the blood particles off from under his chin. He licks it to taste what an asshole tastes like and then quickly spits it on the floor before he turns into one. He smiles a little.

Sir screams hysterically with snot pouring form his nose. Cannon takes each of Sirs ankles into his hands. He easily snaps each one of them placing them into the vices sideways too. Sir bucks up and down hollering in pain. Cannon steps back laughing as he thinks that Sir looks like he's doing the backwards worm like break dancers do on TV. After a few minutes he leaps up on top of Sirs chest staring into his face. Cannon rolls his head in circles as he picks up the sounds of Osiris racing to his ears. He can smell the fear exiting Sirs soul. Sir can see that something has happened to the young Cannon. He quickly realizes that the boy that he once knew is no longer present. With that little bit of sense he tries to plead with him," Listen Cannon I know that sometimes I was a bastard but it was for your own good. I just wanted to make you tough that's all you know." Cannon just keeps moving his head in circles as if he is trying to physically chase something down in his head and then all of a sudden he seems to have found it. Sir stares at Cannon as he keeps his head turned towards the wall with his eyes closed. It is like someone or something is telling him a secret and when he turns back to face Sir his eyes are glowing red. His face starts elongating turning black with teeth protruding everywhere. It is like something is trying to break through his skin. Sir screams and screams in horror as he pisses and shits his pants simultaneously. And then viciously the creature inside the once young loving boy Cannon bites off half of Sir's face, Sir can't scream anymore because he only has half of a mouth. All that can be heard is light whimpers. The whole left half of his face is now in Cannon's stomach. His brain is exposed, damaged more than usual bleeding all down over the table. As the creature positions to take another bite pounding on the garage door brings Cannon back into the drivers' seat forcing the creature to retreat back where it came from but not for too long.

"Bruce are you in there," Sheriff Hunt hollers," If your banging that young Adams girl up the street put some clothes on and save some for me." The Sherriff starts laughing as he walks in the door. Craig and Frank are with him. They burst out laughing too. When the three of them see Sir with his face ripped off and his body contorted in the vices they react. Sherriff hunt draws his Smith & Wesson .38 special +P, Craig grabs a crowbar and Frank pulls out a switchblade and clicks it open with a snapping sound. The three of them crouch low and ready themselves for battle.

"Frank I could give you a citation for that," Sherriff Hunt says," That thing is twelve inches long or more."

Frank smiles and shakes it at him," Made it myself, Sherriff."

Craig is freaking out. He has never seen anyone tore up like Bruce before.

"Would you two be quiet," Craig yells in a frantic voice," I think that whatever did this is still in here."

Just then Cannon pushes a crow bar into the lock on the garage door and bends it into a full circle. The three of them turn to stare at him. They all see that he is covered in blood.

"Boy did an animal get you and Bruce." Sherriff Hunt asks.

Cannon shakes his head yes but doesn't say a word. He wants to but nothing will come out. His lips move in a weird fashion. The men see this and look at one another. He thinks that the Cyclotron may have melted his vocal chords but he isn't sure. He was able to talk to the pastor he thought or did he speak to him in his mind. He was perplexed for a second while Osiris sneakily jumped back in the drivers' seat. When Cannon tried to pull him out he threw him way back this time. Clean back into the unexplored catacombs of his mind. It is a place that looks like a maze of sorts. It is place where someone can lose themselves real easy so Cannon sits back to watch the events unfold. He sees Osiris moving like he's steering a ship while flipping switches.

Bruce starts whimpering a little. Frank runs over to his side where he opens all the vises freeing his limbs. He helps Bruce to sit up on the edge of the table. "There you go buddy are you ok?" he says as he stares into the hole in the side of his head revealing half of his protruding brain. The rumbling inside Frank tells him that it's almost time to chunk.

"Well boy where did the animal go?" Craig yells.

Cannon points at his chest. He taps it repeatedly. Sir whimpers louder as he pulls his twisted wrist up to point at Cannon. The three still can't understand what is going on. Frank takes a big sniff in the air, "My god boys, Bruce shit and pissed his pants."

Cannon waves for the Sherriff to come closer.

"Don't go over there Sherriff," Craig begs," There's something wrong with that little fucker. There has always been something wrong with him and his little retarded brother, I'm telling you. They have the same retard blood as that ass clown Jeb who rides his bike around with his grandfather's world war two flight gear on using an American flag for a cape hollering, me likey, me likey.'"

When Cannon hears the derogatory comment about Mitch he rotates his head back and forth like he did sitting on top of Sir earlier. He almost imitates the motions of Stevie Wonder while he played the piano but in a much slower fashion. It is like he is searching for something in the air. Something he has to get just right before reacting to the environment around him. Kind of like a connection of some sort. Cannon can see Osiris rotating his head while steering.

Sherriff Hunt pokes his revolver against Cannon's face now but he doesn't flinch an inch. He just keeps on rotating his head back and forth in an odd fashion. Sherriff hunt then turns his back to Cannon," Hey this boy is either retarded or on drug-" and before he can finish his sentence Cannon shoves his hand all the way through his back to his chest to show the Sherriff's still beating heart in his hand. Steam comes off the hot 98 degree heart in the cool garage. When the Sherriff collapses to the floor the three others watch in horror as they see Cannon gorge on the heart and then regurgitate the meat. They all can see that his face has elongated full of razor sharp teeth with his eyes are glowing red. A loud screeching sound echoes out from inside the beast coming out of Cannon. Craig runs to the door trying to remove the bent crowbar but it's no use as he is too weak. Frank screams so loud for help as

Sir wobbles on the edge of the table to and from consciousness. He has lost so much blood now that he is slowly fading towards death. Craig is the first to go. He tries to smack Cannon with the crowbar but Cannon rips it from his hand and shoves it way up his anus all the way to the lug end. Craig spins around in circles on the floor trying to remove the bar. Cannon drifts into Sir knocking him off the table to the floor. He rips Sir's tongue from his partially shredded jaw and puts it in his jeans pocket while losing the teeth and fingernails that he had put in the pocket earlier. Frank shoves his switchblade into the beasts' throat and backs away quickly trying to avoid it. Cannon slowly pulls the knife out of his throat, licks off his blood and stabs it into Franks left eye. It makes a sound like a toilet being plunged. When he drops to his knees Cannon rips of his head with one swoop of his claw bearing left hand. In the end the monster in Cannon shreds all four of the men. It eats all of their hearts and burns the place to the ground. Only bones and teeth are found that identify each person that was in the garage at the time. Cannon knight's teeth were found near the pile of bones and his dental records confirm it so he is pronounced dead.

Caustic (kos'tik) [to burn] 1 that can burn tissue
by chemical action; corrosive 2 sarcastic; biting
A caustic substance so as to destroy tissue.

-- A. Dictionary

Slowly I begin to wonder off through an unknown world of bent reality where all physical creations capture my exquisite thoughts as artistic works of perfection. Goose bumps multiply into multitudes of millions of chills aggressively race near and far across my spine, unknowingly hypnotized by the narcotic byproducts of

Nirvana, I have forgotten my identity and why my existence prances atop such a parallel world to the one I could not seem to remember.

--Bran
Bane

CH 13 DRAGONS ARE LOOSE

1

Two-thousand feet below the earth the air is warm and pleasant as long as the fans are circulating but the smell is always a bit dank with a hint of saltiness. That is as long as the East corridor waste fans are blowing at full capacity, blowing the stink of rotten corpses out the stack to the top out.

As tram 79 carrying the Siren squad on the monorail halts to a stop at the City of Cyprus processing facility Garvin peers out the window seeing strange objects. "Girls I think that we better lock and load," Garvin hollers," Because we are not in green territory anymore." Just as he utters his last word a set of doors underneath their feet open to reveal a huge funnel leading into an unknown place. Two of the cadets that stood up to exit the tram disappear into the funnel. The other eighteen young cadets hold on for dear life. Their screams can be heard coming from below. Before the squad can react the tram seats go vertical and they all fall into a straight line holding onto Garvin who is hanging from his rifle sling. When the doors on the bottom of the tram wedge against Garvin's rifle an ear piercing alarm sounds and the light start blinking. The tram shifts sideways as Garvin can hear something approaching above him. He looks up to see his first Plutarch. After almost shitting his pants he aggressively cuts away from his rifle sling and they all fall into the large funnel of darkness.

2

Cannon and the other reapers are dressing in prototype armor that Freckle had placed in a secret location for Cannon to pick up on his way back to the City of Cyprus.

"Where did you get this stuff Cannon?" Roach asks

Cannon looks up inside his helmet to see a heads up display listing across the visor." Well Roach I'm not entirely sure where it came from but Freckle must have known that we would need it and man I am grateful for that."

The suits are one size fits all. None of the cases were marked with anyone's name except Cannon's. Well it wasn't exactly marked. The Guardian actually lit up when they were rummaging through them. In each of the cases is a suit of armor with full face mask, a Guardian like Cannon's but smaller and a ripsicle.

Roach walks over to Cannon," So why is your suit picked out for you and we just get the remainders?"

Cannon knocks on the metal between his legs," Roach they had to specifically make mine with the extra-large cod piece." Cannon busts out laughing. The rest hear and laugh too.

Idle walks over in his new greenish colored suit and holds up the ripsicle to Cannon," How do you think this chainsaw looking thing operates?"

Cannon looks at the handle of the sword. He can see that there are several turbine engines in the grip of it and the blade is made like a chainsaw but thinner. The aggressive teeth are like nothing that he has ever seen but these days there has been a lot of that happening. "I'm not sure Idle," Cannon says," but it looks like a sword for a midget."

Melee accidentally pushes a button on her case. A hologram of a little person pops up," It's made by a midget not for a midget you twit," The hologram says. Melee jumps back away from the case. The man's voice makes them all jump.

They all spin around to see where the voice is coming from.

"Did that hologram just talk?" Roach asks.

The little man in the hologram sneezes. "Yes I am talking to you band of idiots," He says," I am Cachoo Snuffer and this is Burner, Puffer, Scrapper, Mangler and Tickle."

"Tickle?" Melee asks.

"Don't ask," Cachoo replies," We build all types of weapons for any war and our delivery boy Santana drops them off to everyone.

Crass starts busting out laughing. He falls to one knee. "So let me get this straight, do you all live at the North Pole too?" He continues to laugh. The whole crew is laughing now.

"Oh I see how it is,"Cachoo says," you see a little guy on a hologram and it's so funny. Ha-Ha it's so funny isn't it?"

Cannon raises both arms, he waves at all of them to calm down," Listen Sir we are absolutely grateful for these gifts and don't mean any disrespect whatsoever."

Cachoo rubs his little hands down through his long red beard," Listen you all won't be laughing when your asses hit that dirt in the arena so you all better pay attention to what I'm going to say next." Cachoo goes on to tell them all just how their suits work and how the ripsicle and Guardian will only activate with the users blood. He says that the ripsicle's are not for small people but will extend when the time comes and that each one will extend to the persons stature to be height and weight proportionate for balance. And before the crew can ask another question Cachoo presses one of the buttons on his little green suit and the hologram retracts. When melee tries to reactivate the hologram her case melts into a puddle. Cannon picks up his ripsicle from the case but it doesn't look the same. It's four times wider and has a blade at each end.

"We have to get this over with quick people because once Crick collides with that plutonium pellet this place is going up in smoke." Cannon says.

"Plutonium pellet," Idle says," What are you speaking of brother?

Cannon puts the ripsicle in a sheath on his back," I used the God particle on myself in a similar Graviton somewhere else and I substituted a plutonium pellet for Cutlass instead."

"Holy shit Cannon," Sullen shouts," so what do you think will happen to him?"

Melee walks over to Cannon, pulls him down to her level and kisses him." Thank you for sparing my life Cannon," She says," I am forever in debt to you. You know that right?"

Idle is about to speak but is cut off by Nuke," Let's go bitches," He says in a harsh voice," It's show time and I see that the little guys equipped you all pretty well." They all see him wink at Cannon. The seven are loaded onto a mini arc platform that rises to the top of the city and transports them to the arena.

"What the hell is that Knox asshole riding," Hail says," you know I owe that piece of shit for cracking my front tooth last week.

"What did you do?" Crass asks.

"I smacked his sister Jackie's ass a few times," Hail says," and she liked it."

Idle starts laughing wildly. "What day was that Hail?"

"I think Thursday," He replies," Yeah it was thirsty Thursday for sure cause I was drinking and I'm pretty sure that she spiked my brew with that Knell weed shit cause damn I-"

Cannon cuts him off," Are we all really that interested in Knox's stank ass sister when we are about to be mutilated?"

"Well know Cannon," Idle says," I just wanted to ask Hail how my dick tastes before we die." Idle falls into Melee and they both bust out laughing. Crass and Roach are crying. Tears are literally pouring from their eyes. Sullen falls to one knee damn near pissing in his armor suit. When Cannon sees Hail's pouty lips curl up he starts busting it out too. They are all laughing uncontrollably, crying, spitting and the whole nine yards. It's so much that they don't even realize that they just landed right in the center of the arena. Their laughing fiasco is echoing all throughout the arena as Cutlass turns on the microphone on the mini arc. Idle speaks up," listen you think that shits funny? How about Santa and his elves, do you believe that crazy shit?"

Cannon wipes the tears away from his face as he looks up at Idle from one knee," Yeah I can believe because just a little earlier I found out that Jesus was an alien."

Before any of the reapers can respond Cutlass's voice comes across a loud speaker," I'm afraid that Jesus won't be able to help you seven. This is the end of the road for you all."

They all climb off the mini arc and stand back to back. Each of them engages their Guardians, their shields and they fire up their ripsicle's. The sounds from their swords screaming out of the mini turbines echo up into the stands of the arena. The crowd goes crazy because it is the first time that Reapers will be doing battle against their makers.

3

Cutlass spills his chalice of wine all down the front of his ivory skin robe when he sees the weapons that the seven are wielding. Cutlass only wears the ginger inspired robe during the Magnum Opus battles one time during each year. The robe is constructed from the skin of twenty-seven red heads. The stitching is created by weaving strands of red hair together fifty times. It is the most durable of hair colors, Cutlass thinks. The buttons are carved from the big toe nails only unless you are a Kristen from Latrobe and all your toes are gigantic.

Cutlass moves his hand under the table to activate the plutonium devices in the heads of the seven. As he does Nuke walks up. Cutlass waves to the guards to let him in, Nuke wades his way through Cutlass's seven wives. One of them grabs a handful of his ass but he's not sure which one. He plops down beside Cutlass," This is quite a spread that you have going here Cutlass," Nuke says," so why haven't I ever been invited to participate?"

Cutlass looks at Nuke strangely," What do you know about the weapons that those seven are sporting? You were told to only give them basics, not to let them choose anything from the weapons room and especially not the ancient's room," Cutlass yells as he smashes his fist into the table. He gets right up into Nukes face. Nuke turns his neck to look right at him," I didn't do it. Ask your bitch Crick because he is the one who delivered seven cases to them not me. I thought that you ordered him to do it how was I supposed to know?" Nuke has really big cheeks that make his words sound smashed or lazy when they come out and his voice is so deep that he almost has to yell for everyone to hear him talk.

Cutlass plops his lard ass back down in the chair," If the Livid Mother catches wind that a hybrid takes a Plutarch's life you will pay. Hell if they take a Plutarch life here will be an uprising right in this arena," Cutlass pulls the brain implant explosive remote and lays it on the table," It's ok it will never happen because if one of our guys goes down I'll just hit the button.

Nuke had already dropped all seven pellets on the floor when he walked in to see Cutlass.

"Well ok Cutlass, enjoy your show now," Nuke says," I better be getting back to processing the new meat."

Cutlass waves for him to go. "Oh and nuke I'm all out of tongue. Could you please restock my refrigerator?"

Nuke throws him a smirk and walks out.

4

Cannon spins his ripsicle to get a feel for it and when he swings a left thrash the two edged chain sword pulls apart into two. He swings both swords simultaneously loosening up his wrist joints. As the seven anxiously await the enemy, large doors open all around the arena. Knox is already out parading around on a dinosaur looking beast that must weigh 600 tons or more. It has a face of a Tyrannous Rex with claws like an eagle.

"Hey Cannon you ever see any shit like this before?" Idle asks.

"I only have seen stuff like this in video games," Cannon says," Only in video games brother." He readies his swords as his Guardian races up above the arena. Cannon can see everything that the Guardian sees on his heads up display. The part that Cannon doesn't realize is that his suit was not marked because of the two edged sword or cod piece like he joked about but rather designed to keep him contained from turning into the dragon. It was crafted by the midgets to implode the second that he changes. It was the only fail safe that they could use to keep the human race from being decimated by dragons like it has the last seven times over the last thousand years.

Thrashers exit out into the arena in each corner. They drive on large roller balls covered in spikes and their entire bodies are covered in spinning blades.

5

Garvin pulls Viola from the speeding conveyor belt running into a type of stripper machine. Drusilla is not so fortunate as the other six of them watch her get processed. They all fire their weapons into the machines but it doesn't faze it one bit. The mechanical arms rip her S.P.E.A.R suit from her body like a knife passing through warm fudge. Once she is stripped eight burners come in to flash burn away any hair. The only Plutarch that likes to eat hair is Po and he only does it for attention from the ladies. Po eats just about anything. Eunice turns her face away as she catches a hint of Drusilla's burnt hair. Abigail leans into Garvin seeking comfort. Drusilla looks back at her squad for the last time in this novel right before her head is ripped from her neck. They watch as her head speeds past them with the look of fear still across it. Sixteen other heads follow down the conveyor right behind Drusilla's. Ten little arms come out of every part of the wall to whittle away her skin. A large vacuum shoots up into her rectum and removes all the viscera. They all see it slurped up through the ceiling in a clear tube. Two large steel plates slam against each side of Drusilla's decapitated skinless body creating mush. When the two plates pull apart squeegees roll down pushing the mush into mixer. To the left and right of the mixer they see pigs and chickens processed the same way and they are added in with the human meat. On another assembly line they watch as a young man has his bones ripped from the flesh of his body. When they look around they see signs that say boneless, skinless, crunchy and more. Before the six of them can even comprehend what they are seeing before their eyes Nuke grabs Garvin and Abigail by the back of the necks lifting them off their feet. Ruthenia, Viola, Eunice, and Uriah flip their visors down on their SPEAR suits and activate the Razors on their backs. Their lasers are painted all over his face.

"We have to add pork and chicken because your meat is too dry," Nuke says," but that's not to say if you all ate better we probably wouldn't have to do this."

"Put me down you Shrek looking fucker." Garvin yells.

"Hey I take offense to that," Nuke says," do I look green to you?" He starts to chuckle.

Ruthenia sends her RAZOR over to Nuke's head to show him the payload hanging beneath it.

"Listen whatever the fuck you are. If you don't put down my friends I will detonate that big fucking bomb on all of us and I aint afraid to die today."

Nuke drops the two. "Would you calm down please," Nuke says," you on your rag or what sister?"

All the girls look at one another with a strange face and eyes wide open.

"What the fuck are you?" Uriah asks.

Nuke puts his hand to his face. He scratches his chin a little. They all watch as his big eyes roll around in his head searching for the answer. He would love nothing more than to scream I'm an Ogre but he knows that the French one will detonate the bomb on his head. Oh what the hell he thinks. "I'm an ogre just like that cartoon Shrek," Nuke says," that Mike fellow is actually Jesus and he made me in that characters image."

The Siren squad looks at one another. Abigail screams," Cut the shit asshole. We just watched our sister die. Do you think you are fucking funny or something?"

None of them can believe their eyes. All of their minds are racing as they try to comprehend what the hell is happening. Garvin starts putting together that Cyprus rehabilitation is all bullshit.

Nuke shrugs his shoulders, leans up against the wall and pulls out a blunt packed with Knell weed. As he takes in long drags he slides down the wall to their level. "Listen up you Red Bloods I'm not your enemy here. The one you want is Cutlass and he is up in the arena area about to kill a few more of your kind."

After Abigail sees the remorse in Nuke's eyes she walks closer to him. "What is that stinking stuff that your smoking?

Nuke blows several large smoke rings at her. The rings blow through her body. She starts choking but immediately feels the effects of the opiates that Nuke is feeling. "Listen honey get on that platform there with your friends, depress the blue button and it will take you where you want to go."

"Why should we trust you?" Abigail says.

"Listen sister, after I'm done with this blunt I'm going to get the munchies really, really bad and what do you think that I'm going to eat? Hmm?"

Garvin grabs Abigail by the arm. He has to pry her gaze away from Nuke. She wants to kill him really bad. "Abigail lets go now, that's an order," Garvin yells," come on this thing has a point."

"Fuck your orders Garvin!" Abigail screams. She was the closest to Drusilla. She was just like a real sister as the two joined the Navy on one of their buddy systems. If it wasn't for Drusilla Abigail would have never finished the BUDS SEAL training program. When she crawled up to ring the little bronze bell Drusilla drug her ass back to the beach.

The six climb onto the mini arc, Nuke wave's goodbye to them. He sucks in another hit of his blunt, farts, scratches his ass and sniffs his fingers. Now don't pretend that it's disgusting because all of us humans have sniffed a few things that we shouldn't have in our time. He walks down to the mixing pot mumbling under his breath," Better get a leash on that little fiery one man," he plunges his fist down into the pot containing Drusilla, rips it out and takes a bite. When he looks up he sees Abigail painting a laser on his face and before he can react she squeezes off a Nitrite round from her .50 caliber BFG. The six watch as Nuke's brains explode all over the walls of the processing unit. His large body falls into the mixing bowl where his body gets mashed up with the rest of the meat.

6

Autumn and grace are racing up through route 79 in the middle of Pittsburgh where it connects to 376 west. They are running their Suzuki Hyabusa's around 210 miles per hour. They have twenty-two police cruiser trailing behind them despite the fact that their bikes are flashing a green light provided by I.P.C.O and a loud siren. When they jump onto 376 West near the bridge they grab gears and race up around 250 MPH. As they pull away from the PA state troopers a tremendous crackling sound like fifty lighting strikes rips through the Pittsburgh City. When the two look up at the center of the city a purple wave of energy disperses in every direction. Grace screams," Oh shit," as she starts dropping gears but it's too late the crotch rocket starts to come out from under her feet and just when she expects to eat a shit ton of pavement the bike transforms into a round sphere that surrounds her whole body. She can see where she is going through her heads up display on her helmet. She is amazed how the bike saved her from crashing. When she realizes that the sphere drives just like a normal bike does she drops gears to come to a complete stop. She exits her sphere and joins Autumn near the guard rail. The two watch in amazement as the entire city grinds to a screeching halt. The twenty or so police cruisers have all collided into one another to form a huge black and white mess. "What the hell just happened here Autumn," Grace asks.

"I'm not sure Grace but I'll bet my life that this is just the beginning," Autumn replies.

"My dear look at that plane, its, it's going to," Grace puts her hand over her face. She can't believe her eye. She witnesses a Delta 747 plummet into the Liberty Bridge. The fiery explosion sends a shockwave over to their location on the highway. They can feel the heat from the burning jet fuel. "Autumn is this some kind of terrorist attack?"

Cars are flying off the bridge into the Monongahela River, a big rig flips over on 376 East and cars all over the entire area drift into one another like bumper cars without a driver. Explosions with balls of fire jettison out from the small side roads.

"If you mean terrorist as in Plutarch then yes Grace. I would say attack is an understatement here. You remember the Rapture prophecy?"

"Yes I remember it vividly my mother-." Grace immediately thinks of her mother," Do you think that it reached Latrobe?"

"Your living the rapture Grace but it's not going to go down like it's written. The people lying all over the place aren't going to a paradise but rather into the belly of a Plutarch. And to answer your question, who the hell knows!"

"What the hell is that thing flying through the air," Grace asks.

Autumn is already zooming in with her helmet," It's Plutarch technology. Looks like a Knucklehead. Look for yourself."

Grace puts her visor back down and when she zooms in she can see a massive ship collecting people from below. "What do we do Autumn?"

"Well Grace I say we get the hell out of here before it spots us, oh shit too late. Get back in your bike now," Autumn screams as bursts of energy fly past the two. Autumn flips and rolls to get to her bike. A Spector rips up over top the police cruisers. The sounds of tracks hitting pavement bounce off the tall Pittsburgh sky-scrapers. She fires up her bike, spins towards the direction of the Spector and opens fire. Three incendiary tipped missiles shear the big track driving it towards them. "Grace lets head towards Latrobe," Autumn yells through her helmet microphone," let's go get on it quick there are six Teracycles' breathing down our necks."

Grace drops gears and races up 376 West ahead of Autumn," What are Teracycles'?"

"They are the fastest land machine that the Plutarch's build but their armor is light, so don't worry about them. I got your ass covered just go."

As the two rip up 376 Autumn disperses a few hundred metallic marbles from her bike. When the Teracycles' get close enough the magnetic marble stick to them like mini mines and detonate.

Grace looks at the rear camera in her heads up dis-play to see fire and carnage exploding up through the air.

7

Marta, Cutlass's third wife sits a bowl of fresh human crunchy mush down in front of him. He cheers for Knox as he takes three fingers full of the meat. He sucks it from his fingers, rolls it around in his mouth to savor the taste but quickly realizes that something is wrong. "Stop, don't eat that," He screams at his wives," Where in Cyprus did you get this Marta?"

"I received it from the cook my king," Marta says," He delivered it just like he always does during every battle."

Cutlass throws his bowl out into the arena where wild Zippers gobble it up," Guards find the cook now and throw him into the arena. And destroy today's entire meat product. It's tainted."

When Cutlass realizes what he has done in his fit of rage he turns a few shades lighter.

"Is everything ok my Lord?" Zaria asks,

"Yes I'm fine number two just feeling a little under the weather. Maybe you and the others need to return to the quarters until this ends."

Zaria nods in agreement and begins pushing the other wives and the children down the steps to the

V-crest. Cutlass looks into his mounted binoculars on the rail of his box seat enclosure to see another mini arc approaching with humans on it. He picks up the radio," Who ordered another mini arc delivery? Nuke where the hell are you? Nuke you there?"

In his anger fueled rage Cutlass sits on the brain implant remote and activates the charges. When his pet sloth Giorgio climbs in his lap holding one of the glowing pellets he looks down to the floor to see the other five glowing as well. Abruptly he leaps over the edge of his box down to another lever. When he looks back he sees Giorgio chasing after him with the glowing pellet. Cutlass jumps all the way down into the arena. The crowd goes crazy when they see King Cutlass entering the arena. He doesn't even realize that he climbed down that far so fast until Diode approaches with his gold hover chariot. As he watches it approach two Zippers nudge him up against the arena wall. They are licking and snapping their huge turtle like jaws at him. He treads very carefully now around these beasts as he knows that since they have tasted the Plutarch flesh there will be no stopping them once they begin feasting. They're ravenous rage is worse than any other creature on any other world. With their terrible eyesight being the Zippers enemy Cutlass is able to maneuver through the two where he hops on his chariot and heads out of the arena. When he enters the East side away from the action an incredible tremor rocks the entire arena dome. Pieces of the dome roof fall to the ground killing several of the warriors. The mini arc that is carrying the Siren squadron shifts sideways crashing into one of the large pillars in the middle of the arena spilling the six all over the ground.

"How many you get Idle," Cannon asks

Idle shakes his bloody ripsicle at Cannon," I killed twenty or so of those stick like things and at least fifteen of those weird flying things and twenty humans. Dumb bastards are just committing suicide I think."

"Is that it? I'm on at least double that," Cannon replies.

"Yeah but hell your wielding two weapons and you are more than slightly altered now," Idle says.

When Cannon sees that the people who crashed are human he orders the rest of the crew to follow him. The Siren squad immediately starts shooting at everything. They disperse their RAZORS to destroy what they missed. Garvin spins around and lights up Cannon with his AR. The shells deflect against Cannon's armor. Before Cannon can explain Abigail's RAZOR deploys a stint nuke that sends Cannon hurling through the air.

Idle flips open his tinted visor to show them that he is human. When Garvin realizes that they are on the same team he calls off the Sirens attack.

As they get acquainted three human hybrids come upon Melee. She slices one from his asshole to his ears, cuts he head off another and then her Guardian flattens completely out like a dis and shreds the other fella in pieces.

Sullen decapitates a huge Plutarch hybrid with two heads. With the second head in control it grabs Sullen with its huge claws and rips off his arms. The others hear Sullen screaming and open fire turning the beast to a few piles of flesh. Explosions are erupting in every area now.

"Easy guys," Idle says," we are on the same team.

Garvin sees multitudes odd transport vehicles; all makes and models hovering through the air. He knows that nothing like them have ever been made on earth.

"What the hell is this place," Garvin asks," And please tell me we are not stoned because this is the craziest fucking shit that I have ever seen."

The RAZOR's are eviscerating every type of creature they come into contact with. The now six Reapers alive in the arena minus two stand back to back with their ripsicles screaming and their Guardians hovering.

They all fight together with the Siren's killing everything that moves. Idle has to repeatedly flash his helmet visor to clear the blood from his vision.

As Melee helps Cannon up from the ground a huge explosion from Cutlass's box blows several Plutarch's into the arena. Before two of the Plutarch's hit the dirt the Zippers have them in their mouths gorging down. When Knox sees this he knows that the outcome is bad because the Zippers came from the planet Galion the Xenite's home world. Knox arms the Thrasher's and the four mobile bladed machines race after the Zippers. Sparks are flying as the Zippers and Thrashers are in their own battle bouncing against each other. The humans turn around to see Zippers jumping through the Plutarch crowd ripping and tearing everything that gets near their large mouths. As Knox turns to exit the arena himself atop the big dinosaur Cannon drifts the hardest that he has drifted in his life and blows right through the side of the big beast, through the arena wall and down into the main corridor eighty yards from the arena floor. Knox stands up, dusts himself off and races after Cannon. The rest of the reapers wade through the flood of blood and viscera spilling out into the arena from the beast. An odd stench of sauerkraut feels the air. Hail slips on a chunk of fat falling onto a lung.

Cannon entered the beast like a whirling bullet, small entry on one side and a massive hole on the exit end. Plutarch's are screaming in anger as their best clothing is covered in dinosaur blood and viscera. The strange sticks start feeding on the dinosaur meat and begin to grow ten times their size. The sticks that now turned into things the size of big oak trees climb up into the arena stands as well and feast on Plutarch's too. The Magnus Opus is the best fight that the Plutarch arena has ever encountered but unfortunately mass chaos has ensued and the ones who though that they had everything in control are now running for their very own lives. This arena battle is the last that Cyprus will ever see.

8

When Autumn and Grace round the corner near the McKeesport exit they see two F-18 Hornets fire on the Knuckleheads collecting the people in Pittsburgh. When Abraham tanks come barreling down the East side of 376 the two women flip on their chameleon paint scheme so not to be detected. The two pull over to watch the outcome. "Autumn do you see those large transport vehicles spilling out soldiers all over the ground?"

"Yes Grace I do. We can only hope that they are human for everyone's sake."

9

The stealth chopper that is carrying Farouche, Hatchet and precious cargo towards Cyprus crashes in Monroeville. "Hatchet Sir, are you alright," Farouche says," I think that was an EMP blast sent from the Plutarch's.

"I'm sure of it Farouche, the pilots are reporting large ships harvesting people out of Pittsburgh as we speak."

Hatchet pulls himself out of the wreckage. He checks the pilots for a pulse, looks at Farouche and shakes his head no. The two walk down near the Outback restaurant. Once there they see that people are passed out in their cars. Farouche runs over to a young girl in a Chevy Camaro that is still running and bumping into the back of a Jaguar, he checks her pulse," Sir they are not dead but only stunned."

"That makes sense Farouche, they don't want to kill us at all they just want to harvest everyone for dinner. That damn no good lying Cutlass will pay for this bullshit." Hatchet walks back over to the chopper where he pulls an AR-15 from one of the cargo bays. Farouche takes the young girl out of the Camaro and places her in the Jaguar beside the man driving it. When he sees the ring on the man's finger he thinks, 'try explaining this one to your wife buddy,' He laughs, jumps in the Camaro, backs up to get Hatchet who throws two big containers in the back and two AR's. "Better put on your seat belt sir, Farouche looks at Hatchet smiling," I used to be a wheelman for the Behnke family out in California before you recruited me."

The two race up onto the turnpike. "The E-phone is holding up to their end of their bargain Farouche, they said that it would survive an EMP blast and damn Skippy it did"

Farouche swerves in and out of the stranded cars on the highway. "This is like one of those zombie apocalypse scenarios that the government has been stressing about Sir."

Hatchet looks up from texting Juniper on his phone with a white face," Oh shit Farouche, that dragon and Mosby's were in a container under our chopper.

There is no telling where the hell it flew too when we crashed" General Hatchet texts the same information to Juniper, he instructs her to send a few of her Viper squadrons to find the lost cargo and secure it immediately and to full out implement the operation Zeitgeist. He tells her issue a full out martial law plan for the City of Pittsburgh all the way to Latrobe.

10

"Grace, Grace do you see what I see barreling ass towards us," Autumn whispers," If you do go quiet on the com or were dead."

Grace doesn't reply as she has already spotted the Dragon rushing upon them. They both watch as it tears through car after car like a pop can eating the hearts from the stunned people along the highway and within minutes of it feeding on them their corpses have animated. The truth unfolds before the women's eyes as they watch the corpses fight with the Dragon over a heart and when the zombie eats the heart it mutates into a Dragon. They see that the Dragons are not the same but both have different distinctions. One is way larger than the other and its features are different. By now at least thirty zombies have walked past their position.

"Autumn should we-?" Grace's question is cut short when the larger of the two Dragon's starts sniffing around her bike. She wonders if it can smell her inside the sphere. When it sees three zombies carrying a body down the East side of 376 it races after them.

"Fire up now don't fucking hesitate because I'm gone bitch," Autumn hollers as she races West up the highway. She blasts through a large crowd of zombies sending them flying like bowling bowl pins back towards Grace who is right on her ass. Grace swerves to miss a young girl and a vertically challenged male zombie.

11

Cutlass races into the Graviton room where he sees Crick lying on the ground with a blue light emitting from his eyes and mouth.

"Hey Cutlass please let me out of my cage," Lox farts from his mouth," Please Sir before Crick explodes. I beg you!"

In all of his years on Earth and Pluto Cutlass finally shows an ounce of compassion to someone other than himself," There's one catch Lox," He says.

"Anything Cutlass, I'll do anything," Lox begs.

Cutlass busts off the lock on the cage with his iron fist," When I jump through the portal I need you to seal me inside and feed this protocol into the DNA sequencer once I'm gone. Got it?"

Lox agrees, he pulls the little microchip from Cutlass's hand and follows him backwards into the sword of God transport room. It is his first time in the room so he bends over to take it all in.

Cutlass takes off all of his clothes and enters a pod built for a Plutarch. He punches in a code on the inside of the pod. When a jet turbine fires up on the back of the pod Lox runs out near the ancient library. He watches bent over as Cutlass spins round and round on a track attached to the wall until finally a bright light flashes and the pod disappears. Lox runs backwards into the DNA sequencer room. When he tries to work the controls he realizes that they are just too tall for him to see from the ass area so he repeatedly jumps up and down to see the control, inserts the microchip and presses start. Lox hops down from the control area where he heads out the door near the Graviton and as fast as he hears Crick grunt searing pain shoots through every inch of his body. When his mouth opens to scream he feels it turn to ice as he sees a blinding blue explosive force erupt up through him into the City of Cyprus.

12

Several minutes have passed since Cannon blew through the wall. When he skidded to a halt his heads up display went all blue. He tries to move but it's no use. He wonders if the salt mine finally collapsed after all these years. He can remember old asshole Sir telling stories around the bonfire how his great grandfather worked in the mine and how all the old timers were always in fear of the mine roof crushing them. His arms are pinned and all he can see is pitch black. "Can anyone hear me? Hello, are you guys out there too?" And then he can hear Uriel's words penetrate his brain," When you seek death it will flee from you."

13

When Cutlass beams to the planet Pluto every alarm in the entire northern hemisphere goes berserk. The entire royal Plutarch army waits around the old decommissioned transport linked to earth. When they see that the DNA is Plutarch they let it pass inside the atmosphere but with precautions. When Cutlass finally reassembles in the old transport area he realizes that he has been locked in a containment pod. He knows that he will be destroyed for his travesties by the Lord Emperor himself if he finds out what transpired on earth but he hopes that the beasts he told Lox to create eat up the evidence before the armada arrives.

AN ACIDIC DROP OF ICE FALLS FROM CYPRUS

1

At 7:47 PM on a Thursday in May, 2008 the entire world would be changed forever! And a little ten year old girl by the name of Drusilla Castleberry would be forever haunted by the tormenting visions of her loving mother being plucked off route 22 on that Day. And the world around them would know nothing different until six months from that exact day, when a 1/3 of the surface on earth would be infected with the Black Death.

2

The old grandfather clock in the corner of the living room in the Hussey house leaves out a chime that sounds like church bells clanging when the hour strikes 7:20 PM on Drusilla's 10th birthday in 2008. The small brick house situated at the base of the ravine in Echo Valley between Johnstown Pennsylvania and roughly forty miles from Latrobe sits peacefully covered in a fresh blanket of snow. Close to three feet fell that day blanketing the entire area. It was a record snow fall for that time of year in the state. Snow plow trucks could be seen racing up and down all veins leading into Johnstown. The main route 22 was especially cared for as the majority of eighteen wheelers use it to transport goods.

Harry Hussey is outside cleaning off his daughters' 1979 Chevy Silverado step-side bed truck. Harry looks up towards the direction of the old salt mine. He swears that the snow is flowing from that North direction and it is the first time that he has seen it come in that way for two hundred seventy-six years now. And snow in May is very uncommon.

He and his daughter Holley rebuilt the truck from the ground up. The restoration project was her gift for graduating high school. As he carefully cleans away the snow from the hood he spots a dent. It's not huge but he can feel it as he wipes his fingers across it. Just then Holley comes bursting out the front door. She grabs the small snow shovel that her mother Heather bought for her grandbaby Drusilla.

"Dad sometimes I think that you love that truck more than your own children." Holley says. She laughs a little, walks to the passenger side of the truck and starts cleaning a path for Drusilla to walk in," Ha anyone heard from big sis?"

"No we haven't. Heard she was on a mission in Bosnia last. Holley are you sure that you girls have to head down the mountain today," Harry says," the snow is probably way worse at the base and you know how slow Penn-dot is at cleaning roads."

Holley continues to shovel away the snow. She is almost around the back of the truck. The snow is around two feet deep down from the porch to the driveway. She looks to the house where she sees Drusilla opening the door.

Andre Wick probably never thought that the blizzard side effect in May from his little blue Tic-Tac sized implosive would give off such a massive range across Pennsylvania but who knew that it was going to be accelerated by the Graviton and smashed with plutonium.

"Dru don't let the door slam." Holley yells. It's too late though, Dru let the screen door whip back. When the door smacks back against the door jamb a mini avalanche occurs sending several feet of snow from the roof down all over Dru.

"Mommy, mommy," she screams," mommy help me."

Holley runs to her daughters rescue. She is completely covered in snow except for just a little part of her face. Dru huffs and puffs for air a she begs to be freed.

"Oh my, you crazy little turd what did you do?" Holley whispers. She digs Dru out from the small snow grave that the roof covered her in. And as she parts the big white blanket to once again enter the house her mother slams the door too just the same. Another large pile of snow comes rushing down the side of the roof. The two women slide off the side of the small porch out onto the lawn. They are both stunned at first but immediately burst into laughter. They lay there giggling and laughing like two little girls that just heard their first bad word. Dru is perched at the edge of the porch watching her mother and grandmother roll around in the snow below her making snow angels. Dru rolls up a snowball and throws it down at her mother.

"My God Holley you need to visit more often," her mother says," you know Dru is getting so big and your dad and I are getting older and its' been what now-. "Heather is immediately cut off by Holley.

"Mom, do we have to get into this now? Dru and I are about to head down the mountain."

"It's just that we love you both so much. We want to see you more, well that's all." Heather says. Holley pulls herself to her feet. She brushes off the snow and reaches down to help her mother.

"Mom you know why we don't visit that often and I really don't want to get into it again in front of Dru."

Harry overhears the commotion. He walks to the porch, swipes away a few piles of snow around Dru and puts the broom back up on the porch.

"You know Heather if you didn't get knocked up by that two bit thief Alford you would still be living in our house," Harry says," and probably would even had your medical degree by now.

Holley now a burning spitball of fire races to the porch. She pushes right past her father and grabs Dru.

She quickly takes her to the passenger side of the truck, straps her in the seatbelt and walks to the driver's side.

"Daddy you know that I love you very much but this is why I have stopped coming around in the first place." Holley says.

"Holley you can blame your parents all you want but you made the bed in which you lay in know," Heather says," we tried to raise you right but you just never listened. Just like right now!

Holley shook her head, waved her hand and jumped in the truck. She puts her head down and rubs the fuzzy hair on her troll keychain. She starts the truck and cranks up the heater to high. The loud rumble from the 383 S engine sends vibrations up through her loins. The tickle makes her drift off into the past to the day that Alford first approached her. On that day he approached with a dozen roses. She instantly forgave him for giving her gonorrhea. She almost believed that he picked it up from the toilet seat on the portal-Jon at the construction site near the school. She knew that if her parents even had an inkling of that little piece of information they would have castrated Alford for sure. A loud knocking rings out from the outside of the truck. Holley jumps up out of the seat. It is her mother starring through the window at her. Her eyes are filled with tears. It seems that when Holley comes around she is always filled with sadness. If any of them knew that this was the last day on earth that any of them would ever speak again the whole outcome of that day may have been way different.

Holley winds down the window.

"What do you want mother," Holley asks with a hard voice," you just want to lecture me a little more before I go? Can't you see that I have had enough from you two?"

Harry picks up the small shovel that Holley let lay in the yard. He throws it over by his truck, walks up onto the porch and carefully walks into the house. He never lays eyes on his daughter again.

Heather turns her face as the rushing heat from inside the truck dries her eyes. The little peach tree air freshener tickles her nose. She accepts the pleasant odor and turns back to her daughter. She climbs up on the step bar, slides both hands over Holley's hands and kisses her on the cheek.

"I love you with all my heart Holley, "she says as she climbs back down off the truck step bar and heads to the house.

When Holley looks down between her hands she sees a small envelope with a rose drawn on the front of it. It's the same envelope that her mother always gives her when she and Drusilla visit. She opens the letter to reveal six one hundred dollar bills. Tears begin to race down both of her cheeks. The pain is unbearable anymore. It was two years since she and her parents had talked. All she wanted to do was run to her mother and hug her, she wanted nothing more but she couldn't show her weakness. Alford taught her that. As a matter of fact Alford taught her a lot of things. He taught her how to mix the heroine just right with the water before heating on the spoon with the lighter. He even gave her the first injection because she was scared of needles. He showed her how to aerate the syringe before injecting into her vein. And despite the pain that she felt the high was so worth it. It was out of this world. It was a blast all through high school but when she became pregnant with Dru it wasn't a game anymore. And the darkness of reality set in when they tested Dru and found out that she was HIV positive. The two were nothing more than a couple of low life junkies just try-ing to scam a quick buck to get that next fix. And when they stole her father's rare baseball collection and sold it for change it was the end of her relationship with her parents. The day after the two stole from her father they came back to Holley's parents place with all inten-tions to shoot up and screw like every other day before that one. And there they found all of Holley's belongings out in the driveway. The two quickly sobered up for that second as they packed his 1979 Chevy Monte Carlo with all of her things. Holley looked up at the house to see her mother balling her eyes out through the living room window. When her mother put her hand on the window Holley flipped her bird at her and jumped into the car. That was two years ago.

"Mommy, why are you crying?' Dru asks.

Holley stuffs the envelope in her purse. She wipes away her tears, puts the truck into drive and heads down the slippery driveway.

"It's ok baby. Mommy is fine."

"But mommy, why is pap so mean to you?"

Holley starts to sob a little more. She knows that if she had just listened to her parents they wouldn't be in the situation that they're in right now. She looks at Dru and smiles. Dru pulls close to her mother. She hugs her tight.

"Mommy I love you!"

"I love you to sugar."

Holley looks down into Drusilla's big green eyes. The young girl is full of surprises. Despite her infection the virus has not caused any abnormalities yet. She still functions as a normal child and even though her blood is a threat to anyone that gets it in them Holley doesn't tell anyone. She doesn't want anyone to treat her any different. She didn't even tell the nurse at Drusilla's school when she was bandaging up her bloody hand without gloves. Holley wanted to tell. She did really bad want to tell but she knew that Dru would be an outcast immediately. The rumors would start and then all of a sudden a protest would begin and her daughter would have to be home schooled like Retarded Rudy had done to him after the mentally unstable teen ventured out into an alley way near the school and found a box of used syringes. When Nurse Nadine was done being shagged by the girls coach Dorothy they both found Rudy out in the middle of the football field scream-ing. He had shoved a hundred fifty-two used needles into his body that day. He ran around screaming," I'm a porcupine. I'm a porcupine." Which sounded more like, "I'm a pock u pint," but Rudy always tried hard. Rudy Webster was the brother to Ward Webster the school's first string quarter back. After Fridays home game Ward walked out to his 1984 Chevy Camaro Z28 still in his football pads, reached into the console, pulled out his dads Taurus 44 magnum and a can of triple expanding insulation foam. He walked through the parking lot loading the magnums cylinder. When he plopped the last shell into the cylinder he reached the nurse's station where he met up with Nurse Nadine and Coach Dorothy. Dorothy the butch of the two in the relationship was on her knees kissing Nadine's toes when the 280 grain lead slug ripped through her right eye. The warm blood sprayed all over Nadine's face. He forced her down onto all fours, threw up her skirt, ripped over her panties and shoved the nozzle of the triple expanding foam can up her rectum and pulled the trigger. Nadine was screaming God awful noises as the foam burned stretching her insides. When the foam can was empty Ward sat down beside her and waited for the foam to start expanding. Nadine screamed so hard that she passed out from the pain before authorities arrived. One last loud blast was heard. When the police rushed in they found Ward and Dorothy dead and a site that no other person on the planet had ever seen before. There before the officer's eyes was a once beautiful woman ripped and cracked from her rectum to her stomach. Nurse Nadine never practiced nursing again. She is no longer a lesbian and found her faith in God rather quickly. Daily she is reminded of the terror of that day when she cleans the file smelling stench from her colostomy bag. The wheel chair that she is confined to for life makes her hate the fact that she too called Rudy retarded at times.

3

The roads were slick like her father projected as usual. The old coot seemed to always be right for some reason. He was spot on with Alford and even spot on with her future and that infuriated Holley even more as she grasped the steering wheel harder. She had wished that she locked in the front hubs before departing down the heel. The truck was always in four wheel drive until it hit 35 miles per hour and then it kicked out over the 35 miles per hour for fuel economy. And now at 60 miles per hour the light back end of the big truck was starting to kick out from under her. The wind has picked up quite a bit. The snow is blowing against the windshield making it hard to see. As they travel east down route 22 both girls snuggle against one another to keep warm in the old poorly insulated truck. Just then Drusilla sits straight up. She points out the windshield towards her mother.

"Momma, look up there on the hill. What's that bright light? Do you think that is Santa?"

Holley looks up on the top of the ridge near the old salt mine were here great grandfather worked years ago. Her great grandfather Lorca now deceased for quite a while used to tell her and her sister Drusilla about people that lived underground. He would tell them how they had red eyes, blue skin and big sharp teeth. As the thoughts of her grandfather describing evil Smurfs dwelling below the ground she starts to chuckle. She tries to concentrate on driving the big truck down off the mountain but she is fighting off her craving to pull over to catch a quick fix. Holley squeezes the steering wheel as the voice in her head rushes in. It tells her to get the fix. Put it in our vein it screams. I need it. I need it the voice says. Can't you feel it traveling up through your vein like ice? "Stop it, damn it. Stop it," Holley screams as she bites a chunk out of her lip. She doesn't realize how hard she bit down. Blood spews down all over Adolf's flannel shirt.

"Momma, why are you yelling at me? I didn't do anything wrong."

Holley looks away from the road to kiss Drusilla on the forehead when she sees something out of the corner of her eye. As she spins her head back around to see what is in front of the truck she nails it head on. A loud smashing sound echoes in the cab. The entire front of the truck pushes up into the air as the truck slides round and round. After spinning a few three six-ties' the truck comes to rest up against the guard rail in the oncoming traffic lane. When the spinning ends Holley sees that the hood is smashed up on both sides like a teepee but the engine is still running. Both lights are still on to reveal a large black object lying in the middle of the road twenty feet or so from the truck. Holley looks in the rear view mirror to see that traffic is piled up for miles. She can see red tail lights for quite a ways.

Abruptly the two girls see all kinds of animals running past the headlights in front of them. Deer, birds, turkeys, possums, raccoons, squirrels and more run past as fast as possible.

"Momma what are those big black animals coming down off the hill?"

Holley turns from the headlights to see a herd of very large animals coming down off the side of the mountain.

"I don't know what those are baby. They look like overgrown black bears but I have never seen so many together in my life."

The beasts are racing past the truck. Several slam into the passenger side of the truck.

"Baby get daddy's gun out of the glove box. Quickly baby, come on."

Dru hands Holley the semiautomatic .25 caliber pistol. She pulls the magazine out to make sure that it's loaded. She slams it in place, chambers a shell and puts on the safety. If it was one thing that she knew it was how to shoot hand guns. Her father held the state pistol champion title for nearly ten years. She had a few titles too before becoming an addict. The one common hobby that she and her father shared was their love of guns. She especially loved blasting off thirty round magazines through her AR-15 before the ban came into effect. When the government tried to put the assault rifle ban into effect every person that owned one was supposed to either hand it in or due time for being a potential terrorist. And when the I.P.C.O agents showed up at their neighbors house Lorelei Stuckey's place she flat out refused to hand over her weapons. Being an NRA member Harry immediately called the media and the NRA to witness the abuse of power. They came and what they witnessed was amazing. The seventy year old woman came out guns a blasting. She was like an old skinny Rambo all jazzed up on Centrum Silvers or something. After she slain eight agents she took a big pinch of her CuttyPipe chew tobacco, sat in her rocking chair and had a stroke. The cameras show Lorelei wielding the AR-15 like some kind of super soldier. After she emptied her sixth magazine the excitement made her false teeth fly from her mouth at a high rate of speed. Agent Oldham who speaks of the massacre this day owes his life to those old false teeth because as he attempted to enter the house he slipped on the teeth and when he flipped ass over his head smacked against a big green garden gnome. He was knocked out cold. Unfortunately when he awoke all of his fellow agents were dead but there still rocking in the rocking chair was the corpse of Lorelei pointing her AR-15 in his direction. He did not know that she had died so he fired 12 rounds from his 45 ACP SIG into her chest cavity. No one was any the wiser that Agent Oldham shot up the body of a poor dead old woman. No one really knew except Harry who eventually leaked the video to YouTube. But with the rocking chair still rocking you couldn't tell that the old woman was dead. Despite litigations Agent Taggard Oldham was declared a hero. But due to the graphic nature and the uprising of a little old granny that killed eight highly trained agents all on her own the AR-15 ban quickly went away. That didn't stop the government from affecting gun owners the least. They just bought up every round of ammunition that could be fired from an AR-15 and now very few people even own one because they are now paperweights rather than a weapon.

Just as Holley readies the weapon two more beasts hit the passenger side of the truck. This time she caught glimpse of one of their faces. She screams and pulls Dru into her arms. She swiftly reaches into her purse, pulls her cell phone from the pocket and dials Alford but he doesn't pick up.

4

The cold beer is cheap and they go down smooth at the Lake lounge in Derry Pennsylvania. Especially when you are watching sweet babes dance around their poles wearing nothing more than thongs and pasties for breast cover.

"Come on baby shake that ass for me," Alford yells," swing it baby, swing it oh yeah like that." Helen Hussey who uses the stage name Easter Rain dances in front of her sister's fiancé shaking her ass for dollar bills on that night. She doesn't care who throws out the cash as long as she has enough for her fix and her two black babies at home with their father Otis. She spins around the pole, catches Alfords gaze and immediately approaches him.

"Hey baby does my sister know where you are at?" Helen asks.

"No way sexy," Alford replies," I left my cell phone in the car so that the crazy bitch can't get a hold of me."

It wouldn't matter to Alford that he would never see his fiancé or his daughter ever again. Hell he just views them as pains in the ass most times. The only time that he enjoys Holley is when they are making cheap porn for the perverted internet viewers. At one time they had made a shit ton of money. Enough to live comfortably if they had put a little back for a rainy day but their habits got the best of them. A case of Budweiser a day, two packs of Marlboro cigarettes and the large amount of smack drained their account to a negative balance but still here sits Alford handing out dollars to Holley's whore sister while she and her daughter are about to expire.

Helen slides closer to Alford. She rubs her hand down between his legs when no one is looking.

"Hey come on get a lap dance for old times' sakes. It will be like old times before you met Holley. What do you say?"

Alford roots around in his pocket to find the last ten dollar bill to his name. He thinks about it for a minute. He tries to configure how far he can drifting his car home if it runs out of fuel before he gets there. Fuck it he says in his head, I might at least get my dick wet tonight. He grabs Helen's hand. She leads him back to the little booth behind the bar. She puts him in the booth with the door so it can be locked, places a picture in front of the camera of her on a guys' lap as she has done many times before and starts kissing Alford hard.

"You only have ten dollars so this is going to be quick or you give me a little bit of that smack in your pocket, you decide."

Helen leans back against the door. She pulls her thing to the side to reveal a neatly trimmed landing strip right above a perfectly clean shaven beaver. She licks her finger and begins rubbing the tip of her finger in circular motions on her hood. Alford begins to buck a little in his chair as his package throbs uncontrollably. He wants the ass but he doesn't want to give up the smack. He loves it more than pussy and right at that minute he proved it. Any other man in that situation would have cut off a finger or maybe even a testicle to live out that fantasy of boning a stripper in the backroom of a strip club. Alford leans forward, rubs his crotch and then pulls out a small baggie from his left jeans pocket.

"How about, three Percocet's and a pinch of duby, would that tickle your fancy?"

She shakes her head yes. Takes the baggy, pops two Percocet into her mouth, swigs Alfords Budweiser and hen pushes his face into her groin area. The dumb drunk bastard couldn't taste the juices from the other guy that just penetrated her minutes before he put his face there. And the booze must have dulled his senses to the cheese on her breath from the fat Samoan's ball sack that she had just licked on for a quick fifty before the guy before him. There were fifteen or more that Helen sucked, licked or rode that night before Alford put his face in that dirty bottom that evening. And Helen the pig that she is rode Alford to climax unprotected. She was none the wiser that his HIV had grown into full blown AIDS now because he and Holley hid it so well. No one knew about it at all. And before the night ended he shared his needle with her. As a courtesy he left a little smack left over in the syringe for Otis too.

5

Holley slams the flip phone shut. She realizes that her pay as you go phone only has three minutes left on the account. She places the phone in Drusilla's hand.

"Listen baby if anything happens to mommy call pappy ok?" Holley tells her.

Dru nods yes. She squeezes the small cell phone in her hand hard. She is really scared.

"Mommy what are those things hitting the truck?"

"I don't know baby but there looks to be hundreds of them all running somewhere."

Holley rubs her fingers thru Dru's hair. She looks out the window to see one of the beasts sniffing around. When its eyes meet hers it begins thrashing against the drivers' side door. Its claws rip right through the metal like a warm knife through cold butter. The two girls can hear the creature sniffing really loud. Once it gets a good whiff it starts to scream. The ear piercing sounds are like nothing that the two have ever heard before. The sound can only be described as a cross between an eagle's screech and a wolf howling. As it screams and screams more join it. They flip the truck over onto the roof. One by one they take turns shredding the metal separating them form their meal. Drusilla puts her face into her mothers' chest. Holley screams.

"Leave us alone, leave us alone."

As the truck is spun like a play toy an eighteen wheeler carrying cows plows through the beasts. For a moment they turn their attention to the cows. They all leave the truck and begin shredding the bed of the truck. The truck driver puts don the window.

"Hey are you alive in there?" He says.

Holley smashes out the rest of the passenger side window.

"Yes sir can you help us please?" Holley asks.

"By the way I'm Griffith, Griffith Savage," He says.

"I'm Holley and this is Dru."

Griffith chambers a whistler into his Mossberg shotgun, exits the rig and runs over to the flipped truck. He quickly pulls Drusilla from the window, runs over to the passenger side of the truck and places her inside. When he runs back to the flipped Chevy one of the creatures looks up from feeding on one of the cows. It leaps down off the truck in his path. And just as it leaps in the air Griffith Savage pumps a whistler and a shock top round into the beast. The shock top dazes the beast with its 500,000 volt charge until the whistler came up to speed.

Griffith pulls Holley from the truck window.

"What did you do to that thing?" Holley asks.

She looks up in the window of the rig to see a scared Dru starring back at her.

"My sister is a first Lieutenant with I.P.C.O. She supplied me with special rounds in case something weird like this went down."

He looks down at his weapon, chambers another shell and turns to get back into the truck.

"Oh my God, Help me," Holley screams.

Griffith turns around to see a smaller one of the creatures pin Holley to the ground. It shreds open her stomach throwing her viscera all over the ground and climbs up inside her to rip out her heart. He fires two whistlers into its chest cavity and retreats to the truck. And there both Griffith and Drusilla watch in horror as Holley's body appears to come back to life. She sits up and reaches for her heart that was ripped from her chest. Dru tries to open the door but Griffith stops her.

"Mommy, mommy," Drusilla screams," please mommy I love you.

Griffith holds on to the little with every ounce of strength.

"That's not your mommy anymore honey, Griffith says in a low voice," If you go out there you will die.

They both watch on in horror as the now dead Holley eats her own heart. She shoves the meat in her mouth with both hands and sucks out the juice like you would suck the juice from a snow crab claw. Within minutes her body begins mutating into that of one of the other beasts.

Griffith and Drusilla look to the top of the hill to see a series of bright blue flashes with a huge mushroom cloud. Within seconds they along with most of the creatures are vaporized into dust from the thermo nuclear warheads.

KAUSTIK WORLD
DEUCE
NEXT

Visit www.Kaustikworld.com, www.Kaustikworld.info, www.Kaustikworld.net and www.Kaustikworld.org for details on upcoming reads.

Friend Cannon Knight on Facebook to keep up with the latest on Kaustikworld news.